T0363226

THE
ENEMY
WITHIN

Also by Tim Ayliffe

The Greater Good

State of Fear

Killer Traitor Spy

TIM AYLIFFE

THE ENEMY WITHIN

**SIMON &
SCHUSTER**

London · New York · Sydney · Toronto · New Delhi

THE ENEMY WITHIN
First published in Australia in 2021 by
Simon & Schuster (Australia) Pty Limited
Suite 19A, Level 1, Building C, 450 Miller Street, Cammeray, NSW 2062
This edition published in 2023

10 9 8 7 6 5 4 3 2 1

Sydney New York London Toronto New Delhi
Visit our website at www.simonandschuster.com.au

A catalogue record for this
book is available from the
National Library of Australia

ISBN: 9781925640991

Cover design: Luke Causby/Blue Cork
Cover image: viperagp/Adobe Stock
Typeset by Midland Typesetters, Australia
Printed and bound in Australia by Griffin Press

The paper this book is printed on is certified against the
Forest Stewardship Council® Standards. Griffin Press holds
chain of custody certification SCS-COC-001185. FSC®
promotes environmentally responsible, socially beneficial
and economically viable management of the world's forests.

For Tilly Lowes

'Bigotry tries to keep truth safe in its hand
With a grip that kills it.'

RABINDRANATH TAGORE

FIREFLIES (1928)

PROLOGUE

He hit the guy's number and heard a phone ringing on the other side of the apartment door.

No answer.

Trying again, he stared at the flashing screen as it rang out for a second time.

'You in there?'

He thumped the door. Harder. Louder. The noise echoing down the hall.

Nothing.

John Bailey had been standing in the steamy corridor for the last five minutes. Calling. Knocking. Waiting. Where the hell was he? Why would he leave his phone behind?

Pressing his ear against the door, Bailey thought he heard footsteps. A chair dragging. A tapping sound. Then it stopped. It could have been next door. Downstairs. They packed the apartments tightly in this part of Sydney. Doors only a few metres apart. Windowless corridors, trapping the heat. Warm air, laced with smells of spiced cooking and smoke, difficult to breathe. Especially on the top floor, outside apartment 1023.

During his years as a war correspondent in the Middle East, Bailey had been stuck in worse places for a lot longer.

The boot of a car. That bedroom in Mosul with the bloodstains on the wall. The house in Fallujah that had been cut in half by a mortar round while Bailey was hiding inside. Those places were much worse than the humid hallway of the rundown old apartment building where he was standing right now. But the heat was getting to him. A sheen of sweat had formed on his brow, sending a salty trickle into his eye. His throat was dry, his lungs heavy. Bailey looked at his watch: 9.28 pm. He decided to wait outside.

An elderly woman with a box of wine was walking in off the street just as Bailey was walking out. He offered a half-smile. 'Hot one again tonight.'

'Tell me about it,' she said. 'Don't mind the heat so much, bloody smoke that gets me. Are they ever going to put out those fires?'

'Rain's the only thing that'll fix them.'

The woman stopped beside him, squinting and laughing, like he'd just uttered one of the stupidest things she'd ever heard. 'Rain? Can't even remember what it sounds like.'

Bailey sat down on the front steps, the warm breeze feeling surprisingly cool as it tickled the sweat on his neck, his stubbly cheeks. He thumbed through his phone. Checking his messages. Killing time. Anything to distract him from the sinking feeling in his gut.

He heard a voice, someone calling out in the distance, followed by a loud fluttering of birds.

Bailey looked up just in time to see a body falling from the sky.

Leaping to his feet, he fell backwards into the wall, hands hugging bricks, seeking shelter from the arms and legs flailing in the air until, almost in slow motion, the body landed with a loud thud on the footpath.

Bailey froze. Heart drumming against his chest. Arms shaking as he watched the pool of blood spreading across the concrete, gathering in cracks.

He took a step towards the dead guy on the footpath, kneeling down beside him, catching the moonlight on his broken face.

Bailey knew exactly who he was.

CHAPTER 1

It was the summer Australia burned.

A nation stricken by drought, reduced to a giant tinderbox. Hundreds of fires burning since spring. Thousands of homes destroyed. Dozens of people dead. Cars. Sheds. Shops.

Incinerated.

Farm animals. Wildlife. Pets. Even the insects that would have devoured what was left of the smoking carcases.

Gone.

Vanquished by fires so powerful, so aggressive, they created their own weather systems, sending embers leaping through the air, starting new fires in places that couldn't see them coming.

And the smoke.

Acrid, lung-burning, eye-stinging smoke.

It was everywhere, in everything.

Including the warehouse in Surry Hills where Bailey was slowly making his way through the crowd, head bowed, avoiding eye contact with the mostly white men with fashy haircuts, tattoos and ill-fitting stone-washed jeans. Some of them with Australian flags tied around their necks. All of them with hard faces. The patriots.

'Excuse me, brother.'

Bailey felt a heavy hand on his shoulder, turning to see a tall man with a square jaw looking down on him. He had a web tattoo inked into his neck and a spider climbing the side of his shaved head. Thug art.

'Me and my boys are up front,' he said, motioning to get past.

'No worries.'

Bailey stepped aside, nodding at the trail of men with crew cuts and union jacks plastered on their blue t-shirts. He recognised them instantly. The Blue Boys. A far right nationalist group that had recently had its Facebook page shut down after they were caught praising the gunman who had shot up those mosques in Christchurch, killing fifty-one innocent people.

Bailey checked his ticket on his mobile phone. Thankfully, he'd been seated up the back where he could make a quick exit, if things turned ugly. He stared at his ticket a moment longer, shaking his head at the price tag – a thousand dollars to listen to Augustus Strong. The race-baiting doyen of America's alt-right movement and favourite among Neo-Nazis and far right nationalists. What a rip-off. At least Bailey hadn't personally paid for his seat. The magazine had picked up the bill because he was there for a story. Different from the ones he'd spent years chasing in the Middle East. His first article for *Enquirer Magazine*. A feature about Augustus Strong's visit to Australia.

The warehouse reminded Bailey of an old mechanic's garage. Grease stains on the floor. Corrugated iron roller doors tarred with paint and rust. Brick walls chipped and scarred. There were dozens of old warehouses in this part of Sydney. Most of them had been converted into trendy apartments, cafés and restaurants, clothing outlets, or function spaces for parties and events like the one Bailey was attending tonight.

The location of the warehouse had been kept secret, with a message sent out to ticketholders an hour before to let them know where to go. Bailey had made it with plenty of time to spare because the Darlinghurst end of Surry Hills was next door to Paddington, the suburb where Bailey lived in a single-storey townhouse. The warehouse was so close that Bailey had decided to leave his car at home and walk.

The protesters hadn't taken long to get there, either. On his way in, Bailey had counted at least a dozen people holding placards on the footpath outside, and he knew the number would swell. Before Strong had arrived in Australia, he had been front page news after it emerged that the home affairs minister had personally intervened to grant him a visa, despite warnings from intelligence officials that the controversial figure's visit could incite violence.

'Everybody, please take your seats. The event will begin in five minutes.'

A woman's voice echoed through the hall.

'And a reminder to audience members, no photography or recording equipment is permitted. Anyone found to be taking photographs or recording tonight's event will be ejected.'

Bailey plucked his phone from the inside pocket of his jacket, subtly activating a video recording before bringing his ticket back up on the screen so that he had a good reason to be holding his phone, should anyone ask. Steering his way through the crowd, he walked past the row of temporary chairs where he was supposed to be seated so that he could keep filming faces. If he was going to write about Augustus Strong, he needed to know about the people who had paid to hear him speak. How far the tentacles of the alt-right movement had spread in Australia.

When Bailey was done filming he returned to the back row, shuffling past the knees of the people already sitting down, and settled in his seat. Checking that he wasn't being watched, he stopped the video and activated the voice memo app, beginning an audio recording, before slipping his phone back inside his jacket. Out of sight. The sound would be slightly muffled, but it would pick up most of the speech and the crowd's reaction. Experience had told him that.

'Best keep that phone in there, mate.' A bloke in a sharp suit and a fashy haircut was backing into the empty seat beside Bailey, pointing at his jacket. 'Heard the Blue Boys belted some guy for taking pictures at Strong's talk in Melbourne the other night. Ended up in hospital.'

'Probably a reporter from some commie newspaper like *The Journal*,' Bailey said, knowing that his sarcastic dig at the newspaper that had employed him for thirty years would be lost on the bloke beside him. 'Just making sure I'd switched it off.'

'All media's the same these days. Leftist mafia. Out of touch. No idea about what real people want. What we think.'

We.

Bailey had met his first *real person* for the night.

'Tell me about it,' Bailey said. 'World's going to shit. Thank god for truth-tellers like Augustus Strong, eh?'

'Amen to that.'

The lights dimmed as the woman's voice echoed throughout the hall again.

'Please take your seats. Tonight's program will begin in two minutes.'

'I don't agree with everything Strong says, mind you, but by god I'll defend his right to say it.'

The guy beside Bailey kept talking as the last of the crowd hurried to their seats. More men with slogans plastered across shirts and singlets, declaring their allegiances to one group or other. Freedom Front. Real Australia. National Action Coalition. Some of the groups Bailey recognised, some of them he had never heard of before. In any other place he would have had his notebook out, scribbling observations. But not here. Not with a hostile gathering of far right nationalists, including the bloke beside him.

'. . . not really a fan of the outfits and makeup. He's a weird cat. All about the performance, I guess. But he's not afraid to speak the truth. He knows that conservatism is about maintaining a traditional way of life, right? Keeping out not just immigrants but also corrosive influences that eat away at our Aussie values, right?'

He paused, waiting for a response.

'Yeah, mate.' Bailey nodded. 'Strong's good on that stuff.'

The room went dark and the crowd erupted in a loud cheer. Bailey followed everyone else by getting to his feet, cringing at the backslaps he was getting from the man beside him.

'Here we go, brother!'

'Yeah.'

Bailey pumped his fist in the air, feeling like he was betraying every rational thought in his head. The price of fitting in.

Electronic music was blasting from the two large speakers positioned on either side of the stage. A song that Bailey had never heard, heavy with synthesiser sounds. He wondered whether it was one of those fashwave bands. The alt-right's own brand of music.

A cloud of artificial smoke blew across the stage and out strode Augustus Strong, spotlights beaming rays of light like he'd been transported down from heaven. Wearing sunglasses and a bright red blazer, Strong was pumping his arms, revving up the section of the audience chanting his name.

'Strong! Strong! Strong!'

It didn't take long for the entire hall to catch on. An earthquake of excitement for their man.

Bailey had to remind himself that the guy on stage was merely someone who wrote opinion articles for right-wing online publications. He wasn't a politician. He wasn't a businessman. He hadn't starred in movies or had a hit song. He hadn't even written a book. He was just a guy who found an audience through social media by being a contrarian. A self-declared culture warrior who liked to boast and offend. And his targets were always the same. Feminists. Muslims. Socialists. Politicians. The mainstream media and basically anyone who disagreed with him about anything.

During the ninety-minute sermon that followed, Bailey didn't hear anything that would change his view that Augustus Strong was nothing but a great pretender.

When the cheering finally stopped and the house lights came back on, Bailey just wanted to get the hell out of there. But there was one more thing he needed to do.

During his lap of the hall before Strong's speech, Bailey had noticed Chrystal Armstrong loitering by the side of the stage. The publicity queen of Sydney who'd been ignoring his emails and phone calls for the last week. With the event now over, she was gliding down the brick wall towards the exit, where Bailey was determined to catch her.

'Have a good night, mate.' Bailey tapped the chatty man next to him on the shoulder. 'I've got to run.'

'No worries, brother. Good to talk. What did you think of Strong?'

'Solid, mate. Solid.'

Bailey pushed back his chair and slipped through the gap, walking quickly towards the back of the room.

'Chrystal Armstrong,' Bailey said, holding out his hand. 'John Bailey.'

She gave him a blank stare, ignoring his hand, keeping one eye on the security guard nearby.

'I've sent you a couple of emails this week about possibly getting some time with Strong?'

'Sorry, who are you?'

Chrystal had had so much Botox that Bailey wasn't even sure that the words had come from her swollen lips.

'John Bailey,' he said, letting his hand flop by his side. 'I emailed you about an interview.'

'Who are you with?'

The crowd was starting to build around them and Bailey was conscious about not drawing too much attention, especially knowing that journalists like him were not welcome.

Grabbing his notebook, he scribbled down his phone number and email address, tearing out the page and handing it to Chrystal. '*Enquirer Magazine*. It's new. First edition comes out in six weeks. I'm doing a story on Strong.'

Chrystal's face moved, miraculously, with her smile. 'Jock Donaldson's magazine?'

Jock fucking Donaldson.

Of course Sydney's PR queen knew about Jock. The billionaire financier who had grown a conscience in later life, deciding to bankroll *Enquirer Magazine* as some kind of vanity project to 'save journalism'.

'That's the one.'

Chrystal took the slip of paper out of Bailey's hand. 'I'll see what I can do.'

'Hey! This guy's a fucking reporter!'

A hand landed on Bailey's shoulder and he turned around to see a face he knew well. Benny Hunter. The leader of the Freedom Front and Australia's most notorious racist.

'I'm just leaving, mate.'

Bailey tried to move towards the exit, where Chrystal had just done a runner, but Benny had a hold of his jacket. He pulled Bailey close, their faces only inches apart.

'What did you think of our boy Augustus?' Benny said, nodding his chin. Testing Bailey. 'Impressive, huh?'

'Yeah, clever guy,' Bailey said. 'Loved his simple solutions for complex problems.'

Benny took a moment to process Bailey's words. 'Are you getting smart with me?'

'No, mate. Just sharing observations.'

Benny clenched his jaw and Bailey noticed the size of his pupils, guessing that he was on something more than a nationalist high.

'You're a fucking smartarse, y'know that?'

'It's been said.'

Benny pulled Bailey even closer so that their heads touched, momentarily, before letting him go. 'I'm an avid reader, Mr Bailey. I look forward to your article.'

Unnerved by the fact that the leader of the Freedom Front knew his name, Bailey took a step back. 'Glad to hear it.' But he was determined not to be intimidated, despite the posse of skinheads gathered around him. 'You have a good night, gents.'

Bailey started walking towards the exit, adrenalin pumping, bracing for Benny, or one of the other men, to stop him. To finish their conversation with fists.

He made it outside without incident and when he reached the top of the stairs he stopped, turning briefly to check that he wasn't being followed. He was met by a push in the back that sent him tumbling down the half-dozen or so steps to the street. He landed hard on the concrete. Right shoulder aching. Ears ringing. An all too familiar taste of blood in his mouth, reminding him of darker times when he'd been made to understand the meaning of violence.

'Next time watch your manners.' Bailey looked up to see Benny Hunter leaning over him, patting his cheek. 'You never know what might happen.'

'Everything all right there?'

A policeman called out from his position in a cordon that was separating Augustus Strong's supporters from the protesters across the street.

'Poor bloke slipped on the steps.' Benny waved at the cop, pointing at Bailey. 'You're okay, aren't you, buddy?'

'Yeah. Yeah. I'm fine.' Bailey reached into his jacket for his phone, turning the camera towards Benny, who was already walking away. 'Hey, Benny!'

Benny turned around.

'Smile!'

Bailey snapped a picture.

'That's a beauty,' he said, holding up the screen.

Benny took a few steps back towards Bailey, fists clenched, before changing his mind when he noticed the police officer still watching him.

'Cunt!'

He opted to give Bailey the finger instead, before walking in the opposite direction with his gaggle of disciples.

'You all right, mate?' the policeman called out.

'Yeah.'

The policeman turned away to yell at a lone protester who had broken away from the picket line and was trying to cross the road.

'Stop! Stay where you are!'

Bailey couldn't see the protester because the policeman was in the way. But he could hear his voice.

'I know him. That guy on the ground. John Bailey. I know him,' he shouted.

The mention of Bailey's name seemed to be enough for the policeman, who stepped out of the way to let the guy cross over.

'I see you've been making friends.'

The man dangled a bottle of water in front of Bailey.

'Here. Take this.'

'Jonny?'

Jonny Abdo. The former refugee from South Sudan, now a lawyer. It had been so many years since Bailey had seen him that he almost didn't recognise him. A boy back then. A man now.

'Are you okay, Bailey?'

Bailey stood up, rotating his shoulder, a sharp pain pinching his neck.

'I think so.'

'You're lucky that policeman was there. Benny Hunter's a violent man.'

'So I gather.' Bailey accepted the water, shaking Abdo's hand. 'It's good to see you, Jonny.'

'You too.'

'What the hell are you doing here?'

'I came with my students. I'm leading a demonstration against Augustus Strong. He should never have been allowed in the country,' Abdo said, watching Bailey roll his shoulder. 'Sure you're okay?'

Bailey took a mouthful of water, rinsing the blood from the cut on his lip. 'Yeah, thanks. Few bruises. I'll live.'

'Plenty of witnesses if you want to press charges?'

'All good, mate. Good fodder for the article I'm writing.'

Abdo laughed. 'It's always about the story with you, Bailey.'

'It'll get more traction than some drawn out assault case that probably won't go anywhere.'

'I was joking,' Abdo said, frowning.

Bailey realised how defensive he'd just sounded. Standing alongside Abdo took him back to the first time they'd met. A refugee camp in Egypt. Little Jonny Abdo clinging to his mother's legs while Bailey interviewed her about the civil war that had claimed the lives of her husband and three other sons. Getting her reaction to the news that she and Jonny had been granted asylum in Australia. The Abdos had a powerful story to tell. Bailey had written it. But he didn't like the insinuation that newspaper headlines were all that he cared about.

'All good.'

'I'd better get back over there.' Abdo pointed at the people holding placards across the street. 'Make sure this doesn't get out of hand.'

'Hey, Jonny?' Bailey stopped the younger man as he made to walk away. 'You doing okay? How's your mum?'

'Good. We're both good. Mum's retired now, she's . . .' Abdo stopped speaking, distracted by the sound of a glass bottle smashing on the road. 'This country has been good to us. I don't want people like Strong messing that up. I've got to go.'

'You got a card, Jonny? We should catch up.'

Abdo dug his hand inside the pocket of his jeans, handing Bailey his business card.

'I'd like that.'

CHAPTER 2

WEDNESDAY

Bailey liked to start his day with a walk. A lap of Centennial Park and a takeaway coffee on the way home. It always cleared his head after a restless night dreaming about his former life as a war correspondent. The faces of the dead.

This summer Bailey had another reason to walk. The dog.

'She'll be good for you. Keep you company,' his daughter, Miranda, had said on the day she dropped her off. 'And look at her, isn't she beautiful?'

Bailey had watched in horror as Miranda ruffled the ears of possibly the ugliest dog he had ever seen. A greyhound. Skin and bones. Narrow head. White fur not thick enough to hide its pink, spotted skin. Beady eyes staring at him like he was the one who needed help.

'Are you serious?'

Still plagued by guilt from all the years of Miranda's childhood he'd missed, Bailey could never say no to his daughter. Like it or not, he knew the dog was staying.

'What do I call her?'

'Dixie Chick,' Miranda had said, not bothering to hide her smile. 'She's a rescue. Retired race dog. They named her in the shelter.'

'I'm not calling her that.'

'Dad, it's her name.'

'I'm going to call her Campo. Keep it simple.'

'You can't name your dog after a rugby player!'

'Not just any rugby player, sweetheart. That's David Campese you're talking about. Greyhounds are fast. Campo was fast. Makes sense to me.'

'Campo's a man.'

'He was graceful on the field.'

'You're incorrigible.'

Miranda knew her father too well to argue the point. Rugby was Bailey's game and not only did he think that Campese was the greatest winger to ever play, he was also part of the Wallabies' golden era that Bailey would talk about with anyone who'd listen. The name was perfect.

It was still eerily dark when Bailey finished his lap of Centennial Park. The blood red bushfire sun that had been haunting Sydney all summer was nowhere to be seen, hidden by a toxic smoke haze that was irritating Bailey's nostrils and stinging his eyes. The air so thick he could taste it. Or maybe it was the tiny specks of ash blowing in from the fire grounds circling the city.

'Come on, Campo.'

Itching for a coffee, Bailey yanked on the leash when Campo stopped to do one last sniff inspection of the tufts of grass at the Paddington Gates. For an animal that used to race at the track, Campo wasn't much into exercise but if sniffing was a sport, no other dog would have come close.

'Let's go. Come on.'

Although he might struggle to admit it, Bailey had grown fond of Campo. She may have been stubborn but she was otherwise easy. She slept on the end of his bed, never went to the toilet inside and hardly ever barked. Now that he thought about it, Campo spent most of her days curled up in a ball close to him. His four-legged mate. Miranda had been right. It was good not to be alone.

Crossing over to the eastern side of Oxford Street, Bailey stopped when he noticed a man hosing the footpath outside the White Lion Hotel. One of Bailey's old watering holes, when that was his thing.

'What happened here?'

Bailey pointed at the crack in the window and the glass door that had been temporarily repaired with a large square of plywood.

The guy killed the hose, plucking his earbuds out. 'What's that?'

'I was just asking what happened?'

Bailey could see the mess on the footpath now. A dried puddle of black, purple and red. Blood.

'Fight, apparently. Bloke ended up in hospital.' The man knelt down, giving Campo a pat on the head. 'Was she a racer?'

'Yeah,' Bailey said. 'Wasn't any good, apparently. Not surprising. She's as lazy as hell.'

The guy laughed, getting back to his feet. 'Heard that about greyhounds.' He pointed at the dried blood that was clinging, stubbornly, to the concrete. 'I'd better get back to this. They want it done before the foot traffic starts.'

'No worries.'

Bailey grabbed his black coffee from the café on the corner of his street, copping a frown from the waitress with the dreadlocks for not bringing a reusable cup.

'Next time,' he said with a wink. 'Promise.'

'You better. Or I'll make you buy one.'

She had only been working there for a couple of weeks but she wasn't afraid of laying on the guilt.

'That any better for the environment?'

'It will be if you bring it back each time.'

Everybody seemed to have their own personal crusade these days. But she had a point.

The houses in Bailey's street all looked almost identical. Rows of Victorian terraces, each with steel fences, groomed hedges and garages out back too small for the expensive four-wheel drives parked, bumper to bumper, by the kerb. The huge dust storm that had barrelled through Sydney the week before had left a coat of scum on almost every vehicle in the street. It was probably the closest thing these four-wheel drives had come to an off-road experience.

Bailey's townhouse was the black sheep in the street. Overgrown hedge. Rusty gate. Dead fern frowning at the footpath by the front door. The house could have done with a lick of paint too, not that he cared. And the greyhound? Campo was the icing on the cake. Utterly out of whack in an area more prone to the yapping sounds of French bulldogs, cavoodles and pugs.

Bailey dropped a cup of dog biscuits into Campo's bowl in the kitchen and then flipped the lid on his laptop computer, eager to find out more about what had happened at the White Lion the night before. If the victim had been unconscious when he was taken to hospital, he figured there must be a story online. A few clicks of the mouse and he found it.

MAN IN COMA AFTER VIOLENT PUB ASSAULT

A 19-year-old Sudanese man is fighting for his life at St Vincent's Hospital after a brawl at a popular Sydney nightspot.

The Bankstown man was out drinking with friends at the White Lion Hotel on Oxford Street when they were allegedly set upon by a group of men.

The victim suffered serious head injuries and has been placed in an induced coma.

A source close to the police has confirmed that a racially motivated attack was one line of enquiry.

The incident happened at around 11 pm and police are appealing for any witnesses to come forward.

There wasn't much more to the story other than the fact that the victim's identity had not yet been released.

Bailey wanted to know more.

A man of Sudanese background attacked not far from the warehouse where Augustus Strong had been revving up a crowd of far right nationalists. It seemed like too much of a coincidence.

He grabbed his wallet off the bench, sifting through the pile of cards and receipts, eventually finding what he was after. Jonny Abdo's business card. Bailey knew that the Sudanese community was tight in Sydney and Abdo had set up his own law firm specialising in immigration. There was a chance that he would know the victim, or at least know something about him.

Abdo answered after three rings. 'Hello?'

'Jonny, it's John Bailey.'

'Bailey, I didn't expect to hear from you so soon. How's the shoulder?'

Bailey instinctively touched it, wincing at the bruising.

'A tad tender.' There was no point lying, even though he'd been ignoring the pain all morning. But he didn't want to get into it. 'A nineteen-year-old Sudanese kid was bashed up on Oxford Street last night, wondering if you know anything about it?'

'What?' Abdo's voice sharpened. He didn't know.

'Can't tell you more than what I've read online. Kid's in bad shape, apparently. Induced coma. Police are investigating a possible hate crime.'

'Got a name?'

'Not yet. Where'd you and your group go after the protest last night?'

Abdo went quiet on the other end of the phone. He had muzzled the receiver with his hand and Bailey could hear him talking to someone, although he couldn't make out the words.

'Jonny?'

'Sorry, Bailey. I hadn't heard. Let me make some calls. I'll call you later.'

Click.

Before Bailey had a chance to respond, Jonny Abdo was gone.

CHAPTER 3

Benny Hunter was a turd of a man.

Bailey had arrived at that conclusion the night before and he was even more certain of it now, having spent the last hour perched on a stool at his kitchen bench digging around on the internet for any stories he could find about Hunter and the Freedom Front.

They were not hard to find. And none of them were good.

The self-styled far right nationalist had first garnered attention from the media about five years ago for his heavy-handed approach to his job as a union organiser in the construction industry. The first reference to the Freedom Front that Bailey could find dated back to a demonstration against the Australian Government's offshore immigration detention centres at Sydney's Town Hall in 2016. Hunter and his supporters had turned up to disrupt the protest. Punches were thrown, batons swung. Hunter and his crew were taken away in police vans and the media coverage about the protest turned into a series of articles about the newly formed Freedom Front, a hard line nationalist group that espoused the view that 'Australia must rid itself of foreign elements that undermine it from within'. A message that was plastered across its Facebook page.

Crashing other people's demonstrations and intimidating protesters was a tactic that Hunter would deploy again. And again. And again. Protests about climate change, public sector wages, Indigenous recognition – it didn't matter. They were all fair game for Benny Hunter because all he was looking for was a camera to broadcast his racist, Islamophobic, homophobic views.

I'm an avid reader, Mr Bailey. I look forward to your article.

Bailey should have been researching Augustus Strong, but Hunter's sinister comment at the warehouse in Surry Hills had been preying on his mind. It was true that Bailey was a well-known journalist, but he wasn't exactly a household name. He'd always shunned offers to be an 'expert' on television. He wasn't the type of person who got stopped in the street. He was an old-school print man with a name that rang bells but a face that barely anyone knew. For chrissake, the girl at his local café only knew him as the guy who didn't own a keep cup!

Deciding that he had discovered all that he was going to through a search engine, Bailey picked up his phone, looking for a contact he hadn't spoken to in years. Someone who, he hoped, would take his call. He knew she was back working for the Australian Federal Police in Sydney. Only problem was that the last number he had for her was from Kabul. He took a punt and called the AFP switchboard number he found online.

'I'm trying to get in contact with Commander Harriet Walker,' he said to the woman who answered the call.

'The reason for the call, sir?'

'I have some information for her. Information for an investigation she's working on.'

Bailey had mastered the art of bullshitting very early in his career.

'And what is your name, sir?'

'Kenny Baker.'

The woman went quiet on the other end of the line.

'Trust me. She'll know who I am.'

Quiet again.

'Hold the line.'

The call was eventually transferred and Bailey could hear a muffled conversation in the background.

'There's a guy on the phone who says his name's Kenny Baker.'

Laughter.

'You know who it is, then?'

'Yeah. I do.'

'Well. Well. Well.'

Walker was on the phone now.

'I'm guessing that this is a cranky bastard that I used to know, but you're going to need to confirm that it's really you.'

Commander Harriet Walker. Special investigator with the Australian Federal Police.

'The one and only,' Bailey said, suppressing a laugh.

'How the hell are you?'

'I'm good, Hat. Really good.'

Bailey regretted the double emphasis and he could almost hear Harriet thinking on the other end of the phone. Wondering whether or not to go there. In her job with the AFP, she would have known more than most about what had happened in London and Bailey's role in disrupting a terrorist attack and the murder of the woman he loved.

'Glad to hear that, Bailey,' she said. 'Now, to what do I owe the pleasure?'

Harriet was a class act. If she was ever going to rake over the past with Bailey, she'd do it when they were sitting opposite each other. Face to face. Like old friends.

'I need to talk to you about a thing.'

She laughed. 'Of course you do.'

'Are you at city headquarters?'

'Yeah.'

'Can you do a quick coffee?'

'What's it about?'

A person with a job like Walker's didn't just drop whatever she was doing for a catch-up without knowing what it was about. Bailey had to give her something.

'I'm having a dig into far right nationalist groups. Thought you might know a few.'

Bailey could hear Walker tapping away at a keyboard, probably checking her diary. Or doing a quick search on what Bailey was up to. Whether he had already written something that might make meeting him a bad idea. There was always a tension between journalists and cops, even the ones who were friends.

'Martin Place at one o'clock. Lindt Café.'

'Lindt. Really?'

Bailey knew the café she was talking about. Everyone knew the Lindt Café. The place where an Islamic extremist had taken eighteen people hostage in a siege that lasted for sixteen hours.

'It's my local now. And I like the chocolates.'

'Done.'

Bailey checked his watch. It was almost ten o'clock in the morning and he was still dressed in a pair of shorts and a t-shirt from his walk with Campo. He decided to take a shower.

By the time he'd shaved and dressed in his trademark jeans and flannelette shirt, sleeves rolled up to the elbows and an extra button undone to combat the heat, there were four missed calls on his phone. All of them from Neena Singh. The editor of *Enquirer Magazine*.

He called her back.

'Morning, Neens.' Bailey made an effort to sound cheery. 'Four missed calls. What's happening?'

'What's happening?' She sounded angry. 'What's happening is that our new boss is sitting in a café at Bondi Junction alone waiting for us because you find it impossible to keep a fucking appointment.'

Bailey remembered. He had agreed to a 'meet and greet' with the guy who was bankrolling *Enquirer Magazine*, Jock Donaldson. Evidently, Neena was also still pissed at him for being an hour late for lunch with her last week.

'Oops.'

'Oops? What are you, five?' She really was irate. 'I'm parked out front. Hurry up.'

Neena Singh had been a journalist for even longer than Bailey, mostly in places like New York and London, where she had worked on Fleet Street, when it was still a thing. Despite being a good reporter, she had made her mark as a skilled editor who knew how to reverse the fortunes of struggling magazines. She had a sharp wit and an even sharper tongue.

'Good to see you dressed up for the occasion.' She frowned at Bailey's attire as he climbed into the car. 'You look like a fucking hobo.'

He leaned over and gave her a peck on the cheek. 'What are you on about? This is my "number one".'

'It looks like something you'd find on a rack at a charity shop.'

For someone who was usually quick with a retort, Bailey couldn't argue. Because it was true.

Neena glanced across the car, eyes squinting. 'You shop at the bloody Salvos?'

'Only when there's a sale on.'

Neena was still laughing when she swung her sleek BMW onto Oxford Street, ignoring the speed limit as she raced through the back streets of Woollahra towards Bondi Junction. She found a park opposite the bus depot, tapping the clock on the dash as she clicked open her door. 'You're lucky we had a good run in the traffic, we're only ten minutes late.'

'He'll get over it.'

'Bailey.' Neena grabbed his arm, stopping him from climbing out of the car. 'I know you don't like Jock. Just remember though, he's the one paying the bills.'

Bailey knew all about Jock Donaldson. The hedge fund billionaire who had mastered the art of not paying his taxes. Back in the early 2000s, Bailey had done an investigative piece about a law firm in the Cayman Islands that specialised in helping wealthy individuals funnel their millions through offshore companies to minimise their tax. Donaldson was one of them.

'As long as he doesn't interfere with editorial, Jock and I will get along just fine.'

Neena still had a hold of his arm. 'You seriously think I'd let that happen?'

'No,' Bailey said.

'Then cut this shit out.'

'Okay,' Bailey said. 'I just prefer writing stories about guys like Donaldson, rather than having coffee with them.'

'We won't stay long.'

Donaldson was seated at a round table by the window, a copy of *The Australian* stretched open beside a half empty cup of coffee. Dressed in a pink polo shirt and a pair of beige chinos, he looked like he'd just finished playing eighteen holes at Royal Sydney.

'Sorry we're late.'

Jock rocked forward on his chair, using the table to help himself to stand, legs stiff with age. 'Not a worry.' He gave Neena a peck on the cheek. 'I didn't even realise you were late.'

'Jock, this is John Bailey.'

Donaldson locked eyes with Bailey, unloading a charming smile.

'Call me Bailey, everyone else does.'

'Well, Bailey. It's great to have a journalist of your calibre on the team at *Enquirer Magazine*.' He held out his hand and Bailey shook it. 'It's all very exciting, isn't it?'

'Yeah. Thanks for throwing your dosh at it. Tough market, these days. Good to see people investing in journalism.'

'Please, take a seat,' Donaldson said, arms outstretched. 'And let's get you some drinks. The coffee blend is remarkably good, we bring it in from Costa Rica.'

We. Jock owned the café too. Of course he did.

'This your place, Jock?' Bailey asked.

'My daughter's in the hospitality game. It's her place.' Jock waved at a young woman behind the counter and waited for her to come over. 'Katie, this is that reporter I was telling you about. John Bailey. He's part of Neena's team for the magazine.'

Katie couldn't have seemed less interested in meeting Bailey as she wiped her hands on her apron. 'Good to meet you all. New magazine sounds exciting.'

Jock grabbed hold of his daughter's arm, obviously keen for her to stay. 'Katie's just returned from South America where she's been meeting with our suppliers.'

'For the café?' Bailey said.

Katie smiled a rich girl smile. 'We supply over two hundred cafés and restaurants with our imported blends. I try to get over there at least once a year.'

'Right.'

'What can I get you all to drink?'

They ordered their Costa Rican blends from Katie and then listened as Jock continued his proud father routine, sharing how impressed he was with the business acumen of his daughter, before the conversation moved onto the weather, the bushfires, and the dire predicament that Australian politics had found itself in over the past fifteen years.

'No leadership. None,' Donaldson mused.

'Is that why you're throwing your money at a new magazine? To push for better leadership?' Bailey was testing him.

'That's not my role. I won't be pushing anything.' Donaldson's answer was sharp and clear, like he'd been prepped by Neena. 'I've just marked my seventieth birthday and I felt it was time to give a little back. Do something to make our country better. A well-resourced, independent media can be a powerful tool of democracy.' Donaldson paused, staring directly at Bailey. 'We've had enough meddling by media barons. That's not who I am.'

Bailey leaned back in his chair, folding his arms. 'Good to hear, Jock. You picked a good editor in Neena. We're keen to get stuck in.'

'Six weeks until our first issue, I hear you're working on a feature about that American polemicist, Augustus Strong?'

Bailey looked across at Neena, taking a sip of his coffee. 'That's right. Trying to pin him down for an interview at the moment.'

'Chrystal Armstrong's looking after him, isn't she?'

'Sorry?'

'Chrystal's a friend of mine,' Donaldson said, casually. 'I'm happy to give her a call, if you think that might help?'

'Come on, Jock.' Neena laughed, uncomfortably. 'Cards on the table, please. She's more than a friend.'

A seventy-year-old billionaire dating a woman almost half his age. What a cliché.

'Okay. Okay.' Donaldson smiled, palms up. 'We were an item for a while. Not any more. I couldn't keep up!'

'I can arrange my own interviews, thanks.'

'Bailey –'

'It's all good, Neena.' Bailey smiled at Donaldson. 'I do appreciate the offer. I just like doing my own thing, that's all. Stay in my corner.'

Bailey noticed Donaldson's face harden – just for a moment – before he clapped his hands. 'Good, then. Good. Just an offer.'

'Appreciated, Jock,' Neena said.

Donaldson raised his coffee cup like it was a glass of champagne. 'Principled journalists like you two will be the key to making *Enquirer Magazine* a success. Here's to good journalism.'

Bailey followed Neena's lead, picking up his coffee cup to meet Donaldson's, hovering over the table.

Clink.

The most awkward toast he'd ever made.

—

Thirty minutes later, Bailey was getting dropped back at his house, relieved that the meeting was out of the way.

'Thanks for the lift,' he said. 'And Neena?'

'Yes, Bailey?'

'I'll be politely declining the opportunity to catch up with Jock again.'

Neena nodded. She got it. 'Good luck with the story. I'll check in with you in a couple of weeks. We hit the printers very early. I still think you'll get the cover, but let's see how you go.'

Bailey knew Neena well enough to interpret that as her way of telling him that he'd better deliver a strong story.

'I'll get it there. If I get stuck for contacts, I can always call Jock.'

Neena laughed as he closed the door and she sped off down the street.

The conversation about Chrystal Armstrong had reminded Bailey that he should follow up on the numerous emails he had sent her. Augustus Strong wouldn't be staying in Sydney for long. Bailey's window to interview him was closing. He checked his messages. Nothing. Time to call.

'Chrystal Talent Management, Candy speaking.'

'Candy, John Bailey here from *Enquirer Magazine*. I saw Chrystal last night and she said she'd come back to me about a possible interview with Augustus Strong. Are you able to put me through to her?'

'One moment please.'

Pop music started playing through the phone as Bailey was put on hold.

Seconds later the song cut out and Candy was back.

'I'm sorry, but Chrystal is flat out this morning. She says she'll get back to you later.'

'Today?'

'She just said, "Later".'

Bailey doubted that Candy had spoken to Chrystal, or that she would be calling him back. 'Should I leave my number with you again?'

'I think she's got it.'

'Hey, Candy,' Bailey said, 'how about I just give you all of my details again, just in case.'

The phone went quiet, but Bailey could still hear breathing on the other end.

'Sure. What's your name again?'

Bailey gave Candy his details and politely suggested that a returned phone call today would be preferable.

'She'll do her best.'

CHAPTER 4

He still remembers the hostages running down the stairs. Flashes of white light. Heavily armed police rushing in. Windows smashing. Bursts of gunfire. Every second of the chilling finale of the Lindt Café siege captured by a camera at the commercial television studio across the plaza.

Two people died that day, not including the terrorist. Bailey never included murderers in the body count. Not in the countless suicide bombings he'd covered for *The Journal* in Baghdad. The car bombings in Beirut. And certainly not in the attacks on London's transport system back in 2005. Terrorists were cowards. They never got counted.

The attack at Martin Place was the first time civilians had died in a terrorist attack on Australian soil after September 11. As Bailey opened the glass doors of the Lindt Café, he wanted to believe that the siege hadn't changed the city, but he knew that it had. Concrete bollards outside buildings. Tighter security screenings at airports and sports stadiums. Greater powers for police to stick their noses into people's lives, lock up suspects for longer periods without charge. Terrorism had become the drumbeat of life. It affected everyone. Everything.

Bailey looked at the old G-Shock watch on his wrist. The gift from his father that still meant something. It was 12.55 pm.

Their meeting had been scheduled for one o'clock but Harriet Walker was already inside, seated by the window, picking at a plate of chocolates.

'G'day, Hat.'

'Kenny Baker.' She stood up, pulling him in for a hug. 'That was a good one, Bailey.'

Bailey sat down, admiring the woman opposite. Tough eyes. Toothy smile. Latin skin that dodged wrinkles and sunburn. The years had been kind to her, made her more interesting.

'I was impressed that you remembered.'

Walker had been Bailey's source for a story back in 2011 about how the ADF had tried to cover up the deaths of eight innocent Afghan civilians during a raid by Australian soldiers on a farmhouse in Uruzgan. The ADF had mistakenly identified the farm as a Taliban safehouse. Among the dead were a woman and her five children, ages ranging from eight to fifteen years old. Girls. Boys. Cut down by soldiers with bad information, following orders.

Walker had made copies of the ADF's internal report about the incident, and subsequent communications that confirmed the cover-up, getting the documents to Bailey so that he could tell the world the truth about what had happened. The war in Afghanistan was messy enough, it didn't need more lies. Walker had risked everything – career, friendships, reputation – to get those leaked documents into Bailey's hands. To this day, nobody knew that she had been his source on the inside. Nobody would. Bailey never gave up his sources.

Whenever Bailey had needed to contact Walker in Kabul, he'd leave a message with a fake number and a fake name. The name was always some unrecognisable actor who had played a minor role in the first Star Wars film. Bailey had taken a gamble that Walker would remember their system.

'Bit eerie in here after what happened,' Bailey said, tapping the table. 'Come in much?'

'All the time. Made an effort to make this my coffee spot. Normalise the place. Reclaim it.' She pointed at the plate of chocolates. 'And to satisfy my sweet tooth.'

In those short seconds they'd been talking, Bailey was reminded why he'd admired her. She had principles. Her own personal code. 'You're a good egg, Hat.'

'So, why the sudden contact?' She smiled, popping another chocolate into her mouth. 'It's nice to hear from you. I didn't even know you were back in the country.'

'Yeah . . . been laying low.'

Walker waved at the barista behind the counter, before turning back to Bailey. 'You still drink black coffee, right?'

'Good memory.'

'Now, who or what are you looking into?'

Bailey knew better than to bullshit her, so he got straight to it. 'A who and a what, actually. Benny Hunter and the far right nationalist group he leads called the Freedom Front.'

'I know Benny,' Walker said. 'Shit human.'

'What do you know?'

'A bit.' There was hardly anyone else seated at the wooden tables in the café but Walker lowered her voice, briefly scanning for stickybeaks. 'Plenty of people around like him. Angry, young, mostly white men who blame others for their bad lot in life.

The Freedom Front's no different from those Blue Boys and Patriots . . . whatever they're called. A bunch of loud, headline-chasing troublemakers.'

'You're saying they're harmless?'

'No. I'm not saying that at all. Far right nationalists. Neo-Nazis. White supremacists. Whatever you want to call them, they're on the rise. We've seen what individuals can do. Look at Christchurch. El Paso. But it's quite a leap from doing a Nazi salute at a protest to opening up with an AR-15 semi-automatic assault rifle in a mosque.'

Walker had been working as part of an international team fighting people trafficking when Bailey had first met her in Kabul. She was a stickler for details. Facts. And she wasn't someone who'd talk up a threat if it didn't exist.

'You're investigating them now?' Bailey took a stab.

'You know we don't talk about active investigations.'

'You just seem to know more than a casual observer.'

'Who are you working for, by the way?' Walker said, ignoring Bailey's attempts to steer the conversation. 'I saw your name on the list of redundancies at *The Journal*. Awful what happened at that paper. So much fake news around, we need strong mastheads. Any decent reporters left?'

'Plenty,' Bailey said, feeling strangely loyal to the paper that had sacked more than a dozen senior reporters like him in a cost-cutting drive. 'The paper will go on. I'm working for *Enquirer Magazine*.'

She squinted. 'Should I have heard of it?'

'Not yet. New outfit. Investigative magazine.' Their coffees had arrived and Bailey took a sip. 'You can give it a go when the first issue comes out in March. I'm writing the cover.'

'A cover story on Benny Hunter?' she said, sarcastically. 'You doing his PR for him now?'

Just like with Islamic terrorism, news stories about far right nationalism and white supremacists were often used as propaganda to attract more people to the cause.

'Come off it, Hat. Give me a break.' Bailey knew Walker well enough to not get upset by the dig. 'The story's actually about Augustus Strong and his Australian supporters. How the far right movement's growing here, like everywhere else.'

'Right. Sorry, that was a little harsh.'

'We've known each other a long time, Hat. It's all good. I know what you meant. I'd be interested in anything you can get me on Strong too.'

'I can do that.'

'And there's this.' Bailey unlocked his mobile phone, clicking play on the vision he'd secretly taken of the crowd at Strong's talk. 'I only got a couple of minutes. It's not award-winning cinematography, either. But there was a whole room full of far right nationalists at Strong's event last night. Footage is yours, if you want it. Only deal is that you share anything interesting.'

Walker slid her phone across the table. 'AirDrop it to me. No promises, but I'll take a look.'

'Thanks.'

They both placed their phones on the table, sipping on their coffees in silence.

'Bailey?' Walker said, eventually.

'Yeah.'

'Are we even going to talk about her?'

Sharon Dexter.

Bailey knew this was coming. It was probably one of the reasons why Walker had agreed to meet him so quickly. Walker and Dexter had been tight. Good friends. They'd started out in the New South Wales Police together before Walker made the switch to the feds.

'What's the point?' Bailey said, instantly regretting his bluntness.

Walker sighed. 'C'mon, Bailey. I'm not asking you to talk about what happened in London. She was my friend too. And we're friends, aren't we? So I'm asking as a friend, are you okay?'

Bailey could feel that lump in his throat whenever he thought too deeply about Dexter. The one person who had loved him for the complicated, flawed idiot that he was. Gone.

'As good as can be, Hat.'

At least he was being honest.

'Are you talking to someone?'

'Did all that. Moving on now.'

Bailey had hated all those sessions with psychologists. Doctor Jane. Doctor Bob. Doctor fucking prescribe you anything. He had resisted taking any medication but, admittedly, talking about what had happened had helped him to deal with it. Move on.

'How about you, Hat?' Bailey knew that Walker would have been hurting too. She'd lost a close friend. Bailey felt like a selfish prick for only thinking about himself. 'You okay?'

'I think about her all the time, to be honest.' Walker smiled, solemnly. 'She was tough, a good friend to me. Bloody gorgeous too.'

'Yeah, she was.'

Walker leaned down and started rummaging around in her handbag. She placed a set of keys on the table.

'These are yours. Sharon had my spares, I had hers.'

Bailey stared at the keys without saying a word. Dexter had been an only child, her parents long dead. She had left everything to him. He still hadn't gone back to her house in Leichhardt. Not ready for final goodbyes.

'I've dropped in a few times, checking in on the place. Emptied out the fridge. All the perishables. I've been paying the power bill to keep the sensor light working out front. For security.'

'I'll fix you up for that, Hat.'

'I don't care about the money, Bailey. But there's a lot of your things at the house too. Flanos hanging in the wardrobe. Jeans. Blundstone boots.' She laughed. 'You've been wearing the same shit ever since I've known you.'

Bailey forced a laugh. 'Not much into fashion. If the boot fits, right?'

Walker reached across the table, squeezing his hand. 'I'll go with you, if you don't want to go alone.'

He cleared his throat, slipping his hand away and grabbing his cup, draining what was left. 'Keep the keys, Hat. I've got a set. Always good to have spares somewhere different.'

Walker picked up the keys, smiling, staring at them like they were something more, before shoving them back in her bag. 'Sure.'

'When do you think you might get back to me about the video?'

'Give me a day, or two. You on Signal?'

Signal was an encrypted messaging service used by anyone with a secret. Drug dealers. Journalists. Intelligence officers. They all used it. Secure. Untraceable.

'Yep.'

'That's what we'll use.' She handed Bailey her business card, pushing the plate of chocolates towards him. 'One left. Go on.'

'All yours, Hat.'

Bailey's phone started to vibrate, rattling his empty coffee cup on the saucer.

'Answer it.' Walker picked the last chocolate off the plate. 'I'll come back to you soon.'

'Thanks. You go, I'll get this.' Bailey was pointing at the empty plate and cups on the table as he held his phone to his ear. 'John Bailey.'

'Bailey, it's Jonny Abdo. I've spoken to the family of that man assaulted on Oxford Street last night.'

Bailey watched Walker disappear out the door. 'How is he?'

'Not great. Swelling on the brain, busted cheekbone,' Abdo said. 'They're keeping him in an induced coma for at least another day or so, hoping that the swelling will go down.'

'Sorry to hear that, mate.'

'There's more. He was with me earlier in the night. Part of our demonstration against Augustus Strong.'

'Got a name?'

'Can we meet?'

'Yeah. Where?'

'Summer Hill. There's a café called Goblin near the station, can't miss it. One hour?'

'Done.'

CHAPTER 5

It was just after two o'clock and the peak-hour traffic was already building. Heavier than usual for this time of year. The bushfires ravaging coastal towns had forced people to abandon their January holiday plans and the city was heaving. Cars lined up bumper to bumper. Exhausts puffing more crap into the air. The voice on the radio telling Bailey the air quality index was worse than Beijing and that breathing today would be like smoking an entire packet of cigarettes.

He fiddled with the air conditioning settings, wondering whether recycled air or the breeze from outside would be better for his lungs. He had no idea. As a recovering alcoholic, Bailey had pumped a lot more poison through his body than cigarettes. He settled for outside air and gave up worrying about it.

Beep! Beep!

Bailey looked up just as the traffic light turned from orange to red. While he'd been pondering the air, a large gap had formed between his old wagon and the car in front, which was now edging further away along the edge of Hyde Park by the cathedral.

Beep! Beep! Beep!

The guy in the car behind was bashing his steering wheel,

waving his arms and mouthing all kinds of profanities at Bailey for missing the light.

'Settle down, idiot.' Bailey was speaking into his rear-view mirror. 'It's not going to kill you.'

People in Sydney were angry at the best of times but the tension in the smoke-choked city had turned some drivers into raging bulls. There were bigger things to worry about in life than shaving a few seconds off a car trip, like watching your house go up in flames or losing someone you loved. Much bigger things.

Bailey turned up the radio, ignoring the guy behind, who was still shaking his head.

'Hello, dear listeners. You're listening to a special extended edition of the program today as we seek to bring you the latest information about these terrible bushfires. The worst in living memory. What's causing them.'

Here we go, thought Bailey. Keith Roberts – the king of Sydney's airwaves – was about to inject his wisdom into the fire-fighting debate.

'I know there are those of you out there who think that it's all about climate change, that if we didn't have our coal-fired power stations doing their bit to deliver cheap power bills to struggling families, then there'd be no fires. But it's simply not true, dear listeners. I know there are people out there running their own agendas. Playing the politics. But I'll say it again. It's simply not true.'

Bailey made himself listen to Roberts from time to time because, as a journalist, he tried to consume a bit of everything. The left, the right, and even the unhinged. More often than not, Keith Roberts fitted into the latter category but somehow he had the top rating talk radio show in the country. Like him or not, he had a loyal army of followers, which made him powerful.

'Let's bring in our next guest, shadow environment minister, Laura Fleming. Hello to you, Laura.'

'Hi, Keith, how are –'

'Now, I want to get straight to the point with you here, Laura. How on earth can you live with yourself by putting these lies out there about climate change? Aren't people suffering enough? We've got brave firefighters, most of them volunteers, out there holding hoses to flames. People losing their homes. Loved ones too. And you're trying to score political points. Tell me, Laura. Tell me. How do you sleep at night?'

Sometimes guests were merely props on Roberts' show and Bailey knew that Laura Fleming hadn't been invited on to have a meaningful debate about how to deal with the impacts of climate change. She'd been invited on his show to play the punching bag for Roberts' bullying invective. But she couldn't decline the invitation. Politicians didn't dare say no to Keith Roberts.

'You know that's not what I'm saying, Keith,' Laura calmly responded. 'And I don't think you're being entirely truthful with your listeners. There are many reasons why these bushfires are so bad this year. The drought, for starters, and the incredibly dry fuel loads –'

'Exactly. Exactly. Fuel loads. That's exactly right, Laura.' Roberts was sounding smug, interrupting her only to demonstrate that he was in control of the interview. Not her. 'Then why are you going on about all that climate claptrap rubbish?'

'If you'd let me finish my point, Keith. What I –'

'I'll let you tell the truth, Laura. That's what I'll do.'

'Okay, Keith. But what I was going to say was that twenty of the world's hottest years ever recorded have been in the last twenty-two years. Global temperatures are already one degree hotter than they were a hundred years ago. Carbon emissions are still rising and we know that fossil fuels are the biggest driver of the changing climate. We know that because scientists tell us so. All of them. So, what we've been saying is that we'll see more extreme weather events like we're seeing now if we don't do something to –'

'No. No. I'm sorry, Laura, I'm going to cut you off there. If you and the Greens had allowed the states to conduct hazard reduction burns like firefighters had wanted during those winter months then these fires wouldn't be nearly as bad as they are.' Roberts was starting to speak more quickly, a hint of aggression in his voice. Disdain. 'And don't you lecture us about climate change. Scientists this and scientists that. Global warming has always happened. It's the way of the world. Why don't we get to your real agenda here. The plan that you've been secretly hatching with the Greens.'

'What are you talking about, Keith? We don't have any deal with –'

'No. No. You've had your say, Laura Fleming. We've heard your bit. Now it's my turn. It's my show, after all,' Roberts said. 'Australians don't like liars. They don't like secret agendas, or tricky politicians. So just tell the truth, Laura. Admit that you've done a special deal with the Greens to hatch a coup against this government at the next election.'

Bailey's hand was touching the dial, ready to cleanse his ears of the nonsense that was bouncing off the windows in his car.

'I'm talking about your deal to shut down every coal-fired power station in this country. Force businesses into renewables when there's no need. Admit it. We all know that climate change is just some left-wing socialist conspiracy to redistribute wealth and –'

Click.

That was enough for Bailey. He almost felt like he needed another shower, or at least something to wash out his ears. If Keith Roberts really was the voice of the street then the street had problems. The country had problems. Big ones.

Beep!

The light was green and the guy behind Bailey was bashing his steering wheel again.

Time to get moving.

Bailey cut through Surry Hills and hooked past Central, narrowly avoiding being hit by a merging bus at Railway Square, heading west on Broadway. He stopped at a traffic light outside One Central Park just long enough to admire the building's famous heliostat flickering above in the afternoon light, his windscreen catching a spray of mist from the watering system that fed the thirty-five thousand plants that gave the building its big green coat. Sydney could thank a Parisian dreamer for this rare jewel in the city's concrete crown. Most of the other developers let loose during the construction boom would struggle to compete in a Lego competition at a childcare centre.

The traffic was moving slowly and Bailey found himself interrogating the western flank of the city like it was the first time he'd seen it. Sydney University's gothic buildings glowering at the brothels and massage parlours across the road. The pubs and cafés with student meal deals plastered on windows. Billboards hovering in the sky advertising some new streaming service or another superhero character that Bailey had never heard of before.

A few kilometres further along Parramatta Road and the footpath ran dead. It was like developers in Sydney's inner west had downed tools at suburbs like Petersham and Leichhardt. Decaying shopfronts in death throes, if they weren't already six feet under. Windows covered with sheets of old newspapers sandwiched in between shops offering second-hand furniture, musical instruments, wedding dresses and bicycles.

If Australia's economy was flying like politicians had been boasting, who was raking in all the cash? It certainly wasn't the small businesses around here.

Despite the traffic, Bailey made it to Summer Hill with a few minutes to spare. The suburb had an odd mix of federation mansions and slabs of medium density apartment blocks that had been deposited along the rail line. Summer Hill was also popular for having a quaint shopping village and its very own methadone clinic.

Bailey found a car spot out front of the café where he was meeting Jonny Abdo and sat down at an empty table on the footpath. His attention was instantly drawn to a message carved into the concrete telling a former prime minister to do something rather obscene to himself. That was the other thing about most of the people in the inner west. They hated the conservative side of politics, voting Labor, or Greens.

'What can I get you, friend?'

It was Bailey's experience that people who worked in cafés and restaurants in Sydney grew more polite the further west he travelled from the city.

'Coffee, thanks. Black.'

His fourth for the day, not that he was counting. Bailey could drink coffee like water.

'And might as well leave the menu.' Bailey was pointing at the clipboard on the table. 'I'm expecting someone and I reckon that at least I'll eat.'

'Done.'

Bailey had been perusing the menu and he missed Jonny Abdo sitting down.

'Sorry, I'm a bit late.'

'Jonny.' Bailey extended his hand across the table, almost knocking over the bottle of water that had also escaped his attention. 'I just ordered a coffee. Want one? And I'm going to get myself this all-day breakfast they've got here.' He pointed to his choice on the menu as he handed the wooden clipboard to Abdo.

'Breakfast?'

'The stomach wants what the stomach wants,' Bailey said, shrugging his shoulders. 'I forgot about lunch and only had a banana when I got up.'

'Fair enough.' Abdo put the menu on the table without showing much interest. 'I don't have long. I have a meeting around the corner at three.'

'No worries.' Bailey flipped open his notebook. 'What'd you find out?'

Abdo looked nervously at the pen in Bailey's hand. 'The family doesn't want his name in the media. Not yet, anyway.'

'That's okay, mate. This can all be background. I'm not writing for *The Journal* any more. I'm working on a longer investigative piece about far right nationalism. It's why I was at Strong's talk.'

'Okay.'

'I remember you saying that some of the people at last night's demonstration were your students,' Bailey said. 'Are you teaching too?'

'I teach a class at the University of Western Sydney. A couple of lectures each semester.'

'Right. Right.' Bailey was nodding his head, already thinking about his next question, hoping that Abdo wouldn't get defensive. 'Who organised the demonstration, by the way? Was that you?'

Abdo sat back, folding his arms. 'Are you asking me as a journalist?'

'A journalist and a friend.'

Abdo rolled his shoulders backwards, looking up at the sky. 'Does it matter?'

'It wasn't your fault, Jonny. You can't blame yourself for what happened. I'm just after the truth. If I'm going to write about Strong, that also means writing about the people who love and hate him. I write what I see. What I know. So yeah, people holding placards labelling him a racist are part of it. Has to be.' Bailey paused, holding Abdo's stare. 'You're a smart guy, Jonny. You know how this goes. You just need to decide whether or not you trust me.'

They both got distracted by the screeching tyres of a van on the road beside them. The driver waving his arm out the window, screaming at a cyclist. 'Get off the road, you fucking lycra poofter!'

The cyclist gave the driver the finger, pedalling off in the opposite direction.

'People are so angry,' Abdo said, shaking his head, pointing at the van as it sped away.

'Jonny?' Bailey knew they didn't have long and he wanted to get back to their conversation. 'Are we good?'

'I get it.' Abdo relaxed, nodding. 'I was one of the organisers of last night's protest . . . yes. It's not something I do very often. Many of my students had voiced concerns with me about the home affairs minister's intervention in granting Strong a visa. For the government to support a man like this, saying it's just about free speech, misses the point. Strong was caught on camera giving the Nazi salute in America, for god's sake. He knows what he's doing. So we thought it was important to have a presence outside so that events like this don't go unnoticed. That the people who go along can't hide in the shadows.'

Bailey decided to shift gears, knowing that he could follow up about the protest later. 'Let's talk about what happened at the White Lion. What can you tell me?'

'Some of the students said they were going out for drinks afterwards,' Abdo said. 'There must have been about five or six of them.'

'And they ended up at the White Lion on Oxford Street?'

'It seems so, yes.'

The waiter arrived on the pavement beside them. 'You guys ready to order?'

'I'll get the all-day breakfast. Eggs fried.' Bailey turned to Jonny. 'Are you sure you don't want something?'

Abdo looked at his watch. 'I'm sorry. I've got to go in ten.'

'All good. All good.' The waiter picked up the clipboard menu from the table. 'Just the all-day brekky, then.'

Bailey waited for him to leave before resuming his questions. 'What can you tell me about the man who was attacked?'

'Nineteen years old. Matthew Lam . . . Matt. He's in my class.

I helped his parents with their residency applications some years ago. I know the family well.'

'On the phone you told me that he was in an induced coma. What are the doctors saying?'

Abdo pulled a paper napkin from the dispenser, using it to mop the beads of sweat on his brow.

'Are you okay, Jonny?'

'I parked up the road. The heat I don't mind but the humidity kills me.' He finished patting his head, stuffing the napkin in his pocket. 'The doctors say it's too early to know whether there has been any lasting damage to Matt's brain. But they're hopeful.'

'I'm sorry.'

Abdo rested his elbows on the table, leaning forward. 'When you look at me, what do you see?'

'What?' The question caught Bailey off guard. 'What do you mean?'

'I mean what I said.' There was anger in his voice. 'What do you see when you look at me?'

Bailey felt like he had a spotlight pointed at his head. Nowhere to go. No right answer. 'I see the kid I met in Egypt all those years ago. Only he's grown up. No longer afraid. A lawyer. A leader. Against the odds.'

Abdo shook his head, rubbing his eyes.

'What are you doing, mate?' Bailey said, calmly. Gently. 'What do you want me to see?'

'You know.' Abdo pointed his index finger at Bailey, pressing it on the table. 'You know this country isn't the easygoing place that it likes to portray to the world. Any person with skin like mine has a story to tell about being racially abused. Treated differently. In schools. On public transport. Job interviews.

Casual racism, they call it. As if there's a bloody difference. But that's not what happened last night at that bar. This was violent. Calculated.'

Bailey was relieved that they were back talking about the night before. 'What makes you say that?'

'A group of men wearing masks rushed into the bar and went straight for Matt and the others. They knew they were in there. Maybe they followed them after the demonstration? I don't know.' Abdo was speaking faster. Angry. 'Matt's a big man, he must have tried to defend the others. Take them on. They dragged him outside, beating him. Apparently, he fell. Hitting his head on the gutter.'

This was more detail than Bailey was expecting and he was wondering why the police hadn't mentioned any of these details in the media release they'd put out that morning.

'What about the attackers, Jonny? Did anyone at the bar recognise the people who attacked Matt?'

'As I said, they were wearing masks. But from what I've been told, they resembled some of the men we saw coming out of Strong's talk. Their clothes. Builds. But with their faces covered, there's no way of knowing.'

Abdo took a break, taking a sip from the glass of water in front of him.

'What do you want me to do with this information, Jonny?'

'Get it in the media, I don't know,' Jonny said, throwing his hands up. 'It should be out there. I don't understand why the police are holding back information.'

The police would have their reasons. They were probably already talking to witnesses, scouring through security camera footage from both inside the pub and the streets around

Woollahra and Paddington. Releasing too much information in the early stages of an investigation could often be counter-productive, stopping people from coming forward. But if this was a racist attack then the public should know. Men in masks bashing people because of the colour of their skin. This wasn't the country that Bailey knew. Sunlight was always the best medicine, any journalist would tell you that. The public needed to know.

'I'll make some enquiries, Jonny. Talk to some people.'

And by 'people' Bailey meant his old colleagues at *The Journal*. Someone working in daily news.

'Just not Matt's name. Please keep his name out of it, for now.' Abdo stood up, checking his phone. 'I need to get to that meeting. I'll call you if I find out anything more.'

Bailey stood up. 'One more thing, mate.'

'Yes?'

'The people who were with Matt at the White Lion. Do you think they might talk to me?'

'Maybe. I don't know. They're scared, Bailey. Word is getting around about what happened. Families are scared.'

'I get that. But as you said yourself, people need to know.'

'I'll come back to you.'

Abdo nodded his head and left.

'Here you go, buddy.'

The waiter placed a plate of bacon, eggs and mushrooms in front of Bailey. It smelled good, reminding him how hungry he was.

'Thanks.'

He needed to eat quickly. The evening shift would be arriving at the White Lion soon. Witnesses to a crime.

Bailey had just one more stop to make first.

CHAPTER 6

It was strange being back here. The place where Bailey had cut his teeth as a cub reporter back in the 1980s: *The Journal*'s headquarters on Sussex Street. Where someone had always picked up the phone, whatever time of day or night. A reassuring voice to calm Bailey's nerves when he'd called from whatever shithole he'd landed in to report on the Middle East's forever wars. For almost two decades the voice on the end of the line at *The Journal* usually belonged to the paper's chief of staff, Rachel Symonds.

'Just hit the buzzer at the ramp and security will let you in,' Symonds had told Bailey when he'd called to let her know he was dropping by. 'Booked you a carpark downstairs.'

Idling in the traffic, Bailey had plenty of time to think about the past. The watering holes where he went drinking with his colleagues and the hacks from the wire service and radio station whose headquarters were also nearby. The Star. The Covent Garden. The Criterion. That old bar with the name he could never remember, where Labor politicians would get full of booze and drop stories to reporters hungry for a scoop.

The Criterion had been Bailey's favourite boozer. It had character. Walls stained with cigarette smoke. Carpet soaked with so much beer that it was like walking on a velcro blanket. On some Friday nights at the end of a busy news week it was like every journalist in the city drank there, the lack of air conditioning turning the place into a human hot box. Bailey remembered one night in there when it was so hot that the termites couldn't even take it any more, chewing their way through the wood panelling and swarming the bar. None of the journalists bothered complaining to management because the beer taps were still working.

The last time Bailey had found himself on Sussex Street wasn't to visit a pub. A few months back he dropped by merely to collect a cardboard box filled with unopened mail, old notebooks and the picture of his daughter that sat beside the computer on his desk. The day he went to collect his things. The day his redundancy became real.

'John Bailey to see Rachel Symonds,' Bailey said into the intercom at the top of *The Journal*'s driveway. 'She booked me a spot –'

'Mr Bailey! How the hell are you?'

Mick.

Bailey knew that voice. The guy on the front desk who never stopped talking about his kids.

'G'day, Mick. Good to hear your voice. How's the family?'

'Everyone's good. Although my boys are running around the house tackling furniture at the moment. Bring on the footy season, I say.'

Bailey laughed. 'You still coaching?'

'I'll be saddling up again for sure, Mr Bailey. Love it,' Mick said. 'Reserved you a spot on level four. Car spot forty-nine.'

'Thanks.'

Bailey waited for the electric gate to open before easing his wagon down the ramp. *The Journal* shared the building with a big law firm and the parking lot was more like a European car show, with fancy job titles dangling like street signs to deter peasants like Bailey.

Arriving on level four, he paused at the carpark reserved for the editor of *The Journal*. A spot that had once been reserved for his best friend, Gerald Summers. Gerald had been one of the best editors the paper had ever had. The guy who'd transitioned *The Journal* into the digital age, while safeguarding the editorial standards that had made it so great. But like Bailey, Gerald had been let go by the private equity mob that had ripped through the place, firing as many highly paid, and competent, reporters as they could find in their bid to maximise profits and chase clicks and shares. The bean counters had found a willing patsy to saddle up as editor for the next wave of the digital revolution. Adrian Greenberg. The ambitious national affairs editor with a reputation for being a letch with women and for never shouting a round at the bar. The guy would have dobbed in his own mother for a promotion. And Bailey had told him as much on the last day he was there.

'Hey, Adrian?' Bailey had poked his head into the editor's office, where Greenberg was deep in conversation with a young reporter that Bailey had never met. 'Congratulations. For someone who has never had much luck with the ladies, somehow you managed to fuck us all.'

'You're a self-righteous arsehole, Bailey. You know that?'

'Yes, Adrian. I do.'

Bailey smiled to himself, remembering the encounter and the angry look on Greenberg's face, as he settled his wagon into the editor's car spot. One more fuck you for the establishment.

—

'Over here, Bailey.'

Symonds was bobbing tea bags in the kitchen near the elevators when Bailey arrived on the fourteenth floor.

'Fixing us a cuppa.'

Her smile carried an unmistakable hint of regret.

'Rach.'

Balancing two steaming mugs in her hand, she gave him a one-armed hug and steered them into the boardroom, away from reporters bashing away at keyboards and talking into phones. Bailey caught the eyes of a couple of people he didn't recognise, nodding his chin at the few that he did. There were a lot of empty desks, including the one he'd once occupied.

'Have a seat.' Symonds pointed at one of the leather chairs facing the window. 'To what do I owe the pleasure?'

Straight to the point. Another reason why Bailey liked her.

'I know you're busy, Rach, so I won't stay long.' Bailey took a sip of his tea, placing the mug on the table. 'I'm working on a story about far right nationalism and Augustus Strong.'

'A story? Who're you writing for?'

Bailey told her about the new job at *Enquirer Magazine*, Jock Donaldson and the team of reporters that Neena Singh had been assembling.

'That's great, Bailey. Glad you landed on your feet.'

He decided to get straight to it. He knew how busy Symonds was and he'd already noticed her checking her watch.

'I've got some information about that Sudanese kid who got bashed up on Oxford Street last night.'

'Possible hate crime, police are telling us. No one will go on the record. What d'you know?'

'Consider it confirmed. Blokes wearing masks burst in there, singling out the guy because of the colour of his skin. Victim's a nineteen-year-old law student.'

Symonds sat forward, elbows leaning on the desk. 'Go on.'

'His university lecturer's an old friend of mine. Known him since he was a kid. He was with a bunch of students staging a protest outside Augustus Strong's event last night. I'm working on a theory that the guys who bashed him were also at Strong's talk. The kids went up to the White Lion for drinks afterwards. They may have been followed. It's a relatively short walk from Surry Hills.'

'So why are you telling me all this?'

'I'm working on a broader investigative piece. First edition of *Enquirer Magazine*'s still more than a month away. I knew you'd have someone on the story. This information needs to be out there now.'

Symonds' lips pursed. Thinking. 'Got a name for the victim?'

'Family doesn't want his name in the media. Not while he's banged up in hospital.'

Bailey knew that Symonds trusted him, but she couldn't get one of her reporters to write up what he'd told her without confirming a few details first. Journalism 101.

'Will your guy speak to us?'

'Can you give me a minute?'

'Sure. I'll go check on what else we've got.' Symonds pushed her chair back and headed for the door. 'I don't think it's much. I've had someone chasing it all day.'

Bailey waited for the door to close before making the call. Jonny Abdo answered straight away and, surprisingly, it didn't take long for Bailey to convince him to agree to talk on the record.

By the time Symonds had returned, Bailey had Abdo on speaker-phone repeating everything he'd said back in Summer Hill that afternoon. The only thing that was off limits was naming Matthew Lam as the victim. The family still wasn't ready. But the fact that Abdo had agreed to go on the record meant that *The Journal* had a strong story. A community lawyer calling out a hate crime, wanting the police to do more.

'Might get a front page splash with this one,' Symonds said after Bailey had ended the call. 'Give everyone a break from these nightmare bushfires. I reckon the public's getting . . .' Symonds was distracted by someone yelling obscenities in the newsroom on the other side of the door. 'I'd better check on that.'

Bailey followed her through the door as another door slammed down the corridor.

'What was all that about?' Symonds asked a woman working at the computer closest to where they were standing.

'Apparently someone parked in Greenberg's car spot again. Second time it's happened this week. He's not happy.'

Symonds looked at Bailey, the corner of her lip creeping towards a smile. 'You didn't.'

Bailey shrugged. 'It's confusing down there.'

'You'd better get out of here, Bailey.' Symonds was laughing now. 'And thanks for the tip.'

CHAPTER 7

Bailey could hear Campo sniffing and whimpering inside the house before he'd even made it onto his front porch. The dog had almost supernatural senses, smelling his approach from half a block away.

'All right, Campo. Calm down.'

The dog was all over him the second he opened the door, sniffing his knees to see where he'd been, wagging her tail in anticipation of a walk, some dinner, or just someone for her big beady eyes to stare at for the rest of the night. Campo did not like being alone.

With the temperature in the high thirties today, Bailey had left her inside the house. The courtyard out back would have been like a hotbox.

'Come on. We're going for a wander.'

Bailey grabbed Campo's leash, clipping it to her collar, the wagging of her tail gathering speed like a helicopter readying for take-off.

The jacaranda trees lining Bailey's street had already lost their purple bells but their fat trunks were still worthy of a sniff from Campo, who was meandering along the path, tree to tree, depositing small puddles of piss to mark her territory.

'Afternoon, Bryce.' Bailey had only made it halfway up the street when he noticed his neighbour strapping surfboards to the roof of his Range Rover. 'Heading off for a late surf?'

'Hi, Bailey.' Bryce stopped what he was doing, climbing down off the running board so the two men could shake hands. 'Heading up to the house at Blueys for a few days. Need to escape this bloody smoke, it's sending us all mad.'

'Relentless. Hope none of your family or friends have lost anything in these fires.'

'No. We're okay, thanks. Although I heard a few families at the school lost their holiday homes a bit further north from ours. Up near Port Macquarie. Taree.'

'Hello, Bailey.' Jenny Ratcliffe had walked through the gate, her son and daughter in tow, holding out a bag with wine and chips for her husband. 'Thanks, darling.'

'How are you, Jenny?'

Jenny looked stressed, her face flushed and sweaty. 'Fine. Fine. Just struggling with this awful summer like everyone else.'

Bailey could never remember the names of the Ratcliffe children, so he offered them a collective wave. 'How are you, guys?'

'Good thanks, Mr Bailey. You well?'

The Ratcliffes' son answered for the both of them because their daughter couldn't have been less interested in chatting with their neighbour.

'Good thanks . . .'

'Russell.'

Bailey smiled, awkwardly. 'That's right. Russell.'

'Who's this?' Russell said, dropping to one knee, patting Campo on the head, seemingly unperturbed by Bailey's forgetfulness. 'I didn't know you had a dog.'

'That's Campo. Haven't had her long.'

'Campo?' Bryce raised an eyebrow, smirking. 'After the –'

'Yep. She's got a good step on her too.'

'Melissa, are you going to say hello?' Jenny Ratcliffe was giving death stares to her daughter who had a pair of headphones wrapped around her neck and a scowl on her face.

'Hi.'

Melissa faked a smile and climbed into the back seat of the four-wheel drive, lifting her headphones over her ears.

'Teenagers,' Jenny said.

Bailey laughed. 'I remember.'

Russell was still ruffling Campo's ears. 'Nice dog.'

'She's a rescue. My daughter got her for me. I think you're at university now, aren't you, Russell?' Bailey said. 'How's it going?'

'Deferred,' Russell said, getting back on his feet.

An awkward silence followed until, eventually, Bryce cut in. 'Russell's still working out what he wants to do with his life. Aren't you, mate?'

'Something like that. Good to see you, Mr Bailey.'

Russell smiled, climbing inside the four-wheel drive alongside Melissa.

'You too, mate.'

'Bryce,' Jenny said, 'I've locked up. I think it's time to go.'

Bailey left the family to pile into the four-wheel drive, thinking back and trying to remember what Miranda was like at that age, shamefully realising that he didn't really know. Miranda's teenage years were a blur. The years when Bailey had been so focused on his job chasing stories about war and terrorism that he hadn't been much of a father. Being held hostage and tortured by Islamic extremists in Iraq had offered Bailey a painful reminder about the life he'd left behind. The life he'd missed out on. Ten months in captivity had given him a lot of time to think. He had made a vow to himself that if he made it out alive, he'd be a better father to Miranda. Repair the damage of the lost years. Be there for her. And he had.

—

The plank of plywood on the White Lion's front door was gone, replaced by a new sheet of glass. The only sign of last night's violence was a dark stain on the concrete. The guy with the hose had done his best but dried blood was a hell of a thing to make disappear. Or maybe Bailey was just seeing things.

He tied Campo's leash to a pole out front and walked over to the security guard, all dressed in black, checking customers' birth dates and sobriety at the entrance.

'G'day, mate.'

'You're right, go in.'

'I was actually hoping to ask you a few questions, if that's all right.'

'Hang on.'

Bailey stepped to the side, letting a small group of people flash their driver's licences to the all-powerful man on the front door who could make or break their night.

'Happy birthday.' The security guard smiled at a girl who looked like she had come straight from school. 'Take it easy.'

'Thanks.'

The guard waited for the door to close behind them before turning to Bailey. 'Odds on favourite to be spewing in the alley by ten.'

Bailey laughed along with him. Building a rapport – trust – for the questions that would follow.

'So, what can I do for you?'

'My name's John Bailey. I'm a journalist. Just looking into what happened here last night, wondering if you were here and might be able to let me know what you saw.'

'Night off last night.' The guy looked past Bailey's shoulder to the couple approaching, waving them through. 'Enjoy the night, guys.'

'Anyone working who was here last night?'

'Best talking to the manager,' he said, thumb pointing over his shoulder towards the bar. 'Short stocky blonde. Name's Tanya.'

'Thanks.'

There wasn't much of a crowd inside, although it was still early. Just after six-thirty on a Wednesday night. Tanya wasn't hard to find, the security guard's description spot-on. She was loading a tray stocked with notes and coins into the register beside the beer taps.

'Excuse me.'

She looked up. Busy. 'What can I get you?'

'Lemonade would be good, thanks.'

Bailey thought that he'd better order something, giving them a reason to converse.

'Four fifty,' she said, shovelling some ice into a glass.

Almost five bucks for a glass of sugar and water. He could have bought a beer for that price at the RSL down the road. But now wasn't the time to complain.

'Are you Tanya?'

'Yeah.'

'My name's John Bailey. I'm a journalist. I'm just wondering if I can ask you a couple of questions about what happened here last night.'

Tanya stopped the flow of lemonade coming from the post-mix pistol in her hand. 'Sorry, mate. Don't really want my name in a newspaper.' She resumed pouring, placing the glass on the wooden bar in front of Bailey.

'Off the record is fine.' He handed her a ten-dollar note. 'Your name won't come into it.'

Tanya dropped Bailey's change on the bar mat and he put the lot into her tip jar, currying favour.

'What do you want to know?'

It worked.

'Anything you can remember, to be honest. I heard a group of guys with face masks came in and started a fight. Is that right?'

'At first I thought they were going to rob the place, balaclavas and all that.' Tanya looked around the pub, leaning across the bar. 'And I wouldn't quite call it a fight either. They went straight for this group of mainly Black guys and girls. Yelling all sorts of racist stuff.' She looked uncomfortable, reluctant to repeat the words. 'Y'know what I mean.'

'Yeah.'

'Anyway, it all escalated pretty quickly. Our guard on the front door had no chance of stopping them. Not his fault. We've given him a few nights off because he's so shaken up by the whole bloody thing.'

'So, what happened?'

A man appeared beside Bailey at the bar, pondering the beer taps like it was the most important decision of his life. Sydney's craft beer craze had left him with too many options.

'Nicki!' Tanya called out to a woman polishing wine glasses just as the man went to ask a question. 'Could you serve this customer, please?'

Bailey followed Tanya down the end of the bar. 'Bit light on staff, I don't have too much time to talk.'

'No worries,' Bailey said. 'You said it escalated quickly?'

'Yeah. This big Black guy starts pushing them back. A few punches thrown. There must have been six or seven guys with masks. One of them threw a bloody bar stool through the glass,' she said, shaking her head. 'They drag this guy outside and next thing I know he's lying on the footpath, bleeding. Out cold. I called the cops and asked for an ambulance too. Knew it was bad. How is he, do you know?'

'Not great, to be honest. He's in an induced coma. I've been talking to a friend of the family.' Bailey wanted her to know that he was interested in the victim. 'They hope he's going to be okay but won't know for a little while yet. What about security cameras? Any chance I can take a look?'

'Sorry. Cops took all that. Not sure I could show you, anyway.'

'Understood.' Bailey wasn't getting far. Everything she had told him he had already learned from media reports and his conversations with Jonny Abdo. 'What about these guys who barged in, was there anything else about them you remember? Their clothing? Did you glimpse a face?'

'They were clearly all blokes, I think I told you that. Clothes? Jeans. Shirts. T-shirts. Nothing that really stands out.' She paused, face scrunching. 'Actually, there was one thing.'

'What's that?'

Bailey instantly regretted interrupting her. Too eager.

'A tattoo. The big Black guy ripped one of their shirts. He had a tattoo on his chest.'

'Do you remember what it was? A symbol? A word?'

'It was a number, actually. Two numbers. Fourteen and eighty-eight. Written in an odd way.'

Bailey grabbed a napkin off the bar and a pen from his pocket. 'Can you show me?'

'Sure.'

Tanya took the pen and scribbled on the napkin, holding it up when she'd finished: 14/88.

'Fourteen eighty-eight?'

Tanya shrugged. 'That's how I remember it. But, like I said, it all happened so fast that I only saw it for a second. Shirt got ripped as they were dragging him outside. And then he was on the ground, unconscious, and they ran off somewhere.'

Fourteen and eighty-eight. Something about the numbers was familiar to Bailey but he couldn't remember why.

'I need to get back to work, mate.'

Bailey dug into his pocket for a card. 'This is me. If you remember anything else, can you give me a call?'

'Yeah, sure.' She was looking down at the card in her hand. '*Enquirer Magazine*. Haven't heard of that one.'

'It's new. First edition comes out in March.'

Tanya looked puzzled. 'And you're doing a story on what happened last night?'

'Might be part of it,' Bailey said. 'Looking at racism in Australia.'

She laughed, uncomfortably. 'Plenty of it. I haven't seen anything like I saw last night though. Scary thing is . . . the whole race thing doesn't surprise me.'

'What d'you mean?'

'Look around you, mate. Mostly white people around here. I live in Campsie. Full of Asians. Go further west and it's the Lebanese, Iraqis. Sydney's a segregated place these days. Maybe you should write about that.'

The one thing that Bailey missed about being off the drink was the truth talk he heard in pubs. Publicans had the best ear to the street. They knew what was happening in people's homes. What kept families up at night. They also knew how to pick winners at the track and inside parliament.

'Might just do that. Thanks for the chat.'

When Bailey stepped outside, Campo was staring innocently at him, wagging her tail beside a mountainous turd on the footpath.

'She left you a present,' the guard said, pointing and smiling. 'She's good like that.'

Bailey pulled a plastic bag from his pocket, wondering who was the superior partner in the relationship. He bathed Campo, fed her, patted her, and right now he was lifting her steaming turd off the concrete. Bailey couldn't help thinking that if aliens were looking down on earth, monitoring behaviours, they'd probably think dogs were the ones running the world.

CHAPTER 8

It wasn't difficult to find the meaning of the tattoo that Tanya had glimpsed beneath a torn shirt at the White Lion. The fourteen and eighty-eight each had their own specific meaning. Combined together in the way that Tanya had scribbled on a napkin, they were a potent symbol of modern white supremacy, tattooed on prison gangs and Neo-Nazis the world over, particularly in America.

Eighty-eight was the simplest to understand. It was a reference to Adolf Hitler.

Bailey had made the discovery seconds after typing in the words 'far right nationalism' followed by '88' into his internet search browser. With the letter 'H' being the eighth letter in the alphabet, the number '88' was simply the numerical version of HH.

Heil Hitler.

Fourteen was a little more complicated. It was a reference to a guy called David Lane who got handed a 190-year prison sentence for the murder of Jewish radio host Alan Berg, who was shot dead in the driveway of his home in Denver in 1984. Lane was part of a white supremacist group called The Order and, while in prison in the 1990s, he came up with a fourteen-word slogan that became a rallying cry for the Neo-Nazi community.

We must secure the existence of our people and a future for white children.

Lane died in 2007 but his slogan lived on. The 'Fourteen Words' was quoted by the perpetrators of racially motivated massacres in Pittsburgh and Christchurch. The number '14' had been spray-painted across synagogues and the offices of politicians and newspapers. And as Bailey was discovering, it was also a popular tattoo for Neo-Nazis wanting to showcase their anger with ink.

Bailey would award no prizes for creativity, but the fact that someone had decided to pay homage to a white supremacist and a Nazi dictator by tattooing these numbers on their chest was a chilling reminder of racism and hate. In Australia. In Sydney. In the pub up the road from his house.

For the next few hours, Bailey sat on a stool in his kitchen, trawling through the websites, Facebook pages and chatrooms of every Australian far right nationalist group he could think of, searching for references to the 'Fourteen Words' and the numerical homage to Hitler. The Freedom Front. Blue Boys. The 1788 Group. Australia Resistance. The Aussie Liberation Party. Some of them had their own symbols, like crossed swords and fists, but he couldn't find any Australian group that explicitly used the numbers '14/88' together.

As distasteful as he found the ramblings and discussions that most of these groups were involved in online, he found no evidence of violent acts, either. Whoever was responsible for last night's racist attack on Matthew Lam hadn't gone online to boast about it.

It was dark outside by the time Bailey had decided that he was done scouring the web. Dark inside his house too. The only light was coming from the blue and white beam from his computer screen. He climbed off his stool, taking a moment to steady himself, legs stiff from being seated for so long, and switched on the light. The kitchen was a mess. Old newspapers, coffee cups and plates littering the stone benchtop, left to sort themselves. He rubbed his eyes, suddenly tired. He'd fix the mess tomorrow.

Campo had crept up beside him, sniffing his leg. Beady eyes looking skyward, hoping for some dinner.

'All right, Campo. Let's see what we've got.'

He opened the pantry, grabbing a bag of dry food and a can of meat. The dog was a fussy eater but he hadn't had a chance to get to the supermarket to buy her the premium mince she liked. Biscuits and tinned meat would do.

The plate of bacon and eggs that Bailey had wolfed down in Summer Hill was hardly enough to get him through the night. Opening the fridge door, he found a couple of plastic containers half-filled with the rice and lamb rogan josh he'd ordered earlier in the week. Two nights ago? Three? He couldn't remember. He lifted the lid on the lamb, giving it a sniff test. It smelled good. Curry always smelled good. Deciding that the spices had extended the life of the rogan josh, he popped the two containers into the microwave. Fingers crossed.

He settled onto the couch in the lounge room with his steaming plate of curry, switching on the television to catch the latest news about the bushfires. The newsreader telling him that an entire South Australian island was virtually on fire and that two men had been burnt alive in their car as they tried to escape the flames. The updates for New South Wales and Victoria weren't much better. More homes lost. More dead. People stranded without supplies. Fuel lines hundreds of metres long. Government assistance lagging. When would it end?

Bailey was about to switch off the television and close his eyes when another story caught his attention. A speech by the new boss of Australia's domestic spy agency, ASIO. His annual threat assessment. This time the headline act wasn't Islamic terrorism. Australia was facing a new threat – the rise of white supremacist groups. Bailey turned up the volume.

'Right-wing extremism has been in ASIO's sights for some time, but obviously this threat came into sharp, terrible focus last year in New Zealand.'

The director-general was standing behind a podium, talking to a room full of journalists and bureaucrats at the Canberra Press Club.

'In Australia, the extreme right-wing threat is real and it is growing. In suburbs around Australia, small cells regularly meet to salute Nazi flags, inspect weapons, train in combat and share their hateful ideology. These groups are more organised and security conscious than they were in previous years. We continue to see some Australian extremists seeking to connect with like-minded individuals in other parts of the world, sometimes in person. They are not merely seeking to share ideology and tactics.

'Meanwhile, extreme right-wing online forums prolifer-ate on the internet, and attract international memberships, including Australians. These online forums share and promote extremist right-wing ideologies, and encourage and justify acts of extreme violence.

'We expect such groups will remain an enduring threat, making more use of online propaganda to spread their messages of hate.

'While we would expect any right-wing extremist inspired attack in Australia to be low capability, like a knife, gun or vehicle attack, more sophisticated attacks are possible.'

'And what the hell are you doing about it?' Bailey said to the screen.

The newsreader moved on to another story. Something about a new flu-like virus in China that nobody seemed too worried about. Bailey switched off the television.

He looked at his watch: 9.15 pm. It was still relatively early but it had been so long since he'd worked a day like this that he was exhausted. He lay back on the couch, closing his eyes.

Sleep.

CHAPTER 9

'Wait here. I've arranged for someone to meet you.'

Bailey watched Harriet Walker lift the scarf from around her neck and place it on top of her head.

'I'm not staying. Everything you need is in there.' She bent down, tapping the brown envelope on the table. 'Gets back to me, you know what happens.'

'You know I won't let that happen.'

'Yeah, I do. But I felt the need to say it. My arse is on the line now. Be careful.' She stood up, her chair dragging on the dusty floor. 'You need to forget my number for a while.'

'If this is what you say it is, I won't be sticking around long. Might go to London, finish writing it there.'

'Good.'

Walker looked over her shoulder, checking the room. They were alone. A stained globe dangling from the ceiling offering a dim, yellow light. They were surrounded by shelves stacked with rolled carpets and cardboard boxes. The space in the middle barely big enough for the small table and two chairs. Beads were hanging like long strands of hair in the doorway. The only way in. The only way out.

'You going to be all right, Hat?'

'Who knows?' She shrugged her shoulders, faking a smile. 'He won't be long.'

Walker pushed through the beads that separated the room from the carpet shop, the sweet smell of scented tobacco wafting in, irritating Bailey's nostrils. He could hear her saying a few words to the guy smoking the hookah out front, probably handing him a fistful of American banknotes, before the ringing bells of the door signalled her departure.

Bailey wasn't sure who Walker had arranged for him to meet. 'Someone who knows more than I do,' she'd said. 'You can trust him. At least as much as you can trust anyone around here. But you'll get something on the record for your story.'

Those words had been meant to reassure him, but all they did was make him more nervous. Bailey was the type of guy who walked into situations with his eyes wide open, knowing where he was going, what he was doing, who he was meeting. But he trusted Walker. After all, she was the one who'd put her career on the line to tell him about the massacre of innocent civilians during a botched raid on a farmhouse in Uruzgan. And now she had handed him proof.

How long would he need to wait? Bailey had spent long enough in Kabul to know that time had many meanings here. The usual rules around clocks – like scheduled meetings – didn't apply. He decided to rip the top off the envelope in front of him, check whether he really did have the story she'd promised. There was a thick, bound folder inside, the ADF insignia on the front, along with one word: *CLASSIFIED*.

It was all there. Everything she'd told him. Transcripts of interviews. Summary findings signed off by high-ranking ADF officials, pointing to intelligence failures but highlighting the fact that a cache of weapons had also been discovered on the property. Justification for what had happened. Why Afghans had to be killed. He sifted through the pages, speed-reading, taking in as much as he could, pausing only when he came to the collection of photographs. The family. Children. Neat bullet holes in foreheads. Executions at close range. An adult male with rope tied around his wrists but not bound together. Puzzling. Bailey wondered whether his hands had been freed before, or after, he was shot. Another question that he'd put to the military brass before the story went to print.

He couldn't find any photographs of the cache of weapons that the ADF had supposedly found on the property. Evidence supporting the justification for the raid. The killings. A significant omission from the internal investigation that had cleared Australian soldiers of any wrongdoing. Where were the weapons?

The bells in the shop rang again. Footsteps and voices out front.

Bailey hurriedly packed up the folder and had just finished stuffing it into the bag at his feet when the curtain parted and three men walked in, assault rifles dangling from their shoulders. They were dressed in Afghan military uniforms, the nation's red, black and green flag stitched on their shoulders.

Bailey should have been relieved by the uniforms but, if anything, they made him even more nervous. It wasn't hard to get hold of an army uniform in Kabul. The Taliban had made stealing them an artform, sending suicide bombers into crowded bazaars dressed as the soldiers who were supposed to be there to protect people.

'Up!'

The man closest to Bailey gestured for him to get to his feet. Bailey did what he was told, raising his arms in the air, palms up.

'Easy, fella,' Bailey said. 'I'm a friend of Commander Harriet Walker.'

'I know who you are,' the man said, his English polished and clear. 'Legs apart.'

Bailey winced as he copped the kind of overly thorough pat-down that, in most other countries, would have seen this guy arrested.

After Bailey had been checked, the man grabbed the radio from his belt, barking something in Pashto, while gesturing for Bailey to remain standing.

Bailey waited in silence with the men, their stern expressions and dark eyes not filling him with reassurance. There was barely enough room and they were standing so close together that Bailey couldn't help thinking that at least one of them was in need of a bath.

The bell on the door went again. Voices. More footsteps.

Another man with a gun pushed through the beads, holding them to the side for a man in a suit. A man Bailey recognised from countless media briefings and his appearances on television. Afghanistan's Minister for Justice, Abdul Rashid Haleem.

'Minister.' Bailey broke the silence, holding out his hand. 'John Bailey. Thanks for seeing me.'

The two men shook hands before Haleem sat down, gesturing for Bailey to do the same.

'I only have a few minutes,' he said, brushing dust from the elbow of his jacket. 'What do you need?'

'Harriet Walker . . . Commander Walker said you wanted to meet.' Thrown by the question, Bailey stuttered. 'You know about the incident in Uruzgan?'

'The execution of eight Afghan civilians is hardly what I'd be referring to as an incident, Mr Bailey.'

The intensity of Haleem's stare was unsettling Bailey and he wasn't sure that the justice minister had even blinked since entering the room. But he needed to pull himself together, ask the questions he needed to ask before Haleem lost patience with him and left.

'What do you know about what happened at the farmhouse?'

'I know exactly what happened.'

'Are we on the record, minister?'

Haleem sighed. 'That's why I'm here.'

Bailey bent down and grabbed his notebook from his bag, while maintaining eye contact with Haleem. 'And what is your response?'

'The Afghan Government has serious concerns about the conduct of the Australian soldiers involved in the raid. An innocent family was slaughtered, including women and children. We demand a thorough investigation and for that investigation to be shared with us.'

Bailey was unnerved by the response, knowing that he had the report that Haleem was talking about stuffed inside the bag at his feet.

'And do you think that Australia will grant you access to that report?'

Haleem paused, blinking for the first time. 'It would be in Australia's interests to do so.'

Bailey was scribbling down Haleem's every word in the barely legible shorthand that only he could decipher.

'Does this incident . . . will the deaths of Afghan citizens at the hands of Australian soldiers have a detrimental effect on relations between the two countries?'

'A life is a life, Mr Bailey. Thousands of people have been killed in this war. When innocent civilians die for no apparent reason, that is a war crime. We have conducted our own investigation and determined that the people killed had no links to the Taliban, as previously stated by the Australian military. So yes, without proper justice, the unlawful killing of Afghan civilians will have a detrimental effect on relations.'

'Minister Haleem.' Bailey cleared his throat. 'Would it be possible to get a copy of your report about what happened?'

Haleem held up his arm, pointing his finger at one of the men behind him, without looking around. The man in uniform who had accompanied the justice minister into the room produced an envelope from inside his jacket, handing it to his boss.

'This is a summary. It supports what I've told you, with details about the victims. Names.' He slid the envelope across the table towards Bailey, tapping the paper with his fingers. 'You're an experienced reporter, Mr Bailey. I have confidence that you will write the truth. But if I can ask you one small favour?'

Bailey baulked at the word. When a politician of any stripe asked for a 'favour' it was never good.

'What is it?'

'Name the victims. All of them. The victims had names. They had families. Friends. Give them the respect they deserve. Print their names so their deaths don't get lost in this war.'

Bailey was taken aback by the comment. His experiences in Afghanistan had led him to expect something else. Before he had a chance to respond, Haleem was on his feet, holding out his hand. 'And you did not get that report from me.'

'Of course.' Bailey nodded, shaking his hand, watching the men push through the beads and file out of the room. He was still standing when he heard the ringing bell on the door.

Haleem wanted the truth to be out there.

Bailey could give him that.

CHAPTER 10

The vibrating phone on the coffee table sounded like a growling dog and Bailey sat upright, startled, wondering what the hell had gotten into Campo.

Looking around, he spied her sleeping on the rug beside him, before noticing the flashing, humming phone.

'Bailey.'

He caught it just in time.

'Hiya, Mr Bailey, it's Candy here from Chrystal Talent Management. Chrystal wanted me to give you a call to let you know that Augustus Strong is available for an interview with you.'

Candy was sounding much more pleasant than she had earlier in the day.

'Sounds good. When and where?' Bailey said, still trying to focus his eyes.

'Ten-thirty at the Hilton on George.'

Bailey looked at his watch, wondering whether it was morning or night.

It was 9.55 pm.

'Tonight?'

'Yes. Augustus is *really* busy. He's just gotten back from a meeting with some politicians in Canberra but he says he's fine to talk to you. Jet lag, and all that. He's up half the night.' Candy laughed to herself on the other end of the phone. 'Can we confirm that please? I'll need to let Chrystal know you're coming.'

Bailey wasn't about to turn down an interview with the person who was supposed to be the subject of his article for *Enquirer Magazine*. At this time of night, he could make it to the Hilton in ten minutes.

'I'll be there.'

'Good. You'll have twenty minutes with him. Chrystal will meet you at reception and show you up to his suite.'

'Candy, do me a favour and organise a car spot for me?'

Candy went quiet on the other end of the line, like Bailey had just asked her to donate a kidney. 'Shouldn't be a problem.'

—

It seemed that organising Bailey a car spot underneath the Hilton was a problem, and so was his presence inside the hotel foyer at 10.25 pm.

'Who are you again?'

A guy with a name tag that said Richard was tut-tutting to nobody as he searched what he called 'the messages folder' and tapped away on his keyboard.

'My name's John Bailey and I'm here to meet Chrystal Armstrong.'

'I just don't have any record of this. Tracey . . . Tracey!' He was calling out to a woman in a uniform that matched his, waving for her to come over and join the conversation. 'Do you know anything about a meeting with Chrystal Armstrong and . . . and . . .'

'John Bailey.'

'. . . this gentleman tonight?'

'Excuse me, sorry. Sorry. This is my fault.'

Chrystal Armstrong pushed past Bailey, tapping the reception desk with her long, painted, nails, smiling at Richard. 'I'm sorry, darl. We're visiting Augustus Strong upstairs. My stupid assistant was supposed to have let you know.'

Richard had time for one more breathy 'tut' before he faked a smile. 'Sure. Is he coming down to collect you? The elevators are card activated.'

Chrystal held up a plastic card. 'We have one, thank you.'

Bailey followed Chrystal towards the elevators, struggling to keep up with her despite the fact that she was wearing heels so tall that it was like she was balancing on stilts.

'Sorry about the mad dash,' she said when they were safely inside the elevator, her eyes wandering from Bailey's tradesman's boots up his jeans to the red and black checked flannelette shirt that he'd been wearing all day. 'It's been mental.'

'No worries. Did you go to Canberra with him too?'

'Yeah. Awful trip that one. Drive or fly, it's always three hours each way. Makes no difference.' She sighed. 'We flew, of course.'

'Of course.'

'So, you're involved with this new magazine of Jock's, I hear?'

The mention of Jock Donaldson's name annoyed Bailey. He must have put a call in to Chrystal to help arrange the interview. No meddling. That was the deal with Neena. He made a mental note to call her tomorrow so that she could remind Donaldson that Bailey didn't need his help.

'You've been talking to Jock?'

Her lips smiled while her face stood still. 'Yes. He's a darling.'

The elevator doors opened on the sixteenth floor and Bailey followed Chrystal as she raced down the corridor, resuming the cracking pace she'd set downstairs.

She stopped at the door. 'Now, Mr Bailey. A few ground rules. You'll have twenty minutes. I'll be sitting in. Any uncomfortable questions and the interview's over.'

Bailey had been doing this a long time and he'd dealt with 'minders' far more difficult that Chrystal Armstrong. She had issued her instructions with a calmness that told him that people rarely challenged her. Until now.

'Sure. Sit in, if you like.' He returned her smile. 'I'll ask any question I like and he can give me any answer he likes. But I'd hate for you to interrupt the interview, or end it prematurely. From this point onwards, everything's on the record.'

Chrystal's smile vanished and her eyes hardened. 'I'm not here to be a part of your story, Mr Bailey.'

'That's exactly what I was hoping you'd say.'

They were standing at the door, staring at each other, Bailey imagining that Chrystal was contemplating cancelling the interview before it had even begun.

'Jock and I are good friends.'

'Barely know the bloke.'

Chrystal had just played the type of card that probably worked on the typical entertainment reporter that she was used to dealing with, but it had had no effect on a seasoned investigative reporter like Bailey.

After a few more seconds she sighed and put her key card in the door, turning the handle. 'Don't make me regret this, Mr Bailey.'

'I'm not making you do anything.'

She rolled her eyes at him, undoubtedly annoyed at having organised the interview. Too late to back out now.

'Augustus, darling? Are you decent?' Chrystal called out as she walked, slowly, inside.

'Yeah, babe!' Augustus called back. 'Come in!'

Chrystal turned to Bailey. 'Be nice.'

'Of course. I'm really excited about meeting him.'

Bailey winked at her, enjoying watching the concern spread across her face as he feigned the fan boy.

Strong was sitting on his bed wearing one of the hotel's white bathrobes, a plate with a half-eaten hamburger and a few leftover fries beside him.

'Augustus, this is that reporter I told you about. John Bailey.'

Strong climbed off the bed and walked over to them, a hand outstretched to Bailey. 'Hi, bud. Great to meet you. Thanks for the interest in my trip. Australia's been a lot of fun. Just great.'

'Augustus, I thought we'd all sit over here for the interview?'

Chrystal was gesturing towards the lounge area in the adjoining room, where two glasses of water had been arranged on a coffee table in between a pair of armchairs.

'Perfect.'

When they were sitting down, Bailey pulled out his mobile phone, switching it to flight mode and activating the recording device. 'If you don't mind?'

'Of course.'

Strong appeared friendly and charming, which was at odds with some of the vitriol that Bailey had seen on his Twitter account and from some of the other interviews he'd done.

'Now.' Strong clasped his hands together, sitting back in his chair. 'What would you like to talk about?'

'You've become somewhat of a controversial fellow, Mr Strong –'

'Please, call me Augustus.'

'How do you feel about being the pin-up boy for far right nationalist and white supremacist groups?'

Bailey had decided to go in hard but Strong didn't flinch. The seasoned professional. 'All sorts of people like what I have to say. Most people are actually quite ordinary. They're just tired of political correctness. I'm not afraid of calling that out.'

'And what about those critics who say you're racist?'

Strong smiled, like he was enjoying the barbs being thrown at him. 'You see, this is where people misunderstand my words. My positions. Let's take immigration, for example. It's true that I'm dead against Muslim immigration in America, but not because I don't like Muslims, or anyone from the Middle East for that matter. What I'm concerned about is the disintegration, the erosion, of American culture. My country is the greatest country on earth. I'm a proud patriot. What I want is for people to be able to talk openly and honestly about how different Muslim culture is from our own. I want America to hang on to the values, the traditions, we hold so dear. If I get vilified by overly sensitive left-wing fanatics, so be it.'

'So you don't believe that you're racist?'

'Absolutely not. What I am is someone who's brave enough to call out stupidity and political correctness when it damages free speech. When it has a detrimental effect on our society. People often confuse my staunch defence of western culture with some kind of racist crusade. I'm not a white supremacist. It's ridiculous.'

Strong was speaking so quickly and eloquently that Bailey felt like he was listening to a routine that had been rehearsed a hundred times before.

'I'm sure you've heard some of my comments about what happened in Barnsworth, England?'

Bailey had. 'Enlighten me.'

'More than a thousand young girls were raped by Pakistani gangs over a ten-year period. It happened because nobody wanted to talk about it. The police were afraid. Politicians were afraid. Everyone was afraid due to mindless political correctness. Everyone was afraid of calling out these Pakistani Muslim rapists for fear of upsetting people. Spare me!' Strong rolled his eyes, taking a sip of water to oil his larynx, smooth the pipe for the next rush of words. 'Spare me the offence! Had a bunch of white guys been responsible, they would have been called out and hunted down. But because it involved migrant communities it was somehow too delicate to talk about? Come on, Mr Bailey. That's just ridiculous. Ridiculous.'

'So, it's western society that you're standing up for and stopping immigration is a way to do that?' Bailey held up his hand, signalling a two-prong question. 'How does that work the other way around? Westerners moving abroad.'

'Well.' Strong took a moment to think. 'They just shouldn't do it. If we want to protect our western values, they probably feel the same way about theirs.'

'Who's *they*?'

'I know what you're trying to do here.' Strong shook his head, smiling, pointing his finger playfully at Bailey. 'But my answer is simple. *They* are the people who want a different way of life from us westerners.'

'Which is?'

'Freedom.'

'Freedom from what?' Bailey sat back, trying to look interested, like he was hanging off Strong's every word. 'Freedom to offend?'

'Exactly.'

'You want to be able to offend people?'

'I want to protect and defend my First Amendment rights, and the rights of everyone else. To protest. To offend. To stand up for my beliefs without fear or favour.'

Strong was sounding self-righteous now and it was getting on Bailey's nerves. He decided to go back to where he'd started.

'So, why do you court white supremacist groups like The Dawning?'

Strong stared at Bailey, letting his thoughts tick over. He picked up his glass of water, slowly taking another sip.

'Mr Strong?'

The Dawning was an American white supremacist group whose founder – a wheat farmer by the name of Donald Sampson – had recently been raided by the FBI. They'd found stockpiles of weapons on his property and a video recording of a gathering of armed men, all wearing masks, talking about the need for extreme acts of violence to upset the social order and drive out non-western influences from America.

'I neither support, nor condone, the positions of that group.'

'But the problem, Mr Strong, is that there's a photograph of you with your arm around Donald Sampson. A photo taken a year or so ago.' Strong wasn't proving so talkative on this subject and Bailey decided to double-down. 'And if I'm not mistaken, that was the same night when you were pictured giving a Nazi salute?'

'That was a joke. Taken out of context.'

'The Nazi salute is a joke?' Bailey said, emphasising his confusion. 'You'd better explain that context for me, if you don't mind. I'm struggling a bit here. Maybe I've got this wrong.'

Strong coughed, loudly, reaching again for his water.

'Augustus, are you okay?'

Bailey had forgotten that Chrystal Armstrong was in the room and he realised now that Strong's coughing was a signal.

'It's just this cold,' Strong said, getting up from his chair, drinking more water. 'I've got a headache. You know how jet lag can play havoc with you.'

'Take your time,' Bailey said, staying put. 'I don't mind if you need a minute.'

Bailey felt a hand on his shoulder. Chrystal Armstrong was, quite literally, breathing down his neck. 'I think we might need to leave it there, Mr Bailey. It's been a gruelling schedule for Augustus. Maybe you could email some follow-up questions?'

Bailey reached for his phone, slipping it inside his jacket pocket.

'Sure.'

The easygoing, confident showman who had offered the charming greeting to Bailey when he had first arrived was gone. Cut down by a question he couldn't explain. Nowhere to hide. No words left to say.

'One more question, if I may?'

'Mr Bailey, I think we're done,' Chrystal said.

'No, it's okay,' Strong said, earnestly, like he was offering Bailey the world.

'You met some politicians in Canberra today,' Bailey said. 'May I ask who?'

'Sure. I met the border guy.'

'The Home Affairs Minister, Wayne McMahon?'

'Yeah. And a couple of senators from Queensland.'

Bailey knew exactly who he was referring to. Mal Rustin and Sally Paul. The two Liberal National Party conservatives from the north of the state.

'What did you talk about?'

'Immigration. Western values. Things you might expect. Australia and the United States have a special relationship. Two relatively young countries with proud histories. But the same problems with cultural erosion.'

'By "proud histories" you mean white settlement here?' Bailey had one more crack, knowing that people like Strong had a short view of history.

'I think we're done, Mr Bailey,' Chrystal said.

'I'm really tired.' Strong was rubbing his eyes, putting on a show. 'Goodnight.'

Strong disappeared into the bathroom, fingers massaging his temples.

'Follow me, please.'

Chrystal didn't say another word until they were in the hallway on the other side of the door.

'That was fucking pathetic, Mr Bailey.' She jammed a finger in his direction. 'Coming in here, accusing him like that. I'll be speaking to Jock about this.'

'You're a supporter of Augustus Strong, then, I take it? The things he stands for?'

'At least he stands for something, unlike people like you,' she snarled. 'And yes, I think he's brave for calling out immigration. What's wrong with wanting to keep America for *Americans*?

Australia for *Australians*? People like you twist his words. So fucking politically correct all the time.'

'I don't twist people's words,' Bailey said. 'I print them. Just like I'll be printing yours.'

'What?' A look of horror fell on Chrystal's face. 'You're not interviewing me? This is outrageous.'

'You made yourself a part of the interview, Chrystal. And I warned you that everything was on the record. If you're as brave as you say you are, I'm sure your clients won't mind.'

'You can't. You won't.'

'I know my way out from here,' Bailey said. 'You should go check on Strong. Poor bastard sounds really crook.'

—

It was 11.30 pm by the time Bailey made it back home.

He was wide awake so he decided to stay up and transcribe his interview with Strong.

As he thumbed through his phone to find the recording, he noticed a bunch of messages that he'd missed on Signal.

All of them from Harriet Walker.

Got something for you. Meet me 8 pm tonight. Glebe. Eastern end of the park by the water near Jubilee Park playground.

She'd sent another message twenty minutes later.

Bailey? It's getting late. Are we on tonight?

The last message came in at 7.30 pm.

I'm guessing you're caught up. 8 am tomorrow. Same place. Glebe. I'll check my messages tomorrow morning first thing. Please confirm.

Bailey typed a response.

Sorry, Hat. Missed these messages. Confirming 8 am tomorrow. I'll be there.

The speed with which Walker had gotten back to him only hardened Bailey's earlier suspicions that she had already been looking into right-wing extremists. That she may be involved in an active investigation. The video that Bailey had given Walker had prompted her to try to arrange another meeting with him the same day. She must have found something.

The dog had sidled up beside Bailey, sniffing his legs.

'All right, Campo.' He patted her on the head. 'Looks like we're walking in Glebe tomorrow.'

The dog responded with an expressionless stare.

CHAPTER 11

Annie Brooks loved being back at work.

Unfortunately, the tabloid media had been excited for her too. Not everyone was playing nice. One gossip columnist had ridiculed her return to a reporting role in commercial television, questioning whether she was even up to the task. But the criticism only strengthened her resolve to succeed.

Annie loved being on the road. Breaking stories. Chasing leads. It beat the shit out of sitting in an air-conditioned studio, reading an autocue filled with hyperbolic sentences written by ratings-obsessed producers. Being fussed over by makeup artists and stylists to ensure that she looked like someone that viewers could trust. Someone everyday Australians would invite into their homes.

Annie had presented the six o'clock news for almost fifteen years before the network had decided to 'bone' her. When the wrinkles around her eyes meant that – as one TV executive had shamelessly put it – she wasn't 'fuckable' enough any more. Her sacking had initially come as a shock. But Annie had departed with so much cash in her bank account that she hadn't been in any rush to even contemplate what she'd do next.

That next step came in an unlikely telephone call from Bill Russell, the executive producer of *Inside Story*, a nightly current affairs program on a rival network to the one from which Annie had been sacked.

'How would you like to go back on the road?' Bill had asked in that first phone call. 'It's a reporter gig. I don't need a new presenter. But it's what you always loved doing.'

Annie hadn't needed long to think about it. She'd already been out of work for more than a year by the time Bill called. She and Bill had worked together years ago. She trusted him and he was right, her first love had always been 'the chase'. Before being offered the gig to present the six o'clock news – which no reporter could ever turn down – Annie had worked as a correspondent all around the world. Beirut. London. Los Angeles. She'd started her reporting career in Sydney, which was exactly the job that Bill was offering her now, albeit for a current affairs show, rather than the nightly news, meaning she had the freedom to do some investigative reporting and not just chase police cars and ambulances around.

But there was a catch.

'When I ask you to do crime, I don't want any complaints. Got it?'

That was Bill's only caveat for the role. After all, this was commercial television.

'Okay, Bill. But I want the investigative reporting stuff in writing.'

'Done.'

Annie had been in the role for three months already and it hadn't been crime stories dominating her time. It was bushfires. In November, she had held the hands of traumatised residents in refuge centres before going with them to see what was left after the fires had ripped through their towns. It was the same story everywhere she went. Carnage. Memories burnt to cinders. Fires moving so fast that people had barely had time to get out.

The fires kept spreading across Australia in December and by New Year's Eve, it seemed like half the country was on fire. The south coast of New South Wales was particularly bad and Annie had become trapped by a wall of flames glowing in the hills. Ash so thick that day became night. In one town, the panicked residents had driven their cars into a lake to escape the flames. Others sheltered on beaches as the growling bushfire devoured everything in its path. Almost two hundred houses had been lost in one coastal district alone. Cars. Sheds. Businesses. Livestock. Wild animals that had nowhere to run. The people who'd decided to defend their homes. Some of them hadn't stood a chance. Decimated.

It was the fourth week of January and Annie had been back in Sydney for a week. Bill had given her a few days off after the latest fires. Now he wanted her back at work.

'I need you to go and check out a dead body washed up on the sand at Maroubra,' Bill had told her on the phone an hour ago.

'Really, Bill? A drowning?'

Annie hadn't bothered to hide the frustration in her voice. She was tired and the constant smell of smoke in the city, seeping through doors and windows, had left her on edge after her long stint on the fire front. It was like she was still there, walking through the ashes of someone's home.

'Cops are being coy. Could be more to it. And no complaints, remember? This is the first potential crime yarn I've sent you on.'

Annie relented, eager to suppress the diva inside. Think about something other than bushfires. Work also countered the other thing threatening her stability. Vodka. The ups and downs of a reporter's life had made her vulnerable again. She hadn't had a drink for almost a year and it was all she'd been thinking about. She'd even gone back to Alcoholics Anonymous. Two meetings in three days. Seen off the demon. Working would at least help keep it at bay.

'Okay, Bill.'

'Fletch's already on his way. He'll meet you there.'

Todd Fletcher. The cameraman. The guy who'd spent the last few months filming flames and burnt homes with Annie. Fletch had barely had time to catch his breath and reacquaint himself with his wife and two young kids after the shit they'd seen. But getting back to work on a story other than the fires was probably good for the both of them.

—

It was only 8.30 am and most of the car spots were taken along the esplanade at Maroubra Beach. Annie found a spot in front of the surf school, hopping out and heading straight for the police car and the ambulance parked up on the footpath.

Reporters from the networks and the ABC were already there, talking in front of cameras for the breakfast shows. Annie stepped around them, careful not to disrupt their shots, trying to get a look in the back of the ambulance, its rear doors wide open. Empty. The body must still be on the beach.

She kept walking around the pavilion towards the water, spying a white tent on the sand closer to the shoreline. Cops standing around. Two uniforms. A guy in a suit facing the water.

'Annie!'

She turned around to see Fletch walking towards her, his trademark Wests Tigers cap on, balancing his camera on his shoulder.

'Hey, Fletch.' She smiled, nodding her chin. 'Get some rest?'

Fletch laughed. 'Two toddlers at home and a sleep-deprived missus. This is how I rest. Next question?'

'I remember those days.' Annie smiled, thinking back to when Louis was small. When he talked instead of grunted. Teenagers. 'Must have been good to see them.'

'Too right.'

Annie pointed towards the white tent by the water. 'Looks like the body's still on the sand. I'm going to wander down and take a look.'

'What do you want me to do?'

'Get some sequences in the can. Not sure there's a story here for us yet. Bill obviously thinks there might be. If the cops talk on camera, it'll be an all-in. Grab some cutaways.'

'Okay.'

Annie bent down, slipping off her shoes, stepping onto the sand, the sturdy grains oddly cool as her toes cut through the warm surface layer. The tide must have been going out with the forensics tent erected so close to the shoreline. Annie figured the police had at least a few hours to inspect the body where it washed up before the tide came back in.

The two officers in uniform – one male, one female – were keeping watch on either side of the tent, mostly to keep gawkers and the media away. The cop in plain clothes had disappeared inside the tent. Annie could hear voices, but she couldn't see inside the tent because the opening faced the sea.

She walked over to the male officer with the buzz cut, figuring that she had a better chance of getting information from him than the woman.

'How's it going?' She smiled, charmingly. Old habit.

'This is a crime scene, madam. We're asking people to . . . to . . . to keep away from the area, please.'

The guy stumbled mid-sentence as he recognised the person standing in front of him as the woman who used to read the six o'clock news. It happened to Annie all the time. Some news anchors looked so different without their makeup that they had no problem hiding in plain sight. Not Annie Brooks. Her chiselled cheekbones and Nordic eyes made her stand out in any crowd. And even with the wrinkles that had led to her sacking, she was still gorgeous.

'You're Annie Brooks, right?'

Annie smiled. 'Yeah. In a previous life.'

'Didn't like the way they treated you. My folks switched stations after that.'

'Tough business.' Annie wasn't keen on going deep with a stranger, but she had to play along. Build trust. 'Had some good years. Nothing lasts forever, right?'

'I guess so,' he said, relaxing somewhat. 'Live around here, do you?'

'No. I'm working. Saw the tent, came down to take a look.' She paused, hesitantly, knowing that this was the moment when she needed to change up, chase information. But Annie was rusty, second-guessing herself. 'Who found the body?'

No turning back now.

'Couple of tourists sleeping on the beach,' he said, unperturbed. 'They were going for a swim. Spotted her just as the sun was coming up.'

Her.

'Know who it is?'

The cop baulked, suddenly remembering that he was talking to a journalist. 'I . . . who are you working for these days?'

'*Inside Story*,' Annie said.

'Annie?'

A bloke in a brown suit with fraying cuffs emerged from the tent, followed by a woman in a hazmat suit who knelt down beside an open suitcase, bagging whatever it was she'd just scraped from the body in the sand.

Annie recognised him at once. Detective Greg Palmer.

'Greg.'

Palmer stepped around the tent and walked over to where Annie was standing beside the young guy in uniform.

'Been a while. Saw you down Eden way during the fires. On the television. Back on the road, eh?'

'Yeah.'

Annie had first met Greg Palmer in the nineties when she was a crime reporter. Police contacts were everything on that round and Palmer had been good to her, giving her the type of tip-offs that commercial television loved to package up and lead the news. Stabbings. Shootings. Drug arrests. Tip-offs that made the police look good and got guys like Palmer some box tickets at the cricket or backstage passes at a concert. All part of the back-scratching exercise that gave the police good headlines and the nightly news good stories.

'What do you know?' Annie defaulted to the expectation of goodwill from a decades-old relationship. 'Accident or something else?'

Palmer looked from Annie to the guy in uniform, a split second to check that the rookie cop hadn't told Annie anything he wasn't authorised to share. The young buck shook his head, sheepishly.

'You know you can't be here.' Palmer turned serious all of a sudden. A scowl that made Annie feel unwelcome. 'You've got to go.'

'C'mon, Greg.' Annie scrunched her toes, digging them into the sand, holding her ground.

'Sorry, Annie.' Palmer stepped towards her, touching her elbow, pointing towards the esplanade. 'I'm going to need to show you the door on this one. Too early.'

Annie shrugged. 'Can't criticise a girl for trying.'

Palmer turned to the young bloke. 'Left my smokes in the car. I'll escort Ms Brooks off the beach. Don't let anyone else near this tent. And no more chatty chatty. Got it?'

The guy nodded, his cheeks flushing red.

Annie and Palmer walked side by side in silence. When they were well out of earshot, Annie thought she'd give it one more go. 'Not an accident then, hey, Greg?'

'That's my hunch. Pretty early, though,' Palmer said, pulling a pack of cigarettes from his pocket, sparking one. 'Want one?'

'No, thanks. Gave up. Thought you'd left them in the car?'

'Can't talk in front of the young ones,' Palmer said, catching her eye for a second and then looking ahead towards the concrete steps. 'Different world these days. He'd probably fucking report me.'

'So what can you tell me?'

'Off the record?' Palmer stopped at the top of the stairs.

'Of course,' Annie said. 'I just want to know if there's a story for me here. Or not.'

'You've got a story, all right. Not today. But worth a dig.'

'What makes you say that?'

'We've got an ID.'

Annie didn't expect this much. Not so soon, anyway.

'And?'

'Harriet Walker.'

The name didn't ring a bell.

'Who's she?'

'AFP. Someone senior.'

'How do you know that much about her already?'

Palmer's phone started vibrating and he pulled it from his pocket, showing Annie the screen. Number withheld.

'Because my phone has been fucking ringing every five minutes from people I don't know.'

'Feds?'

Palmer shrugged, his face scrunching, annoyed. 'I need to take this. Name's under wraps till you hear from me.'

Annie dug a business card from her handbag, handing it to Palmer. 'Let me know.'

He took the card, slipping it into his pocket as he answered his phone and started walking in a different direction.

Annie watched him for a moment, wanting to listen to his side of the conversation but thinking better of snooping. Palmer had already given her more than she'd expected. She needed to respect that, give him some space.

She headed back towards the ambulance where a policeman had just finished briefing the throng of media. She spotted

Fletch lowering his camera from his shoulder. She caught his eye and pointed to the carpark. Then she pulled her phone from her pocket, dialling Bill.

He answered after two rings. 'Saw it on the television –'

'Bill.'

'Doesn't sound like much.'

'Bill.'

'Sorry for the goose chase.' Bill kept talking, oblivious to Annie's attempts to interrupt him. 'There was just something about this one. My gut talking to me. Maybe I'm losing my edge.'

'Bill!' Annie spoke so loudly that a guy walking past almost dropped his surfboard. 'Can you just stop talking for a second?'

'Right. Sorry, Annie. What is it?'

'I got a name.'

'And?'

'Not on the phone. There's a story here. Not sure what. But there's a story.'

'I knew it!'

Did you, now? Annie thought to herself as she hung up. Bloody producers.

CHAPTER 12

It wasn't like Commander Harriet Walker to be late. A few minutes, maybe. But not the thirty-five minutes that Bailey had been waiting in Jubilee Park. Soon to be thirty-six.

He tried her phone again. This time a call, rather than a text. Voicemail. Something must have come up. He'd give her until 8.45 am and then he was leaving. Nine more minutes.

The edge of the harbour was only fifty metres away and Bailey and Campo had been walking laps on the dewy grass to the edge of the water and back to the playground, where tired parents with takeaway coffees were pushing kids on swings and swapping sleep stories. Bailey could feel their eyes on him too. The middle-aged man loitering by a playground. It was lucky he had Campo with him or they probably would have already called the cops.

Six more minutes.

Bailey couldn't remember the last time he'd ventured down to this part of Glebe and he was observing his surroundings as if he were a painter plotting a canvas.

The giant Moreton Bay fig with hulking branches that stretched across the children's playground, casting twisting shadows across the manicured grass that had somehow maintained its green tinge in the dry. The neatly paved pathways cutting through the park along the harbour's edge. The pram pushers. Dog walkers. Power-walking women striding, purposefully, in lycra, talking on their mobile phones. A running group, its members ignoring the shitty air, sweating it out together in shiny sneakers. A man in a suit riding a motorised scooter, a leather satchel strung over his shoulder.

At the western end of Jubilee Park, Bailey could see the white picket fence of the old cricket ground and the light rail station on the hill. Further round was the Tramsheds complex which didn't house trams any more. The building had been converted into a place for upmarket restaurants and bars for the residents of the million-dollar apartments that had been built on the site of the old Harold Park Raceway.

When did gritty Glebe become so busy? So shiny? So trendy?

'C'mon, Campo.' Bailey tugged on the leash. 'One more lap and then we might call it a day.'

Bailey was thumbing through his phone as he walked, checking news headlines. One story caught his attention. *The Journal* had just published another story about the attack on Matthew Lam at the White Lion Hotel. Rachel Symonds hadn't pulled punches, especially with the headline.

WITNESSES SAY SYDNEY PUB ASSAULT DRIVEN BY RACISM

Everything that Bailey and Jonny Abdo had told Symonds was in the story. The masked men storming in, racially taunting a group of people inside, one of them fighting back. Punches thrown. The fact that the unnamed victim remained in an induced coma.

The story also had some information that Bailey hadn't expected to see in print. Not yet, anyway.

Police are investigating a possible link between the violent assault and an event held nearby earlier that evening by the controversial American polemicist, Augustus Strong.

The group of people attacked at the White Lion Hotel had taken part in a demonstration outside Mr Strong's event in Surry Hills. Police believe the attackers may also have attended Mr Strong's talk.

By the time Bailey had finished his latest circuit, the clock on his phone told him that it was 8.46 am. Still no word from Walker.

It was unlike her not to let him know that she'd been held up, but she was a senior commander in the AFP. Someone with an important job. She must have been needed elsewhere.

—

The drive back across the city was slow-going, which meant that Bailey had plenty of time to listen to the radio. He was flicking through stations, chasing news headlines, when he stumbled across a familiar voice. Augustus Strong. And he was talking to Bailey's least favourite shock-jock, Keith Roberts.

'You're a bloody hero, Augustus. I'm just going to call it out. Let my dear listeners know what I think. Because it's the truth. A bloody hero. A hero.'

Roberts' praise gave Bailey one more reason to dislike him, as if he needed another.

'Well, that's very kind of you to say, Keith.'

'No, I mean it,' Roberts gushed. 'So much bloody political correctness. Say what you think. Say what you believe. Be proud of it, I say. There's a lesson here for us all, dear listeners. Do not be cowed by the left-wing establishment. People like Augustus Strong are shining examples of that. It's been so great to talk to you. When's the next event?'

Bailey was relieved by the fact that it sounded like the interview was drawing to a close.

'I'm heading to Brisbane tomorrow. I've got two talks there. Both sold out of course.'

Wanker.

'And then I'm off to Adelaide.'

'Good. Good. That's great.' Roberts was mumbling along, injecting praise. 'Sold out, that's great. That's great.'

Having only caught the tail end of the interview, Bailey wondered whether Roberts had asked Strong about the story in *The Journal*. He probably hadn't.

'Thanks again for having me, I've really enjoyed our discussion. Not all of the Australian media has been so fair. It seems not everyone is open-minded enough to discuss the things that I really think are important and need to be aired. If there's one lesson I want people to take from my visit, it's the importance of free speech. The right to say whatever you want, wherever you want.'

'Tell me, Augustus. Who hasn't been giving you a fair go? I want to know. I think my listeners should know. Need to know. Free speech. That's the point here. That's the point. If we're going to make this country great again, people need to share their views about the things we've talked about today. Immigration. What we teach in schools. Our way of life, protecting it. So tell me, Augustus. Who hasn't given you a fair go?'

Here we go, thought Bailey. The arsehole was about to name him on Sydney radio.

'I had an unfortunate encounter with a journalist called Bailey. John, I think was his first name. Last night.'

Roberts sighed into the microphone, stifling a laugh. 'John Bailey, eh? Legendary war correspondent. I know him. Know him well. People know him. Left-wing mainstream media guy. People like him are the problem. Bunch of know-alls. Out of touch. They're not listening to what real people out there are thinking. Politically bloody correct. Thank god for people like you, Augustus Strong. Keep up the good work. Thanks for joining me.'

'Thanks.'

Bailey was livid. A public spray by Keith Roberts. It was almost too much.

He swung his car into a side street off Broadway, pulling into a loading zone. Hazard lights on. Bailey was about to make his first ever call to a talkback radio station.

Thumbing through his phone, he found the number to call via the radio station's website, and he was immediately put on hold. After around five minutes, someone answered.

'Street talk. What's your comment or question for Keith?'

Street talk. Roberts was shameless.

'It's Vince from Sutherland,' Bailey said. 'I heard the interview with Augustus Strong. I just wanted to praise Keith for having him on. I want to ask Keith why our politicians won't be more like Strong.'

'Stand by, we'll put you to air in a moment. Remember to turn down your radio and you'll only have around thirty seconds on air with Keith. Okay?'

Bailey could almost hear the happiness in her voice. She'd gotten a good one for Roberts. A loyal sycophant who would tell him why he was so important to the world.

'Got it.'

The radio station was blaring in Bailey's ear – an advertising break – before Roberts was back, barking into the microphone.

'Now, let's take some calls. It's time to hear from you. We've got Vince on the line from Sutherland. Vince, how are you?'

Bailey turned down his radio.

'I'm good, Keith. Good. And sorry, not sure what happened there with your producer, it's actually John Bailey calling. Y'know that left-wing mainstream media guy that you and Augustus Strong were just talking about?'

Roberts went quiet for a few seconds, before composing himself.

'John Bailey. Great of you to call in.'

'As a champion of free speech and all, I thought you'd allow me to respond to Mr Strong's complaint about not being given a fair go.'

'Of course. Of course.'

'That's great, Keith. Good on you.'

During the minutes that Bailey had been put on hold, he'd managed to calm himself down and think about what he'd say. He knew that he wouldn't have long.

'Your listeners may not have seen the footage of Augustus Strong giving a Nazi salute in America. In my interview with him last night, I simply asked him why he thought the Nazi salute was okay.'

'I think that he was –'

'Sorry, Keith. Remember, free speech? I was going to be allowed to say my piece.'

'Yes, of course. Go on. Go on.'

'Well, Mr Strong told me that he was making a joke. But the problem for him is that he made that salute at a gathering of white supremacists, one of whom has just been arrested by the FBI with a stockpile of weapons that he was allegedly about to use in a terrorist attack. That man's name is Donald Sampson and there's also a photograph of Augustus Strong and Sampson standing together with their arms around each other. Friends, it seems.'

'Well, I think that . . . I think that . . .'

For the first time that Bailey could remember, Keith Roberts was struggling for words.

'So, we've got a problem here, Keith.' Bailey was speaking slowly now. Deliberate. 'Mr Strong may be a champion of free speech. But could he also be a champion for racism? For white supremacists? For violence? I know you're a big fan of his, so I thought I'd better ask those questions. Probably good for your listeners to hear your thoughts on that too. Thanks for having me on.'

Bailey hung up the phone and turned up the dial, catching his last few words on the radio. Then silence.

'John Bailey makes some good points there. Good points. We'll be back after this short break to discuss them.'

Bailey couldn't help smiling as he did a U-turn, heading for home, switching off the radio, settling for silence for a while. He took a moment to think about the article he was writing. Maybe he'd ask Keith Roberts for an interview? To properly paint a picture of the rise of far right nationalism and interrogate the influence of people like Strong, Bailey also needed to explore the role of their public supporters. That is, if Roberts was still on the bandwagon.

By the time Bailey was turning into his street, his mind had returned to Harriet Walker.

She'd said she had something for him. Something important enough to ask for a meeting at night in a park only hours after he'd asked for her help. The fact that she had failed to turn up at the rescheduled meeting time of 8 am the next morning was starting to weigh on Bailey's mind. It wasn't like back in Afghanistan where she could lift an entire document, make copies, and hand them over in the back of a carpet shop. The Australian Federal Police Headquarters was a tight facility. Ears and eyes everywhere. If Harriet had bent the rules by accessing information that she wasn't supposed to see, she could be in trouble.

The flashing lights and three police cars parked out front of Bailey's house confirmed that something was wrong.

CHAPTER 13

'Where are you?'

Bailey was speaking into his phone, holding it down so no one could see, not taking his eyes off the cavalcade of police vehicles that had latched onto his house like wasps clinging to their nest.

'Why? Everything okay?'

The guy on the other end of the phone was Bailey's oldest friend. The one guy that he trusted implicitly.

Gerald Summers.

'Bailey?'

A policeman in a suit was standing in the middle of the road, staring in Bailey's direction, checking a notebook in his hand, probably realising that the crappy old station wagon stopped in the street was registered to the name of the same guy he was looking for.

'Gerald, I need you to pop over to my place. Urgently.'

The policeman was walking in Bailey's direction, pointing his finger, gesturing for Bailey to park his car.

'What's wrong, mate?'

'Federal police. I've got three carloads of them parked out front of my house.'

The policeman was getting closer.

'You what? What happened? What's it about?'

'I don't know. Best not get into anything on the phone.' The police officer was close enough for Bailey to see the whites of his eyes. His unfriendly glare. 'Might also need a lawyer, old boy. How quick can you get here?'

'Thirty minutes.'

Bailey hung up, knowing that Gerald would probably arrive in twenty-five. He was like that. Loyal. Gutsy. A man with a plan. It was why he had been the editor of Australia's largest newspaper for so many years. Why he had published stories that had brought down governments, exposed secrets and lies.

Bailey switched off his phone, slipping it into his sock under his jeans, trying to think of another place he could hide it so that the police couldn't confiscate it, if that was their plan.

Click.

Bailey opened his door just as the officer arrived at his window. 'What's going on?'

'Are you John Llewelyn Bailey?'

Bailey stepped out onto the road, closing the door behind him.

'Haven't heard that name in a while.'

Llewelyn was his grandfather's name and the only time it ever got used was when he was filling out official paperwork like travel documents and bank loans.

'Are you John Llewelyn Bailey?'

'I think you know the answer to that question, mate,' Bailey said, not interested in making a friend.

'This way please.' He was pointing towards Bailey's house and the heavy police presence out front.

'You going to tell me what this is about?'

'We'll explain everything in a moment.' He tapped Bailey on the shoulder. 'Let's go.'

Harriet Walker.

This must be about the conversation he'd had with Hat at the Lindt Café the previous afternoon. About what she did next.

'I'd like to know what you think I've done.'

'We'll be the ones asking questions.'

When they arrived out front, Bailey counted six people. Three of them – two men and a woman – were standing around on his front porch, while two others, a man and a woman, dressed more casually, were loitering on the footpath beside the open door of a four-wheel drive.

'Boss, this is John Bailey.' The guy escorting Bailey waved at the older bald guy standing on Bailey's porch. 'Car's parked up the street.'

The bald guy walked down the steps, holding a document out to Bailey. 'John Bailey. We've got a warrant to search your premises for materials relating to a series of stories written by you and published in *The Journal* in 2011 about a raid on a Taliban safehouse in Uruzgan Province, Afghanistan. Stories that also referenced a leaked Australian Defence Force report.'

'You fucking what?' Bailey snatched the document from the bald guy's hand. 'Articles I wrote eight years ago? You're kidding, aren't you?'

The guy didn't answer, leaving Bailey to read the warrant for himself.

The warrant had a 'Local Court of New South Wales' stamp on it which meant that any old judge had signed off on it.

'Michael Keslop?' Bailey said.

'Penrith District Court.'

'You got a judge in Penrith to stamp this?'

'It's a formality, Mr Bailey. The law is the law.'

Bailey shook his head. 'And I'm guessing you're Dominic Harding.' That was the person named as the 'executing officer' in the warrant.

'Correct.'

Bailey kept reading the legalese rubbish that granted a gaggle of AFP officers the right to assemble outside his front door, readying to go in.

The warrant apparently gave them the right to search everything from his handwritten notes and emails, his internet search history, photographs and planning logs.

'This is bullshit,' Bailey said, flicking through pages so that he could take it all in. 'The only place you haven't listed to search is my arsehole.'

'That can be arranged,' the guy who had escorted Bailey from his car piped up.

'You think this is a fucking joke?' Bailey said.

'Calm down, Mr Bailey,' Harding said. 'We're just doing our job.'

'What this looks like is a massive invasion of privacy and an assault on press freedoms,' Bailey snarled. 'This isn't just a fucking job.'

Bailey took a breath and kept reading.

The second page of the warrant was where things got interesting, confirming to Bailey exactly what it was the police were trying to find.

The list stretched across two pages, showing web addresses to Bailey's stories, and the names of anyone, or anything – any words – that may have been used in communications or files that related to the Uruzgan killings. This included Commander Harriet Walker, Abdul Rashid Haleem, *The Journal*, Gerald Summers, Rachel Symonds, Chief of Defence Force, Special Operations Command (SOCOMD) and Special Forces.

Bailey was left in no doubt that the AFP were accusing Commander Harriet Walker of being the person who had leaked information to Bailey. It was written in black and white. But why now?

He kept reading.

The warrant listed a dozen different ways that Harriet may have passed documents to Bailey, or ways in which Bailey may have stolen them, with each allegation referencing some obscure code from the *Defence Act*.

Bailey's meeting with Harriet the day before must have provided the missing link that the AFP had been searching for all these years. A warrant like this one didn't just appear out of thin air. Someone must have revived the old investigation into the security breach that led to Bailey's original stories. Someone must have either seen Harriet and Bailey together at the Lindt Café, or somehow hacked into their messages. Someone with the right connections, or moderately good access to the AFP's databases, could have easily placed Harriet Walker in Kabul in 2011. The meeting at the Lindt Café must have been enough to get the search warrant over the line. Enough to convince a district court judge from Penrith, anyway.

No one was ever prosecuted for the Uruzgan killings. No soldiers, or commanding officers, were even stood down. It was one of the army's biggest alleged cover-ups. At the time, several high-ranking military figures and politicians had called for Bailey's resignation, labelling him a traitor. But Gerald had stood firm, refusing to throw Bailey to the wolves, backing his correspondent's story and questioning the motives of those trying to discredit it.

Afghanistan's Minister for Justice, Abdul Rashid Haleem, was so enraged by the denials coming out of the ADF and the Australian Government that he had, indeed, followed through on his threat to take it to the International Criminal Court, where a special hearing had eventually delivered an open finding. It wasn't the damning conclusion that he had hoped for, but it wasn't an exoneration either. For an often toothless court like the Hague, the finding was enough for the Afghan Government to eject several senior ADF figures out of their country. Another reason that the ADF had it in for Bailey.

Bailey hadn't flinched when he read Walker's name on page two of the warrant. He knew that the AFP were on a fishing expedition and without either confirmation from Bailey that Harriet Walker was his source – which they'd never get – or documentation that proved it, the raid on his home would end up being nothing but an exercise in intimidation.

His confidence took a blow when he made it to the section about the powers of the warrant though. It gave them the right to enter Bailey's house and take forensic samples.

He kept reading, skimming over words that listed, in multiple ways, how these people were about to turn his house, and his life, upside down.

There was one other clause he found deeply disturbing. It related to every electronic device found in Bailey's possession. Computers. Phones. Storage devices. Police had the power to search whatever they wanted. And more.

Bailey was trying not to panic as the words filtered through his eyes and into his brain. The warrant said they had the power to 'add, copy, delete or alter' anything they found on his electronic devices. The words filled him with fear. Those specific powers were mentioned over and over, reinforcing the extraordinary scope of the warrant. They could alter and delete his files? It didn't make any sense.

And then, on page 6, came the clincher. It said that 'the executing officer, and any constable assisting in the execution of this warrant who is a police officer, may use such force against persons or things as is necessary and reasonable in the circumstances.'

The guy standing in front of Bailey had just been granted the power to put him in handcuffs and lock him inside a prison cell on nothing but a whim.

'I'm going to need you to unlock your front door,' Harding said, obviously deciding that he'd given Bailey enough time to think. 'Then you're going to need to give us access to all of your electronic devices. Phones. Computers. Laptops. Anywhere you store information. Passwords to unlock them. Any original materials relating to the Uruzgan stories. And don't play games with me. It's a short drive to the nearest prison cell.'

Bailey was so angry he was almost shaking.

The link that the warrant had made between him and Harriet Walker was an allegation. The raid on his house was about finding the proof. About pressuring Bailey to make an admission. But that would never happen. Bailey always protected his sources.

'Wait a minute.'

Campo. He'd forgotten about Campo.

'I left my dog in the car.'

'What?'

'My dog. I took her for a walk this morning. She's still in the back of the car.'

'Give me your keys,' Harding said, holding out his hand. 'One of my team will get her.'

'No, they won't.'

Bailey turned and started walking up the street, hearing the sounds of footsteps trailing him, turning to see the officer who had escorted him to his house returning with him to his car. He opened the boot of his station wagon and watched Campo take a few awkward goes to get to her feet and then climb, slowly, onto the footpath. Her beady eyes staring affectionately at her master before she gave the stranger a sniff. Checking him out for the both of them.

'Greyhound?'

'Yeah.'

Bailey got down on one knee, attaching the leash to Campo's collar, noticing the drain next to his car tyre. Bone dry and inviting. A place to hide.

'Fuck! A cat!' Bailey yanked on Campo's leash, pulling her back, distracting the officer for a split second as he dropped his phone into the drain, coughing loudly to disguise the sound it made when it hit the concrete a couple of metres below.

'What are you playing at? I didn't see a cat.'

Bailey got to his feet, feeling slightly guilty about startling Campo.

'I'm not worried about you seeing it, mate. My dog clocks a cat and she'll be off like a bullet train. All dogs chase cats but the problem with greyhounds is they can actually catch them. It's not pretty when they do.'

'Okay. Enough about your dog.'

'You're the one who keeps asking me questions about her.'

The guy went to respond but thought better of it, tapping Bailey on the shoulder, pointing at his house.

'Stop pissing around.'

Bailey walked up the front steps of his house without looking at Harding. 'I need a minute to put my dog out back in the courtyard. Get her a drink. Then you can do whatever you fucking like.'

Worried that the scope of the warrant could lead the AFP down rabbit holes that he hadn't even thought of yet, Bailey was trying to buy time so that Gerald and a lawyer could get here. More witnesses. More eyes.

The warrant appeared to be so broad that Bailey feared that anything could be deemed relevant to the years-old investigation. Could other stories he'd written suddenly become more interesting as they sifted through materials on his devices and in his home? Decades of stories – investigations – upended and undermined, ripped to shreds by a local judge's interpretation of a criminal act that had been written at a time when the most common mode of transport was a horse and carriage.

These officers wouldn't just be going through Bailey's work documents. They had the right to search anything they bloody well wanted. Email communications with his daughter, his ex-wife, his friends. Were they fair game too? The thought was terrifying. Personal information becoming public. Things people had no right to know. His medical records. All those sessions with shrinks. His breakdown. Alcoholism. His role in the counter-terrorism investigation that had brought down the FBI's most wanted terrorist. The murder of Sharon Dexter.

Fuck.

Bailey felt like he was in a sauna, panic rising through his body in a rush of heat. He could feel the beads of sweat pushing through the skin on his forehead, blood flushing his cheeks.

Throwing his jacket on the kitchen table, he rolled up the sleeves of his shirt, pausing at the pantry to get Campo one of those pork snacks she liked to chew on, before leading her to the courtyard. Taking his time to fill her bowl with water, gently stroking her head. His only friend. Those calming beady eyes.

'C'mon, Mr Bailey. Now you're just trying to piss me off.'

Bailey closed the door to the courtyard, leaving Campo outside on her own. 'Where do you want to start, then?'

'Laptop. Phone. Desktop computer.' Harding didn't need to quote the warrant, he knew exactly what he wanted. 'And my team will also be searching the rest of the house. Cupboards. Drawers. If you've got a safe, you'll need to open it. Any boxes where you store files. Everything.'

Bailey looked at his watch. It had been around fifteen minutes since he had spoken to Gerald. His old friend lived on the other side of the bridge, hopefully the morning traffic was moving.

'Laptop's there.' Bailey pointed at the computer by the telephone on the kitchen bench. 'It's all I use. Desktop packed up on me a few years ago, realised I didn't need one any more.'

Harding directed one of his officers to get to work on the computer. 'Password?'

'Leichhardt.'

Harding raised an eyebrow, like he was about to ask Bailey why he'd chosen a Sydney suburb as a password, and then thought better of it. Not that Bailey would have told him. Leichhardt was the suburb where Sharon Dexter had lived. Where she had owned a house. The house that she'd left him in her will.

Click. Click. Click.

'Mr Bailey?'

Harding was clicking his fingers at Bailey, who'd zoned out, thinking about Dexter.

'Your phone. I need your phone.'

Bailey patted his pockets, pretending to search for the phone that he'd dropped in the drain up the street, before doing the same with his jacket on the bench.

'Don't play games with me, Mr Bailey.'

'Not sure where it is.'

'Is it an iPhone?'

'Yeah.'

'We can pull the data we need from the cloud,' Harding said, smirking. 'But I still want your phone. Find it.'

'What cloud?'

'Don't get smart. The warrant permits us to go through everything, including data storage.'

Bailey shrugged, looking again at his watch. Twenty minutes since he spoke with Gerald. Hurry up, mate.

'Sorry. Bit of a dinosaur with all that stuff. I don't use the cloud. Don't trust it. I figure if I can put stuff up there then someone else can pull it down.'

'You must back up your files somewhere.'

A statement not a question.

'USB sticks and portable hard drives.'

'Where are they?'

'The drawer in the study.'

'Go get them.'

'No.'

Harding took a few paces towards Bailey, leaning on the bench. He was a few inches taller than Bailey and he was looking down on him, an obvious attempt at intimidation.

'Are you intentionally failing to comply with a search warrant?'

Bailey stood his ground. 'Look, fuckwit. You can grab whatever you like. Consider my house an open book. But you're going to need to sift through the pages yourselves. There's nothing in the warrant that says I need to spoonfeed you people. Don't expect me to make you coffees and serve you lunch. Don't expect me to be a good bloke, either.'

'Sir.' The guy who had escorted Bailey to and from his car was standing in the corner of the kitchen. 'Could I have a word?'

Harding walked over to him and Bailey could hear the two men talking quietly, although he couldn't make out the words.

Eventually, Harding turned back around, a smug look on his face. He pointed to a woman in a suit. 'Watch him. If he moves or tries to do anything suspicious, arrest him.'

'Yes, sir,' she said, looking blankly at Bailey.

Harding and the other officer left the room and Bailey and the woman stood in silence. Seconds turning into minutes. Bailey's legs suddenly tired and heavy.

Minutes later, Harding walked back into Bailey's kitchen holding a mobile phone in his hand with a cracked screen. He had a disturbing, triumphant smile on his face.

'Managed to find that phone for you.'

The other guy must have remembered the drain. He must have heard the phone hit the concrete. Or at least he'd seen enough to make him suspicious.

'Not mine.'

Harding took a few steps forward, pressing the screen so that Bailey could see the photograph of his daughter through the cracked glass.

'So that's not Miranda?'

The bastard even knew her name.

'Password?'

Bailey was in trouble. He'd read the words of the warrant and knew that he needed to give Harding and his officers access to all of his electronic devices. That meant passwords too.

'Twelve. Thirteen. Fourteen.'

Harding punched in the numbers, the glow of the screen flickering on his face as the phone came to life.

'Do I need to search any other drains in the street before we get started?'

Bailey answered his question with silence, panicking at the reality of what was going on inside his home. The realisation that his conversation with Harriet Walker on Signal was only a few swipes and presses away. Wondering whether that would be enough to take her down. Knowing that the raid on his house wasn't about him, it was about exposing the person who had leaked a classified ADF file.

'It didn't have to be this way.' Harding was standing beside Bailey now, metal handcuffs jangling in his hand. 'Turn around.'

'What?'

'John Bailey, I'm arresting you for failing to comply with a search warrant.'

CHAPTER 14

As prison cells go, this one wasn't so bad.

Everything in the room was made of steel and bolted to the floor. Toilet. Sink. Table. Stool. Even the bed he was lying on. The only things that weren't held down with bolts were the plastic mattress and the thin blanket that he had scrunched up and tossed into the corner, fearing that it was crawling with bed bugs.

The small window didn't open but it was big enough to flood the cell with natural light. The yellow dim telling Bailey that it was getting close to sunset, which meant that he'd been locked inside for at least seven hours. More.

Bailey had spent most of the day at Paddington Police Station, lying flat on the wafer-thin mattress, counting mould spores on the ceiling, surprisingly intrigued by the swirling patterns they made. He was trying not to think about what was happening back at his house. His drawers being tipped upside down. Cupboards raided. Investigators scouring through his computer and every storage device they could find. Copying and altering his files. Deleting them. Doing whatever the hell they wanted, thanks to the ridiculous suite of powers signed off by a district court judge in Penrith.

The phone was the thing worrying Bailey the most. The conversation that he'd had with Harriet Walker on Signal. He'd been racking his brain, trying to remember it word for word, wondering whether or not there was anything incriminating in their exchanges. He knew there wasn't a smoking gun that would prove that Walker was the person who had handed him a classified ADF report in Kabul back in 2011. He hadn't even mentioned it. But it didn't stop Bailey's mind from racing. Wondering whether he had missed something. Something that might explain why Walker had disappeared hours after she had scheduled a meeting with him.

A key rattled in the lock. The door to his cell opened.

'Up you get.' A policeman that Bailey didn't recognise was standing in the doorway. 'You're out.'

'What?'

A woman was standing behind the policeman and Bailey could see enough of her bedraggled hair to know who it was.

'Marj?'

Marjorie Atkins. *The Journal*'s legal associate for three decades, who had helped Bailey with some of his more controversial investigations.

'Hi, Bailey,' she said, frowning. 'Sorry it took us so bloody long to get this sorted.'

He slid off the mattress and onto the floor. 'All good. Thanks for coming. Where's old mate?'

'Gerald? In the waiting area, where he's been all day. Miranda's there too.'

Bailey felt sick at the thought of his daughter coming to the police station to help bail him out. 'Who the bloody hell told Miranda?'

'Take it easy, Bailey.' Marjorie grabbed his arm. 'We didn't tell her. There's been some media coverage.'

'What?'

'Excuse me,' the policeman interjected. 'If you don't mind finishing this conversation somewhere else?'

Bailey ignored him. 'What do you mean by "media coverage"?'

'Come on.'

Marjorie turned away from Bailey and followed the policeman down the hall and into another part of the station where there was some paperwork waiting for them, along with a plastic bag with Bailey's belongings inside. Wallet. Keys. Watch. Shoelaces. Belt. The simple things you're permitted to own when you're a person, not a prisoner.

'Marj?' Bailey kept at her while he ripped open the bag, checking that everything was there. 'The media. What's out there?'

'Just give me a minute.'

Marjorie scribbled her signature on several pieces of paper and had Bailey do the same.

'Mr Bailey's free to go.'

'What happens next?' Bailey said, directing his question to the policeman.

'That's up to the Australian Federal Police.'

'I'll explain later,' Marjorie said. 'Let's get you home.'

Home.

Bailey was hoping that Harding and those other heavy-handed pricks from the AFP had left. The thought of them ripping through his house into the night was too much to contemplate.

'It's okay, Bailey. They're gone.'

She must have read the worried expression on his face.

'Dad!'

Miranda spotted Bailey the second he was let through the door to the waiting area. She hurried over and he put his arms around her, closing his eyes, letting himself forget – for just a moment – about the hell of a day he'd had.

'You really shouldn't have come, sweetheart,' he said, pulling back so that he could see her eyes. 'Just the bloody cops over-playing their hand. I've done nothing wrong. Journalism's not a crime.'

'You're right about that, mate.' Gerald was standing behind Miranda and he reached around and put a hand on Bailey's shoulder. 'It's outrageous overreach. I've already registered a complaint to home affairs. Others have too. Newspaper editors, current and retired. The ABC. SBS. All the heads have come out swinging. We'll fight this every inch of the way.'

We.

Suddenly, Bailey didn't feel so alone. The raid may have been happening at his home but the way Gerald was talking, other media outlets must already be viewing today's raid as the assault on press freedoms that Bailey had called out the second he met Dominic Harding outside his front door.

'Thanks, mate. And thanks for calling Marj.'

'Of course,' Gerald said. 'I'm just sorry we didn't arrive earlier. We saw you being driven away in a police van and we've spent the last eight hours in here and on the phone trying to get you out.'

'So, how much coverage is this getting?' Bailey directed his question at Marjorie. 'Please tell me that I'm not the headline.'

'Dad, let's get out of here,' Miranda said, tugging on his arm.

'She's right,' Marjorie said, looking around. 'Let's talk outside.'

The Paddington police station and court house was sandwiched in between residential houses on Jersey Road. Both sides of the street were lined with police cars. Red, blue and white ones with the same chequered stripes. Grey unmarked Fords that you could tell were cop cars by their standard rims. Almost every car spot in the street was taken up by a police vehicle of some description. Hell knows where the locals parked their cars.

Stepping out into the afternoon light, Bailey looked up the road towards Oxford Street, where he could see the corner of the White Lion Hotel. The scene of the attack on Matthew Lam. Those racist bastards had brazenly bashed a Black man less than a hundred metres from a police station.

'You were the nation's top story until about an hour ago,' Gerald said, pulling his phone from the inside pocket of his jacket, lighting up the screen and holding it out to Bailey. 'Then this story broke.'

AFP OFFICER FOUND DEAD ON MAROUBRA BEACH

'What the . . .'

'It's Harriet Walker. Someone killed her,' Gerald said, softly.

Bailey snatched the phone from Gerald's hand, clicking on the story, scrolling down the page, speed-reading words, searching for any mention of Hat's name. Details about how she died.

'Name's not here.' Bailey handed the phone back to Gerald. 'How do you know?'

'Contact in the AFP told me. It'll be out there soon. They're waiting on the family.'

Knowing Gerald, his contact in the AFP was probably the bloody commissioner. He literally had every powerful person in the country on speed dial.

'Any suspects?'

'Too early. Happened before sunrise. She was walking on the beach. Someone attacked her.'

'They're trying to pass this off as a random assault?' Bailey ran his fingers though his hair, looking at the ground, shaking his head. 'Fuck, Gerald. What the hell's going on?'

'Let's talk back at the house.'

Bailey got distracted by a cop in uniform walking up the steps of the big yellow building.

Gerald was right, they needed to go somewhere where they could talk privately. But Bailey had one more question. 'What did your contact have to say about the shit show at my house?'

'Wouldn't go there.'

'I bet they wouldn't,' Bailey said, gruffly.

'Hey, Dad?' Miranda had hooked her arm around her father's elbow. 'How about we get you home? I'll order us some takeaway.'

A feed, along with a shower, was a good idea. 'Yeah, okay.'

'My car's up the street. Ride with me,' Miranda said, nodding at Gerald and Marjorie. 'See you back at Dad's place.'

Bailey's townhouse was just around the corner. Because of all the one-way streets and traffic lights, it would have been faster to walk. But Bailey never complained about spending time with his daughter, even though the seats in her MG Roadster were brutally uncomfortable.

'Everything okay with you, sweetheart?'

Miranda gave him a squinty smile. Sarcastic. 'I'm fine, Dad. Let's not worry about me today, okay?'

Bailey ignored her. 'What about that husband of yours? How's the doc?'

Miranda had married Doctor Peter Andrews in a small ceremony just before the bushfire season. The wedding was the main reason that Bailey had returned to Australia. He wasn't going to miss walking his daughter down the aisle. Not for anything.

'Peter's good. He's great, actually. We think we've found a house we like in –'

'Hold that thought. Stop the car.'

Miranda had just turned into Bailey's street and they both noticed two vans with satellite dishes parked outside his house.

'Damn it!' Bailey bashed the ball of his fist on the dashboard. 'The circus has arrived.'

'What do you want me to do, Dad?'

Miranda pulled over to the side of the road.

'Turn around. Drive away. I think you should go home.' Bailey was talking without taking his eyes off the other end of the street. Eventually, he looked at Miranda. 'Seriously, I don't want you being chased with a camera. Being on the news. Best I run the gauntlet on my own.'

'Why don't you just come with me?' Miranda didn't need much convincing. She was a corporate lawyer who enjoyed her privacy. The last thing she needed was a prime time appearance in the six o'clock news. 'You can stay at our flat tonight.'

'Kind of you, sweetheart. But I need to get inside, see what those pricks did to my house.'

'Okay. Call me if you change your mind.'

Bailey climbed out, tapping the retractable roof of his

daughter's sports car, watching as she did a U-turn and disappeared around the corner. Safe.

'That's him!'

A reporter spotted Bailey when he was three doors away from his house. By the time he was outside three reporters were on him, pushing microphones into his face, cameras lingering behind them like nosy giraffes.

'John Bailey, how do you feel about the way the AFP treated you today?'

'I'm deeply disturbed by what's happened, quite frankly.' Bailey hadn't prepared any words but he felt the need to say something. 'Everyone should be worried. It's a clear assault on the freedom of the press. Now, if you'll excuse me, I've been locked in a prison cell all day. I could do with a shower.'

'Mr Bailey! Mr Bailey!'

A reporter was trying to get him to turn back around as he walked through his front gate, where Gerald and Marjorie were already standing on his porch.

'Do you think there's a link between the raid on your house and the murder of an AFP officer on Maroubra Beach this morning?'

Bailey turned around, glaring at the cameras. 'That's a question you'll need to ask the Australian Federal Police.'

'What do you mean by that? Mr Bailey? Mr Bailey!'

Bailey unlocked the front door and he, Marjorie and Gerald filed inside.

'Not sure that was such a good idea, Bailey,' Marjorie said.

'Yeah, well. Hat was an old mate of mine. Murdered on the same day that the AFP decided to raid my house. She's named in the warrant. Can't be a coincidence. Not in my book.'

CHAPTER 15

ANNIE

'You at home?'

It was Bill. Again.

'Yeah. Why?'

He'd been calling her all day, trying to find a way to cover the story about the dead AFP officer on Maroubra Beach. The six o'clock news would report the death. He needed something else for *Inside Story*, an angle that didn't require Annie burning her police source and naming Harriet Walker as the victim. Not that this was even being considered.

'The AFP's naming Harriet Walker as the victim in a statement at eight o'clock tonight. They've given us the jump on it.'

Annie walked into the kitchen, turning off the stove. The pasta could wait.

'You've got the statement?'

'Yeah. And more. I've got a copy of the AFP warrant for the raid on John Bailey's house. It's linked.'

'What?'

'Harriet Walker's name is all over the warrant. From my reading, it looks like the AFP are accusing her of leaking a defence document to Bailey back in 2011. He broke a story about Australian soldiers killing civilians in Uruzgan.'

'I remember. He won a Walkley for that yarn.'

'And pissed off a lot of people.'

Bailey was good at that, Annie thought to herself. A half-smile crept onto her face before it turned into a frown.

'Annie?' Bill interrupted the silence.

'Yeah?'

'You and John Bailey have a history, right?'

'We're old friends, if that's what you mean.' Annie didn't like the way Bill had framed the question. 'We were in Beirut together . . . at the same time, I mean.'

Annie and Bailey were more than just old friends, although Annie wouldn't have called it a relationship. They'd had a special arrangement. Casual sex. Bed pals. It was a time when they were both living in Beirut and hopping between warzones, Bailey for *The Journal* and Annie for her job in television news. The intimate moments they'd had together were more about keeping each other connected to ordinary life, away from the violence and sadness they were chronicling for readers and viewers back home.

Annie and Bailey also had one other thing in common – booze. For Bailey, that meant whisky. For Annie, vodka. Just over a year ago, they'd reconnected after bumping into each other at an Alcoholics Anonymous meeting in Sydney. They went on walks together. Talking. Listening. Helping each other to keep their demons at bay. Friends.

Then Bailey disappeared to the other side of the world and proceeded to ignore every message that Annie sent him after she discovered that the Australian police detective who had been murdered by a terrorist in London was his girlfriend.

Annie had been imagining Bailey perched on a stool in some dingy bar somewhere, drinking his sadness away. She had no idea that he was back in Sydney, and she couldn't help being more than a little upset that he hadn't let her know.

'Reckon he'll speak to you?' Bill said.

'Don't know. Maybe.'

Annie felt sick at the thought of doing a story on Bailey.

'I'm going to need more than a *maybe* on this one, Annie,' Bill said, coolly. 'This is a big fucking story.'

'You don't need to tell me that.'

'Good. Because you're doing a live hit outside Bailey's house in an hour. Fletch's already on the way. I've emailed you the AFP statement and the warrant. Keep it tight. We break it at seven.'

Annie sighed into the phone. 'Okay.'

'And Annie?'

'Yeah?'

'I want the Bailey interview. It's not going to be tonight, but I want it.'

'That's not going to be easy.'

'I'll text you the address.'

'Don't bother,' Annie said, 'he's two streets away.'

Bill laughed. 'Right.'

Arsehole.

Annie quickly got changed, doing her makeup in the bathroom and pulling her hair into a tight ponytail. The safest option for a television appearance at short notice. She'd stopped caring so much about people judging her looks now that she was back on the road as a reporter. The most important thing was the story, and she needed to give herself some time to read through the warrant and the AFP statement that Bill had sent her.

'Louis!'

Annie called through the closed door of her son's bedroom.

No answer.

She knocked on the door.

'Louis!'

Still no answer.

Using the ball of her fist, she knocked louder, resisting the temptation to barge into a seventeen-year-old boy's bedroom uninvited.

'Louis! I'm coming in!'

'What!'

Finally, a response.

She opened the door wide enough so that her voice could carry through the crack. 'Can I come in?'

'Sure.'

Louis was sitting on his bed with a gaming headset around his neck.

'I need to go out for work for a couple of hours. Home around eight. There's a bolognese on the stove. You'll need to cook your own pasta.'

'Fine.'

Sure. Fine. Whatever.

Louis's three favourite words. So far, he'd only used two of them.

'I love you.'

'Whatevs.'

She sighed.

CHAPTER 16

A box of pepperoni pizza was sitting in the middle of Bailey's kitchen bench surrounded by the scattered pages of the AFP warrant, some of the pieces of paper stained with oil, tomato and round circles made by steaming mugs of coffee and tea.

'Just don't plan an overseas trip anytime soon.'

Marjorie was sitting on a stool, giving him the lowdown about his bail conditions.

'I won't. I haven't.'

'Good.'

'How will they keep tabs on me?' Bailey said, tossing a tired crust into the lid of the pizza box. 'Do I need to report in at a police station or something?'

'Yeah, Bailey. You do.' Marjorie took a sip from the cup of tea that Gerald had made her. 'But it's only weekly.'

'Oh, fucking great. Lucky me,' Bailey huffed, rolling his eyes. 'First, they make you feel like a criminal. Then they treat you like one.'

'We'll fight it, Bailey. We'll win. There's no way you'll get a custodial sentence.' Gerald was sitting across the other side of the counter, pointing his finger into the stone benchtop. 'What happened here today was a bloody disgrace. The court of

136

public opinion already knows it. The other court's just playing catch-up.'

The wise man with the wise words.

'I hope you're right.'

Bailey grabbed another slice of pizza, taking a bite. He hadn't eaten all day and the pizza tasted good, despite the fact that it was cold by the time the poor delivery kid riding one of those stupid electric pushbikes knocked on his front door.

'Just do your best not to antagonise the feds,' Marjorie said. 'Comments like the ones you made outside don't help.'

'I couldn't give a flying fuck about the feds.'

'Settle down, mate,' Gerald said, flapping his hand. 'Marj's just making the point that we don't want to inflame the situation any further.'

'I know this is difficult, Bailey,' Marjorie said. 'I'm just giving you advice on the most sensible course of action.'

'Right. Right.' Bailey was shaking his head, speaking with a mouthful of pizza. 'Sorry, Marj. I'm just racking my brain here. The Afghan stories. Hat's murder. The raid. The timing of it all. There's something more. Has to be.'

'We need to think our way through this, carefully,' Marjorie said. 'I'm doing this pro bono, by the way. You know that, right?'

'Thanks, Marj. Thanks. I really appreciate it. I do.'

'It's fine. Of course it's fine, you know that. But I need to know everything.' Marjorie cleared her throat. 'Gerald told me about the new job with Neena. What are you working on?'

Bailey hadn't given much thought to the piece he was writing about Augustus Strong and far right nationalism. He'd only been thinking of his stories about Afghanistan and the documents that he'd been given by Harriet Walker and the Afghan Minister for Justice, Abdul Rashid Haleem, all those years ago. Whether they could somehow be traced back to Harriet. Her death hadn't changed anything for him on that front. He would take their secret to the grave. Like she had. He just needed to know that the documents couldn't be found.

'Gerald –'

'They're safe, Bailey. Untraceable.'

Bailey nodded gratefully.

Before Gerald had published Bailey's first story about the Uruzgan killings, Bailey had sent him the original files in the post. If Gerald was going to publish a story about Australian soldiers allegedly committing war crimes, he'd need to see the evidence. The documents were probably locked in a safety deposit box somewhere, along with any other secrets that a former newspaper editor kept under lock and key. Bailey didn't need to know where. He didn't want to know.

'Thanks, mate.' He took another bite of his pizza, holding up the slice in front of Gerald. 'This is good. You should have some.'

'So, what are you working on?' Marjorie asked again.

'I'm investigating right-wing extremists. The people getting excited about that Augustus Strong clown's visit to Australia. Interviewed him last night, actually.'

Gerald had said that he wasn't eating but the smell of the pizza was too good and he picked up a piece, casually taking a bite. 'What was he like?'

'As you might expect, full of bluster. Big statements. Scratched the surface and there wasn't much there.' Bailey smiled as he remembered the interview. 'He faked a headache and his PR flunky kicked me out.'

Gerald laughed, almost choking.

'What I don't understand is, why now?' Marjorie hadn't reacted to Bailey's commentary about Strong and she was frowning. 'Why would the AFP suddenly be interested in the Uruzgan stories?'

'Unless it's not about that,' Bailey said. 'Unless this has nothing to do with Afghanistan.'

'What are you talking about, Bailey?' Gerald said.

Bailey ignored the question and grabbed his phone from the bench, punching in his security code. The second he'd arrived home he had scoured through his laptop computer and his phone to see whether the AFP had 'altered or deleted' any of his work. It appeared that they hadn't. Marjorie had demanded a list of the things that they'd copied, mostly innocuous emails and copies of handwritten pages from his notebooks. Bailey's exchange with Walker on Signal was there too, but that hadn't rung alarm bells for him because he'd already concluded that there was nothing incriminating in it. All the Signal chat did was confirm that they knew each other well enough to arrange a meeting.

But there was something else.

'I was due to meet Hat this morning,' he said, still staring at his phone, thumb guiding his search. 'I had asked her to look at something for me. A video.'

'What video?' Gerald had walked around the other side of the kitchen counter and he was standing behind Bailey, staring over his shoulder. 'Bailey? What video?'

'It's gone.'

Bailey looked up, confused.

'What's gone?' Marjorie said. 'What are you talking about?'

'Someone has deleted a video from my phone.' Bailey clenched his jaw, breathing out hard, reaching across the counter towards Marjorie. 'Show me that list.'

Gerald and Marjorie watched in silence as Bailey flicked through the pages again, flinging the ones that didn't interest him across the bench, some of them floating to the floor.

'It's not here. The bloody video isn't on the list.'

Bailey reached across the table, grabbing a copy of the warrant, turning the pages so quickly that he was tearing paper.

'What are you looking for?' Marjorie said.

'This.'

Bailey slammed a page onto the stone, pointing at the paragraph he'd been searching for.

'To add, copy, delete or alter other data in the computer or device found in the course of a search authorised under the warrant.' Bailey was reading – word for word – from the page. 'And that's exactly what they've done.'

'What was it?' Gerald said. 'What did they delete?'

'I took a video of the crowd at Augustus Strong's talk two nights ago. I passed the video to Hat. She said she was going to have a look at it, see if there were any interesting faces in the crowd. You heard the ASIO chief the other day, talking up the threat of white supremacist groups. Hat was interested in the video. From the way she was talking, I reckon she was already part of some investigation into these groups. With her rank, she was probably leading it.' Bailey stopped talking for a moment, massaging his temples. 'I did a deal with her. I gave her the video with the hope that she'd share anything interesting she found. The AFP have been on to these groups for a while. That's why we were meeting this morning. She said she had something for me. Now she's fucking dead.'

'Calm down, mate,' Gerald said. 'We don't know if it's connected. The cops are talking about her death at Maroubra as a robbery, or something. What you're suggesting is a stretch. More than that. It's a big leap, Bailey.'

'Yeah, well. As I said, I don't think it was a coincidence.'

'Think rationally for a second.' Gerald was speaking slowly, an obvious ploy to get Bailey to calm down. 'If the feds are looking into hate groups in Australia, maybe the video had something on it that compromised an investigation? Maybe that's what Harriet was about to tell you?'

'Are you being serious?'

'I'm just speculating. Trying to understand why.'

'Why? Why? You mean why would the AFP be given such extraordinary powers by a judge to literally do whatever the hell they want? Turn my life upside down?' Bailey was so angry that he was shaking. 'There's nothing to understand! It's simple. The AFP have deleted a video from my phone that has no relation-ship to the subject of the warrant, which is a series of articles that I wrote in 2011 about what amounted to Australian war crimes in Afghanistan. A video of far right nationalists couldn't be further away from those stories. They are entirely unrelated. This is absurd.'

'Bailey, I wasn't defending what happened here.' Gerald was doing well to stay calm. 'I'm just trying to look at this from another angle, trying to get a grip.'

'Boys, look at this.'

Marjorie was pointing at the small television in Bailey's kitchen, where they had earlier watched the stories about Bailey on the six o'clock news. *Inside Story* had just started and there was a strap across the screen with Harriet Walker's name on it.

'Turn it up, Marj,' Bailey said.

'Harriet Walker was out walking on Maroubra Beach when she was attacked in what police believe was a violent robbery.' The presenter had a stern look on his face as he delivered the breaking news. '*Inside Story* has more startling revelations to bring you tonight. Annie Brooks joins us now from the Sydney suburb of Paddington. Annie, what can you tell us?'

Annie Brooks was standing directly outside Bailey's house.

'You are fucking joking,' Bailey said.

'Isn't that –'

Bailey waved his hand at Gerald. 'Quiet. Quiet.'

'Good evening, Jim. I'm standing outside the home of the prominent investigative journalist, John Bailey, which was today raided by the Australian Federal Police over a story that Mr Bailey wrote almost nine years ago about an ADF operation in Uruzgan that led to the deaths of eight Afghan nationals. I've seen a copy of the Australian Federal Police warrant and tonight we can reveal that the name Commander Harriet Walker – who of course we have just identified as the AFP officer murdered this morning on Maroubra Beach – is named in the warrant. In fact, it seems very clear that John Bailey's house was raided today due to his connection to Harriet Walker.'

The presenter, Jim Connors, appeared in a box on the screen again as he prepared to ask a question.

'Annie, what more do we know about the connection between Harriet Walker and John Bailey?'

'Well, Jim, John Bailey's story sparked a huge controversy when it first broke in 2011 and it would end up leading to a war crimes investigation at the Hague. Although the ADF's own investigation cleared Australian soldiers of any wrongdoing, the Afghan Government's inquiry accused Australian soldiers of executing eight civilians during a botched raid on what was thought to be a Taliban safehouse. The International Criminal Court would eventually deliver an open finding. Central to John Bailey's story was a leaked copy of the ADF's investigation and today's warrant suggests that the AFP suspect the source of that leak may have been Harriet Walker. Today's raid on John Bailey's home seems to be an attempt by the AFP to find proof. But why would the AFP suddenly be interested in a series of stories from eight years ago? And there's also the peculiar timing of Harriet Walker's tragic death on the same day that the AFP decided to raid John Bailey's home. These are all questions that the team at *Inside Story,* and no doubt many Australians watching, are now pondering tonight. Jim.'

'Fuck this.'

Bailey threw his pizza crust into the cardboard box and charged down the hallway towards the front door.

'Bailey!'

CHAPTER 17

ANNIE

Fletch killed the light that was beaming a white glow across Annie's cheeks and the hedge inside John Bailey's front yard.

'Good cross, Annie.'

'Bit of a rush job. Hope I made sense.'

'You did. Nice and punchy. You got it all in.' Cameramen knew how to pack up quickly and Fletch was already folding his light stand. 'Bill would have been happy for sure.'

A sound over Annie's shoulder caused both of them to jump.

Bailey's front door opening.

The man of the moment stepped out onto his front porch, staring in their direction. Probably relieved that the other television crews had gone, although clearly annoyed by the one that was left.

'Here we go.' Fletch went for his camera, a reflex action from his years in the business capturing moments, making stories.

Annie raised her hand. 'No, Fletch. Don't.'

Bailey slowly walked down the steps and through his front gate.

'Annie.'

The coldness in Bailey's one-word greeting told Annie all that she needed to know about what he thought of tonight's performance on national television. Any bridge that had been built between them after they had been reacquainted at an Alcoholics Anonymous meeting not so long ago was now burning, along with everything else in the bushfire summer.

'Just doing my job, Bailey. You of all people should know that.'

Bailey stood there silently, arms folded, staring at her. Cold eyes, uninviting. His house – his life – now a sorry sitcom for the world to watch.

'Are you just going to stand there?' Annie said, losing empathy with every second that passed. 'Bailey?'

Fletch cleared his throat. 'I'm going to keep packing up, Annie.'

Annie turned to her cameraman, nodding. 'Sure, Fletch. No worries.'

The sky was littered with clouds, making it unusually dark for a summer evening, although not quite dark enough for the driver of the car that was edging along the street to turn his lights on. They both watched and waited for the car to disappear down the end of the street.

'Are you going to say something?' Annie said, finally.

'I don't know what to say,' Bailey said, his hands still tucked under his armpits.

'People usually start with hello.'

Annie's attempt at humour drew a squint from the guy standing in front of her. And a word.

'Hello.'

'C'mon, Bailey. Don't be an arsehole.'

Annie knew all about being the subject of stories, especially when she had been Sydney's most popular news presenter. Even more so when she wasn't. The icing on the cake was when she was hospitalised with a broken jaw after being beaten by her ex-husband. Annie Brooks had lost count of all the times that she'd been the story and she was already tired of Bailey's grandstanding.

'We've both been doing this long enough to know how it works,' Annie said. 'No one likes being the story.'

'You got that right.'

Finally, more than a one-word sentence. Progress.

'You also know that this – that you – are a bloody good story. It's outrageous what happened here today. The feds raiding your home. The ridiculous powers they've been given. I'm sorry, Bailey. I am. It's shit. Really shit. Are you okay?'

Annie stepped towards him. A gesture. She wanted to reach out and touch his elbow, get him to unfold his arms. Remind him that they were friends.

'Bailey?'

'What else do you know about what happened to Harriet Walker?' Bailey said, feet stuck to the concrete like a statue. 'I presume more than what you just told Jim Connors and the rest of Australia on *Inside Story*. And, Annie, don't bullshit me.'

'Not much.' Annie would need to let this one play out. Let Bailey calm down on his own. 'I literally got copies of the warrant and the AFP media release about Walker an hour ago.'

Bailey unfolded his arms, stretching an open palm towards Annie. 'Let me see it. Your phone. Give me a look at the AFP release.'

Annie bent down, rummaging her hand inside the bag at her feet until she found her phone. She unlocked it, spooling through her emails until she found the message from Bill, opening the attachment.

'There's not much there.' She handed him her phone. 'Just a name and the suggestion that it was a robbery.'

'Annie, I'm going to go.' Fletch closed the back door of his four-wheel drive. 'You good?'

'Yeah, Fletch. Thanks for today. Talk tomorrow, okay?'

'Good one.' Fletch was talking over the roof of the four-wheel drive, his attention now on Bailey. 'Like she said, we're just doing our jobs. You take care of yourself, mate.'

Bailey nodded his chin and he and Annie stood in silence as Fletch drove away.

'Good bloke?' Bailey said.

'Yeah. I've only been at work a few months, don't know if I could've handled being back on the road without Fletch. Nice guy. Bloody good at his job.'

Somehow, the conversation had slid somewhere else and, for a split second, Annie felt like she was talking to the guy she had taken walks with in the park. Shared secrets. Like the day she'd told Bailey that she had blown up her sobriety by downing half a bottle of vodka after learning that her violent ex-husband was being let out of prison.

'I'm glad you're working again. Way too young to give it up,' Bailey said, the hint of a smile edging the corner of his cheek. 'And you get to escape that autocue. Be a real journo again. Must have been a shock to the system.'

Annie laughed. 'It was, actually. And no offence taken.'

'You were always too good for that commercial newsreader crap.'

'Again, thanks,' Annie said, dryly.

The sound of someone coughing made Annie and Bailey turn around.

'Annie.' Gerald waved from Bailey's front porch.

'Hi, Gerald.'

'Are you coming in, Bailey?' Gerald said. 'We've still got a bit to talk about. Marjorie needs to push off soon.'

Annie watched Gerald walk back inside the house before she looked at Bailey. The creases in his brow, his sandy blond hair. Eyes glazed by the sad stories behind them. His secrets.

'I'm sorry about Harriet Walker, Bailey. You know, if you want to talk about it, I'm –'

'I'm not talking to you about Harriet Walker.' Bailey stiffened. 'Not on the record. Not on background, either.'

Annie sighed. 'That's not what I meant.'

It was exactly what she'd meant. That sick feeling again.

'Yeah, well.' Bailey flinched, embarrassed. 'I've got a lot going on, Annie. Lawyer's inside. Got to go.'

'Okay, Bailey.' Annie took a punt, reaching out and touching his arm. 'I mean it about a chat. We go back a long way. If you've got someone to talk to, then fine. I'll leave you alone.'

This time she was offering as a friend.

Bailey started walking backwards, running his hand along the top of his unkempt hedge. 'Noted.'

'You've got my number.'

Bailey opened his squeaky gate and disappeared inside his house.

CHAPTER 18

'Have you seen the news?'

Neena was almost yelling down the phone at Bailey.

'What d'you mean? I am the fucking news.'

'This morning, Bailey.' Neena ignored the curt response. 'Have you seen the breaking news this morning about Strong?'

Bailey had checked the morning headlines before running the gauntlet of reporters stationed with satellite trucks in front of his house and heading out for his morning walk with Campo. Other than bushfires, the nation seemed only interested in him.

'In the last five minutes, or five hours?'

Bailey looked at his watch. It was almost ten. He had avoided reading or watching the news since he'd been back, tired of seeing images of his face and house everywhere.

'What's Strong said now?'

'Augustus Strong is dead.'

'What?'

'He was attacked early this morning outside a bloody 7-Eleven on George Street. They're calling it a hate crime.'

Bailey grabbed the remote in the kitchen, switching on the television. A picture of Augustus Strong was plastered across the screen. The prick looking as smug as ever in a publicity photograph of some sort. Now dead. Neena wasn't lying and she appeared to have more information than the newsreader did.

'Hate crime?' Bailey said. 'Where'd you get that?'

'It's just broken online. One of your old colleagues at *The Journal*. Police say they've got a witness.'

Bailey took a breath, wondering how the police had arrived at hate crime.

'Who do they think did it?'

Bailey could hear Neena drinking something on the other end of the phone. Water. Coffee. It was too early for anything else, not that it had stopped Bailey, back in the day.

'A group of guys of African appearance attacked him, apparently.'

Bailey dropped his phone on the kitchen bench, the noise startling Campo, who was curled up on a blanket in the corner, her head shooting up like a meerkat.

'Sorry, Neena. I've got to go.'

He needed to get a handle on what she had just told him, do some digging of his own. It would be a good distraction from the shit show that had rained down on him twenty-four hours earlier.

'Order me a new eardrum while you're at it,' Neena said. 'And Bailey?'

'Yeah?'

'You okay?'

Bailey and Neena had spoken on the telephone late the night before, going over everything that had happened. The boss checking in on the guy who was writing the cover story for the first edition of her new magazine. Wondering whether he should change tack and write something about media freedoms in the wake of the AFP raid instead. Bailey had hated the idea, shooting it down before Neena had a chance to argue her case. He was out on bail. Part of an active investigation. The AFP officer named in the warrant – Bailey's friend, Harriet Walker – was dead. Antagonising the feds with a story about press freedoms was a terrible idea. Even more so because Bailey would end up being the headline. He had been annoyed that Neena had even suggested it.

'I'm fine, Neena. Fine.'

'This story you're writing about Strong.'

Here we go.

'I know. I know.' Bailey knew what Neena was about to say but now wasn't the time to get into it. 'The story just got better. It also just got more complicated.'

'Three weeks,' Neena said. 'You've got three weeks.'

Bailey hung up the phone, grabbing his laptop to read the story in *The Journal* that Neena had been referring to. Checking facts. Reading the police statement that had just dropped on the New South Wales Police media site.

Augustus Strong had been out walking at around 5 am. Alone.

Bloody early, thought Bailey, but he remembered Strong complaining about jet lag playing havoc with his body clock.

He kept reading.

Strong was apparently assaulted by a group of men after grabbing a coffee from a 7-Eleven on George Street. A witness described four men, possibly in their late teens or early twenties, of African appearance. One of them had apparently king-hit Strong from behind, knocking him to the ground. Kicking him. By the time the ambulance had arrived Strong was dead. Wallet in his pocket, full of cash. Expensive watch still on his wrist. Enough to make police rule out a robbery. Enough for them to go straight to a violent, hate-driven murder.

How?

Bailey turned up the volume on the television. The ABC had a reporter down on George Street with footage from the scene. The 7-Eleven. An ambulance. A cop car parked alongside. A crowd of gawkers standing around behind a reporter who was reciting almost word for word the police statement that Bailey had just read.

He switched off the television.

The reporter hadn't told Bailey anything he didn't already know. The poor girl was now chained to the spot, spouting lines from the police media release, while the world was getting on around her. The pitfalls of the 24-hour news circus. Little time to interview bystanders, to find anyone who had been out on the street before sunrise. Bailey needed to get down there to see what else he could find. Ask a few questions of his own.

Bailey's face had been everywhere and if he was going to blend into the crowd in the city, he needed to do something about his appearance. He walked into his bedroom and started rummaging through his wardrobe, looking for the New York Yankees baseball cap that Miranda had given him for Christmas and he had never worn. He found it, tearing off the tag, adjusting the size so that it could fit over his mop of hair, then grabbed a red windcheater off a coathanger to complete his disguise. American tourist. Close enough.

He pulled back the curtain, peering out onto his front porch, searching for the satellite masts that had recently been planted in his street. Gone. And so was the herd of camera operators and reporters. They had probably all been diverted to the breaking news story down on George Street, which was only a few kilometres away. The murder of a controversial international visitor like Augustus Strong was much more interesting than John Bailey.

Bailey pulled down the brim of his cap, zipping the windcheater to his neck, before hitting the footpath out front of his house. He had already decided to leave his car at home and catch a taxi. Driving in Sydney's CBD was a bloody nightmare and the carparks were so expensive that the return taxi fare would probably be cheaper too.

He made it halfway up the street when he saw something that made him stop. Bryce Ratcliffe untying surfboards from the roof of his Range Rover. His neighbour. Someone who undoubtedly would have had thoughts and questions about the raid that had taken place on a house in his street the day before.

Taking a punt that Bryce hadn't seen him, Bailey stepped off the footpath between two parked cars, making to cross to the other side of the street.

'Bailey?' Bryce called out from where he was standing on the four-wheel drive's running boards, his head visible above the roof. 'Bailey, is that you?'

Bailey was standing in the middle of the street and he looked up at Bryce, lifting the brim of his cap. 'How are you, Bryce?'

'Good, Bailey. And you?'

How the hell could Bailey answer a simple question like that after what he'd just been through? *Yeah, I'm great, Bryce. Spent almost eight hours in a jail cell yesterday while police raided my house. An old mate of mine was murdered on Maroubra Beach. And the bloke I recently interviewed for a story just got bashed to*

death down on George Street this morning. I'm great, Bryce. Tip
top. Thanks for asking.

'Had better days, Bryce.'

'I saw the –'

'You're back from up north, already?' Bailey cut him off.
'Wasn't expecting to see you for at least a week, or two.'

Bryce shrugged. 'Something came up and we had to leave
early. But we had a lovely time. Although, it's pretty bleak up past
Forster. Burnt trees everywhere. People lost a lot up there. Very
sad. We're lucky the fires didn't keep charging south.'

'Lucky.'

'How are things with you?' Bryce said. 'I read about what
happened. Bloody ridiculous, by the sounds.'

Here we go.

'Unfortunately, it isn't over yet.' Bailey wasn't about to get
into it. 'I've got to be somewhere, mate. Better keep moving.'

'Sure. Sure.' Bryce waved at Bailey with one hand, while
holding onto a roof rack with the other. 'Take care of yourself.
Anything I can do, just say the word.'

'Thanks.'

Bailey lowered the brim of his cap as far as it would go. The
conversation with Bryce Ratcliffe had just made him painfully
aware of his mood. Grumpy. Irritable. Angry. All justifiable feel-
ings but things he needed to keep in check if he was going to be
able to do his job. His hunch that Harriet Walker may have been
running an investigation into the same groups that he was interested in had only hardened his resolve to keep chasing. Dig deeper.

After making it to the western side of Oxford Street, Bailey
held his thumb out when he saw a cab motoring towards him.
Miranda had been urging him to download the Uber app for

years, but Bailey couldn't be bothered. He was a man of routine. And there was something about the automated world that didn't sit right with him.

'Get me as close to the QVB as you can,' Bailey instructed the driver as he hopped into the passenger seat beside him. 'Don't mind walking a bit. Keen to stay this side of George.'

The inside of the taxi smelled like someone had been using lemon skins as an ashtray and the driver's weathered, wrinkly skin led Bailey to believe that he was a pack-a-day man.

'Easy done. Will shoot down Park.' The driver was speaking without looking at Bailey. 'Gets busy, I can always drop you on the corner of Castlereagh, or Pitt.'

Drivers like this old guy didn't need maps. He knew the city's streets like the hallways in his house.

'Thanks.'

Taxi drivers were also avid consumers of news and Bailey had spied a rolled-up newspaper in the door. He wound down his window, turning his head towards the footpath, so that the driver couldn't get a good look at his face as they zipped along Oxford Street.

'Crossing over George is a nightmare these days. Thanks to that bloody light rail. Morons. Cost three billion, they reckon.' The driver scoffed, changing lanes. 'Three billion!'

Bailey had a feeling the driver had expressed his views on Sydney's light rail before, and like most cabbies, he was keen to offer them again.

'Yeah. Pretty outrageous. Double the budget, right?'

Bailey kept his eyes on the street, the smoky air not as strong as the previous day, but the scent enough to remind him about the fires burning north, west and south of the city. He'd heard a report that rain could be on the way soon. A lot of rain. Enough to douse the entire state. Maybe even put out the fires for good. Bailey would believe it when he saw it. When he felt the specks of water on his cheeks. It had been a while.

'Double? And the rest! Was supposed to be one point three billion. Ended up at almost three. Couldn't organise a chook raffle, that lot on Macquarie Street.' The driver was shaking his head. 'And the track's only twelve kilometres long. Do the maths on that, my friend.'

Bailey stayed silent, knowing that this guy had already done the maths.

'Two hundred and fifty million dollars per kilometre. Half the bloody carriages are empty, mind you. Businesses on George Street had to shut down for years while they built the bloody thing. Won't make it back, some of them. Money well spent, eh?'

'Doesn't sound like it,' Bailey said.

'Got that right.'

Bailey continued to listen to the driver's analysis about all that was right and wrong with Sydney until the traffic ground to a halt on Park Street, as he'd predicted.

'Might jump out here. Thanks.'

Bailey handed him fifteen dollars and told him to keep the change.

After waiting for the little red man at the traffic light to turn green, Bailey crossed over and started down Pitt Street, keeping his face hidden as he passed the back entrance of the Hilton Hotel, where he had been two nights earlier for his interview with Strong. Several police vehicles and an ambulance were parked in the drop-off bay and, through the glass, Bailey glimpsed a bunch of officers in uniform huddled in the foyer.

Bailey needed to keep his distance from the main entrance to the hotel and also the 7-Eleven near where Strong had been attacked. Both would be crawling with police and media. He continued all the way down Pitt and onto Market Street, which would deliver him to George Street well away from the action.

It was late morning and the doors to the old State Theatre were closed, a homeless woman curled up in a blue sleeping bag outside the box office, her trolley filled with all the things she had left. Bailey stopped walking, rummaging through his pocket for a note, bending down and stuffing it inside the McDonald's cup that had the word 'help' handwritten on the side. Bailey had few rules in life, one of them was to never ignore the homeless. Never judge them, either. Cash for people sleeping rough was the only charity that he routinely supported. The only one he trusted. No skimming from back office staff. No ridiculous pay cheques for the celebrities paid to front them.

'Thank you.'

He heard a soft, croaky voice emanate from the blue lump on the concrete.

'Take care, love.'

Bailey put his hands back in his pockets, keeping his head down as he hit the corner of the George Street boulevard. He waited for a tram to pass by – his taxi driver had been right, its carriages were mostly empty – before crossing the tracks towards the Queen Victoria Building, the 130-year-old, green-domed marketplace that took up an entire city block. Sidling alongside the QVB, Bailey stared into the shop windows, reflecting the crowd of media, cops and busybodies that had swarmed the 7-Eleven and the Hilton on the other side of the tram tracks, wondering how close he could get.

This wasn't the first time that violence had shaken this part of the city. Back in 1978, when Bailey was still a schoolkid, a couple of unwitting garbage collectors were killed when a bomb hidden inside a rubbish bin exploded just as they were emptying it into their truck. The explosion also killed a police officer who had been standing on the footpath out front of the Hilton, guarding the dozen or so world leaders who were in Australia for the Commonwealth Heads of Government meeting.

The bomb attack had received so much media coverage at the time that Bailey still had black and white imprints of the aftermath in the archives of his brain. The mangled rear of the garbage truck. Stretchers ferrying the injured and the dead into ambulances. The chipped and blackened arches outside the Hilton. The force of the blast had been so strong that it had shattered the windows of the QVB across the other side of the road.

The Hilton bombing inspired almost as many conspiracy theories as the murder of John F. Kennedy. One of the most popular stories doing the rounds was the one about Australia's intelligence services placing the bomb in the bin as part of a training exercise and forgetting to remove it. But that theory had lost support when a member of a bizarre cult called Ananda Marga confessed to having planted the bomb in an attempt to kill India's prime minister.

Other cult members were later convicted for trying to kill the branch secretary of a Neo-Nazi group called the National Front of Australia. The irony wasn't lost on Bailey. Augustus Strong – the pin-up boy for modern-day far right nationalism – had just been murdered at almost the same spot where a member of the Nazi-hating Ananda Marga group had planted a bomb decades earlier.

There were at least six cameras perched on tripods with reporters standing in front of them, either talking to a presenter in a faraway studio, or practising their lines. Bailey guessed that some of them were from overseas networks like the BBC and CNN. Augustus Strong was a household name. His death would be generating headlines all around the world. Although Bailey couldn't imagine many people missing him.

The 7-Eleven appeared to be open and, with journalists and cops big consumers of both coffee and takeaway food, the little shop was probably doing a roaring trade. Bailey wasn't sure that murder was as good for business for the Downtown Souvenirs and Lowes Menswear shops next door.

Bailey noticed a woman in a suit doing the rounds of the TV crews, pointing her finger at a lone microphone stand that had been set up on the footpath, signalling that a media conference wasn't far away. Minutes later, another half-dozen microphones were crowding the area, with camera operators scurrying to reposition themselves to get the head-on shot that their studio masters would need.

The woman doing all the instructing was now holding up a finger. 'One minute!'

Head down, Bailey started moving towards the crowd that had formed an arc around the makeshift stage on the footpath, waiting for whichever senior police officer was going to walk down from the Hilton foyer a few doors up to brief the media. He wasn't too concerned about being seen because the reporters were all facing the opposite direction. He edged closer so that he could hear what the police were about to say.

Because of the crowd, Bailey couldn't see much on either side of the microphones, but the flashes and pivoting cameras gave him enough warning that the media conference was about to begin. What he wasn't prepared for was the identity of one of the people standing beside the cop with the stars on his shoulders stepping up to the microphone.

'Good morning, everyone, I'm Assistant Commissioner Rick Boulder from the Australian Federal Police and with me today is Detective Chief Inspector Mary Appleby and Detective Greg Palmer from the New South Wales Police, along with Commander Dominic Harding from the AFP . . .'

Harding. What the hell was Harding doing here?

A day after leading the raid on his house, Bailey expected Harding to be sitting around with a table full of geeks and cops trying to make sense of the files and documents that they'd copied. The video they'd deleted from Bailey's phone. He was flabbergasted to see Harding at a media conference about the death of Augustus Strong. What the hell did it mean?

'. . . we'll be providing you with information about the investigation into the death of Augustus Strong, but we're also today announcing the establishment of a joint taskforce to look not only into Mr Strong's death but also the rise in hate crimes we've seen in recent days, weeks and months. As many of you may have read earlier this week, ASIO's annual threat assessment has identified the threat of white supremacist and far right nationalist groups as a major concern for law enforcement agencies.'

'Sir!' an eager reporter called out. 'Are you saying that white supremacists are somehow connected to the murder of Augustus Strong?'

'I'm going to politely ask you to hold your questions until later.' Boulder did well to keep his cool. 'Taskforce Juniper will be headed by Commander Harding, who'll say a few words shortly, with the AFP drawing together some of the best investigators from both state and federal law enforcement, along with our intelligence services. Before we hear from Commander Harding, I'm going to hand over to Detective Chief Inspector Appleby to talk specifically about what happened here this morning.'

Bailey was baffled by what was unfolding in front of him and he found himself edging closer, intent on not missing a word.

'Thank you, Assistant Commissioner. I'm going to be brief today because, as you've just heard, the alleged murder of Augustus Strong is now part of a broader investigation, so there's only so much that I can add to the statement released earlier today.' Appleby looked uncomfortable in front of the microphone. 'At twelve minutes past five this morning a 7-Eleven worker discovered American national Augustus Strong severely injured on the footpath not far from where I'm standing. He'd sustained several significant head wounds. The staff member called an ambulance but unfortunately Mr Strong was pronounced dead at the scene at around five forty-five this morning.'

She paused, brushing a fly from her nose, breathing heavily into the microphone.

'As you'll have read this morning, we have a witness to this crime. Four men, all believed to be in their late teens or early twenties, were seen assaulting Mr Strong and then running from the scene. The men were of African appearance and we are appealing for information from anyone who may have seen a group of men fitting this description anywhere around George Street, or nearby areas, in the early hours of this morning.'

Appleby stopped talking and shuffled awkwardly to the side, making way for Harding.

'Good morning everyone. As you've just heard, we'll be investigating the murder of Augustus Strong as a hate crime. But Mr Strong's violent death is, unfortunately, not an isolated incident. The AFP has been monitoring groups that operate in the shadows of the internet for some time, attracting people who don't share the values that we Australians hold dear.'

Harding paused, checking his audience, prompting Bailey to drop his head so that his Yankees cap could give him some cover.

'Let me be clear. An attack on an individual – or individuals – based on some creed is, most often, an act of terrorism. Ever since the Twin Towers attacks on New York, we've devoted considerable time and resources to disrupting and stopping Islamic-inspired terrorism. But extremists can be radicalised in many ways and today we are dealing with terrorist threats not just from the left but from the right too. The establishment of Taskforce Juniper is a significant step towards combating these new threats building in Australia.'

'Commander Harding! Commander Harding! What are these other *incidents* you're talking –'

'We'll come to questions in a moment,' Harding said, calmly, knowing he had a microphone and that he was talking to a lot more people than the small gathering of reporters in front of him. 'I just wanted to say one more thing. For those of you out there who have been angered by certain things in our society, violence is not the way to make your stand.'

Harding sounded like a schoolteacher and he raised his chin, searching the crowd to see that he had everyone's attention. For a split second, Bailey thought he saw Harding squint in his direction, like he'd seen through Bailey's hopeless disguise.

'I say to the general public, if you suspect anyone you know of harbouring extremist ideals, or you suspect they may be part of a group that could be preparing to do people harm, I'd ask that you come forward. Discreetly. Anonymously. We need to know.' Harding was looking directly at Bailey now. Eyes locked. 'And to you, the reporters who write stories in papers and appear on TV, I'm also asking you to do your jobs responsibly. You may hold vital information that police may need to prevent more violent acts. Work with us. Now, questions?'

'Commander Harding!' The woman who had tried to ask the question earlier was at it again. 'Aly Wong from *The Journal*. You mentioned that Taskforce Juniper will be investigating other incidents. Does that include the violent attack on a Black man at the White Lion Hotel two nights ago?'

'I read your story, Aly, and that is an incident we're looking into. But I don't have any updates at this precise moment.'

Unnerved that Harding may have spotted him in the crowd, and also by the prospect of cameras eventually turning towards him, Bailey decided that he would catch up on the rest of the media conference later. That also meant saving his own questions for another time. Top of his list was trying to understand how Harding had managed to differentiate left-wing and right-wing terrorism. What the hell was the difference? Was he really suggesting that Islamic terrorism was left-wing, with far right extremists being the opposite end of the ideological spectrum? And how did Strong's murder fit into all of this? Are his alleged attackers left-wing terrorists because he's a darling of the right? The distinction was utter nonsense.

What about Harriet Walker? Had Harding just been put in charge of an investigation that she had been running?

And what about the AFP raid on Bailey's house? Was the AFP still interested in finding Bailey's source for his Afghanistan stories?

Too many questions to count. Some of them could wait. Others would require some poking around.

CHAPTER 19

Police media conferences could last for anywhere between two hours and two minutes, so Bailey needed to get moving in case it wrapped up early and one of the many reporters on George Street spotted him. He'd decided to head east and pick up a taxi along the edge of Hyde Park where there was always a steady stream.

'Hey, fella!'

Bailey stopped out front of the State Theatre, where the woman who had earlier been huddled under a blue sleeping bag was sitting up, sipping on a coffee, a copy of *The Journal* beside her, Bailey's head plastered across the front page.

'Thought that was you.' She pointed at the paper and then at Bailey. 'Thanks for the ten bucks, by the way.'

So much for his bloody disguise.

'No worries.'

'Busy morning round on George. Interrupted my beauty sleep.' She smiled, exposing a cut on her lip that reminded Bailey about what it meant to sleep rough. 'That why you're here?'

'Came down for a look.' Bailey wasn't one for small talk with strangers but he wondered whether the woman had seen something. Whether she was the witness who had talked to the police. After all, the attack had happened less than a hundred metres from here and this was her neighbourhood. Her home. 'See anything?'

'Me? No. Not much, anyway. Not pretending I saw more either.'

The comment struck Bailey as odd. 'What d'you mean by that?'

The woman pushed the sleeping bag down past her knees. It was warming up and the sun had a bite in it that was making Bailey sweat. With his cover already blown, he unzipped his jacket, flapping it open to let the air blow against his skin.

'Sounds like some people are telling a few porkies, that's all,' she said.

'About what happened?'

The woman looked past Bailey down towards George Street, and then back up the other way.

'Yeah. The fella with the funny name.'

'Augustus Strong.'

'That's the one.' She laughed, awkwardly. 'Augustus.'

Bailey didn't like looking down on the woman, so he dropped onto one knee beside her.

'Police say they've got a witness who saw four men of African appearance running away from the spot where the attack happened.'

'Heard that too,' she said, smiling at Bailey, flashing two rows of stained teeth. 'Hey, you don't have another spare tenner, do you? Lunchtime soon.'

Bailey hesitated, wondering whether he should cut a deal first. Answers for cash. She didn't seem the type to play the game so he reached inside his wallet where he only had a red twenty-dollar note, handing it over. 'Might get you some dinner too.'

'Thanks.' She snatched the note, stuffing it inside her sleeping bag, out of sight. 'What was your question, again?'

'The police witness. That you?'

She laughed. 'I don't talk to cops.'

'So, who –'

'Margie's the one with the big mouth. Vivid imagination, that one.'

'What d'you mean?'

Bailey looked back down the street, checking that the police media conference hadn't ended and sent a stream of reporters in his direction. It wouldn't be long before news got out that Bailey had sat down with Strong for an interview in the Hilton two nights ago. That information would be interesting to anyone covering the story, maybe even the police.

'I mean, she told them a bunch of bullshit. How could she know these guys were Black when they were wearing balaclavas on their heads?'

'What?'

'They ran right past where you're standing.' She was pointing her arm up the street towards the park. 'Dark hoods pulled down. Last I checked, you can't tell the colour of someone's skin through their eyeballs. That's about all I saw through those hoods. Don't know how Margie reckons she saw a bunch of African blokes.'

Bailey was confused by what he was hearing. Why would a homeless woman lie?

'Where's Margie now, do you know? Think she might talk to me?'

'Who knows?' She shrugged, grabbing her paper coffee cup off the ground, taking a sip. 'Usually sleeps round on George, that's why the police asked her those questions, I guess. They're pretty quick to move us on round there. Because of all the shoppers. It's why I camp outside the theatre. Like my sleep-ins.' She laughed, placing her cup beside her again. 'Uh oh. Speaking of which.'

'Morning, Silvie.' A man wearing a bow tie and black vest appeared out of nowhere. 'We're getting ready for the matinee soon. Time to move on.'

Bailey stood up, ignoring the guy behind him. 'If I have any more questions, where will I find you?'

'Here. There. Around. Depends. The exciting life I lead. Could be anywhere.'

Bailey heard the guy in the vest laugh. 'She'll be here, mate. She's always here.'

Silvie frowned at Bailey, shrugging her shoulders. 'Like the man says.'

Bailey handed her his card. 'In case anything comes up.'

'No phone, Mr Bailey.'

It was the first time she'd used his name.

'Keep it anyway.'

She held Bailey's stare without saying anything, like she was reading his mind, finding the common thread between them. Swapping painful stories.

'Roundtree.'

'What?'

'Margie's surname. It's Roundtree. Usually scabs a feed from the soup van in that little park near St Mary's most nights. Turns up round six. Didn't hear it from me, though. Okay? Won't win me any friends on the street, if you know what I mean.'

'Thanks, Silvie. Mum's the word.'

CHAPTER 20

The little red crosses had turned green above four northbound lanes on the Sydney Harbour Bridge and the traffic was moving freely, which was a relief for Bailey because he was running late. He was supposed to have been at Gerald's house at midday for a meeting with Marjorie to discuss the AFP charges against him. The clock on the dashboard said it was almost 12.30 pm. Gerald was a stickler for time, but Bailey figured that his old friend would cut him some slack, considering his life and house had just been turned upside down.

From a distance, the Sydney Harbour Bridge was like a giant coathanger dangling across a big blue bath of water, hooked on a cloud. Up close, it was all big arches and steel. The view on either side of the bridge was spectacular, even in today's smoke haze. The big cruise ship parked down by Circular Quay. The Opera House. The Manly ferry motoring north-east on one of the world's best commutes. Beyond the train track on the bridge's western flank, Bailey could see the top of Luna Park and the boats parked up alongside the waterfront mansions of the little suburbs that he could never name.

Beep!

Bailey suddenly realised that he was driving almost half the speed limit, angering some knob in a Lancer who had given up on tail-gating Bailey's wagon, and was now flashing his lights, changing lanes.

The city of Sydney had engineered a masterstroke with the Sydney Harbour Bridge. Pity the same couldn't be said for the city's high proportion of road-raging drivers.

'Yeah, okay. Dickhead.'

Bailey smiled and gave a thumbs up to the driver who had sidled up beside him to make his point, mouthing obscenities, waving his finger.

Beep! Beep!

Bailey's smile seemed to only enrage the guy more and he swung his Lancer into Bailey's lane, jamming on his brakes.

'Good one, mate. That's safe,' Bailey said to himself, shaking his head.

The guy dropped his foot on the accelerator and shot off along the bridge. Point made. A win for his narrow little world.

The light turned green just as Bailey arrived at the Military Road exit and he made it through Neutral Bay without even touching his brakes. Gerald lived down near Taronga Zoo and Bailey had been there so many times over the years that he knew all the backroads. Five minutes later he was pressing the intercom outside the big iron gate at the bottom of Gerald's driveway, waiting to be let in.

'It's the convict.'

The gate squeaked open and Bailey waved and smiled at the security camera before driving up the long, snaking driveway. There were two other cars parked in the turning circle outside the double garage, one of them was Marjorie's Mercedes and the other was a Toyota Prius with a rental sticker on the rear window.

Bailey killed the engine, the white pebbles crunching under his feet as he made his way to the stone steps that led to the front door, where Gerald was already waiting.

'Who else's here?' Bailey said, without saying hello.

'Good afternoon to you too,' Gerald said, dryly.

'Sorry, mate,' Bailey said. 'Shitty mood. How are you?'

'Good.'

Bailey arrived at the top of the steps where the two men shook hands.

'Now we've got that out of the way,' Bailey said. 'Are you going to tell me who else's here?'

'Come in.'

Gerald turned around and walked into his house, leading Bailey into the sitting room where Marjorie was perched on a sofa, the AFP search warrant in front of her along with a pile of other papers that Bailey could only guess were somehow linked to him.

'Sorry I'm late, Marj,' Bailey said. 'Didn't mean to muck you about.'

'It's fine, Bailey. Gave me a bit more time to gather our wagons. See what we're up against.'

Bailey got distracted when he noticed the door to the balcony that overlooked the water was open, the pungent smell of cigar smoke wafting in. He could see the edge of a man's shoulder outside, leaning over the railing. The driver of the other car parked in the driveway.

'Never picked you for a Prius driver, Ronnie.'

Ronnie Johnson.

One of the CIA's most experienced field operatives. A former station chief in Baghdad, Kabul and Beirut, where Bailey had first met him beside the charred wreckage of a car bomb more than thirty years earlier.

'Not by choice, bubba. Last rental in the lot. I can barely fit in that thing.'

Ronnie was almost six and a half feet tall and despite nearing the end of his sixth decade on the planet, he'd somehow managed to hang on to the build that had made him one of the toughest tight ends playing college football when he was running around with the Oklahoma Sooners. Ronnie had tried to retire from the CIA a few years ago only to be pulled back into the agency to run a number of special operations in Australia. First, it was Chinese spies infiltrating the Australian Government, before he was assigned into an area he knew better than anyone – counter-terrorism.

Although Ronnie spent most of his time in Sydney these days (often sleeping in Bailey's spare room), he had been working in Canberra the last few months, tying up loose ends on a fledgling Islamic terrorist network that stretched from Syria to London and into Sydney's western suburbs.

'Good to see you, mate.'

Ronnie squeezed Bailey's outstretched hand so tightly that Bailey almost winced.

'You too.'

'What are you doing here?'

'Saw you on the television last night. Spoke to Gerald. Thought you could do with some help.'

'Did you now?' Bailey looked over at Gerald, who shrugged.

'Looks to me like you just poked a hornet's nest, bubba. Lot of angry bugs flying around.'

Bailey wasn't all that surprised to see Ronnie. They were good friends, after all. Ronnie had left Bailey two telephone messages since yesterday and although Bailey knew that the offer of 'help' was genuine, Ronnie's enthusiasm was also likely driven by something else. The events of the past twenty-four hours. The murders of Harriet Walker and Augustus Strong. The AFP raids on Bailey's house. Walker's name on the warrant. Bailey was the common thread, somehow caught in the middle. He knew it. Ronnie knew it too.

'Drove up first thing this morning. Apparently we were meeting at midday.' Ronnie looked at his watch, smirking, puffing smoke out the corner of his mouth.

'Sorry about that. Got held up.'

'Sounds like you were one of the last people to speak to Augustus Strong,' Ronnie said, making it blatantly obvious he knew things.

Bailey scoffed, shaking his head. 'And it sounds like you're not just here to help.'

'American national dies, sometimes I get a call.' Ronnie took another puff on his cigar, this time blowing it towards the water. 'Truth be told, I was actually in my car on the way to Sydney to see you when the call came in. Hell of a coincidence what happened, bubba. And you've known me long enough to know how I feel about coincidences.'

Gerald cleared his throat. 'Ronnie, how about you put out that cigar and come inside so that we can talk properly?'

'I'm enjoying the fresh air at the moment,' Bailey said, eyes stuck on Ronnie. 'What do you think's going on then, Ronnie? I've got my own theories, but I'd like to hear yours. With you here to help, and all.'

Ronnie's head rolled back as he chuckled. 'You're a grumpy bastard, Bailey. Always so bloody sceptical.'

'Yeah?' Bailey was sounding the part. 'Give me a reason not to be? You said it yourself, you had a call about Strong before the guy's body had even had a chance to get cold. My name get a mention?'

'From our people?'

Our people. American intelligence. CIA.

'We knew you interviewed him. I told you that already.' Ronnie answered his own question. 'Strong's an interesting cat. You wouldn't be surprised to learn we were keeping tabs on his visit down under. His talks. Who he's been meeting in his spare time. The guy had good access, by the way. He was down in Canberra yesterday meeting a couple of redneck senators from Queensland.'

'Mal Rustin and Sally Paul. I know about that,' Bailey said. 'And he also met with the Home Affairs Minister, Wayne McMahon.'

Ronnie raised an eyebrow, fleetingly, before his face dropped. 'Good access for a guy who built a career on tweeting.'

'Any idea who killed him?'

'I was going to ask you the same question.'

'Cops saying it was a group of Black guys.' Bailey shrugged. 'I'm not so sure.'

'What makes you say that?'

Bailey thought about telling Ronnie what he'd just learned from the homeless woman outside the State Theatre, but it was a little too early to be sharing. 'A hunch.'

Ronnie stared at Bailey, like he was willing him to change his mind. 'I was sorry to hear about Walker. Good operator. Always liked her.'

Ronnie had known Harriet Walker even longer than Bailey had because of the time Walker had spent in Ronnie Johnson's Middle Eastern playground in the late 1990s and early 2000s. People trafficking. Drug smuggling. Counter-terrorism. The AFP would have worked with people like Ronnie Johnson on all kinds of operations.

'Cops are saying she was killed during a robbery. You buy that?'

Bailey was seeking a rare moment of straight-up honesty from Ronnie.

'No. I don't.'

And he got it.

'The timing of all this, Ronnie . . . as you say, it's all too coincidental,' Bailey said. 'I met with Hat on Wednesday. I left with the feeling she was looking into the same people that I'd been investigating for the story I'm writing about Strong and far right nationalism. By the end of the day she'd lined up another meet. We were supposed to catch up down on the Glebe foreshore yesterday morning. She never turned up because she was lying dead on Maroubra Beach. Then I arrive home to find the AFP on my doorstep.'

'Tell him about the video,' Gerald cut in. 'There's something not right about the reason the feds were searching Bailey's house all day yesterday. Tell Ronnie about the video. The video they deleted off your phone.'

'What video?' Ronnie said.

'I took a video of the crowd at Strong's talk the other night, trying to capture some of the faces of his supporters. I shared the video with Hat to see if there was something, or someone, in the crowd that stood out. The fact she got back in touch so quickly made me think that she'd found something. Something in the video, maybe.' Bailey coughed, clearing his throat. 'The AFP warrant has this extraordinary line in it, something about granting police the powers to delete or change my files and data.'

'Here it is.' Gerald had stepped back inside while Bailey was talking, re-emerging with a piece of paper in his hand, holding it out for Ronnie. 'Have a read of that.'

Ronnie took the slip of paper, squinting his eyes, taking a moment to read.

'Have you ever seen anything like it?' Gerald asked.

Ronnie found the offending paragraph, reading the words out aloud. 'To add, copy, delete or alter other data in the computer or device found in the course of a search.'

'It's bullshit, Ronnie,' Bailey said. 'Utter bullshit. They deleted that video I just described. Gone. No backups. And it has nothing to do with the purpose of the raid, which was chasing my source for a story I broke about the ADF covering up the deaths of civilians in Afghanistan a bloody long time ago.'

Ronnie was nodding his head, staring at the page a moment longer before handing it back to Gerald. 'Walker was leading an investigation into several far right nationalist groups. She'd talked to some of our people about how these groups were connected to white supremacists back in the States.'

Bailey was taken aback by Ronnie's candour. '*Our people*? Are you including yourself in that? Is this what you've been doing in Canberra?'

Ronnie tilted his head, raking his tongue along the inside of his cheek. Thinking. 'I was in Canberra doing what I told you I was doing. Tying up loose ends on your boy Mustafa al-Baghdadi. Checking to see what's left in the web now the spider's gone.'

It was thirty-five degrees outside yet the mention of Mustafa's name made Bailey shiver. He looked across at Gerald, glimpsing the scar on his neck. Another person damaged by that ruthless bastard and his band of fundamentalist followers.

'They're not much different, y'know.'

Ronnie had guessed where Bailey's mind had wandered to.

'What?'

'White supremacists. Islamic terrorists,' Ronnie said, leaning his elbows against the railing, back towards the water. 'They all start out from the same place. Disillusionment. Anger.'

'What are you talking about, Ronnie?' Gerald said.

'The people the political establishment and mainstream media either ignored or pissed off are now part of a mass movement that our eggheads at State like to call *rising populism*. Hungary. Turkey. Brazil. We're seeing it in the US and the UK too. It's growing and morphing into –'

'Here we go,' Bailey said, slightly miffed about Ronnie's sledge at the media. Even though he was partly right. 'Doctor Johnson's here to tell us how the world would have been a better place if only we'd done our jobs better.'

'That's not what I'm saying, Bailey, and you know it,' Ronnie said, shaking his cigar and causing a lump of ash to fall on the ground. 'I'm just talking about the path that got us here and where it leads.'

'Keep going then,' Gerald said. 'I'm always interested in America's view of the world.'

If Ronnie was offended by the sarcasm in Gerald's voice, he didn't show it. 'All I'm saying is that, just like we saw with Islamic terrorism, there's a bunch of angry people out there being drawn to a cause. People who've lost faith in how democracies have been run and they're looking for something different. Someone different.'

'And someone to blame,' Bailey said.

'Exactly. It's a skip and a jump from rising populism to far right extremism. But it's happening,' Ronnie said. 'And these people don't carry placards. They carry guns.'

'The people willing to burn down the house in order to save it.'

Bailey's comment hung in the air for a moment before Gerald chipped in. 'Do you think this is what we're dealing with here? Some kind of attack?'

'That's exactly what I'm saying,' Ronnie said. 'The FBI busted a bunch of Neo-Nazis in Maryland recently –'

'The Dawning?' Bailey interrupted him.

'That's them. The FBI has been investigating The Dawning for some time. Highly organised, they're growing in size. Not just in the States but around the world. Their leader, Donald Sampson, is an old man now but he was an active member of the Ku Klux Klan during the seventies and eighties. For a long time, he appeared to be just your average American racist. But in recent years he's upped the ante, running military-style training camps and preaching in dark web chatrooms about the need for an armed uprising. A race war.'

'How come it took so long to arrest him?'

'I can't answer that question, Bailey. I'm new to this too.'

'Why are you telling us about Sampson and The Dawning?'

'Because Sampson had been talking to people in Australia. Something's being planned here. Something soon. It was one of the reasons why the FBI moved on Sampson. People planning an attack of some kind usually need guns and, as you know, it's not hard to get your hands on an arsenal of high-powered weapons in the United States. Sampson organised a shipment of guns to Sydney. Fuck knows how they got in, but they're here. At least, we think they are.'

'You lost them?'

'The FBI doesn't control Australia's borders, bubba. We told our counterparts here when we knew the guns were on the way, then they disappeared.'

'Umm, boys?'

Marjorie was standing in the open door of the balcony, mobile phone in her hand, with a perplexed look on her face.

'Everything okay, Marjorie?' Gerald said.

'I've just had a call from the Australian Federal Police. They've dropped the case. They're no longer investigating the ADF leak. Case closed. Harriet Walker was their suspect, with her dead they don't have anyone to prosecute.' Marjorie paused, gesturing her chin at Bailey. 'But you're still on the hook for not complying with the search warrant, Bailey. The gentleman I spoke to on the phone was clear about that. But we'll fight it. And win.'

Bailey didn't care about the charges against him. He was more worried about what Ronnie had just told them about a shipment of guns that had gone missing in Sydney and about how Harriet Walker had managed to get tangled up in something so serious that she ended up dead.

'Fuck the charges,' Bailey said, 'they want to push ahead, good luck to them.'

'What are you going to do, Bailey?' Gerald said.

'I'm going to find out who killed Hat.'

Ronnie cleared his throat, stabbing his cigar into an empty coffee mug on the outside table. 'You want to find out who killed Walker, you need to look into those guns.'

'Any suggestions?' Bailey said.

'Those guns didn't just fall out of the sky. They arrived at Port Botany four days ago in a shipping container alongside pallets of Californian oranges. The container somehow made it through customs with the guns inside and then it was loaded onto a truck and delivered to a supermarket produce centre out at Eastern Creek.'

'What are we waiting for?' Bailey said.

'Hold on, I'm not finished,' Ronnie said. 'Two nights ago there was a break-in at the produce centre. Bunch of guys in masks tied up the guard at the front gate, busted open the container and took off with the guns. The van they used for the pick-up was found burning in a nearby park. These guys are ghosts.'

Bailey took a few steps towards the railing, gripping the top of the glass, staring out across the harbour, allowing his mind a moment to think. He turned back around. 'When containers are taken off ships, each and every one of them gets scanned with an X-ray machine. It's not a random process. I've been down there. I saw it in action for that story I wrote years ago about crystal meth coming in from China,' Bailey said, nodding his chin at his former newspaper boss. 'You remember, Gerald?'

'I do.'

'There are three ways a container can bypass the X-ray machine,' Bailey continued. 'One: it mysteriously falls off the ship. Two: through an act of incompetence, the container gets waved through without being scanned. And three –'

'Someone gets paid a wad of cash to let it in.' Gerald finished the sentence for him.

'You don't happen to know the name of the ship and the company that unloaded it, do you, Ronnie?'

'I can go one better than that.' Ronnie smiled, patting the pocket of his jacket. 'I've got the name and address of the customs agent who waved it through.'

CHAPTER 21

ANNIE

The wooden bench across the road from Redfern Police Station was coated with the same dust and ash that was clinging to the rest of Sydney like glue. The city, like the state, was in desperate need of a bath. If the weather report that Annie had heard that morning was right, drought-breaking rain was on its way. So much of it that there were already warnings about flash flooding. Fires to floods. Only in Australia.

Annie dusted the bench with the palm of her hand before sitting down, placing her half-finished coffee beside her. It was her fifth for the day and she had lost interest in finishing it. The caffeine was starting to give her the jitters, much like the feeling she used to get the morning after a bender before she evened herself out with a breakfast juice laced with vodka.

'I've only got a few minutes, Annie.'

Annie hadn't seen Detective Greg Palmer approach and before she had a chance to get to her feet, he was standing on the footpath in front of her.

'Thanks for seeing me.' She stood up, knocking over her coffee in the process. 'It was cold anyway.'

'Bench could do with the rinse.'

Palmer offered a fleeting smile before his face turned serious again. He looked tired. Stressed. Probably wondering what the hell he was doing meeting a reporter on the footpath. The thing that was so urgent that Annie had texted him to request five minutes of his time.

Annie had watched the footage of the police media conference down on George Street earlier that morning at the scene of Augustus Strong's murder, when senior figures from both state and federal police had announced a new taskforce to investigate hate crimes. Annie had noticed Palmer standing beside them. He was a homicide detective who was investigating the murder of AFP Commander Harriet Walker. Annie wanted to know what the hell he was doing there.

'I'll get straight to it. I'm not going to mess you around,' Annie said, ignoring the coffee that was now dripping onto the concrete. 'This new taskforce that's looking into Strong's murder and possibly related hate crimes, is it also looking into who killed Harriet Walker?'

'Taskforce Juniper?'

'That's the one.'

Palmer hesitated. 'At this stage, no.'

It sounded like a lie. Why else would Palmer have been present at the media conference?

'Really?'

'Look, Annie. I know John Bailey's a friend of yours –'

'How do you know that?'

Palmer's face hardened. Annoyed. 'And here was me thinking you meant it when you said you wouldn't mess me around.'

'Okay. Okay.' Annie raised her hands. 'You're right. I'm sorry.

There's just a lot of unanswered questions here, Greg. A lot of things not adding up.'

'Like what?'

'Like why are police sticking to the line that Walker was killed in a robbery? She was as good as named in an AFP warrant as the source of Bailey's stories about Afghanistan. On the same day she gets murdered, the AFP raids Bailey's house. C'mon, Greg . . . something's not right here. A mugging on the beach at dawn?'

Palmer was distracted by something over Annie's shoulder. A flurry of pedestrians, including two uniformed officers, crossing at the lights on Redfern Street. Palmer watched in silence as they walked past where he and Annie were standing and into a burger joint a few doors up.

'Homicide Squad no longer has control of this investigation, Annie,' he said, eventually.

'What does that mean?'

'It means what it means. Someone else's in charge.'

'So Walker's murder *is* being investigated by Taskforce Juniper?'

Palmer paused, knowing that what he was about to say next could have serious ramifications for him down the line. 'That's what I'm expecting. But it's early days.'

'It wasn't a robbery, then.'

A statement not a question.

'No.' Palmer stepped into Annie's personal space, lowering his voice. 'We found her with her keys, phone and cards. Watch. Even the silver chain around her neck. Whoever killed her wasn't interested in hocking her jewellery for drug money.'

A rush of adrenalin shot through Annie's spine, tingling her neck. The feeling a reporter gets when they know they've got a scoop.

'We off the record?'

Palmer huffed, turning his head. 'You know damn well we're off the bloody record.'

'Calm down, Greg. I'm just asking the question. At some point, this is going to get out. I wouldn't be doing my job if I didn't want to be the one to break the news. I'd also add that this is well within the realm of public interest. There's a murderer out there, for chrissake!'

'Lower your voice, Annie.' Palmer was looking around again, undoubtedly regretting having this conversation on the footpath so close to Redfern Police Station. 'I need to get back inside.' He pointed at the little blue neon sign stuck to the side of the building across the road.

'I'm sorry.' Annie was regretting pissing off the best source she had on the story. The only source she had. She needed to get him back on side. 'I didn't mean to push. I won't be running with anything until you give me the green light.'

He bent down and picked up the empty coffee cup from the bench, scrunching it in his hand. Thinking. 'I should book you for littering.'

'I was going to pick that up.'

They laughed together. Tension defused.

'I've got to go,' Palmer said. 'And don't worry, we're good. You'll get your story. I wouldn't be talking to you otherwise.'

'Can I just ask you one more question?'

'Make it quick.'

'Why did you guys suggest it was a robbery in the first place?'

The question made Palmer uncomfortable and it took him a few seconds to contemplate his answer. 'Not my call.'

'It just seems odd to put out the wrong –'

'As I said, it wasn't my call. The feds have been with us on this from the start. Read into that whatever you like. I've got to go, Annie.' He made to leave then stopped, turning back around. Hard eyes. 'I didn't know Walker. But she was a copper. A good one, apparently. Nobody gets away with killing a cop.'

CHAPTER 22

Driving south along Anzac Parade, Bailey was staring out the window at the hulking canopy of trees towering over Centennial Park. There used to be a lot more of them. Centuries-old figs torn down to make way for rail lines, footpaths and tram stops. Sydney's population was growing, tearing away at mother nature's flowing green dress. The city closing in on itself.

Bailey took a left into Darley Road alongside Randwick Gates, skirting the park east up the hill towards Coogee. Sunlight was flickering through the branches, forcing Bailey to squint at the windscreen, trying not to lose sight of the car in front. Ronnie's Prius.

The big Oklahoman took a right turn at the next roundabout before slowing down, his head halfway out the window, searching for house numbers. He jammed on his brakes, pointing his finger at a house on the opposite side of the street, pulling over, leaving Bailey enough room to park behind him.

The two men walked across the road in silence. Both more interested in the Californian bungalow they were about to visit, rather than idle chitchat. A black Monaro with all the trimmings was parked in the driveway and whoever owned the house clearly spent a bomb on keeping it neat. Shiny brickwork. Freshly painted split-gable roof. Timber-framed windows. The hedge lining the driveway carefully manicured, so was the square patch of lawn.

'Not a bad joint for a guy who works on the docks,' Bailey whispered as they arrived inside the sleep-out by the front door.

'Exactly what I was thinking,' Ronnie said, pressing his index finger on the doorbell. 'And, bubba?'

'Yeah?'

'Leave the talking to me.'

'All right, big guy. Your show.'

Ronnie frowned at Bailey, knowing that he was taking the piss. He didn't bother responding, instead leaning on the buzzer for a second time. Waiting.

'Might need to go round back,' Ronnie said.

They stepped out of the shadows of the verandah and into the sun which was burning so strongly that Bailey could feel it nibbling at his skin. They paused at the window by the side of the house, noticing the distinct sound of a television and a blue flickering light, before continuing through the side gate that led into the backyard.

Knock. Knock. Knock.

Ronnie put his knuckles to work on the back door. No answer. He tried turning the handle. Locked.

'Might need to do this the old-fashioned way.' Ronnie dropped down onto one knee, poking the keyhole with the little metal device he produced from his pocket. 'C'mon, you sonofabitch.'

'Getting rusty, Ronnie?' Bailey whispered.

Click.

The door clicked open and Ronnie stood up, winking at Bailey and pressing his finger to his lips.

'Stay close.'

The smell hit them before they even had a chance to step inside. The pungent, nostril-stinging stench of decaying flesh.

Pressing the back of his hand against his nose, Bailey followed Ronnie through the kitchen and into the living area, where a man was sitting upright in an armchair, staring at the television with a blank expression on his face. Had he been alive he would have been watching a repeat of *Midsomer Murders* and probably wondering how so many people could get knocked off in the same small British county. But this guy wasn't watching television. He wasn't watching anything. He was dead.

'Don't,' Ronnie barked at Bailey as he went to pick up the remote control to kill the television. 'Best not touching anything, bubba.'

Ronnie grabbed a handkerchief from his pocket, covering his fingertip so that he could hit the light by the doorframe.

'Fuck me.'

Bailey gagged when he caught sight of the foam dribbling from the dead man's lips. His skin an off shade of purple and green. He had a neat bullet hole in his forehead. The chair behind him wasn't so tidy, pieces of his brain and skull splattered against the fabric, spraying the wall at least two metres away.

'Looks professional,' Ronnie said, seemingly unbothered by the smell and the sight of the decomposing body. He'd seen a few.

'How long ago, you reckon?'

'By the colour of his skin . . . the smell. Two days. Three, tops.'

'What was his name?' Bailey suddenly realised that it was a question he had never asked. Now that the guy was dead, he wanted to know.

'Liam Callaghan.'

'I want to have a poke around,' Bailey said.

'Good idea. But remember –'

'Don't touch anything.'

'You're learning.'

'I don't know how I survived all those years when you weren't around.'

Ronnie ignored Bailey's sarcasm and walked over to the window, peering out. 'We can't stay long. Someone could have seen us walk inside. You take the front of the house, I'll do the back. Intel says this guy lived alone. No partner. No kids.'

Bailey dropped his hand from his nose as he had started to grow accustomed to the stench. He wasn't much interested in the two bedrooms at the front of the house but he poked his head inside anyway, checking for evidence to confirm that Callaghan was the only person who lived here. The lack of photographs of any children or pictures that might suggest that Callaghan was in a relationship led Bailey to think that Ronnie's information was correct. It also explained why nobody had reported his death.

There was a small study off to the side of the master bedroom. Bailey walked inside and around the desk by the window, where a pile of unopened mail was stacked, neatly, beside a space where a laptop computer used to be. He could see that the computer had been there until only recently because of the rectangular dust pattern on the desk and the power cord positioned nearby. Maybe Callaghan's killer had stolen his computer too?

A metal single-drawer filing cabinet sat beneath the desk and Bailey used the sleeve of his jacket to cover his fingers so that he could try to pull it open. It was locked. The front of the cabinet was dented and scratched, leaving Bailey to conclude that someone else had tried to pick the lock with what must have been a screwdriver, considering the damage it had caused.

'Ronnie! In here!'

Ronnie appeared at the door. 'Found something?'

'Not sure. Reckon you can get this thing open?' Bailey was pointing at the filing cabinet. 'Looks like somebody's already had a go. They also pinched Callaghan's computer.'

Ronnie walked over to where Bailey was kneeling on the ground, gesturing for him to get out of the way so that he could have a crack at the lock. It took him longer than it did to get the back door of the house open, but he got it done.

'Tell me what you find.' Ronnie stood up, handing Bailey a pair of pink rubber gloves he must have found in the kitchen. 'Put these on.'

Bailey did as he was told before pulling open the drawer. Callaghan's files were neatly arranged inside with cardboard folders labelling the things he kept private. Files for household bills. Insurance. Tax receipts. Personal documents, including his passport and a curriculum vitae. Bailey withdrew Callaghan's CV, intrigued about what he had done with his life before it had been brutally cut short. Turns out he was a union man who'd had a lengthy career on the docks, making his way up the chain until he landed a supervisor position with customs. Before he overplayed his hand.

Replacing Callaghan's CV, Bailey withdrew the next folder to catch his eye. Bank statements. The printouts were of his quarterly activities and, apart from the fact that Bailey thought his fortnightly pay cheque was a little high for a guy who ticked off containers down at Port Botany, there didn't seem to be any irregular payments. One other recurring transaction caught

Bailey's eye. Callaghan was paying rent to a landlord under the name of Sunshine Inc. Twelve hundred dollars a month, clearly labelled as 'rent'. Bailey wasn't skilled at maths but even he knew that three hundred dollars a week was ridiculously cheap for a house that must have been worth somewhere north of two or three million dollars.

Opening the browser on his phone, Bailey typed the words 'Sunshine Inc' and waited for the cracked screen to load its findings. All that came up was a business offering mental health services in western Sydney and some kind of community action group. He took photos of Callaghan's bank statements with his phone. He'd dig into Sunshine Inc later.

There wasn't much else interesting in Callaghan's files other than the fact that the guy was meticulous at record keeping.

'Anything in those files?' Ronnie appeared in the open doorway.

'Not really. He doesn't own the house but his rent's dirt cheap. If he was getting paid cash to wave through dodgy cargo containers then he was pretty good at hiding it. How about you?'

'Nothing. And it's time to go.'

Bailey clambered off his knees and followed Ronnie through the house and out the back door. His phone started vibrating in his pocket and, not even bothering to check the number, he sent it through to voicemail. By the time he and Ronnie were standing beside Bailey's wagon on the other side of the street, his phone was vibrating again. It was Jonny Abdo.

'Jonny,' Bailey answered, 'how are you, mate?'

'Have you seen the news?'

Abdo sounded agitated. Angry.

'No. What is it?'

'They're endangering my community! Putting people's lives at risk!'

Abdo was in full flight and Bailey was struggling to understand him.

'What?'

Bailey turned away from Ronnie, pressing his finger inside his other ear so that he could focus on what Abdo was saying. 'What do you mean, Jonny? Who are you talking about? What are you trying to say?'

'The police, Bailey. The Australian Federal Police. They're saying Augustus Strong may have been murdered in retaliation for the assault on Matthew Lam on Oxford Street the other night. It's outrageous! The police say they've got evidence that Black men attacked Strong. Have you seen it? Have you seen the evidence? I haven't seen it. Where's the proof? There are CCTV cameras all over the city, but I haven't seen it. Have you? Have you?'

'Slow down, Jonny,' Bailey said, stepping away from Ronnie who was trying his best to listen in. 'Who's saying Strong was killed in retaliation for what happened to Matthew Lam?'

That information was new to Bailey.

Aly Wong had asked Harding about a link between the two attacks at the media conference out front of the Hilton that morning and the AFP commander had played it down. Something must have changed.

Abdo sighed on the other end of the line, taking a breath to calm himself. 'I'm going to read this directly from the article. Hang on.'

'I'm listening.'

'This is quoting Commander Dominic Harding from the Australian Federal Police.' Abdo was sounding calmer as he relayed the words. 'The AFP have now confirmed the murder of American national Augustus Strong is being investigated as a reprisal attack in relation to the violent assault on Sudanese-Australian Matthew Lam on Oxford Street three nights ago.'

Harding. What the hell was he playing at? Abdo was right, thought Bailey, drawing a direct link in public between the two attacks was a dangerous tactic and one that could serve as an incitement to further violence. Surely the AFP were attuned to how these things played out?

'Bailey, you there?'

'Still here.'

'Why would they do this? There are extremists out there. Violent extremists. You've seen what they can do. For god's sake, Matthew's in a coma after being near beaten to death. If the people responsible think Strong's murder was a response to what happened to Matthew then they could do something else. Something worse.'

A race war on the streets of Sydney? Only a few days ago, Bailey would have dismissed what Jonny Abdo was saying as ridiculous. Now he wasn't so sure.

'Where are you, Jonny?'

'I'm at the hospital,' Abdo said. 'That's the other reason I'm calling. The Lams want to talk to you. Matthew's parents. Can you come?'

'When?'

'Now.'

'St Vincent's, right?'

'Yes.'

'Give me twenty minutes.'

Bailey put his phone in his pocket and stepped back from the guy who had been invading his personal space.

'Get all that?'

'Most of it,' Ronnie said. 'And by the way, I don't think he's far off the mark.'

'What do you mean?'

'A race war. It's what these people want.'

'I can't believe we're even talking about this.'

'You going to the hospital?'

'Yeah. What are you going to do?'

'I'd better let people know about the dead guy in there.' Ronnie pointed back at the house. 'He smells bad today. In this heat, we'll have the whole neighbourhood complaining soon.'

'Presuming you'll keep me out of it?'

'Surprised you even asked.'

'Sorry.' Bailey opened the door of his wagon. 'And Ronnie?'

'Yeah?'

'Harriet must have been on to these guys. We need to somehow find out what she knew. The feds won't talk to me for obvious reasons. You got anyone inside?'

'I'll have a think.'

Bailey thought he almost caught Ronnie smile.

'You do that.'

A guy like Ronnie Johnson always had someone on the inside.

CHAPTER 23

Bailey hated hospitals.

That nostril-stinging antiseptic smell. White lights. Lino floors. Waiting around on hard plastic chairs. The inevitable hugs and tears for life, and loss.

The only times that Bailey ever visited hospitals were to either get patched up, or to visit some poor sod who had been on the receiving end of something unpleasant.

Today wasn't any different.

'You coming?'

Jonny Abdo was standing beside Bailey at the reception desk of St Vincent's Hospital where they had just been signed in by Matthew Lam's father.

'Bailey?'

Bailey hadn't been inside a hospital since he'd had the stitches in his shoulder removed after his altercation with a terrorist in London. But that wasn't the hospital visit that came flooding back as he watched a doctor in a white coat walk past. He was thinking about Dexter. The day she was rushed in. The way she left. And then he wasn't thinking about hospitals at all. He was thinking about the smile that lit up Dexter's face, igniting the crow's feet around her eyes. She hated having wrinkles but

Bailey had loved them because they made him believe they'd grow old together. If only he'd told her that. What a fool.

'Bailey?'

'Sorry. Got distracted.'

Abdo grabbed Bailey's arm. 'Are you okay?'

'All good, Jonny.' Bailey felt embarrassed, like he'd made a scene, and turned to Matthew Lam's father. 'Mr Lam, where would you like to talk?'

'First I want you to see Matthew,' he said, gesturing an arm towards the elevators. 'And please, call me Philip.'

The three men caught the lift to St Vincent's intensive care unit and walked in silence to the room where Matthew Lam was being treated. The young man was still in an induced coma and Bailey figured that Philip Lam wanted him to see what that looked like, especially if he was going to be writing about it.

Lam paused at the door. 'My wife's very upset. We won't stay long.'

Matthew's mother was sitting in a chair close to the bed where the young man was lying flat, eyes closed, tubes coming out of him and machines rhythmically beeping all around. She was stroking her son's forehead, barely acknowledging the men at the door.

'The doctors say the swelling has gone down,' Lam whispered. 'They might wake him tomorrow.'

Bailey didn't know what to say but he couldn't ignore the poor woman frowning at him, holding her son's hand. 'I'm sorry to disturb you, Mrs Lam.'

She nodded, returning a sad, friendly smile.

'We'll go now,' Lam said, turning to his wife. 'I'll only be a few minutes, darling.'

The hospital's café was situated in the main foyer by the entrance and Jonny offered to order the coffees while Bailey and Philip Lam found a table. The café was mostly full but they managed to find a place to sit outside where somehow the sweet smell of disinfectant still lingered.

'Please.' Lam gestured for Bailey to choose his seat.

'I'm sorry about what's happened to you and your family, Philip.'

'Thank you.'

In the few minutes that Bailey had known Philip Lam he had concluded that he was a gentle man.

'Good news that Matthew seems to be getting better,' Bailey said. 'What else are the doctors telling you, if you don't mind me asking?'

'The news has been positive. Positive,' Lam said, his tired eyes adding more to his words. 'It appears there won't be any lasting damage. We won't know for sure until he wakes up though.' He nodded to himself, looking away. 'We just hope and pray.'

A chair squeaked on the floor as Abdo sat down and joined them. 'The coffees shouldn't be long. I got them in takeaway cups, Philip. I know you want to get back upstairs.'

'Thank you, Jonny. Thank you.'

The table fell silent again and Bailey couldn't help wondering exactly what he was doing here. He cleared his throat, preparing to ask the question when Abdo jumped in.

'The Lam family would like to talk publicly, John. That's why we've asked you here. There have been many requests coming from television stations and newspapers.'

'Of course. I'd be happy to help. But as you know, Jonny, I don't work for a daily newspaper any more. I'm working for a monthly magazine.' Bailey turned to Lam. 'I'd like to talk to you for the article that I'm writing, but it won't be published for a few weeks. If you're wanting to say something now, something sooner, I can certainly help arrange that for you. What is it you want to say?'

The seconds ticked by as Lam considered his response. 'This country has given me so much. My family. A better life. I'm heartbroken about what has happened to my son. I'm angry too.'

Mr Lam stopped talking when he noticed the waiter arriving with their coffees, placing them in the middle of the table, leaving them for Jonny to distribute.

'Thanks,' Bailey said, accepting his takeaway cup, leaving it to cool down in front of him. 'Go on, Philip.'

'We've lived in Australia for more than twenty years. It's a great country. It's been good to us. But there are things people don't like talking about. Racial issues. They don't like to talk about them because they want to believe they don't exist.' He paused, taking a sip of coffee. His words measured, like he'd been rehearsing them in his mind. 'I brought my children up to understand they'll be forced to endure things other children won't. Because of the colour of their skin, they'll be treated differently. Not always, not by everyone. Second glances in restaurants, more attention from the police. It happens.'

Bailey popped the lid on his coffee, bringing it to his lips, testing the heat. Listening.

'More recently, it's not just sideways glances my children have been getting. My daughter was forced to delete her social media accounts because people were saying unkind things to her. People she didn't even know. She was getting . . . what do you call it, trolled?'

'Yes, Philip. That's what it's called,' Abdo chimed in. 'She was getting racially abused and it turned out it was coming from other students at her school.'

'That's all been dealt with now. The school was very supportive. But it's part of an increasing pattern, I fear, which brings me to my son,' Lam said. 'Matthew's a passionate boy and, despite all I've taught him, he's far less tolerant of this type of thing. He was deeply upset about what happened to his sister. He's the type of boy who fights back.'

'And that's what happened the other night,' Bailey said. 'He fought back.'

'Yes.'

'Is this what you want to say to the media? You want to share your story?'

'More than that,' Lam said. 'I want to call out what's happening. It's time for people like me to have a voice in a conversation that has to be had.'

Bailey was wondering if today's meeting was Jonny Abdo's idea. The activist leader recruiting more people to his cause.

'How long have you two known each other?' Bailey said.

'We met through Matthew,' Abdo said. 'I thought I told you, he's one of my students. I reached out to Philip after what happened on Oxford Street.'

'Only a few days then.'

'Why do you ask?' Lam said.

'I just want to make sure you know what you're getting yourself into, Philip. Speaking publicly can also make you a target.'

'We've talked about that,' Abdo said, giving Bailey a look that made it clear he didn't like the direction the conversation had taken.

'I understand and I appreciate you bringing it up,' Lam said. 'Jonny said you were a good man. I do want to speak out. I want to do it now. If you can't help, who should we speak to?'

Bailey had been pondering that question ever since it had been raised. If Lam was chasing maximum exposure, then commercial television was probably the best way to go.

'There's a reporter that I trust from *Inside Story*. I'll talk to her and come back to you.'

'Thank you.' Lam stood up with his coffee. 'If you don't mind, Jonny said he'll be the contact for the family.'

'That's fine, Philip,' Abdo reiterated. 'John and I can work this out. I'll let you know how we go.'

The two men watched in silence as Philip Lam walked back through the café, disappearing into the main foyer of the hospital.

'Are you sure about this, Jonny?'

'It's time. And remember, we didn't start this.'

Abdo was sounding more and more the activist and an experienced journalist like Bailey knew that people who held placards and led demonstrations were often willing to take risks and go to lengths that other people wouldn't dare. The conversation had also made Bailey think about his own relationship with Jonny Abdo. He barely knew the guy. Apart from keeping tabs on Abdo's career in the years that had passed since he'd arrived in Australia as a child refugee, the two men hadn't really had much contact at all.

'Jonny, I've got to ask you a serious question. I'll ask you only once.'

Abdo's face hardened, sensing Bailey's change in mood. 'What?'

'Do you have any idea who killed Augustus Strong?'

'No. I don't.'

Bailey couldn't think of one good reason not to believe him.

Still, he wasn't so sure.

CHAPTER 24

'You seriously handing this one over?'

Annie was surprised that Bailey would give up an exclusive story so easily.

'As I told Philip Lam, I don't work in daily news any more. I'll use him for the feature I'm writing. Anyway, I figured that, well, I owe you one.'

'For what?'

For being a prick, Bailey wanted to say. Although he wasn't one for casual admissions.

'Family wants an honest reporter. That's you.'

Annie hung on the line like she was about to say something else, before switching gears. Business-like. 'If I'm going to get this up for tonight, I'd better get moving. Who's the contact?'

He gave her Jonny Abdo's details and ended the call, his thoughts already turning to his next move. Finding Margie Roundtree. The witness who had told police that Augustus Strong's killers were Black. She had been on his mind ever since he'd discovered her existence during his conversation with Silvie out front of the State Theatre that morning.

It turned out the soup kitchen where Margie had been known to accept a free meal had four wheels and was staffed by a group of people preparing for the second coming of Jesus Christ. After a simple search on the internet, Bailey had also discovered that a team of volunteers from the Hand of God charity would be parking their van behind St Mary's Cathedral at around 6 pm to hand out hot dinners for the homeless.

Bailey knew that if Margie really was the person who had witnessed Augustus Strong being beaten to death then the police would probably have her holed up in a hotel somewhere. Safe. But Bailey had decided to head down to St Mary's anyway to see whether he could find an acquaintance of Margie's, or anyone who may have heard anything about what had happened to Strong. It was a gamble. But he couldn't think of a better idea.

The Hand of God people were already unloading boxes of food and stacking complimentary bibles in a stand on the grass by the time Bailey arrived at St Mary's Cathedral. They were all wearing green shirts with the charity's logo on the front – predictably, an outstretched hand – with quotes from the bible on their backs.

'How's it going, mate?'

Bailey picked out the person who appeared to be in charge. A tall, skinny guy who looked like he'd had a hard life himself and pulled it back just in time.

'Good, brother.' He stopped walking, balancing a box of apples on his knee. 'We'll start serving food in around fifteen minutes. Still getting set up.'

The response made Bailey uncharacteristically self-conscious about his appearance. Maybe his daughter was right. Maybe the flannelette shirt, jeans and Blundstone boots combo didn't cut it any more. Although his stubbly face and shaggy, unkempt hair probably didn't help.

'I'm not here for a feed,' Bailey said, trying not to sound defensive. 'I'm looking for someone. A woman. Wondering if you might be able to help.'

'We don't give out information about the people who come here,' the man said, doing his best to sound unhelpful. 'If you don't mind, I've got to keep setting up.'

The man walked down the grass to where he and the other people in green shirts were lining up boxes on a table. Bailey followed, careful to keep his distance, not wanting to antagonise him any further because he had a right to be suspicious. Almost half of Sydney's homeless were women and many of them were escaping domestic violence situations. Bailey imagined there would be husbands and partners who went searching for the women who'd decided that a life on the street was a safer bet than living under a roof where they were assaulted and raped. Women who didn't want to be found.

'Sorry, I should have identified myself.' Bailey tried again with the skinny guy. 'Name's John Bailey. I'm a journalist. I'm looking for a woman who may have witnessed a murder.'

Bailey was trying to claw back trust so he decided to go straight for the truth.

'A murder?' The man stopped, lowering his voice as his colleagues walked past to collect more boxes from the van. 'Someone was murdered?'

'You may have heard the news, that American guy, Augustus Strong. Happened early this morning,' Bailey said, relieved that the man was at least talking to him again. 'I just need to ask her a few questions.'

'Heard about that on the radio. What'd you say your name was again?'

'John Bailey.'

'I'm Alec.' He squinted at Bailey, a thought clearly popping into his head. 'You're that journalist who got caught up in that terrorist attack in London?'

Here we go, thought Bailey, a stranger in a Jesus shirt was about to pretend that he knew everything about him. Someone else to save.

'Happened a while ago now.'

'I'm sorry, brother. Hell of a thing.'

'Yeah. It was.' Bailey gave him a look that told him he wasn't his brother and to mind his own business. And then he realised that he was the one questioning a stranger in a park about a woman he didn't know. 'If you don't mind. Old wounds, and all that.'

'Sure. Sure. Sorry.'

'The woman I'm looking for goes by the name of Margie Roundtree.'

Alec shrugged. 'Faces, I know. But I couldn't tell you many names. The type of people who need us don't come wearing name tags, if you know what I mean. And we don't ask.'

'I get that.'

Bailey noticed a few people loitering around the table that was now stacked with boxes of food. Alec had clocked them too and he glimpsed at his watch. 'We need to get started.'

Under instruction from Alec, the volunteers took their positions by the table. One person handing out plates. Others serving scoops of spaghetti bolognese and distributing bread rolls, apples and bottles of water. Alec standing at the end of the line, politely offering bibles for anyone interested. There weren't many takers.

People of all ages were turning up and Bailey wondered whether he might get lucky and that one of the dozen or so women already sitting on the grass and on park benches could actually be Margie Roundtree. The only way to find out was to take a walk and make a few polite enquiries, starting with the three middle-aged women who had managed to get a seat at one of the two tables in the park.

'Excuse me, my name's John Bailey. I'm a journalist and I'm looking for someone called Margie Roundtree. Does that name sound familiar to any of you?'

The women paused their conversation, exchanging glances, shaking their heads. 'Sorry,' one of the women answered for the rest.

'Thanks.'

Bailey moved on, asking the same question of the others he found scattered on the grass making quick work of their plates of food.

No luck.

He noticed a group of younger people sitting in a circle beneath a tree and he wandered over. 'Hey, guys. Sorry to disturb. I'm looking for someone called Margie Roundtree. Name familiar?'

'Nah,' a guy with bad teeth answered, dismissively. 'Never heard of her.'

'Yeah, I know Margie.' A woman who Bailey guessed was aged in her early twenties piped up. 'What's she done?'

'Kaz!' Another one of the women in the group clearly resented Kaz's apparent cooperation. 'Why the fuck are you talking to this bloke?'

'Fuck off, Gemma. I can talk to whoever I want.'

Bailey cleared his throat, dropping onto a knee so that he wasn't looking down on them. 'I'm not here to get anyone in any trouble. I just need to talk to her about something she may have seen. I'm a reporter.'

'You mean that dick who got bashed down on George?'

Kaz again.

'That's the one.'

'Yeah, well. I know nothing about that.' She made a huffing sound through her nose, shovelling a fork full of spaghetti into her mouth. 'Margie sure did all right out of it though.'

Gemma was glaring at her friend. 'Kaz, seriously. Shut up!'

'No, fuck it, Gemma.' Kaz was speaking while chewing her food. 'She's pissed off back to that arsehole who pimps her out, didn't give us fuck all of what she got.'

'What d'you mean, Kaz?' Bailey said, knowing that he needed to push. 'I'm concerned that Margie could be in danger.'

'You think?' Kaz laughed, awkwardly. 'Bitch gets paid and goes straight back to the boyfriend who kicked her out. She's in shit, all right. Won't listen to anyone. Not even her little sister.'

A girl sitting a few metres from the others quickly looked away and started packing what remained of her dinner into her backpack. Bailey caught her just as she was getting to her feet. 'Is Margie your sister?'

'Fuck off, mate.'

'I really need to speak to her.'

'Who the hell are you?'

'I'm a reporter. My name's John Bailey.'

'Cops already took her statement. Told her not to speak to anyone else.'

'Who's this boyfriend they were talking about? If you know she's in a dangerous situation, I might be able to help her. What's your name?'

The girl had tearful, angry eyes. She looked like a kid. Fifteen or sixteen years old. Bailey wasn't even factoring in the years stolen by the street.

'Is everything okay?' Alec appeared beside Bailey. 'Are you okay, Jules?'

'Yeah. Yeah. I'm fine.'

'Jules, I really need to talk to your sister,' Bailey said.

'You don't need to –'

'She needs to get out of there.' Jules was speaking as though Alec wasn't even there. 'I need to get my sister away from him.'

'Where, Jules? Where can I find her?'

'Someone gave her money. I don't know who they are. I don't want to know.' Jules lowered her voice so the others sitting nearby on the grass couldn't hear. 'We were supposed to meet up here tonight. Now. We got enough money to get the bus to Byron. She was just going to say goodbye to him but . . .'

She stopped talking, clearly upset.

'It's okay, Jules. What's happened?'

'That fucking arsehole. She told me she wouldn't touch it. I knew she wouldn't get out of that house without hitting it.'

'Where can I find her, Jules?'

'Jules.' Alec was still standing beside Bailey, checking on his homeless customer. Doing the right thing. 'If you're really worried about your sister, maybe we should call the police?'

'No,' Jules snapped. 'No cops. It'll get her in even more bloody trouble now.'

'Where can I find her?'

Jules went quiet, looking from Bailey to Alec, back to Bailey again.

'There's a share house on Morehead Street in Redfern. Fifty-one or fifty-three. Can't remember. Anyway, that's where you'll find her. When you do, tell her thanks a fucking lot.'

Bailey nodded. 'Okay.'

'Actually. Wait.' Jules zipped her backpack closed. 'I'll tell her myself. I'm coming with you.'

CHAPTER 25

The townhouses were squashed together like plasticine. Almost every home identical. Two storeys high with just enough room for front doors and windows. Tessellated tiled pathways. Tiny front gardens inside arrow-tipped fences. Second-level balconies with steel, patterned railings. Skylights poking through sheets of corrugated iron like pressure valves.

Surry Hills was a place where the rich and the poor lived side by side. Venture up the hill towards Redfern and you could quite literally see the wealth drain away, house by house, until there weren't even houses any more, just tall blocks of concrete stretching into the sky.

'Slow down,' Jules said. 'Might as well park down this end, stay clear of the towers.'

Suicide Towers.

The Redfern housing estate with the nickname that told you everything you needed to know about what went on there. The towers personified all that was wrong with the welfare system. Home to forgotten people. A place where hope often died.

Bailey pulled his wagon to the side of the road, parking in between an old Mercedes and a plumber's van.

He hadn't managed to get many words out of Jules during the short drive to the Redfern end of Surry Hills. Most of his questions had been met with one-word answers.

'Lived in Sydney long?'

'No.'

'Is Margie your only sibling?'

'No.'

He tried one more time as they were getting out of the car. 'Who's in Byron?'

'Mum's sister.'

'Where's your mum?'

'Dead.'

They were standing on the footpath beside a house with a broken fence.

'Sorry to hear that, Jules.'

Jules looked down at the ground, crushing a leaf with her foot. 'Dad lost interest in me and Margie when he got remarried and had a baby with his new wife. She never liked having us around. Guess we reminded her of Mum.'

'I'm sorry.'

Bailey didn't know what else to say and Jules was still looking at the ground.

'My aunt reckons she can get us jobs in a restaurant, or something. Give us somewhere to crash. Probably should go back to school, I guess. Been trying to talk Margie into moving for ages.'

'Sounds like a good move, Jules.'

'Yeah. We'll see.' She shrugged, pointing up the hill, starting to walk. 'Hundred bucks says my stupid sister's smacked out of her mind when we find her.'

'I hope you're wrong.'

The house where Margie was supposed to have been visiting was not hard to find. Jules had called it a share house but it was clearly much more than that. Rubbish in the front garden. Busted letterbox. Paint peeling off the brickwork. Sheets hanging from windows instead of curtains. A guy in a singlet on the front porch sitting on a stained and torn sofa, smoking a cigarette and nursing a longneck of beer. Knee bobbing. Neck twitching. Eyes wide open and alert with paranoia. Probably high on ice.

'Wait a sec.'

They were about to cross from the other side of the street when Bailey noticed two men walking towards the house. They stopped at the gate, saying something to the guy on the sofa who nodded, gesturing for them to join him on the porch. He reached underneath the cushion he was sitting on, handing something to one of the men, who slipped him something in return. Then they were gone. Drug deal done.

'You been here before?' Bailey said.

'Yeah. That's Nicko. He runs the place.'

'Got it.'

Nicko recognised Jules as they were crossing the street and his eyes tracked them all the way through the front gate.

'Who's this?' Nicko said to Jules as he sat back on the sofa, arms spread like an eagle. Arrogance driven by the drugs pumping through his veins.

'My sister here?'

'Who the fuck's this?' Nicko ignored the question, pointing at Bailey without looking at him. 'And I'm not asking a third time.'

Nicko brought his hands together, cracking his knuckles, the muscles in his skinny arms bulging like the eyeballs in his head.

'Calm down, Nicko,' Jules said. 'He's a friend of the family. We're looking for Margie. She here?'

Nicko reached for his beer, sitting back, taking a swig. Seemingly reassured that Bailey wasn't a cop or some do-gooder social worker threatening to interrupt his business.

'Inside with Blake. Upstairs bedroom.' He smiled, patting the cushion beside him. 'Why don't you send the old man in, hang here with me for a bit.'

Bailey went to say something but Jules cut him off. 'No, thanks. I want to see my sister.'

'I'll be gentle.'

Bailey felt like grabbing the longneck out of Nicko's hand and using it to put him to sleep. The guy was a cretin. Drug-dealing scum who had just hit on an underage girl.

'Bye, Nicko,' Jules said, turning towards the open front door. 'Let's go.'

'You better not cause me any trouble in there, old man,' Nicko snarled.

Bailey ignored Nicko's threatening words and followed Jules through the door.

It was dark and humid inside, the air tinged with mould and pot smoke. Jules knew exactly where she was going. Down the hallway, up the staircase, right on the landing, past a bathroom which had clothes and towels on the floor, stopping outside the closed door of a bedroom that, Bailey guessed, opened to the balcony that overlooked the street.

'Let me go in first,' she whispered.

Bailey nodded.

Tap. Tap. Tap.

Jules gently knocked on the door.

Nothing.

Knock. Knock.

She used her knuckles this time. Louder.

'Margie, it's Jules. Can I come in?'

Still no sound from inside.

Jules opened the door wide enough so she could peer inside, before pushing it all the way.

'Margie, I'm coming in.'

She slipped inside and Bailey took over her position in the doorway. The evening sun was strong enough to shine light through the sheet that was pinned to the window frame and Bailey could see two people asleep on the bed, their bodies half-covered by a blanket.

Jules went around to the side of the bed where a woman's long, blonde hair was resting on a pillow. 'Margie. Margie. Wake up.' She was shaking her shoulder, whispering. 'Margie, it's Jules. Wake up.'

'What the fuck?' The bloke in the bed rolled over, sitting up on an elbow. 'What the fuck, Jules? What you doing here?'

Blake.

'What did you give her, Blake? What's she had?'

Jules may have been a teenage girl but she clearly wasn't intimidated by guys like Blake and Nicko. She was smart. Wise for her years. Wisdom garnered through the tragedy of losing her mother and the sadness of her father's rejection. No way to grow up. No way to learn. She had Bailey on her side now and he wasn't going anywhere. Listening in the doorway, he felt drawn to helping her. To be there in a way that he had never been for Miranda when he was off chasing stories in foreign countries, abrogating his responsibilities as a father. Bailey would never get over that feeling of failure, but he'd do his damnedest to make amends. Any way he could.

'Blake? What did you give her?'

Jules tried again.

'Fuck off, would you!'

Blake lay back on the bed, closing his eyes. Margie still hadn't moved.

'Margie. Margie.' Jules shook her sister again, panic rising in her voice. 'Wake up.'

Bailey had had enough. He walked over to the side of the bed where Blake was lying flat on his back, enjoying his drug-fuelled slumber.

'Blake.'

Blake's eyes shot open. 'What the fuck? Who are you?'

'Someone who is about to get the cops in here to raid this house. Search your belongings. Tear this place apart for stolen goods. Drugs. Whatever else you've got going on.' Bailey was trying his best to sound menacing. Force Blake to cooperate. 'Now answer Jules's question. What'd you give Margie?'

'Jules?' Margie was moving on the other side of the bed, slurring her words, still at the mercy of the chemicals that had gripped her body in a dizzying vice. 'Jules? Julie . . . Jules . . . hey, babe. Hey, lil sis.'

Jules sighed. 'Margie, we've got to go.'

'Who the fuck are you?'

Blake went to sit up but Bailey pushed his head back down, holding up his phone. 'Stay there, Blake. One call, mate, and you're fucked.'

Blake looked like he was contemplating Bailey's threat, wondering whether the man looming over him was someone to fear, or fight. Then he sighed, dropping his head back onto his pillow. 'Just fuck off. Take her with you, if you want. I couldn't give a toss.'

'What'd she take, Blake?'

'Just a bit of junk, man.' Blake laughed. 'She's such a light-weight.'

'Margie. Margie. We need to go.' Jules was shaking her sister's shoulder again, trying to turn her onto her side. 'Mr Bailey, can you help me?'

'She's naked under there, you perve,' Blake said, laughing again.

Bailey found a pile of clothes on the floor and handed them to Jules. 'Can you dress her?'

Bailey kept his eyes on Blake as Jules dressed her sister, hoping that the prick didn't change his mind and decide to forcibly evict them from his room.

'C'mon, Margie. You've got to help me here.'

Margie was so out of it she barely had control of her limbs. Heroin highs lasted for hours and her tiny pupils and slurred speech suggested she would remain in her drug-fuelled coma for a while.

'Sorry, sis,' Margie said. 'I'm a bad big sister, aren't I? I wish Mum was here.'

'It's okay, Margie. We're good. We just need to get you out of here.'

It took a few minutes but Jules had managed to dress her sister in a pair of jeans and a t-shirt.

'Mr Bailey, can you give me a hand getting her up?'

Bailey walked around to the other side of the bed, clasping Margie under her armpit, pulling her up and resting her arm around his neck. She was actually quite tall, so Bailey had no trouble balancing her beside him.

'Blake, where's her bag?'

'How should I know?' Blake murmured without opening his eyes or lifting his head. He'd lost interest. 'Over there somewhere.' He clumsily pointed his finger at the window.

Jules found the bag and led Bailey and Margie out of the room. 'You okay with her?'

'All good.'

Bailey took his time negotiating the stairs because he wasn't getting much help from Margie, who still hadn't registered that she was being helped by a stranger.

'Hold up, bitch.' Nicko leapt off the sofa just as Jules and Bailey made it outside. 'Your sister still owes me a fifty. Actually, a hundred. She was shouting Blakey boy.'

Bailey couldn't believe what he was hearing. Nicko was the lowest of the low. 'Are you bloody –'

'It's okay.' Jules unzipped Margie's backpack and Bailey caught sight of a pile of fifty-dollar notes stuffed inside. She handed two of them to Nicko. 'We won't be back. Tell Blake to stay away from my sister.'

'Yeah. Yeah.' Nicko smiled, snatching the money, patting Margie on the head, stroking her hair. 'See you soon, Margie. Whenever you need your Blakey boy or something to make you fly, we'll be here.'

Bailey refrained from saying anything, knowing they just needed to get away. Find somewhere for Margie to dry out. Somewhere safe.

When they were clear of the house, Bailey dug his phone from his pocket, searching for a contact, while he and Jules helped Margie stay upright as they walked up the street towards his car.

The old man answered after three rings.

'Joe, it's Bailey. You home?'

'I knew it was you, dumb dumb. Name showed up on my little screen.' The old priest chuckled down the line. 'Footy's about to start. Almost didn't answer.'

'I need a favour. See you in five.'

CHAPTER 26

Jules climbed in the back seat of Bailey's wagon, fixing a seatbelt around her sister. 'Margie. Margie.' She was clicking her fingers, trying to get her sister talking. 'Margie!'

'She doesn't look good,' Bailey said, spinning his head from the driver's seat.

Margie was mumbling to herself as Jules put on her own seatbelt, letting her sister's head slump on her shoulder.

'I've seen her worse, to be honest,' Jules said. 'By the way, who were you talking to on the phone? Who's Joe?'

'An old priest I know. A guy who has spent his life looking after street kids.'

'We're not street kids,' Jules fired back. 'And you can drop us back near St Mary's. I can look after us from there.'

'I'm sorry, Jules. I didn't mean to offend you,' Bailey said, angry at himself for putting a label on them. 'You've trusted me so far. Joe's a good guy. His place is just around the corner. A place where Margie can dry out. Somewhere you'll both be safe.'

Bailey's initial instinct had been to take them to the nearest hospital but he had to try Joe's place first. The priest had seen enough drugged-up kids in his time to know whether Margie would be okay sleeping this one off, or whether she needed medical attention. Taking the girls to a hospital would create a whole load of trouble they didn't need. Family and Community Services would get involved because Jules, at least, was underage. Their father would get called and if he didn't want them back then they'd get thrown into foster care or a boarding house somewhere. It was a can of worms to be avoided. At least, for now.

'What do you reckon, Jules?' Bailey asked again, catching her eyes in the mirror.

She looked away, staring at nothing out the window.

'Okay.'

Father Joe Henley lived out back of a little Catholic church in Redfern and he always had spare beds for kids in trouble. People like Jules and Margie. The church was only a couple of kilometres away, near Redfern Oval, so Bailey had a slim window to ask Jules about what her sister had seen on George Street that morning. Ask her whether she knew who gave Margie the pile of cash that Bailey had glimpsed inside her bag. He didn't want to have those conversations in front of Joe. He also needed to know exactly what kind of trouble he was delivering to the old man's doorstep.

'Hey, Jules?'

She looked up, meeting Bailey's eyes in the mirror again. 'I know what you're going to ask me.'

'I'm sorry, Jules. I just need to know.'

'It wasn't a group of African guys that attacked that American guy, Augustus Strong, or whatever his name was.' She was talking while monitoring her sister's breathing with the back of her hand. 'We were given money to lie. I told Margie not to take it. It all happened so fast I couldn't stop it.'

'Who told you to lie?'

'Me and Margie had set up on the corner of the QVB. We were asleep when it happened. We woke up to someone screaming for help. They bashed him really bad. Kicking his head on the ground. I knew they'd killed him. No one could survive that.'

'Who did it, Jules?'

'No idea. It was still dark. It wouldn't have mattered anyway because they were wearing masks, like the ones bank robbers wear in movies. Four guys. They bolted straight past us down the street. I didn't think they noticed us but –'

'Julie . . . Julie . . . Jules . . .' Margie was smiling dazedly at her sister. 'I love you, Jules.'

Bailey was steering his wagon with one eye on what was happening in the back seat.

'What happened after they ran, Jules?'

Jules sighed, rolling her eyes at her sister, before catching Bailey again in the mirror. 'A guy appears out of nowhere. Starts talking to Margie. Asking her if she wants to make an easy five hundred bucks. She just needs to tell the police when they arrive that the guys in masks were African-looking, or something. "Black guys," he said. "Just say African or Black."'

'And she said yes?'

'Before I could even stop her she took the money. The guy starts going through our stuff. Gets Margie's ID. Tells her he knows who she is now and if she doesn't do what he said, he'd come back and hurt her. Hurt both of us.'

They drove alongside Suicide Towers, where a policeman was talking to a group of kids standing around with their bicycles.

'What did he look like, Jules? The guy who threatened you, who gave you the money. Can you describe him?'

'Aussie guy. Blondie-brown hair. Kind of trendy looking. Button-up shirt. One of those fashy hipster haircuts.'

Jules was describing the type of men that Bailey had seen at Augustus Strong's talk the other night. He grabbed his phone, typing as he drove, taking a punt on a name and a face that he knew he would find in Google.

He held up the screen so that Jules could see. 'Look anything like this guy?'

'Shit,' Jules said, pointedly. 'That's him.'

Benny Hunter.

'Who is he?' Jules asked.

'He's a Neo-Nazi. Leads a group called the Freedom Front.' Bailey paused, thinking carefully about what he'd say next. 'You already know he's dangerous. I think it's time you told the police the truth.'

'I'm not doing that,' Jules snapped, shaking her head. 'I'm not talking to the police.'

'Jules –'

'You don't understand.'

'Tell me. Why won't you talk to the police?'

'He told us he knew cops. That his police friends would let him know if we didn't say what we'd agreed to say. Why do you think we were heading for Byron? We wanted to get the hell away from all this.' She stopped talking, looking out the window. 'Until my idiot sister felt she had to say goodbye to Blake.'

Bailey was relieved that he'd decided against taking the girls to a hospital. Any call to Family and Community Services may have also triggered a phone call to the cops, which would have most certainly put the sisters in even more danger than they were already in.

'You'll be safe where I'm taking you, Jules. Joe's an old friend of mine. Helped me out when I wasn't that much older than you. He'll feed you and give you a room to stay as long as you want,' Bailey said, trying to reassure the girl in his back seat. 'He won't tell anyone you're there. You'll be safe. Okay?'

Jules nodded. She was done talking, preferring to focus on her sister, hugging her close.

'You'll be okay, Jules. Both of you. I promise.'

The orange dusk was fading to black and the street lights flickered on just as Bailey turned alongside Redfern Oval, the home of one of rugby league's oldest teams, the South Sydney Rabbitohs. Diehard supporters like Father Joe Henley called this footy ground 'the holy land' and although the Rabbitohs played in much bigger stadiums these days, they still trained here, and the fans came along to watch.

'Here we are.'

Joe was standing in the narrow driveway beside the church, waving for Bailey to follow him up the path and park his wagon out back.

The old man had devoted most of his life to helping street kids. Although he'd been a priest for more than six decades, he wasn't exactly loved by the conservative establishment. Joe was one of the renegades who had publicly supported issues like same-sex marriage, while criticising the Vatican's handling of child abuse. The Archbishop of Sydney didn't like him but, with Joe already in his eighties, the church wasn't prepared to cut him loose. He just didn't get invited to many church parties any more, which was fine by him.

Bailey had first met Joe more than thirty years ago when he was studying up the road at Sydney University, wondering what the hell to do with his life after losing his younger brother in a car accident. Joe had taught Bailey to box at the gym he'd set up to give kids a safe place to hang out. A place to learn discipline and respect – for themselves and for others. A place where they could punch out their pain on a heavy bag, rather than the street.

Getting old had never held back Joe Henley and the priest still ran his gym six days a week. He didn't spend much time at the altar any more. Joe was happy for others to wear the robes and teach from the book because his religion was helping people.

'Joe.'

The two men shook hands, only briefly, because the priest seemed more interested in the two girls sitting in the back seat rather than the scruffy journalist who'd transported them to his house.

'C'mon, Margie. Out you get.'

Balancing Margie's arm around his shoulder, Bailey helped the drug-addled girl out of the car as her sister slid across the seat, climbing out beside them.

'Jules, this is Father Joe Henley,' Bailey said, struggling to keep Margie upright. 'And this one's Margie.'

'Call me Joe, love.'

'Hi, Joe. Thanks for helping us out.'

'Don't mention it, sport.'

Joe stood back, his experience with troubled kids telling him not to get in Jules's face. Avoid over-familiarity. Girls like

Jules usually had issues with trust. Joe knew that trust was something that needed to be earned.

'Joe. Joe,' Margie said, laughing to herself. 'Hi there, Joe Joe.'

'This one's high as a kite,' Bailey said. 'Heroin.'

'I see,' Joe said, stepping close, examining Margie's eyes which were rolling about like pinballs. 'Let's get her inside.'

'Good idea.'

'And Jules?' Joe said. 'I've got a room out back for you and your sister. Your own bathroom too. All to yourselves.'

'Thanks, Joe,' Jules said, juggling her and her sister's backpacks. 'I could do with a shower.'

—

The television in the kitchen had been tuned to the rugby league and Bailey felt less guilty about interrupting Joe's night when he noticed that the Rabbitohs weren't playing.

'The stupid nine-a-side game they play in the pre-season,' Joe said, pointing at the television. 'Down to the finals. Battle of the Silvertails.'

Manly Sea Eagles versus the Sydney Roosters.

'Barely watch this game any more,' Bailey said. 'Although with rugby in the toilet I might be forced into it soon.'

'Those fools at Rugby Australia couldn't organise a chook raffle. Bunch of private school boys who like sitting around in corporate boxes. Out of touch. No wonder your Wallabies can't win a game.'

'Don't get me started.'

Bailey could have sat around talking footy with Joe all night but he needed to get moving. Annie Brooks had called him twice in the last half hour and he wanted to hear how her interview with Philip Lam had gone.

'You okay with me leaving the girls here with you?'

'Of course.'

Jules walked into the kitchen, ruffling her wet hair with a towel. She was wearing a clean tracksuit that Joe had dug out from all the sports clothes stacked in his cupboards.

'Thanks for the trackie.' Jules patted her hoodie. 'Perfect fit.'

'How's Margie doing?' Bailey stood up with his half-empty mug of tea, pouring it down the sink.

'Sleeping it off.'

'I need to get away,' Bailey said. 'You okay to stay here with Joe?'

'Yeah.'

'I think you should lay low. For the next few days, at least. Wait till all this settles down. What do you reckon?'

Jules hesitated, giving Bailey the impression that whatever answer she gave him, he probably had twenty-four hours before the sisters did a runner for Byron.

'See how it goes.'

At least she was honest.

'I'll check in tomorrow morning.'

'Okay. And thanks for –'

'You don't need to thank me, Jules. Just look after yourself. Get some rest.'

Bailey wrote his phone number down on a piece of paper and handed it to Jules. He knew she was in good hands with Joe, but Bailey wanted her to know that he wasn't just another person who had abandoned her.

'Call any time.'

She took the slip of paper and shoved it in her pocket, giving Bailey a smile that made him feel sad.

'How about a hot chocolate, Jules? I've got a tin of Milo back there.'

Jules smiled at the old man. 'I'd like that. I'd like that a lot.'

CHAPTER 27

Before Bailey had a chance to call Annie Brooks, a message came through on his phone. It was Jonny Abdo letting him know that Matthew Lam's family had been pleased with the story that Annie had managed to pull together for television. 'Community happy too,' the message had read. Bailey was relieved because even though he had trusted Annie with the Philip Lam interview, he'd seen stories about racism backfire on reporters before.

Bailey dialled Annie's number and she answered almost straight away.

'I've been trying to call you.'

'And I'm calling you back.' Bailey tried to sound chirpy. 'Were you ringing about your story?'

'Yeah. I think it went well, but you never know.'

'It went well.' Bailey reassured her. 'Got a message from Jonny Abdo. Family's happy. Community too. Sounds like a lot of people watched it.'

'That's good. Where are you, by the way?'

'On the way home.'

'Might want to re-think that one,' Annie said. 'The other reason I was calling you, there's a TV crew parked outside your house along with a reporter from the *Tele*. They're chasing a comment about the AFP charges still hanging over your head despite the whistle blower investigation being canned.'

Bailey hated being the story and the last thing he felt like doing was running a gauntlet of reporters at his own front door.

'Hungry?'

'Starving.'

'Meet you at The Paddington in fifteen. I could murder a chicken.'

Annie laughed. 'See you there.'

—

It was after 8.30 pm by the time Bailey was walking up Oxford Street towards the restaurant. He wasn't much of a cook and The Paddington was the type of place he went when he was looking for a hearty meal to replace all the breakfasts and lunches he'd been skipping. The guy at the front door recognised him and directed him towards the back of the dimly lit restaurant where Annie was already sitting at a small wooden table beneath a painting of a cow.

She noticed him just as he reached the table, standing up and giving him a hug. 'Hi, stranger.'

'Annie.'

Just as they were sitting down a waiter arrived with two glasses of iced water, depositing them on the table before letting them know that he'd be back to take their order soon.

Annie tapped Bailey's glass, smiling. 'On the rocks, right?'

Alcoholics were allowed to joke with each other about elephants in rooms.

'You know me too well.'

They each sipped on their drinks, leaving the buzzing noise of the mostly full restaurant to occupy the awkward silence that Bailey hadn't expected.

'Well done with the interview,' he said, eventually.

'Thanks for setting that up. Led *Inside Story* tonight. You see it?'

Bailey took another sip of his water, draining almost half the glass. 'Not yet. What'd he say?'

'Philip Lam? Nothing overly surprising. Spoke lovingly about his son, how what happened to him has caused pain for the broader community too. Nice man. Eloquent. He's hurting, though.'

'Any change in Matthew?'

'Philip was hoping they might wake him up tomorrow. Could be a couple more days though. Doctors are worried about brain damage.'

'Poor bastard.' After his conversation with Lam at the hospital, Bailey figured the interview had run exactly as Annie had described. 'Speak to anyone else at the hospital?'

'Just the lawyer, Abdo. He seemed pretty eager to get on camera, to be honest. Knowing he led that protest the night Matthew Lam was bashed, interviewing him made sense. Didn't hold back though. I've already had a couple of newspaper journos call me chasing his number.'

'What'd he say?'

'Just some big statements about racism. The hidden cancer in Australian society. People too proud and defensive to talk about it.' Annie paused, taking a sip of her water. 'Had some good one-liners. Wouldn't be surprised if we start seeing a bit more of him in the media. A natural.'

Bailey went to say something but he was interrupted by the waiter who had returned, notepad and pen in hand, ready to take their orders.

'What would you like, madam?'

Annie looked at Bailey. 'This place was your idea, why don't you order for the both of us?'

Bailey smiled, not bothering to look at the menu in front of him. 'Half a chicken, fries and some broccoli to share. And better get some of that gravy you guys do on the side.'

'Good choice.'

Annie laughed as she watched the waiter walk away with their menus. 'Chicken and chips?'

'I'm a simple man.' Bailey finished his water, crunching a piece of ice between his teeth. 'Trust me, you won't be disappointed.'

'I've got something for you too,' Annie said, the smile on her face flattening, before morphing into a frown. 'I didn't want to mention it on the phone. It's about Harriet Walker.'

'Go on.'

'I've got a contact close to the investigation. She wasn't killed in a robbery.'

'Never thought she was.'

Although Bailey didn't have any evidence to prove it.

'Well, I can confirm your instinct was right. When the police found her she had all of her valuables. Watch. Necklace. Bank cards. Her killer wasn't interested in making a quick buck. They just wanted her dead.'

'Why are the police still calling it a robbery?'

Annie shrugged. 'My contact's just as confused about that as you are. Someone from higher up made that call, could have been the feds. Don't know why. Don't know who.'

Bailey knew of police putting out misinformation in murder investigations before. A tactic often deployed to play mind games with a killer.

'I don't get it.'

'Tell me about it.' Annie shook her head, leaning forward on her elbows. 'That's all I know.'

Bailey folded his arms, staring at Annie without responding.

'I can see your mind ticking over from here,' she said. 'Anything you'd like to tell me?'

'Harriet Walker was investigating right-wing extremists. Neo-Nazis. I shared some information with her and we were due to catch up again to go through what she'd found. Instead, she turned up dead.'

'Shit, Bailey. I'm sorry. But you can't . . . you're not –'

'Hat was a senior investigator in the AFP,' Bailey said, sharply. 'She knew what she was doing.'

He didn't want to admit that he felt at least partly responsible for Hat's death. Another person who had died because of him. Annie Brooks understood Bailey well enough to know about the demons inside his head. The faces of the dead. Now he had one more.

'Who do you think killed her?'

'I can't answer that. But I suspect there's someone on the inside who was working against her. Undermining her investigation.'

And about an hour ago, Bailey had been told by a frightened teenage girl that a Neo-Nazi called Benny Hunter had a friend in uniform. State or feds, he had no idea. But the revelation had been bothering him. Sending his mind spinning in different directions.

'Maybe Hat was getting too close?' Bailey said, lowering his voice. 'Maybe the raid on my house had nothing to do with my source from those stories about Afghanistan?'

'That's a hell of a conspiracy, Bailey.'

He shrugged, looking around to check that none of the other diners had cottoned on to their conversation and were listening in. 'That contact of yours in the cops, you talking state or feds?'

Annie paused, considering her response. 'State.'

'Trust him?'

'He's old school. Been around even longer than you and me. Never got caught up in that dirty shit back in the eighties. As far as I know, he's squeaky clean.'

'So you trust him?'

'Yeah, I do.'

'Good. Because I might need your help with something down the line.'

Bailey was thinking about Jules and Margie. The sisters were being guarded in Redfern by an 82-year-old priest. At some stage, they might need more help. Protection. If Annie had someone inside the New South Wales Police that she trusted, that person could come in very handy indeed.

'Care to tell me any more about that?'

Bailey was relieved to see the waiter arrive with a plate of roast chicken and a bowl of fries.

He smiled. 'You beauty.'

'Greens are on the way,' the waiter said.

'Thank god for that,' Annie said. 'I'm going to need to jog an extra lap of the park in the morning if we get through all this.'

Bailey smiled, popping a chip in his mouth. 'Don't worry, we'll get through it.'

The waiter returned with the broccoli and Annie waited for him to leave before returning to the topic at hand. 'What were you about to tell me about the police?'

'Let's eat.' Bailey ignored the question, cutting into the chicken, offering to deposit some onto Annie's plate. 'Breast?'

'Sure. We done with shoptalk, are we?'

'I reckon.'

Once he'd finished stocking Annie's plate with chicken, chips and broccoli, Bailey piled most of what was left on the plate in front of himself.

'You've got to try some of this.' He held up the gravy boat he'd just indiscriminately poured over all of the food groups on his plate.

'I'll pass.'

The two reporters spent the next few minutes eating in silence. Bailey didn't want to talk about work any more but he didn't want to get personal, either. Annie was more than a colleague and there was a period in their lives when she had also been more than a friend.

The conversation turned to small talk. Annie's son. Bailey's daughter. The extraordinary length of the bushfire summer. Inevitably, they started reminiscing about Lebanon.

'Beirut feels like a long time ago now,' Annie said. 'Remember that little bolthole apartment you had above the market near the US embassy? I don't know how you stayed in that shoebox for so long. How long were you there in the end? Three years?'

'Six. I loved that apartment. So close to everything. May not have been flash, but it had everything I needed. Back then newspapers had smaller budgets than you TV people. Living in a five star hotel for months on end wasn't exactly roughing it.'

Annie laughed. 'Wasn't my decision.'

The Australian commercial television networks mostly based their international correspondents in big gateway cities like London and Los Angeles and they'd only spend time in places like Beirut when they were covering an ongoing story or investigating a new one. Lebanon in the 1990s seemed like the centre of the world. Political assassinations. Tensions with Israel. Iraqis flooding into Lebanon after fleeing Saddam Hussein's brutal regime. Ongoing military battles between Lebanon and Syria. Hezbollah seemingly at war with everyone. Annie had good contacts and she was the type of reporter who broke stories. It was also why she had gotten on so well with Bailey.

'The world seemed crazy back then,' Bailey said. 'Sad thing is, it's even crazier now.'

A squinty smile spread across Annie's face. 'Remember that day the windows blew out in your apartment? I was in the bloody shower, you had to carry me out of the bathroom because of all the broken glass.'

How could Bailey forget? The morning after another bender. They'd been out most of the night drinking at the Marriott Hotel with a bunch of United Nations guys, stumbling back to Bailey's flat for a nightcap. The unspoken arrangement back then was basically booze and sex. No more, no less. Moments of intimacy to remind each other of what life was supposed to be about.

Bailey could still picture her in the shower. She had a habit of leaving the door open just enough so that he could glimpse her naked body inside. Annie's not so subtle way of reminding him that he was one of the luckiest men in Beirut. Annie Brooks was beautiful back then. She was beautiful now.

'Lucky it was summer. I had to sleep with open windows for almost a month, it took so long to find someone to fix the glass.'

'Life's a bit of a blur from those days,' Annie said. 'We had good times though, didn't we?'

'Yeah, Annie. We did.'

Bailey wasn't sure where this conversation was headed but he was suddenly feeling uncomfortable, shifting in his chair, looking for the waiter.

'Are you okay?'

'Fine.' He answered without looking at her. 'I'm just buggered. Been a long day.'

Annie kept talking but Bailey wasn't listening any more. He was holding up his hand, trying to get the waiter's attention. 'What the fuck's wrong with this guy?'

Annie reached across the table, touching his hand. 'Bailey? Did I say something wrong?'

The touch on Bailey's skin brought him back to the woman sitting opposite, painfully aware of his sudden change in mood.

'Sorry, Annie. It's just . . .' He stopped talking, tapping the table. 'It's just that I haven't had a dinner like this in a long time. Not saying that this is anything. Not saying that we . . . it just got me thinking, y'know.'

Annie's arm was still stretched across the table and she rested her fingers on top of his hand. 'It's okay, Bailey. I get it. I know things have been hard.'

'Yeah.'

After another period of silence he slipped his hand from under hers, sitting back in his chair. Staring at the woman on the other side of the table. The wrinkles around her eyes and her cheeks adding stories, making her even more interesting for a guy like him. Only Bailey wasn't ready for Annie Brooks. He wasn't ready for anyone.

'Hey, Bailey,' she said, waiting for him to look at her. 'It's okay to talk about her, you know that, right?'

'Yeah.'

How could Bailey talk about Sharon Dexter when he was still having daily conversations with her in his head?

'Have you thought about speaking to someone? Sometimes it helps.'

'Did that. I'm good.'

Bailey noticed the waiter heading towards their table. Finally.

'How was everything?'

'Good, mate. Can I get the bill?' Bailey said. 'We're done here.'

CHAPTER 28

They were moving him again.

He didn't know where. He didn't know why. He'd stopped asking questions a long time ago. Stopped wondering why he'd been taken. Why they were keeping him alive.

'Get in.'

Now they were ordering him to share the boot of a car with a dead man.

Bailey shook his head, his shackled hands gripping the edge of the car, refusing to budge.

He knew the butt of the rifle would come. He didn't care. It was the only thing that made him feel alive. Like he still had control over what was happening to him.

Crack!

He fell to his knees, the blow making him unsteady, splitting his cheek, warm blood trickling down the wrinkle in his cheek and into the corner of his mouth. The metallic taste another signal that he was a person. Not just someone's prisoner.

'Get in!'

Bailey shook his head again, spitting a glob of blood into the sand.

'Fuck you.'

The vacant stare of the dead guy in the boot had put Bailey in a defiant mood, giving him a rush of power he hadn't felt for a long time. The power of being.

Crack!

This time the rifle butt found Bailey's gut, knocking the wind from his lungs, leaving him gasping for breath.

'You want to be like him?'

The guy with the gun pointed at the crumpled, lifeless body lying face-up in front of them. White vacant eyes frozen in fear.

'Fucking animals.'

The rifle butt was airborne again, arm cocked for one more go.

'Okay. Okay.' Bailey held up his arm, knowing he'd made his point. 'I'll do it.'

'Go!'

Bailey climbed in, catching a whiff of his travelling companion. The man they'd killed with a single bullet to the head. A neat hole right between his eyes. It had happened only hours before. The smell engulfing the boot of the car wasn't decomposition. It was a mixture of sweat, piss and shit. The poor bastard's final shame.

This was how Bailey got around in Iraq in those days. In the boot of a car. Only he was more used to being alone. Not breathing in the odours of a dead guy.

The car bumped along the road for an hour or more before it skidded to a stop.

He heard car doors opening. Footsteps crunching sand. Keys jiggling. The boot clicking open. White light momentarily blinding him.

'Where are we?'

No answer.

Colours started to emerge through the white.

Blue. Yellow. Orange. The colours of Iraq.

The guy from earlier was standing over him, a second man at his side.

They were talking to each other in Arabic, arguing about whether to leave Bailey inside until, finally, they agreed they would.

'There! Stay! Stay!'

They pushed Bailey to one side, dragging the dead man out of the car, pausing when they had him at the tailgate, each grabbing an arm and a leg, swinging him into the air.

Bailey leaned forward to see where they'd discarded the body, the smell of rotting corpses slapping him in the face, burning his nose. He climbed onto his knees, peering between the two men at the horror in front of them. A pit filled with bodies piled on top of each other. So many it was impossible to count.

Men. Women. Children.

Murdered.

'What the fuck?'

The sound of Bailey's voice made the two men turn around.

'This is what happens when you try to escape.'

The guy who'd hit him earlier lifted his rifle again, spinning it around so that the butt was inches from Bailey's head.

'Go to sleep, dog!'

Crack!

Darkness.

CHAPTER 29

SATURDAY

The air was so thick with moisture that Bailey was dripping with sweat by the time he finished his second lap of Centennial Park with Campo. Beads of smoke-laced water were stinging his eyes, making his t-shirt cling to his body, accentuating the little gut that refused to flatten no matter how much bloody exercise he did. Meals like last night's chicken and chips obviously didn't help.

Rain had been bucketing on bushfire zones in Victoria and the south coast of New South Wales and now it was edging further north. The elusive rain that was finally putting an end to the bushfire summer was forecast to hit Sydney tomorrow and the clouds looked like dark grey balloons ready to burst.

Tomorrow was Australia Day and you wouldn't find one person who would complain about the rain coming down on their annual public holiday. Everyone and everything had had enough of the blistering dry, along with the smoke that had become the torturous scent of summer. Despite the rain, the citizenship ceremonies, barbecues and Change the Date rallies were expected to go ahead. People were just being advised to pack raincoats.

Bailey had decided to walk a second lap of the park this morning so that he could clear his head from the nightmare that had interrupted his sleep. Bloody Iraq. His first nightmare in a while. He'd forgotten how violent and unsettling they could be.

They walked slowly up the hill towards Paddington Gates, allowing Campo ample time to sniff the brown grass and the gaunt, shrivelled trees as they went. The dog was just as tired as Bailey was and she was loudly panting, her tongue drooping out the corner of her mouth. Greyhounds were bizarre animals. They could sprint one hundred metres faster than any other dog on earth but ask them to walk a few kilometres and they nearly shut down.

When they finally arrived outside Bailey's local café he knelt down, steering Campo towards the bowl of water that was always kept full on the footpath.

'There you go, Campo. Have a drink.'

The dog greedily slurped back water as Bailey stepped towards the café's takeaway window.

'Two long blacks, thanks.'

Bailey tapped his card and ignored the eye roll from the waitress who didn't bother reprimanding him about the fact that he had – again – turned up without a reusable cup. Instead, she seemed only interested in the change in his usual order.

'Get some company last night, did we?' She smiled and winked at him.

Surprised by her cheekiness, Bailey couldn't help but laugh. 'Yeah. He's probably still snoring in my spare room.'

'Oh.' She looked disappointed.

It had been late when Bailey had arrived home the night before but he knew the big Oklahoman was staying over because of the cigar stub and pizza box in his kitchen.

He thanked the girl for the coffees and commentary and headed towards his house. It was just after 7 am when he opened his front door. The lights were on inside, which wasn't surprising because, like him, Ronnie was an early riser.

'Big fella, you here?'

'Out back!'

Ronnie was sitting in Bailey's courtyard, thumbing through the newspaper with a plate of toast beside him.

'That for me?'

'Yeah.'

Bailey handed Ronnie his coffee.

'You're a good man, bubba.'

'Anything in there about Walker?'

'Nothing. Story about racism on the front page linking that Matthew Lam kid to Augustus Strong.'

'And?'

'No different to what we knew yesterday. Print playing catch-up.' Ronnie licked his finger, flipping through the pages. 'Nice little piece about you though.'

Ronnie held up the paper, revealing a photograph of Bailey underneath a headline that read: AFP TO PROSECUTE VETERAN REPORTER DESPITE CASE BEING DROPPED.

'What's this veteran reporter crap? Makes me feel like an old man,' Bailey said.

'You're no spring chicken, bubba.'

'Piss off, Ronnie. Anyway, I couldn't give a toss about that now. Good luck to them.'

'You must have really annoyed this Harding fella,' Ronnie said. 'Clearly doesn't like you.'

'Yeah, well. You didn't expect me to roll out the welcome mat when he decided to rip through my house, did you? And what do you mean, he doesn't like me? You spoken to him?'

'No.'

The last time Bailey had seen Ronnie they were standing outside the Randwick home of the corrupt customs agent they'd found sitting on his sofa with a bullet hole between his eyes and his brain splattered all over the wall. Liam Callaghan had allegedly waved through a shipping container packed with Californian oranges and guns. Ronnie was supposed to have been chasing information from his contacts in Australian intelligence and law enforcement circles. He may not have spoken to Harding, but he'd spoken to someone.

'Get anything from your sources?'

Ronnie munched on his toast. 'Not yet.'

Ronnie Johnson had a long history of working closely with Australian intelligence agencies. ASIO. ASIS. ASD. AFP. They were just the organisations that people knew about. There were so many arms of Australian intelligence that you needed the entire alphabet just for the acronyms and initialisms. Ronnie knew how to navigate that exhaustive list and get what he wanted. Bailey was surprised that he didn't already have something to share.

'Really?'

'Really.'

Bailey took a chair beside Ronnie, placing his cup on the table. Campo appeared beside him and started turning in circles, looking for a place to lie down. She shunned the doggy mattress by the door and settled for the cool bricks in the courtyard, resting her head on Bailey's shoe, closing her eyes.

'Never picked you for a dog person.'

'Neither did I.'

The two men went quiet and Bailey was hoping that Ronnie might eventually pipe up to tell him that he had, at least, found a skerrick of information that might be interesting. But he didn't. So it was left to Bailey to share what he had discovered the evening before.

'I think I know who killed Augustus Strong.'

Ronnie stopped chewing his mouthful of toast. 'Go on.'

'Benny Hunter.'

'The Freedom Front guy?'

'Yeah. He may not have done the deed himself, but he was part of it. Possibly organised it.'

'Theory, or fact?'

There was a tone in Ronnie's voice that annoyed Bailey. He let it slide. 'Fact.'

Bailey told Ronnie about the Roundtree sisters and how Benny Hunter had paid them to tell police that a group of Black men had attacked Augustus Strong on George Street. About how Hunter had threatened the girls, telling them he had a friend inside the police. He told him about the soup kitchen down by St Mary's Cathedral, the Surry Hills smack house, and the fact that Jules and Margie were now being looked after by an old priest in Redfern.

'You've been busy,' Ronnie said, finishing off his toast. 'Not sure it changes things right now though.'

'Bullshit.' Bailey had raised his voice and Campo's head shot up, wondering whether something was wrong. 'What do you mean it doesn't change things? It changes everything. We've got a witness who has implicated Benny Hunter in Strong's murder.'

'The same witness who told police it was someone else.'

Ronnie was right. The girls' evidence was rubbery at best and although it should inevitably lead to Benny Hunter being hauled in and questioned, it wasn't enough to risk asking the girls to amend their statement. Especially if there was someone inside the force close to Hunter.

Bailey hunched forward, frustrated by Ronnie's assessment, knowing that he was right. 'But this information could be useful, right? Surely, you've got someone in the feds who'll throw you a bone? You've been working with these people for bloody decades.'

A fresh cigar was sitting on the table and Ronnie picked it up, lighting a match, his head disappearing in a white cloud as he puff-started the stump. Eventually, he let his hand and the cigar dangle by his side. 'I'm not trying to be a downer here. I'm just processing this in my head. Playing both sides. This lead on Hunter's good. I might be able to use it.'

'Might?'

'We need to get a handle on Walker's investigation. Find out who else was working it, how far they'd gotten. Who they were looking into.'

'Hunter,' Bailey said. 'I'm pretty sure the Freedom Front was on her list. We talked about him when I met her at the Lindt Café. She had something for me, I'm positive about that . . . something so good it got her killed.'

'Tell me, what's the motive for killing Strong?'

'I've been thinking about that ever since the girls told me about Hunter.'

'And?'

Bailey reached down and pulled on Campo's ear, giving her a pat. 'Stick with me, this is going to sound a little out there.'

'I'm listening.'

'You said something to me yesterday about a race war. How the FBI reckon the leader of The Dawning was preparing for a race war. You said Donald Sampson had been running training camps, building support all over the world through online forums. And he's the guy who shipped the guns to Sydney.'

'Right.'

'Well, making it look like a bunch of Black guys were responsible for killing Augustus Strong is surely going to rev up far right extremists. Bring more people to the cause. Possibly even provoke a response. I mean, Strong was the pin-up boy for the alt-right. I know it sounds far-fetched, but it's possible, isn't it?'

'It's possible.'

Ronnie stood up, his chair screeching across the bricks.

'Where are you going?'

'To make a trade.'

'Hang on.'

Ronnie stopped at the door. 'What?'

'Don't forget, if these guys have someone on the inside, it could be more than one. Careful who you trust.'

'This is my world we're playing in, bubba. And I've been doing this a heck of a long time.'

The expression on Ronnie's face made it clear that he didn't appreciate the advice. But Bailey didn't care. 'One more thing, Ronnie.'

'What?'

'Keep the girls out of it.'

Ronnie left without saying another word.

CHAPTER 30

Bailey had reached the point in his investigation when he needed to get writing. Plot the story he had so far, his cast of characters and incidents of crime. He knew that he wasn't just writing about Augustus Strong and the rise of far right nationalism in Australia any more. He was on to something bigger and now was the time to get some words down while he waited for the police to do their job and lead him to the places he didn't already know.

He flipped the lid on his laptop, boiled the kettle and got to it.

Apart from a 'check-in' call from Gerald and a message from Annie Brooks to thank him for dinner the night before, Bailey's phone stayed unusually quiet for most of the day.

Fuelled by coffee from the plunger in his kitchen, he had managed to write almost five thousand words by evening. It wasn't exactly poetry, but it was a good start on the article that Neena had commissioned him to write. Bailey had spent most of his career racing to meet tight deadlines and although he was writing a much longer article, he was enjoying the extra time to think and chase. Today's writing session meant that he was on track. The cover story for *Enquirer Magazine*'s debut issue was destined to be a cracker.

The chicken and chips from the night before had provided him with enough fuel to make it through most of the day without needing more than the piece of toast he'd eaten for breakfast. But by 7 pm, just as the computer screen was starting to hurt his eyes, he was starving. Most of the contents in his fridge looked questionable and there wasn't much to choose from in his pantry, either. He managed to find a tin of baked beans with a respectable use by date and some bread that could be improved in the toaster. It would do.

Two mouthfuls in and he was interrupted by his vibrating phone. Jonny Abdo's name flashing on the screen.

'Jonny, how are you?'

'I think I might be in trouble.'

Bailey sat up, holding his phone to his ear with one hand while rubbing his eyes with the other.

'What's happened?'

'My personal details are out there. Someone has published all of my details on social media. Facebook. Twitter. I'm everywhere.'

Abdo was clearly rattled but Bailey was struggling to get a handle on what he was talking about. 'Your personal details?'

'I've already told the police. They did bloody nothing, of course. Just took my details and said they'd look into it.'

'Look into what?' Bailey still didn't have a clue what Abdo was talking about. 'You need to slow down, Jonny. Explain to me what's going on.'

Abdo sighed heavily into the phone. 'Do you know what doxing is?'

'No idea.'

'It's when someone posts your personal information on the internet without your consent. Both my home and work addresses were put out there this afternoon by a white nationalist group that calls themselves the Blokes Brigade. They even posted the licence plate and model of my car!'

'Why would they do that?'

'They must have seen me talking about racism on the news last night,' Abdo said. 'This is what these groups do. Try to intimidate you. Shut you up.'

Bailey walked into the kitchen while listening to Abdo, flipping the lid on his laptop, putting his phone on speaker and placing it beside him so that he could start typing. 'Where'd you say they published your info? I'm sitting in front of my computer.'

'Just type in the words Blokes Brigade and my name. You'll see.'

Bailey did as he was told and he was directed to a Facebook page where there was an image of Jonny Abdo beneath the words, GO HOME TRAITOR! Abdo's name and addresses were published there too, along with a short article quoting some of the things that he'd told Annie Brooks on *Inside Story*. The last line of the article sent a chill up Bailey's spine.

Maybe someone should pay this guy a visit. Over to you, patriots.

'This isn't good, Jonny. This isn't good at all.'

Bailey was speaking while reading some of the comments below the post about Abdo. There were at least a dozen or so, mostly unimaginative racist sledges from people with odd pseudonyms like 'Gate Crasher' and 'Mountain Goat'. But some of the comments were more extreme, with one person calling for Abdo to be 'dangled from a tree'.

'I'm not sure what to do.'

'Where are you now?'

'I'm on my way home from the hospital.'

Bailey started to formulate a plan. 'Go home, pack a bag. I'll jump in the car now and meet you. You can stay at my place tonight.'

Abdo went silent on the other end of the phone.

'Jonny? You still there?'

Nothing.

'Jonny?'

Breathing. 'Okay.'

'And Jonny?'

'Yeah?'

'Anything looks strange outside your place, just do laps around the block until I get there. Most of these guys are cowards who like to talk tough on the internet. But there are some violent bastards out there too.'

'Thanks, Bailey.'

Bailey had never been to Jonny Abdo's place but he didn't need to ask for his address. It was staring at him from the computer screen on his kitchen bench. Abdo lived in an apartment in Bankstown, around forty minutes' drive from Paddington. If Abdo was on his way home from St Vincent's Hospital, then Bailey would be up to half an hour or so behind him. He needed to get moving.

He grabbed his car keys and flew out the door, dialling Ronnie's number as he jogged along the street to the spot where he'd parked his car.

'Come on. Come on. Pick up.'

Ronnie didn't answer so Bailey left him a garbled message telling him to call back, urgently. If he couldn't trust the police then Ronnie Johnson was the person he wanted to watch his back.

CHAPTER 31

'Oh my god.'

A woman's voice.

'Oh my god. Oh my god. Oh my god.'

Distressed.

A hand landed on Bailey's shoulder.

'Are you okay?'

A man's voice.

'Buddy. Buddy.' The man was now tapping Bailey on his back. 'Are you okay?'

Bailey didn't answer. He couldn't take his eyes off Jonny Abdo's lifeless body. His eyes, plastered open in fear. The pool of blood growing like a contorted halo around his head. The left side of his face caved in, broken by the impact of hitting the concrete. Bailey had seen dead bodies before but not like this.

'Did you know him?'

The man was kneeling down beside Bailey, his voice softening.

'Yeah, I knew him.'

Minutes earlier, Bailey had been knocking on the door of Abdo's apartment. He had figured that the lawyer had just gone out to get some takeaway. The guy had been at the hospital and may not have had a chance to eat dinner. It had made sense. Bailey had decided to wait on the steps of the apartment building so that he wouldn't miss him when he got back. From his position at the entrance he could also monitor people walking in and out of the building. See if anyone had been encouraged by the Blokes Brigade to pay Jonny Abdo a visit.

'Think he jumped?'

Hearing the man's question startled Bailey back to the present. He got to his feet and stepped past Abdo's body closer to the road, looking up at the balcony from which the lawyer had just fallen ten storeys to the ground.

Bailey turned to the woman and the man who were both standing beside the body. 'Did either of you see anyone else come out that door?'

The woman didn't answer because she was talking into her phone. Alerting police. Asking for an ambulance. Although there wasn't much that the paramedics could do other than scoop the dead body off the footpath.

'Mate!' Bailey tried again, this time directing the question at the man. 'Did you see anyone come out of that building?'

'No,' he said. 'No, sorry, I didn't. I –'

Bailey didn't wait for him to finish his sentence, sprinting up the front steps of the apartment building and into the foyer. Ordinarily, there would have been two options for Bailey to choose from to get to the upstairs floors, but the 'out of order' sign on the elevator door had reduced those options to one. The stairs.

Taking the steps two at a time, he'd made it up the first flight when he heard a loud thud below. The sound of a heavy door closing. There was a small window on the landing and he stopped, peering through the glass, spying two men running through the carpark at the rear of the building. A carpark he had no idea was there. The building must have had another exit on the ground floor. Bailey had missed the two men by only seconds. Leaping down the stairs, he took a right at the bottom where he guessed the exit would be. The door was literally only a few metres from the staircase below a dusty neon exit light that clearly wasn't working. No wonder he'd missed it.

Pushing open the door, Bailey started running between parked cars trying to get his eyes to adjust to the darkness as he looked for the men he'd seen through the window. He was certain they were men by their body frames and the way they moved.

The only light outside was coming from a dim, flickering lamp in the corner of the carpark. It was reflecting off vehicles in a way that made it impossible to see inside windows. Bailey stopped in the middle of the driveway. There must have been around fifteen or twenty car spots and every one of them was taken. Using the palm of his hand to block the distracting light, Bailey watched and listened, alert to any sign that the two men were still out here.

Nothing.

No movement. No sounds. Only the whistle of his breath, the hum of the traffic, and the distant echo of a magpie song.

An engine started and the headlights of a hatchback came on directly in front of him. High beam. Blinding. The engine revved into gear and the car lunged towards him, leaving him no time to get out of the way. He jumped into the air, landing on the bonnet, rolling onto the windscreen, bouncing onto the gravelly dirt. Lying on the ground, he watched the red tail lights of the car race down the driveway and disappear into the traffic.

Dusting the dirt from his sleeve, Bailey rolled onto his back, allowing his body to play catch-up and report any injuries he may have sustained during the hit and run. His hand was burning after breaking his fall on the gravel, but his wrist and fingers were moving all right. His shoulder was also aching and his ribs were sore but that could have been the lingering bruises he'd suffered earlier that week when Benny Hunter had pushed him down a staircase.

A phone was flashing on the ground a few metres away and Bailey patted his pocket, realising it was his. It took Bailey a few goes to get to his feet and by the time he made it to his phone the call had already gone through to voicemail. It was Ronnie Johnson and he was calling again.

'Where are you?'

Ronnie was allergic to pleasantries.

'Bankstown. Jonny Abdo's dead.'

Bailey wasn't much better. Straight-talking saved time.

'We need to meet and – what?'

'Abdo.' Bailey took a breath, wiping his sweaty brow with the back of his hand. 'Jonny Abdo's dead.'

'What the hell?'

Ronnie obviously had something else on his mind but Bailey's news had just trumped the next thing he was about to say.

'A white supremacist group published Jonny's details on social media. He got doxed, or whatever the hell they call it. I came out here to pick him up. Was waiting outside his building. Poor bastard lands on the fucking footpath beside me.'

Bailey was walking down the driveway towards the front of the apartment building. He could hear sirens in the distance. Police. Ambulance. Emergency sounds howling together into the night.

'What the hell, bubba?' Ronnie said. 'You don't think he –'

'No. He was pushed, I'm certain about that.'

'How so?'

'Because the two guys who did it just tried to run me over in a fucking hatchback.'

The sirens were getting louder, which meant the paramedics and the police were getting closer. Bailey didn't want to be there when they arrived. He didn't like the prospect of spending the rest of his night being quizzed about why he had come to Abdo's apartment, and what else he knew about the people who may have killed him. Especially if there was a corrupt cop involved.

'You should get out of there.'

More people had come out of the building and they were standing in a semi-circle around Abdo's body. Some of them hugging each other and crying. Abdo clearly had friends inside these apartments and news of his shocking death was spreading fast.

'That guy!' The man who had been talking to Bailey earlier was now pointing his finger in his direction. 'He was outside when he fell.'

'Ronnie, I've got to go,' Bailey said into the phone.

'Wait!' Ronnie said, sharply.

'What?'

'The reason I rang. Harriet Walker. I've been tracing her last movements and I know where she went before she was killed.'

'What does that mean?'

Ronnie cleared his throat. 'You need to get out of there, Bailey. Now. Hang up the phone. Meet me in Leichhardt.'

'Leichhardt?'

'Sharon Dexter's house.'

'What?' The mention of his dead girlfriend's name stopped Bailey's legs from working and he turned his back on the crowd of people that were all now staring at him. 'Why are we meeting at Sharon's house?'

'Because Walker visited there around midnight the night before she was killed.'

'Ronnie, I don't get it. Why would she –'

'I'll explain when I see you. Now hang up the phone and get the hell out of there.'

Bailey ended the call and walked over to the guy from earlier. 'I need to talk to you.' He grabbed his arm and pulled him away from the others. 'Did you see the car that just sped down the driveway? The hatchback? White, I think.'

'Yeah. Yeah, I did. It turned into the road right in front of us. Didn't get a good look inside.'

'The victim. The dead guy over there.' Bailey pointed at Abdo's corpse. 'His name's Jonny Abdo and those guys in the hatchback killed him, I'm certain of it. And they just tried to run me down in the carpark out back. Did you get a licence plate?'

A sharp pain shot through Bailey's head and he rubbed his temples with his fingers, momentarily closing his eyes. Maybe he'd hit the ground harder than he thought.

'Only a partial. DGX or maybe DCX . . . one? I think there was maybe a nine in there. Are you okay?'

Bailey ignored the question. 'That's good. That's good. Tell that to the cops.'

'What? Where are you going?'

'I can't be here right now. I've got to go.'

The man grabbed Bailey's arm around the elbow. 'Wait. Why? You can't leave. What's your name?'

'Sorry, mate.' Bailey brushed away his hand. 'I've really got to go.'

Before the man had a chance to respond, Bailey turned around and jogged off down the street, peering over his shoulder only once to make sure that he wasn't being followed.

His car was parked around the corner and he climbed in, starting the ignition as he fastened his seatbelt, ducking his head when he noticed the blue flashing lights of a police car in his side mirror. He waited for the cops to pass before he spun his wagon out onto the street, doing a U-turn so that he wouldn't need to drive past Abdo's building. At this time of night he would make it to Leichhardt in around twenty minutes.

He had another phone call to make on the way. Annie Brooks answered after two rings.

'Hello, stranger.'

'Annie. Sorry it's late.'

'What's wrong? You're panting like you've just run a marathon.'

Ordinarily, Bailey would have laughed at that. The thought of him finishing a marathon was ridiculous. He could barely walk two laps of Centennial Park.

'Jonny Abdo was killed tonight. Thrown from the balcony of his apartment block in Bankstown.'

'What? When did it happen?'

'About ten minutes ago. I came here to meet him.'

'You were there?'

Bailey ignored the question, focusing instead on the things she needed to know. 'He'd been threatened. Someone posted his personal details on social media. Address and all that. Some white supremacist group.'

'He was doxed.'

Bailey wasn't surprised that Annie knew about doxing.

'I think you should get here, Annie. It's a big story.'

'Please tell me you didn't see it happen.'

Bailey's silence answered the question.

'Jesus, Bailey. You okay?'

'I'm fine.'

He didn't want to think about it any more. He wanted the image of Jonny Abdo's mangled body to disappear from his mind.

'Have you given a statement to the police?'

'No.'

Bailey turned on his indicator and wound down his window to let some cool air in to his car.

'Are you driving?' Annie said. 'If you're a witness to what happened, the police are going to want to talk to you. Leaving the scene of a crime is not a good idea.'

'I know what I'm doing.'

'Okay.' Annie paused, waiting for Bailey to say something. When he didn't, she went again. 'Where are you going?'

'I'll text you Abdo's address. You should get moving. I'll talk to you later. I've got to go.'

'Bailey –'

He ended the call and clumsily typed Jonny Abdo's address into his phone while steering his car, sending it as a text message to Annie, before throwing his phone into the back seat. He didn't want to look at it any more. He didn't want to answer any more calls.

All he could think about was Sharon Dexter.

When he had last visited Dexter's house, she was still his girlfriend and she was still very much alive. He had been avoiding this moment for months. Now he didn't have a choice.

CHAPTER 32

Leichhardt was the type of suburb where young families lived. Mostly inside compact houses with white picket fences. The planes flew low over this part of Sydney but nobody seemed to complain about the noise because Leichhardt was a place that had everything. Good transport links. Shopping centres. Parks and playgrounds. Schools and churches. And enough Italian restaurants and cafés to have earned the nickname 'Little Italy'.

Bailey had spent so much time with Sharon Dexter during the year before she died that her little grey cottage had become a home they'd shared together. He liked Leichhardt. The people. The houses. The history. The suburb had a persona that made people feel welcome. Like they belonged. Sydney's infamous hipster eye-rollers didn't work behind bars and cafés in this part of town. Bailey could order a coffee from his favourite place on Norton Street and talk about rugby with the Azzurri-loving barista who remembered his name and cared about what he had to say. Leichhardt had started to feel like home in a way that he had never felt in Paddington, where he had owned a house for decades. In Paddington he had mostly known dysfunction. A place he had treated like a hotel during the decades he'd spent living in the Middle East and Europe, only returning home to visit his daughter. When he did finally move back to Sydney on a permanent basis he was a broken man and his house became a place where loneliness lingered. Where one-night stands were the only form of intimacy he knew. Where he would sit around listening to the same Stones records, drink himself to sleep and wake up with the carpet stuck to his cheek, ready to repeat the routine all over again.

That was before Sharon Dexter re-entered his life and gave him another good reason to get sober. Get his shit together. Be a better man. A better father. Someone who was capable of sharing days and nights with other people. Bailey and Dexter had been building something in Leichhardt that wasn't even close to being finished before it came tumbling down.

He parked his car a few doors up from Dexter's cottage and turned off the ignition, taking a moment to prepare himself for what was to come. To walk inside knowing that she wouldn't be there. That she wouldn't open the door after a late night chasing criminals, slide into bed beside him, wake him for a chat. Or a cuddle. He was always up for either.

Tap. Tap. Tap.

Ronnie was standing beside Bailey's car, knuckles knocking against the window, puffing on a cigar.

Bailey opened the door, climbing out. 'Mate.'

'How long you been sitting there?'

'Just arrived.'

'Sounded like a shit show in Bankstown,' Ronnie said. 'You all right?'

Bailey was anything but all right but it wasn't because he'd just seen Jonny Abdo fall out of the sky and land on the footpath in front of him. He was on edge because he was about to step inside his dead girlfriend's house for the first time since her death. The ending that he had been avoiding. The finality of loss. He never saw her body after she died. He didn't attend her funeral. He never got to say goodbye. The lawyer taking care of Dexter's estate had tried to contact him several times but he had always fobbed him off because he didn't want to know. Bailey still wanted to see Dexter in his dreams and converse with her in his head. As crazy as that would have sounded to others, he was hanging onto whatever tiny strands of her that he could find. If Bailey could still imagine Dexter's voice, see her face, then she was with him. Nobody could take her away.

'Bubba?'

'Yeah,' Bailey said, finally. 'Let's do it.'

He locked his car and walked towards Dexter's house without saying another word. He had so many questions for Ronnie but he would park them while he dealt with the warm rush of sadness that had come over him. Unclipping the latch on the gate, Bailey pushed it open, the squeaky hinge and the overgrown hedge another sign that this was a dead person's home.

Bailey still had Dexter's key and he slid it into the lock on the front door, leaning his head, briefly, against the wood, before turning the key and opening the door.

Ronnie coughed behind him and Bailey turned around to see the tall man bending down, stubbing his cigar into the garden bed next to the tessellated tiled pathway.

'Don't leave that there,' Bailey said.

'Okay, bubba.'

Taking a step inside, Bailey flicked on the light, illuminating the narrow hallway that led to the kitchen and the lounge room out back. He stopped, staring into the house, expecting to smell something that would remind him of Dexter. Her shampoo. That perfume she wore on the rare occasions she'd put it on. The scent of cigarette smoke when she'd had a bad day and stolen a puff. He couldn't smell anything other than the musty scent of a vacant home.

Bailey's boots clomped loudly on the floorboards as he walked down the hallway. He paused at the closed door to Dexter's bedroom, grabbing the handle, turning it a fraction before deciding that he wouldn't go in. Not yet.

'What do you think Walker was doing here?'

'Just give me a minute,' Bailey said.

Ronnie was keeping his distance. The two men had been in London together when Dexter was killed and now they were inside her home.

Bailey moved on from Dexter's bedroom and kept walking into the kitchen, flicking the switch for the downlights. Only two of them came on but it was bright enough to see. Dexter never needed much but the things she bought were nice. Like the matching black kettle and toaster and the trendy lamp shade that dangled above the kitchen table. Bailey had been with Dexter on the day she'd bought that lamp shade, wondering why the hell anyone would spend three hundred dollars on something like that. He remembered exactly how she'd responded when he'd questioned the purchase. How it had made him smile.

'How much money have you wasted on Rolling Stones records over the years?'

'I think *wasted* is a little harsh,' he'd said.

'Bailey, you own four copies of *Exile on Main Street*.'

He had never been much good at debating Dexter. Not that he'd cared about trying.

'Are you okay?'

Ronnie was standing beside Bailey in the kitchen.

'Yeah. Haven't been here in a while,' Bailey said. There wasn't much point in lying.

'Not a bad joint,' Ronnie said.

Bailey wasn't about to tell him that Dexter had left the house to him in her will. It didn't feel right. So he moved on to Ronnie's question from earlier.

'She was looking after the place.'

'What?'

'Walker. She and Dexter were mates. Hat told me she'd been looking in on the place from time to time.'

'Right.'

Ronnie walked past Bailey and found the switch for the lamp.

'Nice light.'

Bailey laughed to himself.

'Something funny?'

'No.' Bailey's frown wiped away the memory and he changed the subject. 'You said on the phone that Walker was here the night before she was murdered. How'd you know?'

'I've got ways and –'

'Ronnie.'

'Okay.' The CIA veteran smiled. 'A guy in the feds owed me a favour. Gave me the tracking data from Walker's phone. Mapped her last movements. Pings from cell towers, and all that.'

'I know how it works,' Bailey said. 'Is that all you got?'

'Unfortunately, yeah.'

'Some favour.'

Ronnie ignored the slight and turned his back on Bailey, walking around the room. Touching things, picking them up, putting them down. A small clock. A picture frame of Dexter as a much younger woman in uniform with a medal pinned to her chest.

'I couldn't get my hands on a copy of the investigation she was working on,' Ronnie said without looking at Bailey. 'And my guy was very cagey about it.'

'What do you think that means?'

'It means I'm not entirely sure Walker's colleagues knew much about what she was doing.'

Bailey didn't know what to make of what Ronnie was telling him and he also didn't like the fact that Ronnie was touching Dexter's things.

'Why do you think Walker was here so late the night before she was killed?'

'I don't know. Maybe she thought she'd find you here?' Ronnie looked away from Bailey, still touching things. 'Memories and all that. You told me yesterday you'd missed a meeting with her that night. Maybe she was trying to find you?'

'Doesn't make sense. She'd already rescheduled our meet for the following morning.'

Ronnie shrugged, dragging a chair across the floorboards, sitting down at the kitchen table. 'No idea then.'

Bailey joined him at the table, checking the time on the old G-Shock strapped to his wrist: 10.58 pm. He leaned forward, elbows on the table, closer to the bowl of fake plastic fruit that Dexter had thoughtfully positioned below the lamp.

'What the –'

There was something in the fruit bowl that shouldn't have been there, nestled in beside the fake lemons, apples and oranges. A small Star Wars figurine. R2-D2. Bailey picked up the miniature robot and held it up for Ronnie to see.

'Didn't know Dexter was into Star Wars,' Ronnie said.

'She wasn't.'

The figurine was small enough to fit in the palm of Bailey's hand and he was holding it up to the light, inspecting it from all sides, trying to figure out what the hell it was doing in Sharon Dexter's house.

'Give me a look,' Ronnie said.

Bailey tossed the figurine across the table and when it landed on the wood R2-D2's dome head popped off and a USB stick spilled out.

'Bingo.' Ronnie grabbed the USB, holding it out for Bailey to see. 'Clever girl.'

'Shit,' Bailey said.

'Shit indeed, bubba.'

'What do you think's on there?'

'Let's find out.'

CHAPTER 33

ANNIE

'Not a problem, thanks guys.' Annie was speaking to someone in a studio control room on the other side of the city. 'Have a good night.'

She had just finished her last live cross for the evening. The midnight national news update. Jonny Abdo's murder was the lead story and Annie and Fletch had to hang around for one last hit after already filing copy and photographs for the website, crossing into several earlier news programs and gathering interviews and footage for tomorrow night's *Inside Story*. The media was a hungry beast. Thanks to Bailey's tip-off, they had broken the news of Abdo's death and both Annie and Fletch were keen to own the coverage, no matter how late into the night. But a live cross into a three-minute news update felt like a stretch too far.

'I'm cooked,' Annie said. 'You okay, Fletch?'

'All good, Annie,' Fletch switched off the bright lights that had been shining on Annie for hours. 'Studio happy?'

'Yeah. Let's pack up and get out of here.'

Annie never complained about working late but she was tired and couldn't help worrying about leaving Louis at home by himself at this time of night.

'If you need to get moving, I can sort this.'

She pulled out her earpiece as Fletch unclipped the little microphone fastened to her shirt.

'No way, Fletch.'

Annie and Fletch had worked in the field so often during the summer that they'd developed a rapid pack-up routine. They could have tripods, stills and video cameras, light stands and sound equipment packed and stacked on Fletch's portable stand within minutes. There wasn't any satellite equipment to pack away because high-speed broadband had allowed them to beam into the studio via a bunch of SIM cards attached to the camera.

'Seven minutes,' Fletch said, smiling and looking at his watch. 'I reckon that's a new record.'

Beep! Beep!

'Fake news, dickheads!'

Annie gave a sarcastic wave to a guy who was giving them the two-finger salute out the window of an old tradie's ute.

'Another fan, hey, Fletch?'

'They love us round here.'

The media had been copping a bad rap in recent years and the car horns and abuse had become an unfortunate part of working in the field.

'Where'd you park?'

Annie pointed down the street. 'Just around the corner. You?'

'Other way. You right to –'

'I'm a big girl, Fletch.'

The cameraman laughed and held out his hand for a fist-bump. 'Good show.'

'Story's got legs.' Annie tapped Fletcher's knuckles. 'Bill will want us chasing early tomorrow, so get some rest.'

'Talk to ya later.'

Fletch flipped his trolley onto its wheels and headed up the street, away from the crime scene that had been established on the footpath out front of the building where Jonny Abdo had earlier plummeted to his death. Police tape had been used to cordon off the area and a forensics team was still wandering around, taking notes, measuring the distance of Abdo's fall to support the theory that he had been thrown from a balcony on the tenth floor.

'Any updates, Greg?'

Detective Greg Palmer was tapping away at his phone as Annie sidled up to the police tape.

'Same as I told you earlier,' he said, the irritation of a long night hardening his voice. 'Looking for two suspects. We've got a good lead on their car. Doing our best here, Annie.'

'Sorry, Greg. Wasn't meaning to have a go. I'm done for the night. Thought I'd check in before I left. I'll be on this again tomorrow.'

'Okay.'

The look on Palmer's face made Annie think that he was regretting being short with her.

'Mind if I check in with you in the morning?'

'Text me. No guarantees I'll come back.'

'Understood.'

'Annie?'

She had already started walking away when Palmer stopped her.

'Yeah?'

'The killer or killers were inside Abdo's apartment, we know that for sure.'

'How?'

Palmer hesitated, like he hadn't yet made up his mind about what he was about to say.

'Greg?'

Annie took a few steps towards him so that he could speak without anyone listening in.

'Background only. Okay?'

Annie nodded.

'We found a swastika spray-painted on the wall.'

'What the hell's going on in this city?'

'Fuck knows,' Palmer said, noticing a woman in a hazmat suit staring at him. 'I'd better get back to it.'

Annie also took the forensics lady's goggling eyes as a cue to move on but before turning to walk away Annie looked up one more time at the building. At least a half-dozen people were hanging over balcony railings, staring down at the crime scene, probably wondering what Abdo had done to deserve to die. Annie knew something about the motive that the residents didn't: that Jonny Abdo may not have done anything to provoke someone to want to kill him. He may have been murdered simply for the colour of his skin.

The footpath was getting darker as Annie walked up the side street where she had parked her car. She made it about one hundred metres from the corner when she became aware of the fact that she wasn't alone. Someone was walking about twenty paces behind her.

Casually turning her head while her legs kept moving, she saw the dark silhouette of a man. She hadn't noticed him earlier when she was walking under the bright lights of the main road, but she noticed him now. The hum of the traffic no longer disguising the scratchy sounds of rubber soles on cement. Footsteps getting closer. Gathering pace.

Quickening her stride, Annie fumbled inside her bag for her keys. Her four-wheel drive was so close that she could see the moon bouncing off the roof. She pressed the button to unlock the doors and the lights flashed on. Stepping between two parked cars, Annie walked onto the road so that she could quickly jump in the driver's seat, lock the doors.

She altered her grip on her keys, sliding a single key through her fingers, making a fist so the little piece of metal was pointing like a knife. The closest thing she could muster to a weapon.

The footsteps followed. Closer. Louder. Almost running.

'Excuse me?'

Annie wrenched open the door but it was too late. The man was beside her.

'I think you dropped this.'

A young guy in a tracksuit was holding Annie's notebook out to her, a polite smile on his face.

'Oh, thanks, thank you.'

Annie didn't realise that she had been holding her breath and her words came out fast, startling the man. She loosened her grip on her keys, relieved that she hadn't just punched a stranger in the eye with her makeshift weapon.

'You okay, lady?'

Annie took the notebook, offering an awkward smile. 'Yeah, yeah. Sorry. It's just late and you . . . you gave me a fright.'

'No worries,' he said, walking away. 'Have a good one.'

Annie climbed in the car and threw her notebook and bag on the passenger seat, locking the doors. All she wanted to do was get home, check on her son and climb into bed.

It was too late to call Louis but Annie had exchanged messages with him about half an hour earlier when he'd said he was going to sleep. With school not being back, she'd been worried that he may have snuck out to meet some of his more troublesome friends, rather than stay home to play computer games like he'd said he would. In around half an hour she'd know.

There wasn't much traffic on the road so the drive back to Paddington was relatively painless. The air conditioning in the car felt cool against Annie's armpits and neck, making her uncomfortably aware of how much the humidity had made her sweat during the walk to her four-wheel drive. She had a mild headache which she put down to the long day, drinking from the bottle of water that she kept in the door of her four-wheel drive.

By the time she turned into her street it was almost 1 am. Most other people were already tucked up for the night and she couldn't find a car spot out front of her house. She eventually found one big enough for her four-wheel drive a couple of hundred metres up the street. She killed the engine, taking a moment to see whether there was anyone else around. Grabbing her notebook and bag, she climbed out, locking the doors. Even though she was the only person on the footpath, Annie's newfound paranoia made her jog the short distance to her house. By the time she arrived out front she was feeling quite stupid, shaking her head and laughing.

She pushed open her front gate, triggering the sensor lamp on her porch, igniting the path to her door in a dim yellow light. She only made it two steps along the path before something forced her to stop. Something that shouldn't have been there. Something frightening.

Words.

Three words.

Sprayed in red paint across the front of her house. So big they stretched from the eaves, across rendered bricks, the window, all the way to the door.

LYING

JEW

BITCH

'Oh my god.'

Annie fumbled with her keys as she sprinted up her front steps, almost falling against the door, struggling to stop shaking long enough to get the key in the lock.

'Louis!'

She yelled her son's name the second she opened the door, running up the stairs to his bedroom.

'Louis!'

She pushed open his door and her son was sitting upright in the darkness.

'What the fuck, Mum?'

He was rubbing his eyes, staring blankly at the crazed woman who had just flicked on the light and landed on his bed.

'Are you okay?'

'I'm fine,' he said. 'What's happened?'

She reached forward and put an arm around her son, pulling him close, kissing the top of his head.

'Did you hear anyone outside? Has anyone been here?'

'No. Why?' He was wide awake now and sounding annoyed. 'What's the time?'

'One o'clock. Get up, Louis. We're not staying here tonight. Get up!'

'What's happened?'

Annie stood up, placing a hand on her son's shoulder, pointing her finger. 'We need to go. Pack a bag with some clothes for tomorrow.'

'Why? Is it Dad?'

The mention of her ex-husband made Annie suddenly aware of the fact that she needed to hit pause and explain to her son what was happening. He couldn't think that this had anything to do with his father. The man who had beaten her. Barron had been released from prison not so long ago and he wasn't permitted anywhere near Annie or their son.

'I'm sorry, Louis. I'm sorry. This has nothing to do with your father. I don't even know where he is. Queensland, I think. Away from here.'

She was rambling.

'Then what is it? Why do we have to go?'

'Someone has vandalised the front of our house. Graffiti. It's got something to do with the story I've been covering. We just shouldn't stay here tonight. It may not be safe.'

Louis and his mother were tight. As tight as a mother and a teenage boy could be.

'Okay, Mum. But where are we going?'

'Somewhere close.'

Annie picked up her bag from the floor, rummaging around until she found her phone, searching for the name of someone she knew she could trust.

He answered after two rings.

'Annie?'

Bailey sounded wide awake, like he was up working.

'Something's happened. Can Louis and I stay with you tonight?'

'Are you okay?'

'I'll explain when I see you.'

'Want me to come get you?'

'No. See you in five.'

CHAPTER 34

Bailey was waiting on his front porch when Annie and Louis walked through the gate.

'Give me that.'

He took her bag, catching her eyes, eager to know what had happened. Not wanting to ask the question in front of her son.

'Sorry about this,' Annie said.

'Are you okay?'

'Yeah.'

'G'day, Louis.'

Bailey held out his hand to the teenager he had seen before but had never properly met.

'Hi, Mr Bailey.'

'Just call me Bailey,' he said, winking at Louis, shaking hands. 'The mister makes me feel like a school teacher.'

Louis returned a tired laugh and Bailey could see by the kid's puffy eyes that he was keen to go back to sleep. 'Come inside. I've thrown some clean sheets on the bed in the spare room.'

Bailey pushed open the front door and they could see Ronnie sitting in the kitchen down the end of the hallway with the blue light of a computer screen on his face. He waved his hand, clearly not interested in the guests.

'Ronnie's helping me with some research,' Bailey said, noticing Annie staring at the big guy. 'Working late.'

'Is it connected to –'

'Mum,' Louis said, 'can we go inside?'

Relieved by the kid's interruption, Bailey led them down the hallway, pushing open the door to his spare room and placing Annie's bag on the bed.

'Is that Ronnie's stuff?'

Annie was pointing at a duffle bag and a pile of clothes in the corner.

'Don't worry about him. He's on the couch tonight.'

Annie frowned, embarrassed. 'Let me get Louis sorted and I'll come out.'

Bailey left the mother and son alone and returned to the kitchen where Ronnie was now standing by the sink, filling the kettle.

'There's shitloads of files here, bubba. Whatever Walker was thinking, looks like she dumped everything she had in a hurry. Not sure we're even going to put a dent in it tonight. Could take days or weeks to piece it all together.' Ronnie was now spooning coffee into Bailey's plunger. 'And what's she doing here, again?' He lowered his voice. 'Sensitive material here. You sure you want a TV reporter sticking her beak in?'

Bailey stepped closer to Ronnie so that he could keep his voice low. 'She asked for my help. I wasn't going to leave her hanging. Anyway, I trust her and I –'

'You guys done talking about me?'

The two men hadn't noticed Annie walk into the kitchen and she was standing beside the fridge, arms folded, half a smirk on her face.

Ronnie coughed. 'Annie.'

'Ronnie.'

'Thanks for the room.'

'Not a problem.'

'How's Louis?' Bailey said.

'A little rattled. I'll go back and check on him in a sec. You sure this is okay?'

'Of course, it's fine. Now, what happened?'

'Someone sprayed racist graffiti across the front of my house. Must have seen me on air tonight or read my story online about Abdo.'

Annie stopped talking and looked over her shoulder, stepping back into the hall to see that her son hadn't come out of the room.

'That cop I told you about, he was in Bankstown. Told me off the record that someone drew a swastika on the wall of Jonny Abdo's apartment. Presumably whoever killed him,' she said, lowering her voice to a whisper, speaking quickly. 'Lam. Augustus Strong. Now Abdo. Hell knows what's coming next.'

'What'd it say?'

'What?'

'The graffiti. What'd it say?'

'At my place?'

'Yeah.'

'Lying Jew Bitch.'

'Nice,' Bailey said, clearly meaning the opposite. 'Notice anything else? Sign of a break-in?'

The kettle started rumbling and Ronnie lifted it from its cradle, pouring the boiling water into the plunger, steam billowing out the sides. 'Want a cup, Annie?'

'Bit late for me. Got anything herbal?'

Ronnie stopped pouring for a moment, forcing a smile, probably wondering how he'd suddenly become the waiter. 'I'll check.'

Bailey pointed at the pantry, amused. 'I think there's some chamomile or something back there.'

'Thanks.'

'What have you done about the graffiti?' Bailey said, glancing at the USB stick and the two laptop computers shining light on his kitchen table. He didn't care for a visit from the police tonight. State or feds. 'We're going through some sensitive stuff here and, well –'

'I think whoever did it was just trying to intimidate me,' Annie said. 'I called that detective on the way over here, told him I won't make a statement tonight. That Louis and I had somewhere else to stay.'

'Did you –'

'Don't worry, I didn't say we were coming here,' Annie said, placing a hand on Bailey's forearm, giving it a squeeze. 'The detective said he'd send some uniforms around to check out my place, make sure there isn't anyone hanging around who doesn't belong. I'm going to meet him there tomorrow at seven when we've both had some sleep. Bill's going to meet us there too. With a camera.'

'I bet he is.'

Annie tilted her head to the side, frowning. 'Don't be like that. This is part of the story. Anyway, I want it put on the record. People need to see this stuff. Bill said he'll have someone clean it off as soon as it's been captured in daylight.'

Ronnie handed Annie a steaming cup of tea without mentioning the blend. 'It's hot.'

'Thanks.' Annie took a whiff, smirking at Bailey. 'Ginger and lemon, I'm impressed.'

'You and me both.'

Ronnie carried the plunger to the table where there were already two cups waiting to be filled. He filled them both and sat down, eyes back on the screen.

'So what are you guys looking at?' Annie wagged her finger at the computers. 'Or are you going to play secret squirrels on me?'

'That's up to him,' Ronnie said without looking up.

'What do you say, Bailey? Going to loop me in?'

Bailey joined Ronnie at the table, sitting down in front of the other laptop screen, in no rush to answer. 'Take a seat.' He gestured to one of the empty chairs, picking up his coffee, taking a sip, nodding his chin at the big guy. 'That's good.'

Ronnie didn't care about the coffee and he was getting agitated. 'Bubba, this isn't a –'

'Settle down, mate. We're all pushing in the same direction here.'

'Suit yourself,' Ronnie grumbled.

Annie sat there, patiently waiting for Bailey to tell her what he and a supposedly retired CIA agent were working on in his kitchen in the middle of the night. It had to be something.

'You mentioned three names earlier.'

'Abdo, Strong and Lam.'

'You need to add one,' Bailey said. 'Harriet Walker.'

'What about her?'

'I've gotten hold of the investigation she was running into

far right nationalist and white supremacist groups in Australia. Her files.'

'How did you –'

'Doesn't matter.'

Annie tried a different tack. 'You mentioned her investigation at dinner the other night. You're now certain that's why she was killed?'

'Yes.'

It was the first time Bailey had answered the question so succinctly.

The USB stick that Walker had planted at Dexter's house contained a link and a password for a secure online portal that appeared to have everything relating to her investigation. Bailey had already seen enough to lead him to think that Walker was close to blowing the lid on a highly organised and sophisticated extremist network that had money, power and, more recently, a shipment of high-powered military assault weapons.

'Hat had been tracing extremists through the internet,' Bailey said. 'Connecting them to groups here and overseas, often by their white nationalist rhetoric and the handles they used in Facebook discussions and on messaging boards on the dark web.'

'8chan?'

'Yeah.'

Bailey wasn't surprised that Annie knew about the dark web. Messaging boards like 8chan had supposedly been created to protect free speech but instead they had become safe havens for paedophiles, racists and criminals to share, sell, recruit and roam. The 8chan site was also where manifestos and live stream videos of violence had been shared by the white supremacists responsible for massacres in Christchurch and El Paso.

'There are plenty of groups named here. Some I know. Some I've never heard of before.'

'Like who?'

Bailey was driving his laptop with a mouse and he was pushing it around, clicking and searching for something.

'Come here.' He waved for Annie to come closer. 'I'll show you.'

Annie placed her hot tea on the table and leaned in beside Bailey, close enough so that he could smell the perfume on her neck.

'Meet the Lucky Lads,' he said, tapping his screen. 'There are literally hundreds of pages like these. Screenshots of websites, images and conversations.'

They were looking at a screenshot of the Lucky Lads' Facebook page, which was adorned with photographs from inside what appeared to be the group's clubhouse but looked more like a garage gym because of the weight-lifting equipment, boxing bags and tattooed men in singlets. The walls were adorned with union jacks and confederate flags, along with a poster of a black eagle perched on a swastika.

'Who are these guys?' Annie said.

'Your garden variety white nationalists. A reporter from *The Journal* wrote a story not long ago, tracing the Lucky Lads to a house in Concord where they apparently meet on Thursday nights. Probably still do.' Bailey clicked his mouse a few more times, bringing up a page that showed a conversation involving the Lucky Lads and a photograph of a bunch of guys with fashy haircuts. 'These groups all talk to each other, it seems. Attend each other's gatherings. Recognise anyone?'

'Benny Hunter.' Annie spotted him instantly. 'You think the Lucky Lads are an offshoot of Hunter's group?'

'Don't know,' Bailey said. 'Ronnie and I've been sifting through materials relating to at least a dozen or so groups like the Lucky Lads and Hunter's Freedom Front and there are plenty of references that suggest they've been trying to organise themselves for a bigger, more united movement. And Benny Hunter's name keeps popping up.'

Bailey still hadn't told Annie what he'd discovered about Hunter's involvement in the murder of Augustus Strong. That Hunter had bribed and threatened the Roundtree sisters to tell the police that a group of Black men had beaten Strong to death on the footpath outside the 7-Eleven on George Street. Now was the time to share.

Leaning back and folding his arms, Bailey turned so that he could look Annie in the eyes. 'There's something else.'

'Bubba, not sure this is a good idea,' Ronnie said.

'She needs to know, Ronnie,' Bailey said, shaking his head. 'If these guys are orchestrating some kind of race war, then the truth needs to be out there very soon. We're racing against the clock now. We don't know what's coming next.'

'What are you guys talking about?' Annie said.

Bailey told her what really happened to Augustus Strong on George Street, only leaving out the fact that the Roundtree sisters were now staying with an old priest in Redfern. Although he trusted Annie, the fewer people who knew the whereabouts of the girls, the better.

'Jesus, Bailey. You really think Hunter's capable of that?'

'I do.'

'And what did you mean earlier by "race war"?'

Bailey clicked his mouse a few more times, turning the screen so that Annie had a better view. 'That's Donald Sampson.'

Bailey tapped the screen, pointing at the photograph of an old man in handcuffs being led out of a farmhouse by men and women in FBI jackets. 'One of America's most famous racist arseholes. He's been leading a group called The Dawning for many years. An offshoot of the Ku Klux Klan. He's been communicating with groups all over the world, including Benny Hunter. This guy's the real deal. Batshit crazy. He's been running military-style training camps, preparing his followers for some kind of armed uprising. And he sent a shipment of guns to Sydney.'

'How d'you know that?'

'We know,' Ronnie said.

'And you think Benny Hunter has the guns? And this other theory of yours about what happened to Strong, if that's true, why haven't you told the police?'

Annie was directing her questions at Bailey, judging him with her eyes, clearly wondering whether he was prioritising his story above the safety of the public.

Bailey stood up, his chair squeaking across his floorboards. 'Because an Australian Federal Police officer was murdered and we think the person, or people, responsible may be on the inside.'

'Federal police?'

'Yes.'

'How do –'

'And it's not just the feds.' Bailey was back clicking his mouse again. 'Ronnie and I've been at this for hours. From what I can see, Harriet Walker was close to blowing the lid on a network connected to money and power. We've got people boasting about politicians being paid off. We've got –'

'Mum!'

Bailey stopped talking at the sound of Louis's voice.

'I better check on him,' she said, already on her way.

The two men sat in silence while they waited for Annie to return. It didn't take long.

'Louis is pretty rattled,' she said, folding her arms like she was cold. 'It's late, guys. I think I need to go be with him.'

'No worries,' Bailey said. 'We'll keep it down out here. We're going to keep working. Try to piece all this together. Get some rest. We can talk more in the morning.'

Annie put a hand on Bailey's shoulder, giving it a squeeze. 'Thanks for letting us stay.'

Bailey touched her hand, catching her eye for a moment. 'Go get some sleep.'

'Night,' Ronnie said without looking up as Annie left them to it.

Bailey looked at his watch: 2.15 am. 'How're you feeling, Ronnie?'

'Fresh as a daisy.'

CHAPTER 35

Sunshine Inc.

The name was popping up all over the place in a collection of receipts and statements that Walker had grouped together in a sub-folder in the secure portal she'd used.

'Ronnie, I think I've got something here.'

'What is it?'

It was 5.30 am and the two bleary-eyed men had been reading through documents, scribbling down notes, trying to connect dots, for hours. Finally, a breakthrough.

'A money trail.'

Bailey remembered something else and grabbed his phone, searching for the bank statement he'd copied back at Liam Callaghan's house in Randwick.

'That customs guy, Callaghan. He'd been paying ridiculously low rent to a business called Sunshine Inc. I made a copy of his financials.' Bailey was speaking in an excited whisper. 'The same company's listed on an invoice for a shipment of Californian oranges. Can't be a coincidence. Walker was on to these guys. She was close,' Bailey said. 'And there's more. Political donations. Harriet had documents with "Sunshine Inc" listed on a register of Liberal Party donors and on a separate fundraising event for the Home Affairs Minister, Wayne McMahon.'

Ronnie poured himself the dregs from the latest brew of coffee. 'Did Walker discover who owns Sunshine Inc?'

'Can't see it. Not yet, anyway.'

'I think I've found something too. That –'

'Hold on.' Bailey sat bolt upright as a message flashed on his screen. 'A conversation's started.'

'What?' Ronnie stood up, placing his cup heavily on the table beside him, splashing coffee on yesterday's newspaper. He brought his laptop to the opposite side of the table so that he could see Bailey's screen. 'A conversation? Where?'

'A message board. I've had the one with the most recent traffic open for the last few hours.'

While Bailey was still talking, a series of photographs hit the screen. Abdo's dead body on the footpath. A swastika sprayed on the wall of the dead man's apartment. A picture of Annie's vandalised house. All posted by someone calling themselves Aussie Patriot.

'This is how they do it,' Ronnie said.

'Do what?'

'Posting it this way, they know it'll get out there. Reporters jump on this shit. Helps with the propaganda. It's what you people never understand. The headlines and stories you write. You do exactly what they want. Deliver messages.'

'I'm not up for one of your rants about the state versus the media.'

'You don't have to like it, but it's true.'

Bailey went to say something but another message appeared below the photographs, grabbing his attention in a way that not even the image of Abdo's dead body had before:

Brothers and sisters. We've been building towards this day. The race war has begun. Australia Day will be remembered as the day we started to take our country back.

'Who the hell's Wise Elder?' Ronnie said.

Wise Elder posted again:

Remember the Fourteen Words.

'How many people are seeing this?'

'You only know someone's there when they post something. These dark web boards are virtually untraceable. They are . . .'

Ronnie stopped talking because Wise Elder had just written something else:

We must secure the existence of our people and the future for white children.

'Australia Day. The fourteen words. This is a rallying cry, Ronnie. Something's going to happen. Today.'

'Hang on.' Ronnie sat down, spinning his laptop so that Bailey could see, keeping one eye on Bailey's screen in case another message appeared. 'I've got something here.'

'What is it?'

'That video you said was deleted from your phone the day the feds raided your house. I think I've found it.'

'Show me.'

Bailey watched as Ronnie opened a '.mov' file on his screen and a video popped up, shaped like a rectangle. Filmed on a mobile phone. It showed the inside of the warehouse before Augustus Strong had taken the stage, the shaky footage capturing the motley crew of people who had paid for a seat that night.

The video lasted for just over a minute and the two men watched in silence all the way to the end.

'Anything?' Ronnie said.

'Play it again.'

Bailey knew there must have been something incriminating in the footage. There had to be. Why else had Harding deleted it?

'Focus on the people. The faces.'

Bailey rubbed his eyes, trying to focus as he watched the video for a second time. He caught sight of Benny Hunter and his crew but there wasn't much else.

'Fuck it.' Bailey bashed his fist on the table. 'There's got to be something. Again.'

The video started for a third time and Bailey was staring so hard at the screen that for a split second his vision went blurry.

'There!'

'What is it?'

'Give it to me.' Bailey grabbed hold of the laptop and used the keyboard to scroll back a few seconds. 'You're kidding me. What the hell's he doing there?'

'Who?'

'That guy.' Bailey leaned forward, tapping the screen on a freeze frame of Hunter with his arm around a guy that Bailey recognised. Hunter had the man in a headlock, tapping his cheek, speaking into his ear. Smiling. 'The young bloke with Hunter. Russell. His name's Russell Ratcliffe. He lives in my bloody street.'

'He's a member of Hunter's Freedom Front?'

'No idea.' Bailey pushed back his chair, standing up, rubbing his eyes. He looked at his watch: 5.46 am. 'What do we do? Wait until sunrise then bang on their door?'

'We're not waiting for the sun.'

Before Bailey had a chance to respond, Ronnie was charging up the hallway towards the front door. Bailey grabbed his keys and set off after him, doing his best to close the front door quietly behind them so they didn't wake Annie and Louis.

'Which house?' Ronnie was speaking over his shoulder because Bailey still hadn't caught up. 'Which house, bubba?'

'Wait!' Bailey grabbed Ronnie's arm, making him stop. 'Hang on a second, would you? We can't just go charging into my neighbour's house demanding to speak to their son.'

'Why?'

'What's the game plan? What do we say?'

Ronnie was almost a foot taller than Bailey and he was looking down, scowling. 'I know exactly what I'm going to say. I'm going to tell them to get their kid out of bed so he can tell us everything he knows about Benny Hunter and why they look like best pals.'

Bailey had given himself a chance to think and he knew that Ronnie was right. The most recent post they'd read about Australia Day was disturbing and if there really was something coming – another act of violence – then they didn't have much time.

'Okay. Okay.'

They only needed to walk another twenty or so paces before Bailey pushed open a wrought-iron gate, leading Ronnie past the tall hedge that separated the Ratcliffes' townhouse from the street, up the steps to their front door. Ronnie pressed his finger on the doorbell, holding it down, a loud buzzing noise echoing inside and outside too.

'I think that's probably long enough,' Bailey said after the bell had been ringing for at least ten seconds. 'I'm pretty sure they know we're out here.'

The sound of footsteps and a light coming on inside the house confirmed it.

The door flung open and Jenny Ratcliffe appeared, dressing gown pulled tight across her chest, squinting at the lamplight on the porch, a startled look on her face.

'John?' Jenny's panic turned to confusion at the sight of Bailey standing there with a large man beside him. 'What are you doing here? Something wrong?'

'Hi, Jenny. Sorry to disturb.'

Bailey did his best to sound polite.

'Who is it, Jenny?'

Bryce Ratcliffe's voice sounded from the second floor, followed by footsteps as he made his way down the stairs in a pair of boxer shorts and singlet.

'It's, it's our neighbour. John. John Bailey and . . .'

Before Jenny had finished her sentence her husband appeared beside her at the door. 'Bailey? What are you doing here?'

'Sorry, mate,' Bailey said. 'We're wondering if we can come in for a minute. Need a quiet word.'

'What about? What's happened?'

Ronnie cleared his throat. 'Where's Russell?'

'What?' Bryce said. 'What's this got to do with our son? Has something happened? And who are you?'

'I'm Ronnie.'

Bailey held out his arm, blocking Ronnie from getting any closer. 'Ronnie Johnson. He's an old friend of mine and he's been helping me with a story that I've been working on. An investigation. It's why we're here. I think Russell may have gotten himself into some trouble. Is he here? I'm so sorry about the time. Bloody early, I know.'

'It's not even six in the morning,' Bryce said, clearly miffed. 'Couldn't this have waited until a more reasonable hour?'

'Where's your son?' Ronnie asked again.

'He's not here,' Bryce said, gripping the door with his hand. 'Are you going to tell me what this is about?'

'Where is he?'

Ronnie was answering questions with questions, impervious to the concerned looks on the faces of the parents inside the house.

'Staying with a friend. He's twenty years old, not a boy any more,' Bryce said, looking at Bailey. 'Why do you want to speak with him?'

Ronnie went to say something but Bailey cut him off. 'I'll explain, Bryce. Honestly. If you'd just let us come in for a few minutes, there's something you need to know.'

Bryce's shoulders slumped and he loosened his grip on the door, opening it a fraction wider, stealing a look at his wife, who was standing behind him hugging her dressing gown. 'Okay. But please be quiet. We'll go into the kitchen. Our daughter's asleep upstairs.'

The two unwelcome guests followed the Ratcliffes down the hall and into a lounge area that adjoined the kitchen. Bailey could see the backyard through a large bay window, the moonlight shining on a neat garden, lawn and small wooden shed. The Ratcliffes' block must have been two or three times the size of Bailey's and he imagined that his little townhouse would have probably fitted on their back lawn.

Bryce switched on the light, killing the view outside, gesturing to a flower-patterned sofa. 'Take a seat.'

Bailey and Ronnie sat down as instructed, waiting for the

Ratcliffes to do the same on the identical sofa on the other side of a glass coffee table.

'So what's so bloody important that you felt the need to ring my doorbell at stupid o'clock?'

Bryce hadn't softened his stance during the short walk from the front to the back of his house and he clearly wasn't about to offer them a cup of tea and a biscuit.

Bailey cleared his throat, tapping Ronnie's leg to let him know that he'd kick things off. 'There's no easy way to tell you this. Russell's been hanging around with some pretty unsavoury characters.' Bailey paused, knowing he was dancing around the words that he needed to say. 'White supremacists. Neo-Nazis. A group that may be responsible for the recent spate of racially motivated violence.'

'What?' Jenny gasped, her right hand touching her lips. 'Russell isn't involved in anything like that!'

'I'm sorry, I know this is difficult to hear,' Bailey said, 'but it's true. We need your help to find him because we have reason to believe more violence is being planned. Some kind of attack. We don't know. Russell may be able to help us. He may know things.'

'No. No. You've got this wrong,' Jenny said, looking at her husband, who was sitting beside her in stony silence. 'Russell wouldn't be involved with those people.'

'I know this is hard, Jenny.' Bailey was trying his best to persist with a diplomatic approach that would have been irking Ronnie. 'We're not guessing here. We have footage of Russell with a guy called Benny Hunter. They don't just know each other, they're friends. You may have heard of Hunter. He's been in the news. He's a white supremacist who leads a group called the Freedom Front. Russell was with Hunter earlier in the week. Did you know that Russell went to see Augustus Strong speak?'

Jenny was shaking her head, not wanting to believe what she was being told. 'No. No. Not my Russell.'

Bryce put his hand on his wife's leg and left it there. 'Jenny. Jenny, wait.' He was shaking his head. 'We knew that Russell had changed. We knew it, Jenny. We did.'

'No, Bryce. Don't.'

Jenny started sobbing.

'Where's Russell, Bryce?' Ronnie joined the conversation. 'Clearly you know something and, being honest with you, I'm losing patience. Fast.'

'What is it exactly you do, Mr Johnson?' Bryce said, defensively.

'This and that.'

'Ronnie and I are old friends,' Bailey said, trying to deflect attention away from any more questions about Ronnie's curriculum vitae. 'He's had a lot of experience with situations like this in his old job in . . . in law enforcement.'

'As the man said, we have good reason to believe something violent's about to happen,' Ronnie said. 'It's time for you to tell us everything you know about your son.'

'What d'you mean by something violent?' Bryce said.

'That's a question we can't answer because it hasn't happened yet.' Ronnie was getting more blunt with every second that passed. 'A Black man was murdered in Bankstown last night. Another kid's in a coma after he was bashed at the pub up the street. More violence is coming. Something bigger. Worse.'

Bryce was glaring at Ronnie. 'Like what?'

'I'm not going to sit here speculating with you, pal,' Ronnie said. 'You saw what that white supremacist maniac did in

Christchurch. Fifty-one people dead. The Walmart massacre in El Paso. Twenty-three dead. You getting it?'

Bailey liked how Ronnie recited precise numbers. Not rounding up. Not rounding down. The exact numbers of people who died. Like every victim counted.

'You don't seriously think that –'

'We don't know anything for sure,' Bailey cut in. 'All we know is these people have the capability to do something very bad.' He was thinking about the guns. 'That's why we need your help. Why we need to find Russell. He may know things. He may not. But right now he's a link we need to find.'

Jenny stood up, almost shaking. 'Bryce, can I have a word? In the kitchen?'

'Sit down, Jenny,' Ronnie said. 'No one's going anywhere. You're hiding something. I can see that. Russell may not have done anything wrong. He may be the good boy you think he is. But it looks to me like you're protecting him. Now answer the man's damned question. Where the hell's your son?'

Jenny sighed, sitting back down. Shaking. 'We haven't seen or spoken to Russell in days, okay? He took off from our holiday house at Blueys. Said he was coming back to Sydney. We don't know what he's been doing. Who he's with.'

'Darling, we need to tell them.' Bryce let out a long breath, reaching for his wife's hand, clasping their fingers together. 'We need to tell them what we found.'

Jenny was nodding her head, resigned to what was about to happen, needing a moment to prepare. She cleared her throat, laughing nervously, knowing there was no humour to be found. 'Like any mother, I do my fair share of snooping around. Cleaning up, mostly. Gathering his dirty clothes, replacing them with clean ones. That's when I might sometimes take a look. See what my boy's been doing in his room.'

'And?' Bailey said.

'The bloody internet. YouTube. Russell would sit around all day and night watching videos.'

'What kind of videos?'

'I don't know . . . videos about conspiracy theories. Things like that. You know how young people are these days. They hate authority. Questioning everything and anything.'

Jenny was sounding like she was already making excuses for her son.

'Tell us more about these videos, Jenny,' Bailey said. 'What was he watching?'

'I can't believe this stuff's allowed to stay up there. They sound so convincing. People with their own channels. People who ramble about philosophy. Immigration. History. War. Russell watched hours of this stuff. Hours and hours. And I also found a book.'

'What book, Jenny?'

'Darling, tell them,' Bryce said, calmly.

'The book's called *The Great Replacement*,' she said. 'Written by someone called Camus.'

'Renaud Camus.'

Bailey had learned all about Camus during his research about where far right extremists get their inspiration.

'Yes. A Frenchman,' Jenny said. 'I started reading the book. It was quite confronting. John, you know him. Who is he?'

'Renaud Camus is a conspiracy theorist who believes the white European population is being replaced by people from the Middle East and Africa. He's often cited as an inspiration for far right nationalist groups. And terrorists.'

Bryce's face almost matched the white wall behind him. 'There's more. Jenny, tell them.'

'Jenny?' Bailey said. 'What else did you find?'

'Printouts of manifestos. The one by that Australian man in Christchurch. The boy in Texas you mentioned.' Her voice was cracking as she held back tears, like sharing this information had made her realise how potentially dangerous her child had become. 'We were going to talk to him. We were –'

'What? You never confronted him?' Ronnie didn't bother hiding the fact that he was judging them. Whether it was through love or weakness, Jenny and Bryce had failed in a basic duty to society. Protect one another. Do everything within your power to stop bad things from happening. Protect good people from getting hurt. For a guy like Ronnie Johnson, they'd just crossed a line. 'How long ago did you find this stuff?'

'A few weeks, it wasn't long,' Bryce said. 'But it's not like we did nothing, either.'

'What'd you do, Bryce?' Ronnie didn't bother trying to conceal the contempt in his voice.

'I told an old acquaintance of mine. Someone in the Australian Federal Police. He said he'd talk to Russell, find out whether he was just getting a little carried away, or whether there was really something for us to worry about.'

A name was blaring in Bailey's mind, but he had to be sure. 'What was the name of the policeman?'

'Commander Dominic Harding. We went to school together. He was the year below me. I asked around and we had mutual friends. Someone put us in touch and he agreed to have a quiet word with Russell. They met a couple of weeks ago and Commander Harding called me to tell me there wasn't anything to worry about. That Russell was just a young man still learning about the world, discovering himself.'

'Did he now?' Bailey said.

Harding. The guy was everywhere. In everything.

'Okay, Bailey. We need to move.' Ronnie knuckle-tapped the table. 'Bryce. Jenny. You need to tell us right now if you have any idea about your son's whereabouts. If I learn you've omitted anything, I won't believe it was an accident. And when I come back here you're going to see a side of me that you can't imagine possible for someone who has ever worked in the law.'

Even Bailey was shaken by Ronnie's words and Bryce looked like he was about to wet himself.

'There's one more thing,' Bryce said, sheepishly.

'Get it out, Bryce,' Ronnie growled.

'Not long after we found those manifestos, I put one of our old phones in the glove box of Russell's car so I could track his movements.'

'You what?' Jenny said to her husband, obviously unaware.

'For chrissakes, Jenny!' Bryce leapt to his feet, squeezing his eyes tightly shut, placing his hands on his head, rubbing his temples. Taking a moment. He turned to look at his wife, who appeared to have shrunk in size on the sofa. 'I wanted to know where our son was disappearing to late at night. I had to know. For him. For us. I'm his bloody father.' He took a breath, calming down. 'I activated a tracking program. Just like the one in Russell's phone when he was at school.'

'Is the phone still active, Bryce?' Bailey asked.

'No. The battery died a week or so ago.'

Ronnie breathed out hard. 'You were monitoring his movements. Where'd he go?'

'Nowhere that made any sense to me.'

'Was there an address where he visited more than once?' Ronnie said. 'I need you to think, Bryce. Think hard.'

'There was one place. A house.'

'Where, Bryce? Where was the house?'

Ronnie got to his feet, pulling a small notepad and pen from the inside pocket of his jacket. Slamming it down on the coffee table.

'Write it down.'

CHAPTER 36

A band of dark grey clouds had transformed the morning, drawing a curtain on the moon and everything else up there, turning Sydney black. The sun would be rising soon but it wasn't going to get a look-in today because an almighty storm was gathering.

No rain yet. Not a drop.

But the air was hot and thick with moisture and the sky was shimmering with electric light. The change was coming. Bailey could hear it whistling in his ears, feel it in his bones.

'I'm driving.'

'Fine,' Ronnie said, stopping on the footpath beside his Prius. 'I just need to grab something from the rental.'

Ronnie popped open the boot, grabbing a black bag with one arm, his bicep bulging with the weight.

'What's in there?'

'Things we might need.'

Ronnie slammed the boot closed, locking the car, and resumed walking along the footpath towards Bailey's wagon, not wanting to engage in a conversation about the contents of his bag. Bailey wasn't much interested either. He knew that Ronnie had a gun in there. Or guns. He also knew that Ronnie knew how to use them. They were about to knock on the door of a house that was connected to a white supremacist group and a shipment of automatic weapons. Turning up empty-handed would have been a bad idea.

'Wait in the car,' Bailey said, unlocking Ronnie's door. 'I need to go inside.'

'Why?'

Bailey left Ronnie's question on the footpath and slipped inside the house, quietly opening the door to the room where Annie was sleeping alongside her son.

'Pssst. Pssst. Annie?' he whispered. 'Annie, you awake?'

A shadow sat up in bed. 'What is it?'

'I need to talk to you.'

Bailey stepped back from the door and walked into his kitchen where Campo was doing paces around the table, whimpering at the flashes in the sky, spooked by the storm.

'Come here, mate.' Bailey got down on one knee, patting his dog on the head, rubbing her ears. 'It's all right, you sook.'

'Something wrong with Campo?'

Annie was standing behind him, pulling back her hair.

'Doesn't like storms. There's a big one coming,' Bailey said, getting to his feet. 'That's not why I needed you.'

'What is it?'

'Ronnie and I have got a line on a bloke who's been running with Benny Hunter's crew. We think they're planning something today.' Bailey could see that Annie was about to ask him a question and he held up his hand. 'I don't have time to explain. I may need you to call that cop friend of yours. Just not yet. Not until we know what we're dealing with. I don't want to risk these guys finding out we're coming. I'll let you know.'

'This doesn't sound like a good plan, Bailey. Not at all.'

'We know what we're doing.'

'Do you?' Annie put her hand on Bailey's arm, squeezing it, making sure she had his attention. 'These people are dangerous, Bailey. You know that . . . and you're not a cop.'

'It's okay. I've got Ronnie.'

'Bailey –'

He started walking towards the front door. 'Remember, don't call him until I say so. And Annie?'

'Yeah?'

'Let Campo sleep in the room with you, would you?'

On any normal day, she would have laughed. 'It's just gone six. I'm not going back to bed. I'll stay up with her.'

'Thanks.'

Ronnie was on the phone when Bailey climbed into the driver's seat beside him.

'I know it's early but I'm cleaning up your fucking mess.'

Whoever was on the other end clearly didn't appreciate the 6 am phone call. By the way Ronnie was speaking, he didn't care.

'That's right. The address in Bronte I just gave you. I want to know who lives there. I don't care how you get it. I need it in ten.'

Ronnie hung up, slipping his phone into the inside pocket of his jacket.

'Who was that?' Bailey said, turning the key and pumping the accelerator.

'A friend.'

'Didn't sound like one.'

'Yeah, well. I was being liberal with the reference. Guy's an arsehole and he owes me.'

Bailey steered his wagon into the street. He had glimpsed the address on the slip of paper that Bryce Ratcliffe had handed Ronnie earlier and he knew exactly where they were headed. A house on the hill above Bronte Beach. Less than ten minutes' drive.

'Why'd you need to go back inside?'

'Wanted to check on the dog. Doesn't like storms.'

Ronnie laughed like he didn't think Bailey was funny. 'Bullshit.'

Bailey shrugged, eyes on the road. 'What can I say? She's gotten to me.'

'The girl or the dog?'

Bailey didn't bother answering, deciding to shift the conversation somewhere else, pointing at the bag that Ronnie had dumped on the back seat. 'You stored that in a hire car?'

Ronnie laughed, this time for real. 'Safer than inside your place with your friends in the feds dropping by.'

They drove past Paddington Gates in silence and it stayed that way as Bailey sped along the freeway below the Junction, up Bondi Road. A few specks of water landed on the windscreen but it wasn't enough to call it rain. More like dribble from the sky.

They were almost on Bronte Road when Ronnie's pocket started vibrating. He answered. 'Get it?' He waited a few seconds before speaking again. 'Good.' Another pause. 'No.'

Ronnie slipped his phone into his pocket. 'It's Harding's house.'

'Of course it is,' Bailey said, suddenly feeling nervous. 'What else did he tell you?'

'Wanted to know if his debt had been settled,' Ronnie said, smirking. 'I told him it hadn't.'

—

Bronte Beach was nestled in a gully two beaches south of Bondi. Tourists didn't come here often because, other than a headland walk, the surf wasn't much good and it didn't have a pub or shopping precinct either.

Two kinds of rich people lived in Bronte. The new money folks who had done it all themselves and the inheritance babies whose ocean views got served on platters made of silver. Bailey figured that Commander Dominic Harding had been handed his start in life because there was no way a police officer could afford a house around here. Either that or he'd been on the take for years.

'Kill the lights, bubba.'

Bailey had turned off Bronte Road and he was driving slowly down a steep hill on the southern side of the beach, searching for Harding's house.

'That's it.' Ronnie pointed at a driveway hidden beneath a canopy of trees. 'Keep driving. Park down the hill. We'll walk up.'

Bailey did what he was told and the two men climbed out, huddling beside the open rear passenger door where Ronnie was rummaging through his bag.

'You're going to need to follow my lead,' Ronnie whispered.

'Sure.'

It was a public holiday and the residents of Bronte appeared to be enjoying a sleep-in because the windows of the houses around them were black and Bailey hadn't glimpsed a single soul on the street. That would change very soon. It was well after 6 am and the early bird exercise groups would be rising with the sun, whatever happened with the weather. It was also Australia Day, which meant citizenship ceremonies, cultural festivals and community barbecues.

'What's the plan?' Bailey said.

'Put this on.' Ronnie handed Bailey a bulletproof vest that looked more like a heavy singlet. 'Take off your shirt. Goes underneath. Close to the skin. Concealable.'

Bailey didn't argue because Ronnie was already slipping off his shirt, putting on a vest of his own. When he was done he turned his attention back to Bailey. 'Give me a look.' He undid the velcro corners of the Kevlar, pulling them tight against Bailey's skin. 'Better.'

The vest felt cool. It was so thin and tight that it was barely noticeable and Bailey wondered whether it was actually capable of stopping a bullet. Hopefully, he wouldn't need to find out.

Ronnie punched a code into a metal box inside the bag, clicking it open. He withdrew a Glock from inside, loading a cartridge, flicking the safety on and off.

'Remember how to shoot one of these?'

Bailey's mind flashed back to London. Kensal Town. The magazine he'd unloaded on the street. The terrorist who'd tried to kill him.

'Bailey?'

'I'm not carrying a gun.'

'Don't be stupid. It's for your own protection.'

'This is Sydney, mate. Not the wild west.'

Ronnie held Bailey's gaze for a moment longer. 'Suit yourself.'

'So, what's the plan?' Bailey returned to his original question.

'I'm going to head up there and take a look around. House's at the bottom of a long driveway which means one way in, one way out.' Ronnie stuffed the Glock into the back of his pants, closing the car door. 'You stay here. Wait for me. I'll be back in a few minutes once I know what we're up against. At some point, we're going to need to call the police, we just can't risk Harding being tipped off by a bent cop. We don't know how far his reach goes. Who else might be involved.'

Bailey was relieved to hear Ronnie mention the cops. Whatever they were trying to achieve here, he couldn't help thinking they would be outnumbered. Alerting the police – or Annie's detective, at least – was a good idea. But he'd wait.

'Okay.'

Bailey watched Ronnie walk up the hill and slip down a driveway that wasn't Dominic Harding's, reassured by the small comfort of knowing that the CIA veteran had done this before. That one of them knew what they were doing.

He leaned his back against the car, checking his watch: 6.25 am. He stared at the digital screen until the number ticked over again. Ronnie said he'd only be gone for a few minutes. A few meant three but nobody ever used the term like that.

Despite his lack of sleep, Bailey's senses were charging. He could hear cars in the distance. Waves crashing into sand. Morning birds squawking at the day. The smell of smoke that had poisoned Sydney's air for months was gone and Bailey wondered whether the great southern blaze was finally out. One threat extinguished as another one began.

Taking a deep breath, Bailey held the air for a moment, before letting it join the southerly that was gusting up the road, twisting and turning between houses. He shivered. The wind suddenly cooler than before. A flash of lightning over the water. A rumbling sky. The change had arrived. The rain would be here soon.

He pulled out his phone, deciding to type Harding's address in a message to Annie so that it was ready when they decided it was time to call in the cavalry. Cops they could trust.

Click.

Bailey felt the cool metal barrel against his head.

'Phone. Now.'

A man's voice. Familiar. Behind him.

Bailey had only managed to type the word 'Bronte' but he hit send anyway.

'Fucking smartarse.' Benny Hunter snatched the phone before Bailey had a chance to lock the screen. 'Who's AB?'

Bailey had a habit of only using initials in his contact list for personal friends. A habit that had just paid dividends in a way he hadn't anticipated.

'No one.'

Whack!

Bailey's ear started ringing as it recovered from the open palm that had just slapped the side of his head.

'Next time it'll be the butt of the gun. Got it?'

Bailey grunted an acknowledgement, hoping that Ronnie was watching from the shadows nearby. Ready to take back control.

'You alone?'

'Yeah.'

'I don't believe you.'

'Yeah, well. If you want me to get started on all the things I don't believe, we'll be here all day.'

Whack!

Luckily, Bailey had only copped the open palm of Hunter's hand again. But now he had two ringing ears.

'I'll try again. Who else's with you?'

'Just you, Benny.'

Hunter went quiet and Bailey was preparing himself for another whack to the head.

'You're a fucking smartarse, you know that?'

'It's been pointed out.'

'Move.' Hunter shoved Bailey in the back with his gun.

They walked in silence towards Harding's place, down the sloping driveway.

'Keep going.'

Bailey was staring into the bushes on either side of the steep drive without moving his head, hoping that Ronnie was out there. Watching. No sign of him yet.

A dim light was shining at the end of the driveway by the front door, a van parked outside, making Bailey wonder how many people were here.

'That way. The steps.'

Hunter diverted them off the driveway and onto a stone staircase that dropped into the bushland by the house.

'Where are we going?'

'Keep walking.'

The steps were uneven and Bailey was taking it slow in the darkness. About thirty metres below he could see a small house that looked more like a granny flat, or a shed, shadows moving through the windows.

Trying to get a look at Hunter's face, Bailey twisted his head. 'What are you planning?'

'Turn around.'

'Why'd you kill Strong, Benny? I thought he was one of you people.'

'I said shut up.'

Bailey knew that Hunter was his best chance of finding out what these lunatics were planning because guys like Harding were good at keeping secrets. Hunter, on the other hand, had made a career out of boasting in front of cameras.

'So, Harding's the money man? Must be family dough, eh?' Bailey went again, rolling the dice that Hunter wouldn't use the butt of his pistol on a steep stone pathway. 'I know all about Sunshine Inc.'

'You have no idea what you've walked into. No fucking idea.'

Talking was good. The sound would carry through the trees, up the path. Let Ronnie know that Bailey had been captured, that he needed help. That it might be time to call in the police. The real ones. The cops who protected and served.

'I've read all that shit you guys post. Your conspiracy theories about some kind of cultural invasion and how white people are the master race.' He interrupted himself with a laugh. 'That's the amazing thing about white supremacists. Not much supreme about them.'

'Shut your mouth.'

'Your good old-fashioned racism. Fear of the unknown. I don't like it, but I get it. I can see where it comes from.'

'I'm warning you.'

'But the white supremacy stuff about a master race. It doesn't add up.' Bailey kept talking. Making noise. 'I'll give you some examples. Paper. Gunpowder. Printing. Guess who invented these vital tools of society? A hint, it wasn't the white fella. It was the Chinese. And what about the flying machine? Music? Hospitals?' Bailey paused, waiting for a response. Nothing. 'And coffee? You must know who invented coffee? No? All right, then. Muslims. All those things I mentioned. Magic from the Middle Ea–'

Crack!

This time Hunter used the butt of his gun, the blow sending Bailey scuttling down the last few steps, landing heavily on the paving outside the door to the little house. He took a moment to lie still, waiting for the pain and the dizziness to subside, feeling the back of his head, knowing the pistol had pierced the skin, hoping it wasn't too deep. There was a warm, wet slick in his hair. Not much. He couldn't pinpoint a gash. It must have been a tiny cut. But he was bleeding.

He looked up, squinting at the bloke who had just hit him for a third time. 'What is it with you and pushing me down steps?'

'I warned you, didn't I?'

Hunter was standing over him, his gun only inches from Bailey's face.

'Benny! What the hell are you doing?'

Bailey turned to see Harding standing at the door, arms raised, wondering why Bailey was lying on the ground with a gun to his head.

'Stop messing about. Get him inside!'

Hunter grabbed Bailey under the armpit, pulling him to his feet, pushing him towards the open door where Harding was waiting for them.

'John Bailey.' Harding made a tutting noise with his tongue. 'You just couldn't keep your nose out of this, could you?'

'What'd you expect? Turn my house upside down off the back of a flimsy warrant. Murder my friend.' Bailey felt like taking a swing at him but he knew how that might end. 'Deleting the video was sloppy though, Harding. You should've picked on somebody else.'

'Get him inside,' Harding growled.

'Go.' The muzzle of Hunter's gun was pressed into Bailey's shoulder blades with even pressure to keep him moving.

As soon as Bailey stepped through the door he could see that there wasn't much to the place. Bathroom. Kitchenette. A lounge room just big enough for a table, sofa and the television that was mounted on the wall. It was the kind of cottage where the help might live.

'Over there.' Hunter directed Bailey towards a wooden chair beside the sofa. 'Sit.'

Bailey did what he was told and watched as Hunter got down on one knee, using plastic zip ties to secure his arms to the chair, pulling them tight.

'Back in a moment.' Hunter stood up, slapping Bailey on the cheek. 'Don't go anywhere.'

'I'm tied to a chair, Benny.'

Hunter glared at Bailey for a few seconds, probably wondering how he'd allowed him to get under his skin and whether he should pistol-whip him again. He went to say something but thought better of it, turning around and walking out of the room.

The sound of male voices flowed from the kitchen. Harding. Hunter. At least one other voice, maybe two. He couldn't be sure. They were speaking so quietly it was impossible to make out the words.

Harding appeared in the open doorway, looking back towards the kitchen while he finished his conversation. 'It's uploaded? Good. Good. He needs to get moving.'

Something had been uploaded. What was it? A message? A video? And who else was there? The questions running through Bailey's brain.

'All right, then.' Harding walked into the room, rubbing his hands together, smiling at Bailey. 'The waiting game.' He pointed at the television. 'Soon we can watch it here, together.'

Bailey went to say something but a figure in the doorway had hijacked his attention.

Russell.

The son of Bryce and Jenny Ratcliffe. The kid who lived in Bailey's street.

Not a kid any more.

Wearing black combat gear, Russell was dressed for war. Ballistic vest. Helmet. An assault rifle slung over his shoulders. Pistols strapped to his side, his ankle. Cartridges clipped to his torso.

'What the fuck?'

Bailey mouthed the words but hardly any noise came out.

Harding and Russell locked hands, grabbing each other's shoulders. The muscle hug.

'Good luck, brother.' Harding patted his cheek, fiddling with a small camera fixed to his helmet. 'Wait for the last minute before you turn this on. The live stream begins automatically. Okay?'

Russell nodded.

'And remember, stay out of sight in the van until you get there. Benny will get you right up close. You know what to do. The park. Beach.'

Bailey felt a warm sick rise in his throat. 'Russell, you don't have to do this.'

'Yeah, I do.' Russell's dead eyes confirming how far gone he was. 'For all of us.'

Russell left the room followed by Hunter. The door to the house opening and closing. Footsteps on the path. Wheels in motion.

Bailey kept watching the hall as though Russell was still there, hoping he was coming back to tell him that he was just playing some kind of sick party trick. That it was all fake. The military fatigues. The guns. That he wasn't about to go and kill a bunch of innocent people. Live stream it on social media.

And where the hell was Ronnie?

'We didn't have a choice, you know.'

Bailey hadn't noticed Harding settling himself on the sofa, elbows on his knees, leaning closer for a chat.

'Everybody has a choice,' Bailey replied. 'You're nothing but a coward.'

'Coward?' Harding shook his head, making that annoying tutting sound again. 'You really don't get it, do you?'

'No. I get it,' Bailey said, almost spitting his words. 'You're looking for someone to blame for your pathetic life.'

'This isn't about me. This is about my country. I've been watching it for decades. The crime. The cultural erosion. I know exactly who's responsible,' Harding said through gritted teeth. 'Australia's being destroyed from the inside. Taken over. This is about preservation. Protecting our way of life. We're the ones brave enough to fight.'

'You're a terrorist, Harding. No better than an Islamic Nation suicide bomber who straps on a vest.'

'A terrorist?' Harding looked genuinely surprised. 'We're part of a global movement that's getting more popular by the day. People like you in the mainstream media don't get it. You don't understand real people any more.'

'Real people?' Bailey cut in. 'What does that even mean?'

'It means you're out of touch. The elite. The left. You've already lost. Can't you see that? Turkey. Brazil. Austria. Hungary.

The United States. The Philippines. The UK.' Harding was proudly rattling off every nation that had been touched by the rising tide of populism. 'This isn't some flash in the pan, my friend. We're building here in Australia too. It's only a matter of time. The politics of yesterday is gone. Failed. We've expended enough blood and money on foreign wars, taking in refugees only to see them take up arms against us.'

'You're simplifying everything to suit your extremist cause. Make you feel good about being a racist murderer,' Bailey said.

'No. No. No.' Harding was waving his finger at Bailey like he was a naughty child. 'You think this is just about race. It's not.'

'Enlighten me,' Bailey said, almost spitting the words from his mouth.

'Big business is to blame almost as much as the left-wing political classes who first opened the door to immigrants. For big business, it's about cheap labour. New migrants are coming here and doing the low-paying service jobs we need. But their children don't. Their children's children don't. They use our education system, healthcare, to infiltrate our way of life. Attend our universities. They become bankers, media barons, and more and more we're seeing them taking our positions in parliament, where they slowly seek to change our country. Erode our culture, our heritage. Replace us.'

'And killing people's the answer?' Bailey said.

Harding tapped the arm of the sofa. 'Today's a wake-up call. Like Christchurch. Oslo. El Paso. It may take time, but we're in this for the long game. There'll be more days like today.'

'And what about Augustus Strong?' Bailey still didn't understand why the American was among the dead. 'All that crap you just rattled off, it's the type of gibberish that made Strong the pin-up boy for extremists like you.'

'All talk,' Harding said, shaking his head. 'Augustus Strong was all talk. He joined us here only a few days ago. Rattling on about his brand. His followers on social media. Only interested in himself. We couldn't have pretenders like that in our cause.'

'So you had him killed?'

'Benny's idea. It wasn't part of the plan. But we shared too much. Strong couldn't be trusted. And look at the headlines it gave us.'

Harding was laughing now. Deranged, eye-rolling laughter.

'You're nothing but a fucking psychopath.'

Knock. Knock. Knock.

Jolting upright, Harding stopped laughing, his neck spinning towards the door. He stood up, confused. Reaching inside his jacket, he pulled a pistol from the holster beside his chest.

He pointed his gun at Bailey. 'Who's out there?'

'No idea.'

Knock. Knock.

'Make a noise and you're a dead man.'

Harding moved towards the door. Opening it.

'Back!'

Ronnie.

Bailey knew that voice and he had never been so glad to hear it.

'Back up!'

Harding was walking backwards, balancing his pistol mid-air, slowly stepping into the room, edging closer to Bailey.

Ronnie appeared in the doorframe, his arm flexed tightly around Russell's neck while he held his Glock to the young man's temple.

'Stop there!'

Ronnie was ducking down, his head concealed by Russell's helmet, protecting him from the bullets from the gun that Harding was pointing in his direction. With his arms tied behind his back and a full complement of body armour, Russell was the perfect human shield.

'Where's Benny?' Harding said.

Russell couldn't speak because he had gaffer tape wrapped tightly around his head, covering his mouth. Struggling to breathe. Each sniff of air sounding desperate and distorted as he tried to blast the mucus from his nose. It was a hell of a time to have a cold.

'Benny won't be joining us,' Ronnie said.

In one quick movement, Russell rammed his elbow into Ronnie's gut, distracting him long enough for Harding to slip behind Bailey, kneel down and hold a gun to his head.

'Do that again and you're a dead man,' Ronnie said to Russell, flexing his arm more tightly around his neck. The young man's face turned red as he struggled to breathe.

'Who are you?' Bailey felt Harding's words on his neck while watching Ronnie's eyes, trying to read his next move.

'Nobody.'

The two men with guns were less than five metres apart. Point blank range.

'All right, nobody. It seems we're at somewhat of a stand-off here.' Harding sounded alarmingly confident. 'I tell you what's going to happen. Bailey and I are going to walk outside. It's the only way nobody gets hurt.'

'Is it?'

With a knife in his hand, Harding reached forward, his face

shielded behind Bailey's back as he cut through the zip ties across Bailey's wrists.

'Get up,' Harding said, his hand tapping Bailey on the shoulder. 'Up!'

Bailey did as he was told, watching Ronnie, wondering what the big guy was waiting for.

'I'm going to ask you to move out of the way so that we can get through that door.'

'That's not going to happen,' Ronnie said. 'Sorry, bubba.'

'What?'

Ronnie dropped to one knee behind Russell and fired his gun.

Bang!

The bullet hit Bailey in his chest, forcing him to slump forward, exposing the top half of Harding's torso.

Gunfire engulfed the room. Voices. Yelling. Windows smashing. Bodies hitting the ground.

Then silence.

Ears ringing. Vision blurred.

Bailey couldn't breathe.

The bullet had blown the air out of his lungs and he felt a sharp pain in his chest. He had no idea how many rounds had been fired. Five. Six. Ten. He just knew that he'd been hit. He looked around, trying to count the bodies. How many were still standing. How many had hit the deck. Shadows were moving in the smoky air and the acrid smell of gunpowder was burning Bailey's nostrils. He ran his hand across his chest, feeling for a wound. Moisture. Blood. Hoping that the bullet fired from Ronnie's gun was stuck in the Kevlar vest and not buried beneath his skin.

'Fuck!' Bailey was rolling around on the ground, coughing and clutching his chest, trying to move Harding's bloodied corpse from his legs. 'You bloody shot me, Ronnie. You –'

Bailey stopped talking when he caught sight of Ronnie slumped against the wall, holding his arm, blood on his hand.

'Ronnie.' Bailey crawled towards him, coughing. 'Mate, you okay?'

'Fucking arsehole got me. Hit me in the arm.' Ronnie was already clambering to his feet, gritting his teeth to hide the pain.

'Where's Russell?'

There was a bloody patch on the floor where Russell had just been, and red splotches leading all the way to the screen door which was now flapping in the breeze.

'He's gone.'

CHAPTER 37

The hill was a sea of black houses with yellow windows. The residents of Bronte abruptly woken by gunfire. One loud bang could have been ignored, reasoned away as a backfiring car, or thunder. The gunshots that had shaken the tiny house in the scrub had been enough to wake the entire neighbourhood, forcing panicked residents to their phones. To alert the police because guns didn't get fired around here. Ever.

Bailey knew the average response time to an emergency call was twelve minutes. If they got lucky it could be half that. Bailey wasn't banking on it. Not on Australia Day, when cops in uniform would be stretched from one place to another. Events. Parties. Protests.

They were on their own.

'Stay behind me. Stay close.'

Bailey was chasing Ronnie up the steps, trying not to worry about the arm that was dangling by Ronnie's side, dripping blood on stone.

'Can you see him?' Bailey whispered.

The sun had appeared between the ocean and the clouds and there was just enough light to see the other trail of blood. Russell's blood. Leading to the driveway.

'No,' Ronnie said, panting and waving his gun. 'Stay low. Head down.'

Bailey had a gun too. Harding's. Prised from his dead hand. The warm metal foreign to Bailey's fingers, his palm. He didn't like holding it. Ronnie hadn't given him a choice. After seeing Russell dressed like Rambo, Bailey hadn't bothered arguing.

'This way.'

They followed the splotches of blood along the driveway towards the van, which was puffing exhaust smoke, engine humming, its deflated tyres collapsed on the concrete. Benny Hunter's body lying lifeless nearby. Ronnie's handiwork, no doubt.

'It's over, Russell!' Ronnie yelled. 'Van's no good!'

They stopped moving, leaning up against the van. Listening.

'You need help, Russell.' Ronnie lowered his voice. 'We need to get you to a hospital. You've lost a lot of blood.'

Nothing.

No movement. No sound.

If Russell was somewhere nearby, he was staying out of sight.

'Let us help you, mate,' Bailey added. 'Think about your mum and dad. Your sister, Melissa. Harding was just using you. It can all end now. Before it gets out of hand.'

Tapping Ronnie on the shoulder, Bailey pointed to the other side of the van where he thought he'd heard something. Ronnie raised his gun, gesturing for Bailey to do the same.

Bailey's boots crunched loudly on the sandy concrete. Arriving at the rear of the van, he poked his head down the side, glimpsing Russell sitting on the wall by the driver's door.

Bailey slid his finger across the trigger of the gun, preparing to do something he had never been trained to do.

'Russell?' Bailey tried to sound calm. Reassuring. Neighbourly. 'This can end right now. Let's get you to a hospital.'

Russell was holding his rifle with both hands and he stood up, head twisting towards Bailey.

'Drop it!' Ronnie's voice boomed and Bailey could see the top of his head hovering over the roof. 'Last warning, Russell! Drop the gun!'

The next rounds of gunfire were so quick and loud that they sounded like an earthquake. Flashes of rapid fire erupting from Russell's automatic weapon. Bailey only managed to squeeze the trigger once and he had no idea where the bullet went as he dived for cover. He was on his knees, crawling up against the van's back wheel, expecting to see Ronnie crouching nearby. But he was gone.

'Mr Bailey!'

Russell's voice.

'Drop your weapon! I don't want to kill you too.'

Russell was moving around the van towards him, one foot dragging on the ground. Clearly injured. Just not enough.

'Last chance, Mr Bailey,' Russell said. Closer.

Bailey stood up, leaning against the van, peering around the side. Pointing his gun.

Band! Bang! Bang!

The sound of the bullets burrowing into metal panels made Bailey realise that his pistol was no match for the killing machine in Russell's hands. A semi-automatic assault rifle shipped from America and carried by soldiers in warzones.

'The gun! Throw it where I can see!'

Bailey tossed his gun onto the ground and seconds later Russell was beside him, pointing his rifle at his face.

'Where's your car?'

'Where's Ronnie?'

'Dead.'

'What?'

'We're leaving.' Russell pushed the hot muzzle into Bailey's cheek, sizzling the sweat on his skin. 'Your car, take me to it. Unless you'd prefer to die. I'll count to three. One. Two –'

'Okay. Okay.' Bailey pushed the muzzle away. 'It's around the corner.'

'Walk.'

The injury didn't appear to be slowing Russell down and he kept pushing the rifle into Bailey's back, ordering him to quicken his stride.

Reaching the top of the driveway, Bailey stopped and looked back towards the van. The house. The steep, bushy embankment. Searching for any sign that Ronnie was alive. He imagined the big man diving away from the hail of bullets, just like Bailey had done. If Ronnie was dead then surely his body would have been lying on the drive?

'Which is it?'

Another shove in the back.

'The wagon.' Bailey pointed at the old yellow bomb that had brought him here. 'There.'

After forcing Bailey into the driver's seat, Russell climbed into the back, pushing his gun into Bailey's rib cage. 'Drive.'

'Where are we going?'

Bailey turned the key, twisting his rear-vision mirror so that he could see his passenger. The helmet. The military fatigues. The rifle on his lap. Eyes raging with adrenalin.

'Bondi Beach.'

Russell was sitting in the middle of the row, ducking down, maintaining a clear view out the front windscreen. A clear shot at his driver.

Shoving it in gear, Bailey turned the car into the street, performing a U-turn under instruction, steering through the winding hills that hovered above Bronte. Within minutes they were turning onto Bondi Road, edging closer to the country's most famous beach. A place where people flocked – rain, hail or shine.

'Why are you doing this, Russell? You're ruining your life.'

Bailey tried again to get his passenger talking. Find a connection. Anything to get the young man to rethink what he was about to do.

'Harding's dead, you know that?' Bailey said, trying to catch his eyes in the mirror. 'Let's end this. You're not a bad guy. There's time to turn this around.'

'Shut the fuck up!' Russell snarled. 'People like you. The media. You're part of the problem. I'm glad you're here for the ride. You can learn something. What it means to really believe in something. Do whatever it takes. I'm giving you the story of a lifetime.'

Large droplets of water started splattering on the windscreen, just enough for Bailey to turn on the wipers.

He noticed the footpaths getting busier the closer they got to the beach. People carrying surfboards. Walking dogs. Jogging. Families striding together in raincoats. Bailey imagined Russell running at them with his gun, firing with purpose, trying to kill as many innocent people as he could, just as those other white supremacist lunatics had done before.

Bailey was running out of options. If he couldn't talk Russell back off the ledge, what else could he do?

He took his foot off the accelerator as they approached the sweeping bend that would deliver them to the southern end of the beach, where Bailey could see several large, white marquees in the carpark down by the esplanade. It wasn't even 7.30 am and there were already hundreds of people down there, huddled around barbecues and a stage where dignitaries would give speeches and musicians play songs.

'Don't slow down. What are you doing?' Russell said. 'Turn right at the roundabout. Drop me in the carpark.'

'I'm not going to let you do this.'

Bailey felt the gun push against his head and Russell sat up, not caring about being seen.

'Yes, you are.'

A four-wheel drive appeared alongside and Bailey glimpsed the face of the driver, her mouth agape at the sight inside Bailey's car. Children in the back seat. A man leaning across the woman's lap, phone to his ear. Probably calling the police just like Bailey imagined half of Bronte had done. Still no sirens. Where the fuck were the police?

Russell's eyes left Bailey as he fiddled with the camera on his helmet, activating the live stream. Sensing an opportunity, Bailey slipped on his seatbelt and dropped his foot onto the accelerator, the back wheels slipping as he skated around the bend.

'What are you doing?' Russell said, panic rising. 'Bailey? Bailey!'

With his foot to the floor, Bailey was beeping his horn and flashing his lights as he sped down the hill, not slowing as he entered the roundabout on Campbell Parade, side-swiping another car, bouncing onto the opposite side of the road.

'Stop!'

Bailey had found his target. A light post on the corner of the roundabout. He hit it head-on at seventy kilometres an hour, Russell flying through the front windscreen, his rifle leading the charge through the glass, Bailey's head smashing against the steering wheel, seatbelt slicing into his neck.

The blaring sound of a car horn brought Bailey around and he lifted his head off the steering wheel, killing the horn, staring through the shattered windscreen, searching for Russell in the smoke that was billowing from the crumpled engine. Blood was rushing from Bailey's nose, running down his forehead into his eyes, making it difficult to see. His neck ached and as he went to open the door his right arm didn't respond. The joint of his shoulder wasn't right. Numbing pain that he remembered after a spiteful tackle on the rugby field.

Using his left hand to wipe his eyes, he noticed something moving in front of him on the grass. Russell. On his knees, swaying and trying to get up. Bailey yanked on the handle of the car door with the hand that worked, pushing it open, falling out and onto the road. He rolled onto his side, pushing himself up off the ground, oblivious to the people staring at him from the footpath, the grass and the shops on the other side of Campbell Parade. Wondering what the hell had just happened. What was going to happen next.

Staggering across the footpath, Bailey made it onto the grass, where Russell was lying down again, barely moving. The post from a sign that had been advertising the Australia Day festivities impaling his stomach. His shirt was torn open revealing a tattoo on his chest, the artwork bloodied but easy to see. Four numbers.

14/88

The Fourteen Words. Heil Hitler.

Bailey was staring at the guy who had bashed Matthew Lam almost to death at a pub in Paddington. Someone linked to the murders of Augustus Strong and Jonny Abdo.

Warm-up acts for a Bondi massacre.

Dropping to his knees, Bailey wrenched away the weapons still attached to Russell's body. Rifle. Knives. Pistols. Throwing them out of reach on the grass.

Russell went to say something but all he could manage was a gurgling sound. He gave up, slumping onto his back, eyes staring at Bailey, suddenly realising this was it. His life was over. His grand statement reduced to a media story, then a footnote, before it became nothing at all.

Watching the life fall from Russell's eyes, Bailey searched his emotions, desperate to feel something for the pathetic extremist on the grass. He found almost nothing. No sadness. No grief. Only pity. Because Russell Ratcliffe had died a long time ago. The moment he started believing the lie.

Bailey lay back on the damp grass, staring at the clouds, the drops of water floating down. His shoulder randomly clicking back into place, sending another pulse of pain through his damaged body. Bruises. Cracks. A busted nose. The things that happen when you drive a car head-first into a steel pole. When your head thumps a steering wheel. If only he'd followed his daughter's advice and bought himself a better car. Something nice.

Something modern. Something with an airbag. Maybe he wouldn't be feeling so rough. Then again, Russell may not have careened through his windscreen and been impaled by an Australia Day sign if Bailey had owned a car with an airbag.

He closed his eyes and heard sirens in the distance, getting louder. Cars skidding to a stop. Doors opening and closing. Footsteps running. He knew that he needed to get up but he didn't want to move. He just wanted to lie there and let the raindrops fall on his face. Breathe the smoke-free air.

'Bailey!'

He opened his eyes, hoping the voice he'd just heard wasn't a dream.

'Bubba, you okay?'

Ronnie was next to him, kneeling down, a makeshift tourniquet around his bicep.

'I thought you were dead.'

'It'll take a lot more than a sonofabitch like that to take me down.'

Bailey went to laugh but the pain made him stop. 'All right, tough guy. Help me up, would you?'

Bailey held out his good arm and Ronnie grabbed his hand, pulling him up.

A loud blast of thunder grumbled from the sky and the rain that had started a few minutes earlier was now pelting down. The grey curtains that had been dangling over the sea were giving Bondi a drenching it hadn't seen in years, sending people running for cover.

The rain had also plastered Ronnie's shirt to his body and Bailey could see where the bullet had entered his shoulder. 'You need to get that looked at. Is it the only one?'

'Copped another two in the vest before I dived down the embankment. Sorry I left you.'

'You didn't leave me,' Bailey said, holding his gaze to let him know.

'John Bailey?' A guy in a raincoat appeared behind Ronnie. 'I'm Detective Greg Palmer. Are you all right?'

'Yeah. I'll be fine.'

'We've been to Harding's house. Just missed you. Mr Johnson filled me in on the way down. Thanks for sending Annie that text. We got some emergency calls from residents in Bronte who were woken by the gunfire. Put two and two together. Then we got a call about a guy with a gun.'

Bailey wasn't up for the debrief. Not yet. 'Can I go?'

'We need to get you to a hospital. But we're going to need to talk to you later. Both of you,' Palmer said, gesturing to Ronnie too.

'Figured.' Bailey nodded, tapping Ronnie's chest with the back of his hand. 'Good luck with him.'

Palmer laughed, like he was expecting it. 'Interviews can wait. There's an ambulance over there.'

'You head over, bubba. I'll catch up. Looks like you might need a minute anyway.' Ronnie pointed at the ambulance, where Annie Brooks was standing in the pouring rain, staring in their direction.

Bailey was already walking away as Ronnie pulled out his mobile phone, taking pictures of Russell's dead body and the small arsenal on the grass. Capturing the scene for the Americans. Close-ups of the semi-automatic rifle with the bump stock attachment that would have helped Russell fire his weapon faster. Kill more people.

The door of the ambulance was open when Bailey got there and a paramedic in a blue uniform was standing in the rain.

'Mr Bailey, I'm Kath.' She tapped the inside tray of the ambulance. 'It's bloody pouring. Let's get you inside. Check you out.'

'Give me a second, Kath.' Bailey turned to Annie. 'You all right?'

'Am I all right?' She squinted and held back a laugh. 'You look like you've been to hell and back.'

'Nah.' Bailey smiled. 'Seen that place. This wasn't it.'

'Everybody back! Back!' Another cop had taken charge and she was ordering half the street to shut down, keeping gawkers at bay. 'Further! Further!' The rest of the cops were only metres away but the sound of the pelting rain was drowning her words. 'Shut it down! The entire road! The diversion, now! Shut this down!'

'Police wouldn't let me onto the grass,' Annie said. 'You okay?'

'A few bruises. I'll obviously need a new car,' he said, trying not to laugh because of the pain.

'Mr Bailey.' Kath touched him on the arm. 'We should get going.'

Bailey looked at her for a moment before turning back to Annie, pushing his bloody, wet hair out of his eyes. 'Okay.' He could see Ronnie walking towards them and he knew it was time to go. 'What are you going to do?'

'Work.' Annie held up her smartphone. The broadcasting tool that would deliver her to the masses as soon as she decided it was time. Not yet. Annie had made her choice. 'Which hospital, Kath?'

'Vinnies.'

'Up for a visit later?'

He let Annie's question linger for a moment while he climbed, awkwardly, into the back of the ambulance, taking a seat on the stretcher.

'As long as you don't ask me for an interview.'

EPILOGUE

Five days later and the rain still hadn't stopped. Hundreds of millimetres had fallen on almost every corner of the state. A fire-extinguishing, drought-breaking downpour.

The bushfires may have never wreaked havoc on the Sydney metropolis but the smoke haze had taunted and threatened the city for months. Thanks to the rain, people could breathe clean air again. Unfortunately John Bailey wasn't like other people and for him the air didn't taste so good. Another threat still lingered and it would require more than rain to fix it.

'I don't understand what this meeting's all about. If the story's not ready, what are we doing here, Bailey?'

Neena Singh was remonstrating with Bailey outside the café at Bondi Junction where they had met Jock Donaldson a week and a half ago. Bailey had requested an urgent meeting to discuss the article he was writing for the magazine and he hadn't given anything away.

'And what happened to your face?'

It was a fair question. Bailey had two black eyes and a steri-strip across his nose. He looked like hell.

'Car accident.'

The police had managed to keep Bailey's name out of what had happened at Bondi Beach on Australia Day and, because of the rain, the usual flood of social media videos had been reduced to a trickle. Somehow none of them featured Bailey. There was no hiding the fact that Bailey's car had been the one to have slammed into a light post on Campbell Parade but so far nobody had linked the licence plate to him. Now wasn't the time to out himself.

'Let's talk inside,' Bailey said, peering through the glass. 'I can already see Jock out back.'

Bailey dropped his umbrella into the bucket by the front door and walked inside. Donaldson was sitting at the same table they'd sat at last time, a coffee and a newspaper in front of him.

'Don't get up, Jock.'

Donaldson lifted his reading glasses off the tip of his nose, dropping them onto the paper.

'Good to see you, John.' The two men shook hands and Donaldson frowned at Bailey as he sat down. 'You look like you've been in a fight?'

'Fender bender in my car. Long story.'

'Hi, Jock.' Neena gave Bailey a dirty look as she went around to the other side of the table, giving their financier a peck on the cheek, sitting down. 'Sorry to drag you out in the rain.'

'I'd planned on dropping by to see my daughter, anyway.' Donaldson nodded his chin at Katie, who was manning the coffee machine behind the counter. 'So, John.' He smiled at Bailey. 'Neena said you wanted to discuss our cover story. When do I get to read it?'

'Should be up in a few hours.'

Donaldson had been rocking the handle of his walking cane from side to side and Bailey's response made him stop. 'Sorry?'

'What are you talking about, Bailey?' Neena clearly wasn't amused.

Bailey glanced at the face of his watch. 'The story will be up on *The Journal*'s website in around two hours.'

'Neena?' Jock was scowling at his editor. 'Care to tell me what's going on?'

'If this is your idea of a joke, Bailey,' Neena said, 'it's not funny.'

'Sorry, Neena. I really am. There was no other way.' Bailey shifted his attention back to Donaldson. 'This magazine's not going to happen because we've got a few problems, don't we, Jock? Or should I call you *Wise Elder*?'

Donaldson said nothing, squinting his eyes. Sizing up an adversary he hadn't seen coming.

Bailey glared right back at him. 'All the money in the world and it was never enough. But what I don't get is all that hate, Jock. Where does it come from?'

'I have no idea what you're talking about.' Donaldson tried to appear calm. 'What is this nonsense?'

'Bailey, you really need to explain yourself,' Neena said. 'Who or what is *Wise Elder*?'

'Wise Elder is the pseudonym used by a white supremacist who's been bankrolling Neo-Nazis in Australia and around the world. Trying to unite them together to form some kind of global movement. Isn't that right, Jock?'

'This is ridiculous,' Donaldson said, forcing a contemptuous laugh. 'I give you money for a magazine. Your first story's connected to this very bloody topic. You're sounding like a madman!'

'Am I?' Bailey fired back. 'As Neena well knows, a key tactic of these groups is to get publicity any way they can. What better way than to feed an idea you knew made sense for a simple reporter like me. Whose idea was it for me to write the piece about far right nationalism and Augustus Strong, Neena?'

Neena's pale face was enough for Bailey.

'Just as I thought.' Bailey kept going. 'Matthew Lam. Augustus Strong. Jonny Abdo. And then your finale, if that's what you want to call it. Arming Russell Ratcliffe with the weapons you'd smuggled from California, sending him to Bondi Beach for an almighty statement on Australia Day. Hitting the crowd that had gathered for a citizenship ceremony and a multicultural breakfast. That's some plan, Jock.'

Donaldson used his handkerchief to dab at the beads of sweat escaping from his bald head.

'You might have gotten away with it too.' Bailey wasn't looking at Neena any more. Only Donaldson. Studying his facial movements as he unleashed the truth on him. 'But you got sloppy with Sunshine Inc. Did you really think no one would link it back to you?'

'I have no idea what you're talking about.'

'I've got to admit, you're bloody good at hiding money. Off-shore bank accounts. Trusts. But Sunshine Inc? That *was* sloppy. You should have known people would dig into Liam Callaghan's finances. Try to figure out who killed him and why.' Bailey kept at him. 'Turns out Callaghan was a meticulous bookkeeper. Almost missed it, to be honest. The only reason I decided to take a look at Sunshine Inc was because Callaghan was paying the company ridiculously low rent to live in such a nice house.'

'I've had enough of this.'

Donaldson folded his newspaper and leaned on his cane, pushing his chair back.

'You didn't think about the other people you'd take down, did you, Jock?' Bailey decided to up the stakes. 'The other lives you'd ruin. Friends. Family.'

Donaldson sat back down, slapping his paper on the table, folding his arms. Saying nothing.

'I thought you might want to be sitting down for this part.' Bailey grinned with a knowing intent. 'The house that Callaghan was living in last sold in July 1996, almost twenty-five years ago. Sunshine Inc was registered as a company three weeks later. So for three short weeks, the house was in the name of Elisabeth Sandford.'

Donaldson's face dropped.

'Who's Elisabeth Sandford?' Neena asked.

'Jock's ex-wife. Number two, or was she number three, Jock?' Donaldson didn't answer. 'Doesn't matter. What matters is that the house hasn't been sold since, and it was transferred into a company called Sunshine Inc. Elisabeth sends her regards, by the way,' Bailey said, smirking again. 'You set her up with a lovely home in Bowral. It appears she was happy to look the other way as long as the money kept coming. Who could blame her? She trusted you. Even when you did the rich man thing and dumped her for a younger woman. But Elisabeth had no idea what you were up to and, quite frankly, she was horrified when I gave her an inkling. Even more so because the events of the past few weeks exposed the truth about her brother. Someone she'd idolised. Commander Dominic Harding.'

'So what?' Donaldson scowled. 'So one of my companies owns property in Sydney and one of the tenants happened to be a corrupt customs official.'

'I never said Liam Callaghan had done anything illegal, Jock,' Bailey said, tightening the vice. 'Police have suppressed Callaghan's identity. His crime.'

'He was a tenant in one of my properties.'

'I've dug into all your properties, Jock. All thirty-five of them. Not counting the number of apartments you own in those buildings in Parramatta. Do you know the names and occupations of all your tenants, or just Callaghan? And why the discounted rent?'

Donaldson responded with silence, which Bailey took as his cue to keep going. Bury him in his hole. Because he'd saved the best for last.

'You've just admitted that Liam Callaghan was one of your tenants, which means that Sunshine Inc is, in fact, a company owned by you. Care to explain why Sunshine Inc appeared on the invoice for a shipping container that arrived in Sydney not long ago filled with Californian oranges and guns?'

Donaldson left his newspaper on the table this time as he pushed back his chair, standing up. 'I think we're done.'

'Sit down, Jock.'

A big hand landed on Donaldson's shoulder, pushing him down into his chair. Ronnie.

'Who the hell are you?' Donaldson said, pushing away Ronnie's hand.

'A friend of Harriet Walker's.'

The name caused Donaldson's cheek to flutter.

'You've always had friends in high places but they can't help you now,' Bailey said. 'You won't get sympathy for being involved in the murder of a decorated officer from the Australian Federal Police. And, as you'll soon discover, people loved Harriet Walker.'

Bailey coughed, swallowing hard, surprised by his physical reaction after mentioning his dead friend's name. 'Going after Hat was a bad idea. I presume that was Harding. That he'd cottoned on to her investigation and realised how close she was to tearing you lot down. So you had her killed.'

Bailey stopped talking, searching for an answer in Donaldson's eyes. An admission of guilt.

Nothing.

'This is where you really came unstuck, Jock.' Bailey kept at him. 'Getting Harding to raid my house was a bad idea. But I get it. I know why. Harding must have known that Walker and I had met the day before. That we were sharing information. So you needed to know what she'd given me. The raid on my house didn't yield much. But Harding found the video I'd taken of the crowd at Augustus Strong's talk and decided it was a problem because it identified Russell Ratcliffe. The kid lived in my street. I know the family. So Harding deleted the video.

'I'm not the type of guy who ignores something like that. Deleting that video made me more than curious. Made me think the raid wasn't about my old Afghanistan stories at all. That Harding had abused his power at the Australian Federal Police to do something he knew was wrong. I couldn't let that go, Jock. It's not in my nature. I've spent my life chasing stories. I never let go. Like a dog with a bone.'

Bailey laughed, awkwardly, taking a breath. 'Don't bother calling your mate at home affairs for help. Wayne McMahon will be hard-pressed trying to explain all the money you've donated to his campaigns over the years and why he let you talk him into granting Strong a visa to enter the country. He'll be running from you like you've got the plague. And if there's one thing politicians are good at, it's throwing discarded friends under buses.'

Donaldson was shrinking into his chair as he listened to Bailey's attack. The untouchable billionaire suddenly reduced to a frail old man, captive in his own café.

'Benny Hunter's dead and we don't need to get into how you and him became close. I'm figuring that was Harding's doing, although he's also no longer around to confirm. Or maybe you found each other in a chatroom? Doesn't matter. Needless to say, the cops are already all over Hunter's Freedom Front. The Lucky Lads. Blue Boys. Any group that links back to him.'

Bailey sat forward in his chair, elbows on the table, stealing a glance at Donaldson's daughter who was staring at them from behind the coffee machine. 'Now let's talk about the shipping container with the guns that Callaghan smuggled through Port Botany for you. Your connection to Donald Sampson. The deal you managed to get over the line before he was arrested by the FBI. Someone was on the ground in the United States for that one, weren't they, Jock? Someone with money and time. Someone you could trust?'

Donaldson clenched his jaw and his eyes glistened with loathing.

'I can't believe you involved Katie in all this.' Bailey was shaking his head, keeping one eye on Donaldson's daughter in case she had cottoned on to the conversation and did something stupid. 'Sending her on jaunts overseas under the guise of your coffee business. She's your daughter, Jock. What were you thinking? I didn't tell Elisabeth, couldn't risk it. When a mother discovers that her ex-husband has coopted their daughter into being a terrorist there's no telling what she'd do.'

Donaldson wasn't looking at Bailey any more. He was staring at his daughter, exchanging unspoken words. She put down the coffee portafilter in her hand and started towards the door.

'The FBI shared thousands of surveillance images with cops back here and guess who turned up in California at a restaurant with Sampson a few days before those guns were packed into a shipping container alongside pallets of oranges?'

Detective Greg Palmer was sitting at a table by the door and he stopped Katie before she could make it outside, grabbing her by the arm.

'Let go of my daughter!' Donaldson stood up, sending his chair crashing to the floor. 'Get your hands off her!'

Donaldson's booming voice stopped every conversation in the café, attracting every gaze.

Bailey was on his feet. 'Game's up, Jock. You're done.'

Police in uniforms poured into the café, urging people to stay calm and remain seated while they did their job. Palmer had already put Katie Donaldson in handcuffs and he handed her off to a uniformed officer.

'I'll fix this, Katie! Don't talk to anyone! Wait for a lawyer!'

Katie managed one more look at her father – a hopeless glance – before she was steered through the door.

'Probably the last time you'll see her.' Bailey's words were laced with a retribution that surprised even him. 'Terrible price to pay for doing what her father told her.'

Donaldson lunged at Bailey with his cane, losing his balance and falling clumsily onto the table, sending cups and saucers, glasses and a bottle of water, spilling and smashing on the floor.

'You're pathetic,' Bailey said, looking down on Donaldson, who was wriggling around on the floor trying to get up.

'Jock Donaldson.' Palmer appeared beside Bailey, helping Donaldson to his feet. 'I'm Detective Greg Palmer from the New South Wales Police.'

'Get your hands off me. I don't care who you are.'

'I'm arresting you on charges of conspiracy to murder, financing terrorism and also for your alleged involvement in the planning and execution of an act of terrorism. You have the right to remain silent and to refuse to answer questions. Anything you say or do may be used against you in a court of law.'

'I said get your hands off me!'

Donaldson tried to push Palmer away as he was explaining his rights and the detective reacted by twisting Donaldson's arm behind his back, pushing his head down so that it touched the table while he cuffed him.

'Aaargh!' Donaldson cried out as Palmer pulled him up off the table with his hands locked in metal. 'I'll have you fired! Do you know who I am? Do you?'

'We know exactly who you are, Mr Donaldson. It's why you're in handcuffs,' Palmer said.

He turned to Bailey, Neena and Ronnie: 'Stay here a few minutes while I put this prick in the wagon. Cameras outside and all that. Might want to steer clear.'

Bailey had tipped off Annie Brooks to be there for Jock Donaldson's arrest and Palmer was right, there was no way that Bailey and Ronnie would want to be a part of this story.

'Back in a moment.'

'No worries,' Bailey said, patting Donaldson on the shoulder. 'They're going to love you in prison, Jock.'

Donaldson said nothing.

'Not bad, bubba,' Ronnie said as Donaldson was led away. 'I reckon you might have chosen the wrong career. What you've put together for Palmer looks watertight. This guy's going to spend the rest of his life in a cage. His daughter too.'

'You did all this?' Neena sounded incredulous.

'Sorry, Neena,' Bailey said. 'Before I knew it, I was in too deep.'

After Bailey had gotten the all clear from hospital, he'd spent the last five days doing what he did best. Diving headfirst into a story. Piecing it together. Harriet Walker's investigation had given him more than a head start. She had been on the cusp of lifting the lid on a global white supremacist movement driven by hate and financed by a dark web identity known as Wise Elder.

Bailey had managed to find the final pieces of the puzzle and when he'd finished writing his story he'd decided to share the article, along with Walker's files, with Detective Greg Palmer so that today's arrests would happen. So that justice would be served. *The Journal* was the logical place for a long investigative piece like this to be published and, not surprisingly, the paper's editor, Adrian Greenberg, had graciously accepted the article, despite making it clear that he still hated Bailey's guts.

Annie Brooks had led the way in reporting the story about what had happened at Bondi Beach, referring to Bailey as 'the unnamed driver' who had been forced at gunpoint to take Russell Ratcliffe to Bondi for his planned attack. Annie reported that the driver had 'heroically crashed' the car into a light post, risking their own life and causing Ratcliffe's death. It was sensational stuff.

It was inevitable that Bailey would be unmasked as 'the driver' – whether in court, or by a diligent reporter – and he'd already promised an on-camera interview with Annie for *Inside Story* when it happened. Until then, he'd enjoy his relative anonymity while it lasted.

'Have a seat, bubba.' Ronnie had been picking up the chairs around the table with his good arm and he plonked himself in one of them. 'We're going to need to wait out the shit show.'

The people in the café had lost interest in Bailey, Ronnie and Neena and they were crowded by the door, watching through the glass as Donaldson was led into a police wagon, ducking his head away from the microphone that Annie had shoved in front of his face and the camera that was capturing his ignominy.

'Anyone know how to work that thing?' Bailey pointed at the coffee machine.

'Don't look at me.' Ronnie leaned back, pulling a cigar from the sling that was supporting his bandaged shoulder, sparking it. 'I'm sure the cops won't mind.' He blew a cloud of smoke at Bailey, smiling.

The police wagon took off and Palmer came back through the door.

'Get it all?' Bailey said to Palmer as he unbuttoned his shirt, wincing as he tore the tape that had fixed the recording device to his hairy chest, handing it to the detective.

'We got it, Bailey.' Palmer carefully wrapped the cord around the device and put it in his pocket. 'You should get out of here. I can catch up with you later.'

Bailey didn't need to be told twice and he was already on his feet before he remembered the other thing that had been on his mind.

'Any word on the Roundtree girls?'

'Safe as houses. Arrived in Byron at their aunt's place last night,' Palmer said. 'I know a cop up there who'll keep an eye on them.'

Bailey had taken the detective to visit Jules and Margie at Father Joe's place in Redfern a few days ago to reassure the girls that they weren't in any trouble. That this frightening chapter in their lives was now closed. Their mother's sister had offered to take them in up at Byron Bay. Help them get their lives back on track. Back to school. A fresh start. Palmer had organised a car to drive them north, saying it was the least he could do. Unsurprisingly, the girls' father didn't stand in the way. He'd given up on parenting his daughters years ago.

'That's good news, Greg. Appreciate it.'

Bailey still had Jules's number and he'd check in with her from time to time too.

'Mind if I come with you to the station, Greg?' Ronnie said. 'Got a few things I need cleared up for the motherland.'

'Sure.' Palmer sounded cagey, but he didn't bother arguing. 'Ms Singh, we're going to need to get a statement from you. One of my officers will come and see you shortly.'

Neena was still in shock about what she'd just witnessed and she nodded her head. 'Sure.'

'I'm off then.'

Bailey didn't bother with a goodbye and he didn't wait for the others to give him one either. He just stuffed his hands inside his jacket and walked outside into the rain, grabbing his umbrella, popping it open, slipping through the crowd, eager to get away from the action.

'Hey, Bailey?' The pelting rain had suppressed the sounds of Annie's footsteps hitting puddles on the footpath behind him. 'Wait up!'

He stopped. 'Get the shot?'

'We did. Thanks for the heads-up. I'm about to go live for the morning news.'

'Big story, Annie.'

She stepped closer, sheltering under Bailey's umbrella. Their faces only inches apart. 'You must be relieved it's over. You okay?'

Exhausted by another story that had almost killed him, Bailey could only shrug. Too tired for anything else. 'I'm always okay.'

A lie.

'Annie!' Fletch was waving at his reporter from outside the café. 'We're up!'

Annie gestured to Fletch that she'd be there in a minute, turning back to Bailey, the cloud from her breath touching his cheek. 'Catch up later?'

'Sure.'

'What are you going to do now?'

'I thought I might take Campo for a walk.'

'In this?'

Bailey held out his hand, catching droplets falling from the sky, watching them splatter on his skin.

'There's something about rain that makes me feel alive.'

ACKNOWLEDGEMENTS

The act of writing may be a solitary exercise but it's never truly something that you accomplish alone. Thanks to the wonderful team at Simon & Schuster Australia, particularly Fiona Henderson for her encouragement and our countless plotting sessions, and to editor Deonie Fiford, for her brilliant suggestions and edits.

Some of the subject matter in this book is sensitive so I can't publicly thank many of the people who helped me with often very small details involving intelligence, policing, customs and the law. As we've seen in Australia and around the world, journalists can often become targets for shining lights in dark places. I want to thank all those reporters who've stared down often powerful detractors to report the truth. Don't stop.

Thanks to Candice Fox for her advice and for reading early chapters of this book, and to Stan Grant for our conversations about books and writing. Thanks to Randy for his Star Wars expertise and to my draft readers – the eagle-eyed David 'Mac' McInerney, Gavin Fang and Tracey Kirkland.

I want to thank my agent Jeanne Ryckmans for kick-starting this exciting journey with me and staying the course.

And lastly, I'm eternally grateful for the love and support of my wife, Justine, and our little people, Penelope and Arthur.

ABOUT THE AUTHOR

Tim Ayliffe has been a journalist for more than 20 years and is the Managing Editor of Television and Video for ABC News and the former Executive Producer of *News Breakfast*. He has travelled widely and before joining the ABC he worked in London for British Sky News. A few years ago he turned his hand to writing global crime thrillers featuring former foreign correspondent John Bailey. He is the author of *The Greater Good*, *State of Fear*, *The Enemy Within* and *Killer Traitor Spy*. When he's not writing or chasing news stories Tim rides bikes and surfs. He lives in Sydney.

COMING SOON

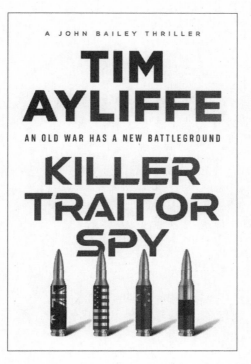

A JOHN BAILEY THRILLER

TIM AYLIFFE

AN OLD WAR HAS A NEW BATTLEGROUND

KILLER TRAITOR SPY

Praise for *Killer Traitor Spy*:

'A carefully crafted, propulsive thriller that
sails uncomfortably close to the truth.'
Michael Brissenden

'Ayliffe is a master of the genre.'
Sulari Gentill

'Torn from the headlines and relentlessly paced.'
Matthew Spencer